WHERE THE TREES WEEP

'There are things that burn me now
Which turn golden when I am happy.
Do you see the mystery of our pain?
That we bear poverty
And are able to sing and dream sweet things'

From *An African Elegy*
Ben Okri

Dedication
To all those denied their right to vote

WHERE THE TREES WEEP

DOLORES WALSHE

WOLFHOUND PRESS

First published 1992 by WOLFHOUND PRESS
© 1992 Dolores Walshe
Wolfhound Press receives financial assistance from The Arts Council / An
Chomhairle Ealaion, Dublin, Ireland
British Library Cataloguing in Publication Data
A catalogue record for this book is available from the British Library
ISBN 0-86327-319-X
Cover design: Fiona Lynch / *Typesetting:* Wolfhound Press
Printed in Great Britain by Cox and Wyman Ltd, Reading, Berkshire
WOLFHOUND PRESS, 68 Mountjoy Square, Dublin 1,
and Wolfhound Press (UK), 18 Coleswood Rd, Harpenden, Herts AL5 1EQ

Acknowledgements: I wish to record my heartfelt thanks and appreciation
to the following organisations and sources which furnished me with material
and information in the course of my research:

Irish Anti-Apartheid Movement; Amnesty International; Oxfam; Volunteer
Missionary Movement; Catholic Institute for International Relations; The former
International Defence and Aid Fund for Southern Africa, now the South African
Legal Defence Fund (SALDEF); Unicef; Concern; The Kairos Document, Johan-
nesburg 1986; Trocaire; International Conference on Children, Repression and
the Law in Apartheid South Africa, Harare, September 1987, convened by the
Bishop Ambrose Reeves Trust (BART); Willem C. van Manen, member of the
Amsterdam Bar, for his 'The Passtoors Trial' report to the International Com-
mission of Jurists and its Dutch section; Report on 'Police Conduct during
Township Protests,' Aug–Nov 1984, by the Southern African Catholic Bishops'
Conference; Officers of the Irish Defence Forces who have been exposed in their
peace-keeping experiences to some or other of the types of situation depicted in
this book.

A very warm thank you to Kader Asmal for his unceasing generosity of spirit.
My heartfelt gratitude to Louise Asmal for constant access to the wonderful data
bank she carries in her head. I very gratefully acknowledge the advice and
assistance of the late Nkululeko Sandile Trevor Vilakazi.

I know no words which would express my debt of gratitude to the very many
brave individuals who helped me in the course of my research, individuals as
ordinary and extraordinary as those whose children, relatives and friends have
been detained, tortured and murdered, individuals whose courage, humour and
generosity of spirit have saved me more than once, in the course of writing this
novel, from despair. For their own protection, they must remain anonymous.

It is with great humility and admiration I thank 'The Iron Keeper': my debt
is incalculable.

I am also very grateful to the novelist and poet Ben Okri, for his kind
permission to quote from 'An African Elegy'.

Very many thanks to my editor Mary Montaut, to Josephine O'Donovan,
Seamus Cashman, Fiona Lynch and all the staff at Wolfhound Press.

Lastly, I gratefully acknowledge a bursary received from the Arts Council,
Dublin, which kept me afloat during part of the writing of this book.

Chapter One

I

'*And a tree grew in Emma's womb.*' The words rustled in her head, old roots in a burial of rain, the 'and' suggestive of a life lived prior to the rooting of the tree, a life she could not remember.

Her belly sprouted branches weeping blood-bright with sloes. In the distance, the dog lifted his snout to the moisture in the wind and breathed. Turning, he moved through the darkness, tracking the bloodness of musk.

So, always, was the dream dreamed, her sleep giving birth to it, not in the long nights after the child had died, but later, much later when she thought the memory of the deed could not be exhumed.

Each time she woke marooned in sweat, alone: without Sipho, without the half-formed embryo that had been flesh of his flesh. Time passed, but the dream would not leave her, growing instead as the tree grew sapling-sweet in the dream, the dog slavering as he tore it limb from limb, making her womb a death chamber. In the end she faced it, for the dream was truth, swelling from the shadows of sleep, sapping the hollow-eyed flesh of her days.

By her own hand it had been done: the anaesthetised hours in a clinic to sanitise its death, its pulse faltering in her illegible signature under the polite eye of the reception nurse. For days, she and Sipho had warred over it. In the end, he had gone away, his walnut skin taut with hatred. Before he had gone, he'd given her a piece of paper. 'In case you change your mind,' he'd said, forcing her fingers round it till she held it in a tight, pink fist. But his dark eyes were bleak with the judgement of her set face.

Now Emma unfolded the shivering paper, staring at the number he'd written down: local, somewhere in the city, Hampstead, perhaps? But dialling it would only be the first step. If she wanted to see him again, she would have to find a way to get to Africa. And the way would of necessity be devious.

* * *

Sophie Chamberlain stood looking out the study window at the broad sweep of lawn stretching to the silver birches, the grass still frosted under the pale eye of the sun. To the north, towards London, the sky bulged with cloud.

It surprised her to find how much she still missed Nobby, his quiet bumbling presence at breakfast-time setting a pattern to her days. Now that he was dead it seemed pointless to eat in the dining-room, the rasp of her knife across the toast becoming a death-rattle echoed in the walls. Instead she got James to bring her a tray by the fire in the study, the flames warming her arthritic hands as she tried to break the mould of memory.

Over breakfast this morning, she had finished going through Emma Harford's portfolio, an impressive selection that testified to the woman's journalistic abilities. There was no doubt about it, she could be useful, very useful: a full-blown series of articles on South Africa in these censored times ... why, it'd be an absolute blessing.

Sophie crossed to the desk to re-read the letter Emma had written. Something in the tone of it didn't quite ring true. Sophie chewed the small, fleshy lump inside her bottom lip. Her son, Thulatu, went by many names. One of them was Sipho. This woman knew her son in one of his identities, that much was certain. Yet, in all the written information she'd given, she never mentioned his name.

Sophie frowned. Not that Thulatu himself had been any more forthcoming when he'd phoned her from Durban last evening, no direct admissions from him either.

'Let her come, though not to Jo'burg or Durban,' was all he'd said. But his voice had been glacial.

'Who is she, this Ms Harford?'

In the silence, she thought they'd been cut off. 'Hello, hello? Thulatu?'

'Keep me out of it, Mother. For the present, will you?'

She'd sighed, biting back her next question as he swiftly engineered an end to the call. He would tell her only what he wanted her to know, and only when he felt he wanted her to know it. It was a trait in him that had always amused Nobby. But then, Nobby hadn't been his father.

'Frankly, my dear, apart from the colour of his skin, he's exactly like you, it's the damnedest thing.' Nobby had laughed often, as though it were a huge joke. Still, she'd been lucky, all things considered. If Nobby hadn't been Nobby, she'd never have had Thulatu in the first place. But if Nobby hadn't been who he was, she'd never have been able to keep her son either. She drummed her fingers on the desk. Life had a queer habit of leading you round in circles, like the contours mapped on a mountain, the upper reaches made possible by the ground lower down. She and Nobby had been like that, each climbing about their own contours, yet locked in the solid mass of a marriage that had never been consummated in the physical sense of the word.

In the beginning she'd been bitter, blaming herself when the man she'd married couldn't make love to her. The posting to Africa had seemed to offer them a second chance, coming at a time when they'd both begun to despair. And the trip had indeed proved a watershed. Her mouth twisted in a wry smile. Though not in any possible way she could have imagined.

The moment she'd discovered that Nobby preferred the company of men had been the darkest of her life. She closed her eyes, remembering how she had run from it, through the orange grove until she'd reached Malathi's house. Still she could see him, sitting on the stoep, smoking a clay pipe, gazing with astonishment at the wall of trees as she broke through, breathless and weeping. Thulatu had been conceived there, in the whispering dark among the scent of ripening oranges.

From the moment she'd known she was pregnant, she'd begun planning the deception, she and Nobby closing ranks like discreet lovers locked in a lifelong secret tryst.

And tomorrow her son would come again, his first visit since Nobby's death. How she yearned for it! Yet before that, Emma Harford had to be dealt with, she ought to be well on her way here by now. What had been between this woman and Thulatu? She was itching to know. A pity he'd asked to be kept out of it, or she might've had her answer this afternoon. Sophie placed the letter in the portfolio and closed it. The interview would be a long one.

* * *

The house was in the heart of Sussex, a two-hour drive from London. Emma was unprepared for the sheer palatial scale of it, the mellow stone wall pacing her for miles before she finally reached the gates. Closed.

She sat looking through the Mini's cloudy windscreen as the engine whimpered into silence. Whatever words might have been carved into the stone pillars had long been overwhelmed by ivy. Above each pillar on a wide plinth, a sphinx gazed with mystic eyes into the distance of another world: as inscrutable as the future, or the dream instinct that drove her, overriding logic.

Rolling down the window, she lit a cigarette, reluctant to make the next move. The sudden stillness, in the wake of the engine's whine, was unnerving. Opposite the gates, a dark line of trees brooded on the edge of the deserted roadway. She had the distinct feeling she was being watched. Scanning the wall and gates, she tried to track it. It was then she spotted the camera.

Christ, she was crazy, the whole thing was crazy. She shivered in the blast of cold air invading the small interior. Didn't even know who she was to see. When she'd phoned the number, mentioning Sipho's name, the Nigerian had agreed to meet her. But when she'd gone to see him, he'd been unforthcoming.

'You must understand, Miss Harford, the need for ... discretion.' He had paused, the patina of his dark skin heightened against the cream silk of his shirt. Discretion. She'd tried to hide a grin. The language of the diplomat. Pure cloak and dagger. But now that she'd arrived, it was no longer comic, the high electronic lens peering from a network of ivy, trained on her with the patience of a cat which senses its prey. Better get out. Inaction might appear furtive.

The driver's door gave a piercing shriek as she pushed heavily against its warped hinges. A black explosion of crows burst from the trees, hurtling towards the sullen sky. She swore aloud, more from panic than anger. This, she thought, heading toward the gates. This is what it will be like. Heart going into overdrive every time I'm given more than a passing glance, do I want this? But she kept moving, the word back in her head again, pacing its insistent beat against the measure of her footsteps: tor-ture-torture-tor-ture. Sweat trickled between her breasts as her hand hovered over the intercom bell. Leave, she thought. Now.

'Yes?' The word barked belligerently from the speaker, thrust full in her face. A crackle, like showers of spittle trailing it.

'Eh ... Miss Harford.' She stared foolishly at the speaker. 'To see ... I, I have an interview.'

'Face the camera, please.' There was no courtesy in the rapping English tone.

She glanced up at the blank gaze of the lens. The cold eye of some faceless interrogator.

'Yes. You are expected.'

Turning at the sudden whirr, she caught sight of the small sign on the gates as they plunged inwards. 'Armed Response,' the carved words gold-leafed in a classic script, as though to soften their impact. Grimacing, she hurried back to the car. But her fear was gone, replaced by a strange sense of detachment that would carry her through until the hour she finally stepped on South African soil.

The engine screamed as she forced the stick into gear, lurching forward through the gates. Christ, a real rattletrap, the exhaust riddled with rust, belching smoke and wind with equal dexterity at the walls of withered rhododendrons lining the drive. Armed response. As long as nobody mistook her for some kind of threat.

The checkpoint took her by surprise as she rounded a bend, the electrified fence glinting in a sudden spear of sunlight. The armed guard was some distance ahead, his hand raised in a gesture she couldn't mistake. Who were these people? The Nigerian had told her nothing other than to give her a small hand-drawn map of the area fifteen miles south of Guildford, an 'x' marking the precise location of her appointment, the time written neatly beside it.

Professional, whoever they were. She stood apart while the young guard searched her car with an amused grin.

'Almost as old as this place,' he said, nodding at her when he'd finished.

'Where am I?' She looked up at him as he held the door and the warmth in his eyes was suddenly masked.

'Holbrook Hall, Madam,' he said, walking back toward the small concrete office. Madam! She couldn't have been more than ten years his senior. Disgusted, she rammed the gearstick into second as the barrier lifted.

Holbrook Hall. Now, where had she heard ...? Yes. Lord and Lady Chamberlain. Hadn't one of them died? She'd read something somewhere. Fairly recently? Ignoring the guard's renewed amusement, she coaxed the Mini spluttering and coughing past the checkpoint. Madam!

Another two miles, the drive ribboning through undulating meadowland dotted with clumps of oak and chestnut. Far to her right a medieval spire jutting from a small copse. On her left, swans rising in a cloudburst over the stippled grey of a lake.

Rounding a bend she came within sight of the house. She stared, the word 'house' seeming ludicrous in the face of what she saw, the vast edifice thrusting from the earth in a symmetrical design of towers, battlements and parapets, its classic columns supporting carved stone porches and balconies. Resplendent.

She tried not to think of the picture her car made approaching such a place. The tyres gorged on the gravel as she slid to a halt before the worn granite steps and she sat for a moment, eyeing the imposing entrance dubiously. To have come from the Nigerian's dusty little office in the London embassy to this. Incomprehensible. Perhaps she should try finding a back entrance? 'Emma, you're a peasant,' she murmured, grinning as she climbed out.

Nobody should be this rich. The steps took her by surprise, the same flinty stone of her grandmother's cottage in the Welsh mining village all those years ago.

'Miss Harford? This way, please.'

One half of the heavy door was already open, a pale man eyeing her disinterestedly, sleek as a penguin in his black suit. She followed him through the ceremonial hall, footsteps echoing on the flagged Italian marble, the ornate sarcophagus seats hugging the walls beneath a dizzying array of gilt-framed oil paintings, lavish tapestries.

He paused before a dark panelled door at the far end, knocking softly, his lips the width of a platypus beak as he gestured for her to enter.

Inside, the spines of a myriad books flickering in the firelight, deep bay window framing the outside day, the room ripe with the smell of old leather. A frail, elderly woman was poking logs in the Adam grate with a brass fire iron.

'Ah, Miss Harford. You've arrived. Do sit down. No, no, over here where I can see you.' A small hand flitted towards the fireside chair opposite her own. On a low table between them lay a bulging file, a silver tray set for two.

Emma stared at the lined face before her, the bird-cage fingers gripping the solid pot to pour. Somebody's grandmother. Was it possible? For some reason she couldn't fathom she'd expected a man. Or at least a more ... prepossessing woman.

'Is it ... you I've come to ...?'

'Yes. Drink your tea, child. You look half frozen.'

Child! Emma grinned, thinking of the young guard. 'You're not ... what I expected ...' she began, feeling foolish.

'Nor are you.' Bright eyes regarded her over the delicate rim of a teacup. 'You seem much younger than ... let me see ...' the fingers scrabbled at the file, '... thirty-eight, isn't it? Tell me why you want to do this.'

The directness took Emma by surprise. 'You are ... Lady Chamberlain?' she asked, partly to gain time, partly as a pointed reference to the lack of any kind of introduction.

'Yes. And I never shake hands — too many arthritic lumps. Well, my dear?' Sophie refilled the cups, sharp eyes twin beacons in the craggy layers of her face. Emma recalled what the Nigerian had said, 'Honesty. If you give anything less with this person, then I can assure you, Miss Harford, you won't stand a chance.'

She saw what he meant. For a moment she struggled, but the old woman's gaze was unwavering.

'Guilt,' she said at last, staring into the fire. The logs spat viciously in the silence that followed.

'Don't despise it, child.' The tone was gentle.

'I don't.' She didn't add that it was what was in herself she found hateful.

'You were born in South Africa?'

'Yes.'

'Your parents were Irish?'

Emma baulked at the prompt. Turning from the fire, she said, 'My mother. My father was Welsh. But you have all the details, I think.' She glanced at the file.

'I think not.' Sophie Chamberlain leaned forward grasping a log from the wicker basket. Let her come, Thulatu had said. But Sophie was damned if she'd conduct the interview as though the conclusion were foregone, despite her love for her son.

This part of her task was never easy. Yet she found she was relishing the challenge the young, jean-clad woman posed. A Renaissance face, she thought. And the eyes. Their shadowy lustre fixed on some inner star. Different from most of those who sought her help. It wasn't often a white one came. So spare with words it was positively irritating. No happy medium. They either talked too much or almost not at all. Once, when she had complained of this to Thulatu, he had said, laughing down at her, 'It's probably this place, even your queen would find it a trifle daunting!' Sighing, she tossed the log onto the fire. If only Thulatu hadn't made her promise not to mention him.

'Facts, my dear.' Sophie's fingers pecked the file. 'But you can fill in the details.'

'May I?' Emma was lighting the cigarette before the old lady could respond. Ashamed as she was of her need, the small ritual calmed her.

'The riot in Winsgate last month,' she began, the words tripping easily as she had planned them. Somewhere in the room a clock ticked into existence, as though it were racing to some sort of conclusion. Inexorable, Emma thought. Like the riot squad, batons drumming on the faceless shields, homing in on the inevitable hour of chaos.

'Contrary to what was reported, less than a quarter of those demonstrators were black.'

The old lady's eyes flickered, more as a gesture of acknowledgement than surprise.

'That Pakistani boy who's on the critical list. He wasn't even part of it. Standing on the sidelines, cheering the demonstrators on. Smiling, laughing as though it were some kind of parade.'

'You were there?'

Emma nodded, trying to keep her voice neutral. 'One of the few whites arrested. And Martin Burnett. A photographer. We work together a lot. They confiscated Marty's film. Broke his camera.' Her lips twisted. 'Accidentally. We were ... cautioned ... to say the least.' She paused to control her rising anger, feeling again the indignity of the strip search, the probing fingers, the questions about her Irish connections. Afterwards, when she'd sought to lodge a complaint, the implacable eye of the Chief of Police.

'But you carry an Irish passport, Miss Harford. In the interests of public safety you can hardly expect us to believe that you were there to compliment our police on their restraint?'

The police knew the work she did. Every detail. Every back issue of *Focal Point* she and Marty had sweated to print.

'They threatened a court injunction to stop us printing any of it. I presume you saw the official version all the papers carried?'

Sophie Chamberlain nodded. 'And the young boy?'

Emma dug her nails into the palms of her hands. It had been the boy who'd brought her the first dreams, the warm rush of his blood against her sweater as she'd caught him, stirring her memory, drenching her with guilt.

'A police baton. Two vicious blows. Marty caught it on camera. For all the good it did him.'

There was a hiss as the fire enveloped a trickle of sap from the log. The heat was suddenly oppressive. Emma waited. But the old lady said nothing.

'We were held for ....' She stopped. 'After we were released, I went to see the boy's family. His parents are still in Pakistan. He was living with his aunt. Zaleth, that's the boy, had won a scholarship through one of those cultural schemes. He was attending the London Polytechnic. He'd been in England three months. She, his aunt, kept saying the same thing over and over. "If he had not come here, he would be well. We come here, so full of hope that at last we can make a life for ourselves, but it is a lie. We are afraid here, always afraid. Every time there is trouble, you know? It is the black skin, always the black skin that becomes the scapegoat for you English. How do I tell his mother this? Tell me how?" ' Emma paused.

'What did you say to her?'

'Nothing. I said nothing. What could I say? We both knew she was right. I tried to persuade her to bring an action against the police, but she was too afraid. She said the police had been. They told her several eye-witnesses had identified Zaleth as one of the rioters who'd thrown rocks, attacked the riot squad. When I checked, it turned out the 'witnesses' were three young whites who had been arrested when the crowd surged forward, refusing to allow the police barricades to divert the march.' Emma's mouth tightened. How many times had she encountered it? — the travesty so subtle it was becoming an art form.'The aunt lives on a council estate. As it is, she is barely tolerated. She's afraid to speak out, afraid of what the neighbours might do. She even begged me not to reveal that she'd agreed to see me.'

'So what did you print?'

'Nothing. Not a damn thing,' Emma struggled to keep her voice level. 'Oh, there's an enquiry going on. But the outcome is a foregone conclusion. The police raided our office. Confiscated all our equipment. Some irregularity in our licence, they said. According to the lawyer, they can pussyfoot for months. Besides, I'd been looking into the high number of young black males ending up in special sections of mental institutions, being administered drugs their white counterparts wouldn't be given. All my paper-work on that was confiscated too.' Emma grimaced, remembering the months of painstaking research.

'But in the meantime,' Sophie's eyes narrowed, 'what started out as a peaceful, orderly march by hundreds of people protesting against unemployment and poor housing, has been portrayed as a riot led by blacks.'

'Well, who in the media is willing to stick their necks out and admit that police harassment of the demonstrators seemed to indicate a racial bias? Or that reportage itself was biased?' Emma's tone was bitter.

'I don't doubt your sense of outrage. But your desire to go to South Africa. Why now? Why not ...' Sophie Chamberlain glanced through the file ... 'ten years ago, when you first started writing about racism?'

So. The explanation hadn't been enough to let her off the hook. Nor, apparently, had the details of her mother's death she'd given in the file. The old lady wanted more. Emma gritted her teeth, wondering how to phrase it. But she wouldn't talk of Sipho or the abortion unless she was forced to it.

'How old were you when you left Pretoria?'

'Twelve. The orphanage agreed to release me into the custody of my father's family in Wales.'

'Then you must remember quite a deal.'

Quite a deal. Too much. Emma jumped up, moving to the window. Except for Sipho, it was all in the file. What was it that the old lady wanted? Outside, across the bright sward of lawn, a clump of dishevelled birch stood, a few stubborn leaves rusting on the branches.

'Yes.' Emma breathed shallowly, keeping her voice light. The need to beat around the bush, a few anecdotes told in just the right tone, then the words about her mother, unemotional, slipped into the conversation, bland as the next breath. But only if necessary. 'The day the sisters took me to the airport—. There was an old white woman, I've never forgotten her, she must have been seventy, marching up and down outside the Supreme Court, two boards strapped to her like an overall—.' She paused, seeing again the frail back bent with the weight of her slogans as the old lady leaned into the whipping wind.

'Last month, when the boy, Zaleth—. I kept thinking of that woman, what it must have cost to do a thing like that. Though she was protesting about the injustice of the pass laws, even the blacks were avoiding her, stepping round her like she was some kind of embarrassing mess on the pavement.' Emma swallowed, wanting to weep. The whites had done the same when the dog had savaged Mama, stepping around her bloodied stillness on the pavement as though she weren't there. When Emma had told Sipho about it, he'd said they couldn't look because it meant admitting what they kept their dogs for. She rubbed her eyes, seeing again the savagery of the timberwolf, colourblind once the scent of blood filled its nostrils, its training submerged in the swift unleashing of brute instinct.

In the silence, the clock reasserted its presence, each second dripping about her with the persistence of memory, gathering in pools until it threatened to engulf. She stared out across the landscape, a jumbled coverlet spread before her, something frightening in its secretive folds and curves.

The old woman's voice was gentle, as though she'd been reading her mind. 'How soon did your mother die after it?'

Emma took a deep breath, keeping her voice even. 'Five weeks and three days. They took me to see her in the hospital each Sunday, but she never regained consciousness after the heart attack.' She paused, struggling to contain it, but her voice, when it came, was acid. 'One of the sisters told me my mother was a virtual saint, that she'd reap her reward in heaven for going to help a poor coloured woman like that, that it was more than God would expect of any ordinary white.' She closed her eyes, remembering how she'd kicked out viciously at the nun, screaming fuck-God-fuck-God-fuck-God till the cowled face turned white as the nun fainted.

Sophie stared at the clenched back. How had a twelve-year-old managed to deal with a thing like that? She glanced down at the photocopy of the mother's death certificate in the file. She could only make out 'pulmonary embolism.' Under the doctor's illegible curlicues were some words written in a childish scrawl: 'It was the dog that kiled my mother.' Her throat thickened as she registered the misspelling.

Sophie tapped the file. She hated prying any deeper, but if this woman was to go to South Africa, the words had to be said, she had to face what she might be letting herself in for. And why now? A whole quarter of a century later? Why? The question hadn't been answered yet.

Emma heard the old woman tapping the file, but she didn't flinch as the words probed her back. 'They are still training dogs to attack natives, you know that, child? All the time you've been living here, they've been training them. Why have you waited till now?'

Emma closed her eyes. Oh, if only the boy had never bled on her, her sleep would've gone on being sleep! Why now? She couldn't answer it without speaking of the savage in herself, the same monstrous thing rearing its ugly head in the dreams, killing the child as it had killed her mother. She wouldn't, couldn't talk about it to this stranger. Some truths were only for self-inspection. She wouldn't mention the abortion, or Sipho, even if it meant losing. The decision made her light-headed, courageous, as though she'd had a few drinks on an empty stomach. But she mustn't lose, she mustn't! The old lady must be convinced! She had to see Sipho again, she had to find him. She began to speak, the words tumbling recklessly.

'Why now? An accumulation of guilt, I think. Here, in Europe, the prejudice is so ... well disguised. Insidious, even. And there's a limit to how much we want to read about our failings. Besides, if there's a special offer on South African fruit in the market this week, who's going to turn it down? Especially when our politicians tell us that sanctions would just impose further hardship on the blacks? At least if I write about South Africa, I'm free to make a living, historical record of the truth. The dream of most journalists. And it will be tolerated here, encouraged even, because it is the story of somebody else's mess. Perhaps coming at it sideways is the only way we can stomach truth.' She paused, breathless. Sometimes she was startled to find herself functioning so craftily, times when she seemed to stand on some kind of periphery, watching herself perform.

Behind her, silence. The clock became relentless in the vacuum. Emma swivelled, catching an odd expression on the old lady's face. But as swiftly as she tried to decipher it, it was gone, leaving her with a vague sense of discomfort under the steady gaze.

Sophie sighed, searching the desperate face. It was the first time she had failed. Whatever moved this woman was going to remain a secret, that much was certain. And not a single word about her son. She'd have to try working on Thulatu when he came tomorrow, she was damned if she'd let him keep her in the dark about this one. She closed the file. Let her come, he'd said. As if he knew the reason. Suddenly, she saw it. He did know the reason why this woman wanted to go, he knew because he was the reason. She stared hard at Emma. My God, was it really so simple that she'd almost missed it?

'You know, I could ask why you ... I could ask you the same question,' Emma blurted, uneasy under the shrewd gaze.

The calm eyes widened. 'You could, child.' Sophie Chamberlain picked up the file and carried it across to the oak desk dominating the far corner of the room.

'I mean, you must have started ... somewhere ... for some reason ... I mean, we all have our ....'

'Reasons?' the old lady supplied helpfully.

Emma felt the heat in her cheeks. 'I, I mean—.'

'Conviction is a misleading word, don't you think? Come and sit here by my desk. Merely the outward ... manifestation, shall we say? Where have I put that blasted diary?' Papers and books were pushed aside in the search. 'What's more interesting ...' Sophie Chamberlain stopped suddenly, delicate head tilted, a bird tracking the rustle of an insect in the earth ... 'crucial ...' she stressed, '... is the root of the conviction, what it stems from, because that, my dear, is what will bring you through.'

Emma stared. 'Bring me through ...?'

'Living in South Africa.'

Emma uncurled her fingers. The palms of her hands stung where the nails had bitten deep.

'Then you'll help me?' She tried to keep the relief out of her voice, knowing there would be no more questions. Something had softened in the old lady, the hard edge gone from the line of her mouth, the edge that could have turned this interview into a battle of wills, and won.

'That root had better be strong.' The eyes demanded utter commitment. To what? Emma was wary of saying anything which might upset the sudden balance she sensed had been achieved between them.

'How soon?' She sat up straight, denying the impulse to lean forward.

'Let me see. Today's the—. I'll make an appointment for the fourteenth. A Doctor Rutledge, he's in Bellvue, here's his card.' Without looking up, she held out the white rectangle, scribbling frenetically as Emma took it.

'Doctor?'

'Have you ever had a typhus shot?'

'Typhus?'

'Fortunately, it won't take me long to clear you with our people.'

'What about the cultural ban? Won't they—?'

The old lady raised her head, smiling. 'I shouldn't think there'll be any problem, not when they know what you're about.'

'Look, I probably should've mentioned this earlier—.' Emma paused, embarrassed. 'I'm afraid I've very little money—.'

'You'll need a passport, of course. Best not to take any chances on your own.'

'But I've done nothing wrong—.'

'Nothing other than to declare yourself through your writings as a strong opponent of racism. Not exactly the kind of career that makes you enamoured of the South African government: that magazine of yours isn't unknown in the South African Embassy, child.' Sophie Chamberlain's laugh was gleeful. 'Though it hasn't been known to grace the coffee tables in reception. No, a new passport is essential.' Her pen scratched busily. 'I'll give you an address to go to. Then there's the residence permit. I'll arrange that myself. How long?' The old lady shot her a glance. Emma, having fished a notebook from a back pocket, was trying to keep up.

'Don't!'

Pencil poised, Emma looked up startled.

'No notes.' The voice was firm.

'But I write everything down.' She grinned. 'The journalist in me.'

'Not this time. And you take nothing to South Africa, nothing, you understand?' The tone brooked no argument. 'If you're ever picked up by SAP, there'll be nothing to incriminate you.' A thin gold band slid from a finger-joint back toward the knuckle as the old lady tapped her forehead. 'This is your notebook. Rely on it, use your eyes, your ears, that's all.' Her voice was grim. 'It'll be more than enough, I can promise you. Now, I'd also like you to see Dan Whittiger, he's a psychiatrist, among other things. He'll brief you on police interrogation methods, that ... sort of thing.' She paused. 'It's unlikely that you'll be detained, still, best to take every precaution.'

Emma tried to nod. The gesture seemed more like a reflexive twitch she couldn't control. Her feet felt swollen, suddenly stifled in the light sneakers; she wanted to flee but her legs were leaden weights in some peculiar tug of war between thought and action.

Littered with the stamp of the old woman's integrity, the desk yawned between them, a vast gulf leaving Emma stranded in her own shame as the efficient voice droned about her ears. She sat on, redundant, while Sophie made and received calls, stopping now and then to bark instructions at the sepulchral voice of her male secretary coming over the intercom. Emma shivered. With a voice like that, perhaps it was as well Sophie kept him secreted in some ante-room. The old lady's energy was unflagging, and it was late in the evening before she was satisfied that all the necessary arrangements were sufficiently under way. In the end, at her insistence, Emma agreed to stay overnight.

'Don't you ever get tired?' she asked as they sat at last eating dinner in the cavernous dining room, the glitter of the crystal chandelier pale in comparison to its reflection blazing from the burnished wood of the old refectory table.

'Lonely, perhaps, but ... tired? Whatever from?' Sophie raised her wispy eyebrows, but her tone was teasing. 'Have some more salmon, child, perhaps it'll revive you!'

Emma laughed, relaxing despite herself as Sophie began to talk about her own childhood.

'I was what was known as a "late" child, which is to say I was too late to be considered as a candidate for inclusion in Mother's and Father's incredibly busy lives.' Sophie sipped the chilled wine as she talked on, and Emma found herself wondering at the lack of bitterness in her tone. Not just 'late,' but an only child, she'd been dispatched from boarding school each summer to French and Italian holiday camps, bleak summer schools run on rigid disciplinary lines spawned in the early part of the century to meet the needs of wealthy parents wishing to unload their offspring. Though the old lady spoke of it all lightly, Emma sensed the misery and solitariness inherent in such an upbringing. It struck a responsive chord in her own memory, the later part of her childhood spent with her Welsh grandmother, a dry, taciturn woman whose sudden outbursts of anger had terrified her. She was now a little tipsy, as much from the wine, she thought, as the conversation.

'A strange and lovely evening,' she suddenly blurted. If she were sober she'd have blushed at her own words. But Sophie nodded, smiling, patting the back of her hand. They talked on then, into the small hours, the sense of something shared forging a bond of sympathy that prompted Sophie to ask as they moved at last from the dining room, 'My dear, won't you change your mind about this?'

Emma stood in the huge shadowy hall, bleary-eyed. 'What?' But even as she asked, she knew what Sophie was referring to.

'You don't have to do any of this.' Sophie touched her hand to Emma's cheek.

'But I want—.'

'Whatever you want, it seems to me that after what happened to your mother, Africa already owes you a debt. Not the other way around. Why don't you sleep on it, child?' The anxiety in Sophie's face took Emma by surprise. She felt a rush of warmth, of gratitude even. Leaning swiftly, she kissed the old lady's cheek. 'Thank you,' she whispered, not trusting her voice, 'but I won't change my mind.' Turning, she hurried towards the butler waiting impassively at the foot of the wide marble staircase to show her to her room.

By the time she left after breakfast the next morning, her destination within South Africa had already been decided. Hurtling down the drive, her mind swarmed with instructions. Three weeks. Just as well. No time to breathe. Or reflect. Rounding a curve too quickly she found herself gazing into the bared teeth of a chrome radiator. Grasping the wheel, she sheered crabwise into the grass verge as the silver chauffeur-driven hulk eased past. In the back, a coloured man sat, his face large, fine-boned, eyes fixed in amusement on some inner point of reference as he worked to fasten a stiff clerical collar about his neck.

'Well, fuck you too!' Emma hissed when she could breathe again. She stared at her hands trembling on the wheel. The features had not been unlike Sipho's. Or was it the subtle shading of skin which tricked her? Though the glimpse had been brief, blurred almost in the speed at which both cars had been travelling, it was enough to spark the old longing. Fool, she thought. Let it die. *Requiescat in pace.* She coaxed the car back onto the drive, trying to make light of it. She could always hare after the sometime priest, persuade him to perform a funeral service. For whom, my daughter? For lost lovers, Father, and .... No. Drop it. Thin ice. Anyway, he was no priest, she'd swear it. A cheat, come to lighten the old lady's pockets. Sipho had talked with disdain of one such man: an exiled black who claimed to have spent five years on Robben Island working side by side with Mandela in the lime quarry. A week after someone had spilled the beans, he'd been fished out of a quiet stretch of the Thames by a policeman on night duty, a rambling note found in his room reiterating his claim. He'd been telling his story for too long. In the teeth of death he was unable to relinquish it. That is what happens, she thought. We become the fabrication. Hers, too, had been lethal. The spillage from her womb. But the dreams had taught her to stop blaming Sipho, the dark urge of his anger.

* * *

Thulatu rubbed the groove in his neck where the starched collar had bitten. A relief to get the damn thing off. As the car rounded the final curve, bringing the house into view, he leaned forward, sliding back the glass partitioning him from the chauffeur.

'Well, Rafiq.'

'In all the glory, Sir.' The elderly driver gestured at the house.

'Less of the "Sir".' Thulatu tapped his shoulder. Rafiq was one of the hand-picked few who knew the truth. Thulatu stared ahead, drinking it in. No matter how infrequently he came, the feeling was always the same. Coming home. It would be nice, once, to come up the drive as the man he was instead of the son of the old African retainer the Chamberlains had, in their generosity, brought back with them to England to be civilised and educated. But not even when Nobby had died, had Sophie been tempted to declare him openly. A lot more could be achieved for Africa by the cover they maintained.

Yet, for all his pleasure at being here, soon he would long for a glimpse of the green walls of sugar cane sweeping from Durban to the low forested hills that screened the distant townships from the sensitive eye of the city. The tug of history, more compelling than birthright. And the tug of his son. His daughter too, though he knew he would never have the courage to own her. He smiled, pulling the photo from his breast pocket, unable to resist the urge to look at it yet again. Up till now, he'd only ever seen her in the distance; the white family she'd married into weren't in the habit of courting coloured friends. The pale face stared back at him, the dark eyes and hair not unlike his own. But it was her mother she truly resembled, the same fair skin, the same doll-like features set in the delicate face. Uncanny, as though her mother were still alive. Sophie would be thrilled to see a photo of Mia at last. And he'd Babo to thank for it, she'd taken it specially for him the last time she'd been to dinner with her brother and his wife. Not that he'd have it for long. He grinned as the powerful wheels spat the gravel onto the steps before the hall door. His mother would pounce on it as soon as he produced it, insisting it belonged in the little private family album she kept separate from the tomes of horsey Chamberlains dating back to the year dot. Perhaps he shouldn't show it to her till tomorrow, have the pleasure of it for one more day. When he got back to Durban, he'd ask Babo for the negative, have another one printed for himself.

* * *

Sophie had just returned the receiver to its cradle, when the door swung inwards.

He stood still, watching her. It was in this woman his feeling of coming home was rooted. The day that she was not here, already she was in her seventies — he broke off, winded by the thought as she hurried towards him. For a long time they held each other. He was struck by the changes ten months had wrought.

'A starved sparrow. What're you trying to do, shame me?' He pressed his lips against the wisps of white hair.

'If I could do that, I'd have my son here with me. You're early, I wasn't expecting you for another—.'

He heard the faint tremors in her voice and waited for her to regain control. She didn't like him to witness what she considered her moments of weakness.

Later, sitting by the fire, she told him of Emma. 'You just missed her, she left right before you arrived.'

He looked at the sharp gaze tracking his face. Had his mother kept Emma overnight, deliberately, hoping to see the two of them together? He wouldn't put it past her. 'How unfortunate.' His tone was mocking, but he was careful to keep his face expressionless as he stared into the flames. She talked on, giving him time, he thought, time to come in his own way to telling her. Yet he couldn't talk about

Emma. Not tonight. He'd thought by now he had it under control. But her face staring at him from the professional photograph in the portfolio, brought it all back, his hatred for her, for the thing that she'd done, writhing in his gut. He sighed. There were times when he cursed the colour of his skin. Perhaps he'd do better to curse his choice in women, choices which had cost him two of his children. Well, thank God he had his son. If it weren't for Thabo, Emma's abortion would have driven him mad. He tightened his grip on the brandy glass, trying to forget how he'd begged, begged her, please, please don't kill it, Emma, Emma, it's a life, a life, flesh of our flesh, it's got a brain, Emma, a mind forming even as we speak, dreaming its first beautiful dreams, I'll take it, love it, feed it, clothe it ... cherish, oh how I'll cherish it, Emma, please, please! He closed his eyes, trying to blot it out. Whatever he told Sophie about the whole affair, he wouldn't tell her that. Thinking of it still left him feeling his stomach was ripped, his insides exposed to the raw sun. What was Emma up to? What? Whatever twisted purpose she had in trying to contact him, she was in for a shock. He didn't plan on seeing her till it suited his purpose. And then, God strike him if he didn't make her suffer for what she'd done, suffer as he'd suffered, as he still suffered, as he would always—.

'... Thulatu?'

Sophie's voice brought him back.

'I said, I've decided to send her to Rhaumsfontein, don't you think that's the best—?'

'Dick will have a fit. He's always considered his mission clinic there to be a one-man show.'

'Well, you asked me to keep her away from you.' Her eyes were hawkish. He sighed. She'd plague him the entire trip if he didn't say something. 'Tomorrow, Mother, we'll talk about it then.'

She nodded, dropping it. 'Tomorrow' would lengthen into several, but in the end she'd find out or know the reason why. 'When does Dick get back from California? Couldn't you have a chat with him, explain what she's about?' Sophie reached across, and patted his knee coaxingly. 'I'd like her to go to him, he's been there longer than any of the others.'

He put his glass down on the table. 'From what you've said, she's penniless, it seems. Did she give you any idea why she wants to go now?' He kept his tone casual.

'I rather thought you could answer that one for me.'

He stared back into the fire, refusing to meet her eyes.

'Don't worry, I'm not going to harp. As long as you tell me before you go back. Rudi's done his homework, she's been well vetted. And she's a fine journalist, I'll grant you. Painstakingly honest.

Courageous.' Her fingers tapped the file between them. 'You'd have to be blind not to see that. Besides, there are photostats in there of two jobs she's been offered recently, apart from freelance—.'

Thulatu tried to keep the annoyance out of his voice. 'What's this? The Emma Harford Fan Club? I don't need to be reminded of her ...' his lips curled '... attributes.' He was sorry as soon as he said it, his mother's gaze trained on his face. He sat forward, picking up the brandy, making a fuss of swilling it about the glass. When he spoke again, his voice was even-keeled. 'A pity you didn't think of sending her to the Cape. They're more accommodating—.'

'But you said yourself this priest in Rhaumsfontein was overworked, the conditions you described—.'

'Yes, I know, but Dick actually likes to work on his own, he's not very good with women, most particularly white ones.' Thulatu forced a laugh. 'I think he sees them as a pampered species. He made short work of the two ladies the Black Sash sent him last year—.'

'Well, you're going to have to help her out, it's worth it, surely? In six months she'll be back here with new material, fresh, unbiased, and most important, uncensored. I've already talked to Harvey. He says if we can come up with a series of articles, he'll do a major feature, running over several weeks.'

'I won't be her babysitter, Mother.'

Sophie fidgeted. She didn't like the look on his face. There was bad feeling, too much of it, in the sudden glitter of his eyes. 'You're the one who knows her, who said to let her come.'

'Yes. We can use her, we can't afford to look a gift-horse in the mouth where the struggle's concerned. But that's all.' His voice was hard.

'No it's not. I happen to like her. I won't have her used, just to further the struggle. She's sort of ... lost-looking, for all her qualifications. Like it or not, I'm insisting you keep an eye on her. Besides, as you've just said yourself, it's in our own interests.' She leaned forward, anxious to change the subject. He was tense, tired from the long trip. She'd give him time to unwind before she tackled him again. 'Now tell me how my grandson is.' She relaxed as his face brightened. He pulled out the photos of Thabo. Someone had snapped him during a student protest march, his dark fist raised in defiance as he challenged the camera.

'Oh, I wish he'd finish his studies first! Then he can get involved in the struggle. He'll never become a lawyer if—.'

Thulatu passed on quickly to the next photo. Pointless trying to explain to Sophie the new philosophy. Once, he had attempted it, but she couldn't take on board the idea that it had become a children's struggle. Or wouldn't.

Nor could he blame her. It took the heart of a Boer to contemplate the children being fleeced of their childhood in police cells. Thank God Thabo had escaped it. For those who hadn't .... Hardened. Something forever crystallised in the dark, watchful eyes.

'Thulatu? You're not listening. I said, if that boy had a mother, he wouldn't be like he is. She'd soon knock some sense into him. Education is everything, doesn't he know that, for goodness sake?'

Thulatu roared with laughter. 'He says it won't give him a vote. And that's not how politely he puts it. How can you argue with that!'

II

When the waiter came to refill his glass, Dick refused the wine. His mother was seated towards the far end of the trestle table, slowly getting pissed. He would have to drive.

At the tables all about, conversation vibrated in the Californian heat, the overhead canopies strung between spruce and pine, full-bellied sails in the merest whisper of wind. Despite his boredom, his lack of appetite, he forced himself to eat. Seventeen years with people who walked a tightrope of poverty and hunger had left him with nightmares about wastage.

Luckily, he'd been placed at one end of the table, his gaze forced to confront no one in particular. The women on either side had long since given up on him. They were discussing the merits of something. Idly, he kept an ear to their conversation.

'... that's when I decided. My second husband, Ron? It was all his idea really.'

The left-hand voice laughed. 'According to my ex, having my colour chart done was what broke up our marriage. No, don't get me wrong, it wasn't the money, he was good that way, I'll say that for him. Why, one time, up in Tahoe, he blew more than a thousand on one a those silver dollar machines? Sometimes he'd win, but mostly he lost, right down to the last dollar. I kept telling him it'd happen, but he just kept feeding those dollars in, like that crummy machine was some kinda ... cow or something, with four or five stomachs, y'know?'

'Aw-haw? You couldda had your colours done twice for that—.'

'Yeah, when I think of it. I kept walking round that machine, wondering where all those dollars were going, musta been a hole in the floor or something. Anyway, we split up soon after I had my colours done.'

Unable to resist, he stole a glance at the left-hand voice. Her colours had certainly been 'done': a perfect epiphany of pink and lilac traced through the clothing into the lipstick and onto the fingernails. No worse than his mother, really, the living embodiment of Autumn in muted ochres, rusted browns, shades of withered leaves. The human canvas, a rich source of income for failed artists. Selling like hot cakes in the midst of a famine. God, how he wished he were back in Africa. He watched the preparations get underway for the fashion parade. A wooden dais threaded a path between the diners, so that nobody should miss a close-up of the latest in designer wear.

A hundred bucks a ticket. He was still staggered by it.

'But, honey, the *proceeds* are going to the Star of the Firmament, surely you see—.'

'And what d'you think they're going to do with the money? C'mon, you tell me.' He'd banged his fist on the breakfast table, upsetting a glass. 'For Chrissakes, they're paying their goddamn taxes with it! Don't you know when you're being conned?' Seeing the triumph in her eyes, immediately he'd been sorry, knowing it would open the same old floodgates.

'There's no call to swear at your mother. What kinda son'd swear at his mother, what kinda ... *priest!* You shouldda stayed here with your mother, instead a going to that *heathen* hell in the first place. Seems that place is teaching you nothing but swearwords and ... and *sour* ways! Why, you'll be lucky if you don't catch AIDS!'

He'd stared at her, dumbfounded. 'Wha—, what did you just say?'

'You heard me.' She was swabbing at the spilt juice with a cloth. 'That's where it comes from in the first place, all those black people being promiscuous. There was this *doctor* talking on the Johnny Carson Special ....'

He held his breath until the ringing in his ears alarmed him. Somehow, he'd have to call a halt. Control it. He sucked air into his lungs in long, deep draughts.

'Listen, Mom, sit down, will you?' Wrapping his blunt, pink fingers about her wrist, he tugged gently. 'In a couple a days I'll be gone again, no, don't let's start on that, just let's try making the time pleasant as we can for both of us, huh?' He tried to peer into her face, but she kept her head down, the rich auburn curls deceptively childish. Close to her scalp, the grey roots were pushing forth. Nature admits no counterfeit. It was difficult to feel compassion. She had never mothered. She had ... managed him. The reference to AIDS. Did she still have lingering doubts about his sexuality? Laughable really. Almost. He cringed when he recalled what she'd put him through during puberty.

'Listen to me,' he said leaning towards her. 'That stuff about AIDS, that's a load a hogwash, racist hogwash, y'hear?'

'D'you have to go back so soon?' The real cause of the friction between them. By now he was immune to the plea in her voice.

'Couldn't you take, one a them, what's-its? Sabbaticals?'

'What is it you want? A consecrated robot on your arm, blessing everything in sight?'

In the silence, the refrigerator hiccupped, then settled to a long, agonised whine.

'Lots of people take sabbaticals, not just priests, doctors even, and *dentists*.'

When he didn't answer, her voice became plaintive. 'Is that too much for a mother to expect from her *son*, her *only* child?'

'Listen,' he said. 'I'll come to this fete thing, this garden farce, okay?'

'If that's meant to distract me, I am not ... *moved*.'

But he could see she was pleased. He followed it up quickly. 'You can show me off to your friends, I'll be so charming you—.'

'You'll talk to Hettie? If you could only be *nice* to her, she's so fond of you, y'know?'

He had promised. But by evening his enthusiasm had waned. Hence, her inebriated state. Somehow he got through dinner under Hettie's reproachful gaze, as she sat consoling his glassy-eyed mother.

A young Hispanic in a short black frock and frilled apron began clearing their table. He rested his gaze on her thin arms, filled with a sudden longing for the dark, hungry faces of his own people, the immediacy of their needs, his life's blood.

There was something odd about the way she was clearing: a surreptitious storing of the larger chunks of food, steak, generous helpings of vegetable, sweetmeats, in one of the big serving vessels. When she had cleared everything, she came back for the dish.

Excusing himself, he wandered after her into the giant marquee. The heat greeted him like a blast from a furnace, the smell of food and stale sweat choking his nostrils. A small, red-faced man was whipping about, barking orders at the groups of dark-skinned women preparing desserts, stacking dishes, filling garbage sacks. From another opening at the far end, waiters flitted in and out, popping corks, grabbing the sweet, white Napa wines to be served with dessert.

Suddenly the red-faced man's attention was arrested. Dick followed his gaze, seeing the young girl move with the dish into a shadowy corner opposite, the grassy floor heaped with items of clothing, shabby pocketbooks, frayed shopping bags. It was partially screened from the main arena by a heap of cardboard food cartons. The changing room. Dick's mouth curled. By the time the man stood behind her, the girl was already stooping to empty the food into a plastic bag. The man watched her for a moment, then reaching out, began to massage her buttocks. She froze, a bobcat caught in the beam of a headlight, her face a struggle between revulsion and, what? The desire to keep the food? More than that. Fear. Dick saw it clearly: her need to work, her illegal status making her the perfect prey. Marin County. Land of plenty. Rich pickings for the rich, while the poor were smelted into new gold. No different from South Africa, except here they were doing it more discreetly.

Anger clenched in his throat, Dick moved forward. He would have to be careful. She wouldn't thank him if he lost her her pay.

'Hey, you there!' His drawling voice, deliberately raised, turned more than one curious head. The hand dropped instantly from the girl's buttocks as the man swung to face him. Dick addressed the girl. 'You manage to find something to wrap that food?'

Straightening, she stared at him uncomprehendingly. Come on, don't blow it now, he thought. He turned, smiling at the man.

'My dogs,' he said. Thank the Lord he wasn't wearing his collar. 'Got six Great Danes. Eating me outta house and home. You ever kept dogs?'

The man frowned, unwilling to be drawn in. 'Naw, I—.'

'I tell you, it's an expensive business.' Dick laughed. 'I never pass up on the leftovers. Why, you wanna know something? Once, couple a years back, I was up Sonoma way—.'

'Listen bub, I ain't got time—.' The man was backing off, gesturing towards the din behind him.

'Sure thing.' Dick laughed raucously. 'I'll just be picking up my doggie bag from the little lady.'

He turned to the girl. Already the man was out of earshot, bawling fresh orders as he thrashed back into the hub of activity. He held out his hand. 'I'd better take it, just in case he's watching.'

Wordlessly, she handed it to him, eyes wide.

'I'm at table fifteen. I'll leave it under my chair.' He winked, catching the ghost of her smile before he turned to walk from the tent.

'Hey, Misterr! Tsank you!' The low words reached his ears as he neared the exit. Without turning, he raised his hand in a gesture of acknowledgement.

Outside, the fashion show had begun, the air filled with appreciative murmurs as the first models twitched like stick insects in their autumn furs, mincing along the dais in time to the music. Someone had served him a large wedge of cheesecake.

'We didn't know what to order, you were gone so long. Then your Mom said cheesecake's your favourite, so we took the liberty, okay?' The lilac epiphany beamed, her breath thick with tobacco as she tried to make herself audible above the commentator's shrill voice. Nodding his thanks, he glanced at his mother's rapt expression. She was gazing cross-eyed at the furs designed to brave winter in the Antarctic. Silently, he cursed her. She knew he hated cheesecake.

* * *

Before he left, she gave him another gold cross and chain. It was heavier than the previous one.

'Mind you don't lose it like you did the other one.' She stood, folding and refolding his shirts in the suitcase. She wouldn't come to the airport, but she insisted he phone his father.

'Lord knows when you two'll get to see each other again.'

'That should keep him happy.' He spoke without rancour. Neither he nor his father ever had much to say to each other.

'You shouldn't *talk* about him like that. Just because we got divorced doesn't mean—.'

'All right, all right, I'll phone him.'

But his father was out. Fortunately. Save them both squirming their way through awkward formalities.

Silently she drove him to Larkspur to catch the ferry, the evening air cool enough to have the windows open. From the gardens, came the hiss of lawn sprinklers; behind it, the first faint notes of the crickets. Browsing above the houses, the yellow hills where he had teased lizard, frog and rattlesnake. Soon the rains would come, wash them green. He would never see them again. The thought, unbidden, startled him.

'You won't leave it so long, next time, will you?'

'No,' he lied. Why had he come? He hadn't been forced to. He had not even needed the vacation. He had never been one of those who cracked under stress, a valuable asset in the eyes of the church, and more particularly, the ancient order of friars in Europe to which he was attached.

The ferry was in. As he stood with her for a moment, ticket in hand, he felt a sense of regret, a vague need to salvage something.

'*I'll* miss you,' she said.

He smiled. 'You always stress the wrong words.' He put his arms about her shoulders. But there was no give in her.

As the ferry reversed out into the bay, he looked back. Already she was getting into the car, her face turned toward Sausalito. He pictured her back in the apartment, remote control in hand, flicking from one evangelical channel to another, the television becoming a pulpit. Or had she only done it to punish him while he was there?

Like the list, pinned to the kitchen wall: all the churches in the state of California, each one that she'd joined crossed out in thick red felt-tip, soon as she'd moved on to the next. And the notes left lying in strategic places after every argument: 'Must remember I am not *speaking* to him,' or the one after their last row, 'Must remind him that charity begins at home, it *says* so in the Bible.'

God in heaven, such relief to be out of it, a forty-four-year-old ape who couldn't figure out what it was his mother would not forgive him for.

The ferry lumbered relentlessly, the sun's last rays, lava trapped in foam. San Quentin eased past like a bloated whale, the string of men a blue-beaded necklace in the exercise yard. Violence, he thought. Regenerating in a savage breeding-ground. Across the bay the city's business sector prodded the sky, a monolithic stab at civilisation. Home of the free and the brave. On Monday mornings, right across its vastness, the pledge of allegiance chorussed in classrooms. Every heart beats true. To form. The image came again, swiftly: the young girl in the tent, the soft bulge of her flesh straining against the fabric as she bent over. He stared across at Alcatraz, trying to blot it out. Fortress of nothing, he thought, locked in the sea. But the girl's image could not be shaken. He felt the familiar tingle in the back of his neck, a sense of constraint in the dark suit, and shifted uneasily. The ferry bucked suddenly, driving the spray in his face. Like a cold shower. He grinned. And his mother had doubts about his sexuality.

III

Emma stared down at the yellow tailing dumps and mine heaps as the plane dipped towards Johannesburg, engines thrumming noisily. Some were in disuse, the tops covered in rubble, or concreted over. The city itself was divided by the gold-bearing ridge of the Witwatersrand running east to west, a labyrinth of towering cubes and rectangles spreading to suburbs of well-defined gardens in the north, the blue sky locked in the kidney swimming pools. Earlier, as the plane had first lost altitude, to the south she'd glimpsed a vast complex of squares, barely discernible through a thick layer of smog. Soweto? She had strained eagerly to peer towards Rhaumsfontein to the west but the distant landscape merged in a blur of light and shade.

Security was tight at Jan Smuts. Armed guards everywhere. Confidently, she stepped through the electronic beam, submitting her handbag to the metal detector. It would take a far more sophisticated instrument than they possessed to detect the poison in her heart. Black and white mixed freely in the queues for passport control. No sign of apartheid here. Except all the administrative staff was white, as though there were no Africans in South Africa other than those visiting. She shook a little as the middle-aged official perched on his high stool within the glass cubicle studied her passport, his blue gaze flicking to check her surname on the small computer level with his knees. She answered the few desultory questions he put to her with her lips parted in what she hoped was a smile. But he seemed more intent on keeping his queue moving, his eyes already on the person behind as he handed her documents back.

Sweating a little, she walked out into the foyer, the large sign, 'Welcome to South Africa,' greeting her effusively, the walls adorned with magnificent Safari posters: springbok, cheetah, elephant, wildebeest. A small, wizened black porter came trundling towards her and she shook her head, smiling politely.

According to Sophie, she would be paged by whoever was to meet her.

She sat, smoking cigarette after cigarette until she felt nauseous, but though she waited a long time, nobody called her name over the intercom. All about her, people greeted people, or moved with purposeful faces towards the exits. What if nobody came for her? She felt oddly bereft. Maybe nobody would come, maybe she was stranded here, Christ, why didn't someone come, her ears were addled from listening to the muffled voice making announcements over the air, her heart leaping every time a name sounded similar to her own. She took a few deep breaths, finally thinking to check at the information desk.

The girl was friendly, advising her to look on the notice board. And there it was, how stupid could she be, the message phoned in, transcribed on a standard airport memo: 'Ms Emma Fitzgerald' — Sophie's idea to take her mother's maiden name for the new passport — 'Unable to meet you. Taxi to city centre bus rank, mini bus to Rhaumsfontein terminal, north three blocks, east one block, Church of the Holy Cross, Portacabin at rear.' Unsigned. She blinked away the tears of relief. So. She hadn't been forgotten. She re-read the message, suddenly niggled by the terseness of it. No apology, no attempt at any kind of courtesy. Apart from which, she'd need a frigging compass. Charming.

She was still seething less than an hour later as the taxi wove its way through a seedy entertainment strip close to the city centre. It reminded her of Soho. Here, the faces were mixed; black, white, the euphemous Cape coloured, Indian, Asian, some other skin shades, subtle bone structures that reminded her of aboriginals. 'Hillbrow, Miss,' the driver informed her when she asked. 'It's often called the grey area,' he said and laughed. He was coloured.

'Why?'

'It's officially a white area, you see those blocks of flats? Many blacks and coloureds live there among the whites. They work in the bars and cafes, the night clubs, it's convenient for everybody, even the bosses, so nobody talks about it, that is the way.'

The mini bus turned out to be a Kombi-van that had seen better days. She grinned. It would've made her own old Mini, which she'd sold for scrap, look positively healthy. All the passengers were black, the line operating as a taxi service between township and city. It took her a while to persuade the driver that this was the bus she needed to board. Her cheeks were burning under the eyes of the other passengers, some curious, some openly hostile as comprehension finally dawned on the driver. He clapped a hand to his brow, a smile cracking the ice in his gaze. 'Ah, you want the Roma church?' She nodded, unsure of what he meant, but relieved when he reached out to haul her bag on board. His words seemed to set the minds of the other passengers at rest, a couple of them even smiling as they made room for her to sit. Roma? She lurched in unison with every other body on board as the bus frog-leapt, then settled into a series of jumps and glides as it headed out into the early evening traffic. Roman Catholic, that must be it. She grinned. It wasn't often in her life she found herself glad to cling to religion.

A couple of hours later, she dragged her case from the bus and stood shivering in the biting wind as the battered mini bus turned back towards Johannesburg. Terminal. She made a face. A heap of rubble on the edge of a ghetto. At least she had no difficulty in deciding which route faced north. Surrounding her on three sides was the dusty, brown scrub grass of the veld, interspersed with clumps of thorn-bush. Ahead, lay a wide, rutted track weaving through rows of tin huts stacked like ingots in the last rays of the sun, the wind whistling grotesque parodies in the corrugated roofs. The two black men who had endured with her on the bus to the end had vanished while she stood to gather her bearings. Ahead, the street was empty. There was no footpath.

She began picking her way gingerly around the muddy potholes. 'North three blocks.' A real euphemism, that. A huddle of shacks strung together with cardboard pallets, rusted corrugate, bits of rotting wood, the shadowy gaps between each cluster, alive with sounds that made her skin bristle. And the stench. She tried to breathe shallowly, lessen the invasion in her nostrils. Like being stifled in a sewage pit, so bad as she passed a row of tin latrines that she stopped breathing altogether, afraid she'd be sick. Around the latrines, the earth was a quagmire of yellow silt, here and there a startling green profusion of grass and weed, the process relentless.

Deeper into the shanty town, she met a gaggle of old women and children about a communal pump. The raised voices stilled as she approached. She licked her dry lips, again feeling the heat in her cheeks. It was like being under a microscope. None of them spoke English. Awkwardly, she made some signs, her eyes a question mark. The children, dirty, barefoot, gaped at her, languidly brushing away the flies homing in on the glistening snail tracks of dried mucus about their nostrils. Her stomach hove and she turned again quickly to the old, gap-toothed woman gesticulating wildly in what Emma hoped would be the direction of the church.

Walking on, it came to her what the women had been arguing about. The pump had not been working.

Church. She stared at the squat structure, the drab exposure of concrete blocks, the roof the same corrugated sheeting as the huts. A small cross on the wooden door gave the only clue to its function. Her spirits rose. By comparison with its surroundings, it seemed a virtual palace. The door was locked. She peered through one of the windows. The gloomy interior housed rows of wooden benches arranged horseshoe fashion about a large concrete structure. The altar?

Round the rear of the church, the large Portacabin lay brooding in the half light. No sign of life. She tried the door. It too, was locked. Terrific. She dropped her suitcase and slumped wearily onto the concrete block which served as a doorstep. What the fuck was she supposed to do next? She chafed at her hands, trying to ease the numbness. He knew she was coming, this Dick Carruthers, else why had she received the message at the airport? She was freezing. Hungry, despite the filthy odours the wind shoved in her face. And if she didn't get to a loo soon, she'd wet herself. Loo. The cabin was raised more than a foot off the ground, perched on concrete blocks. Swiftly, she got on her knees, peering into the shadows beneath. She crawled the length of it, searching feverishly.

No dark shape that would indicate any kind of pipes, any outlet. No toilet. She closed her eyes. The latrines she had passed earlier. The strange growth about them. The stench.

Swiftly she went around the back of the cabin, cursing her decision to come. The wind drove the grass tickling against her skin as she squatted and she leapt, terrified it was some insect. She turned her face from the steamy urine splashing between her thighs.

When she stood, re-zipping the jeans, she realised she was crying. For herself, for Sipho, for the child she had killed, for the hopeless eyes of the old women who kicked at the sullen pump, the lack-lustre gaze of the toddlers who dragged their skirts, the lines of patched hovels groaning in the wind, the dark spaces between the clusters teeming with rodent life. No one deserved this, no one, Christ, was this a life? Wiping her eyes, returning to sit on the step, she felt it, as tangibly as the darkness thickening the sharp contours of the church, a gathering within herself, a sense of something beyond anger, shame, solidifying to a hard core.

She must have dozed. When she first became aware of the sound, she realised it had been there for some time, a wavering sigh threading through the wind, its tentacles reaching into the stupor which numbed her. Eyes open now, she listened: a low wailing in the distance, drawing ever nearer, till it was the muted roar of an ocean, rising, swelling on the wind, carrying into every crevice of the township, the ground beneath her feet thrumming in unison. Was she dreaming?

Mesmerised, she stood, the strange chant a tumult of grief, unbearable loss, reaching out, drawing her irresistibly into its web. Her skin prickling, as though it were alive with insects, she moved around the side of the church.

A mass of people surged through the street in an endless flood, the voices raised as one. In the near darkness, she did not find one white face. Warily, she stepped back into the shadows. If anyone spotted her, a white, worse, a total stranger.... She pushed the thought aside. It didn't bear thinking through. All the same, perhaps she should take some precautions. Swiftly, she returned to the doorstep. She'd leave her things around the back of the cabin, keep watch from the rear.

But where was her bag? Kneeling, she scrabbled about behind the doorstep, her hand closing gratefully on the soft leather.

'Ms Fitzgerald?'

She screeched in terror, the sound swallowed by the crowd. Still on her knees, she twisted to face the threat. A dark bulk standing over her.

'Been waiting long?' The accent unmistakable. It had to be the priest. Besides, he knew her name. She heaved air into her lungs.

'A while. I got here, the place was closed—.'

'We had a funeral planned for this morning. A kid, shot by one of the riot squad. The whole town wanted to attend. But the police showed up, threatening to detain anyone who wasn't immediate family.' His laugh was short. 'They'll never get it through their heads, for Africans, everyone is family. Anyway, I cancelled the funeral. We waited till the cops left, then we buried him.'

'So that's why you couldn't—?'

'You planning on staying down there forever? Perhaps you feel the need a some penance?' His voice was dry.

A wise crack. She gritted her teeth. 'I mislaid my handbag.'

'Well, that's a relief. I've had it up to here with pious ladies who come to tell me how to run my clinic.' The warning in his voice was unmistakable.

Emma rose. 'Look, if you want an argument, we can have it tomorrow. Right now, I'm freezing, I'm tired, and I'm hungry. Besides, I don't believe in God.'

She didn't know why she'd tacked that on, perhaps to shock him.

'Right, if you're through with the sob story, let's get inside.'

The bastard! She stood stiffly as he lit the small gas lamp.

A makeshift office, a few, paltry medical supplies on a shelf. In one corner, a table with a two-ringed primus, a couple of cooking pots, a plastic basin. Overhead, a cupboard.

'This is the clinic?' She tried to keep her voice neutral.

'Well, yeah, the supplies end of it. I hold the sessions in the church. This place isn't exactly what you'd call roomy.' Leaning over the desk, he was a small, powerful bulldozer, his pen gouging a sheet of paper.

'How often?' She sat on the chair in front of the desk.

'Twice, three times a week. Outside that, you'll still get people calling to the door every day.' He didn't look up.

'Couple a doctors show up from Lenasia once a month, if we're lucky.'

'Lenasia? That's that Indian location outside Jo'burg?'

'They got an outreach service, a mobile clinic. They give us as much help as they can. Takes a bit of organising, but men like—.' Dick broke off, unaware of whether she had actually met Thulatu yet. Better play it safe till he knew a little more about her.

She didn't seem to have heard him. She was looking about uneasily. 'Where do I sleep?'

'Through there.' He nodded at a door near the table. 'You'd probably be better off staying in Jo'burg, coming out here a few times a week. That's what the Black Sash women did.'

So. He didn't want her here. She stood, moving through the door, stifling the urge to accept the escape route he offered. An old camp bed with a plastic mattress was shoved tight against the far wall, a frayed sleeping bag tossed on its surface, its dull colour defying definition. She looked at it, bemused. To her left, a small closet hugged the partition adjoining the office. Perhaps some shelves, or a hanging locker? She stared, hardly daring to believe it. Reaching out, she lifted the lid. Instantly, a strong odour of chlorine invaded her nostrils. A chemical toilet. She closed her eyes. The small, unassailable dignity of it.

Outside, the grouse was still scratching, the pen an assault on the page. She picked up her suitcase, began moving again towards the room.

'Well?' He looked up.

'Well what?' Emma slung her handbag across her shoulder.

'As you can see, I've no facilities to speak of.'

'Where do you sleep?'

He jerked his head towards the door behind him. 'In there.'

Emma walked into her own room. 'Good,' she called back. 'If you snore, I won't be able to hear you.'

His enraged snort carried through the thin wall. 'Fuck you too,' she thought, too weary to undress. She lay down, pulling the sleeping bag across her. As her eyes closed, she realised she still hadn't eaten.

IV

'Reverend Moses Jabolani?' The uniformed clerk at passport control studied the photo, then scrutinised Thulatu carefully.

'Yes.' Thulatu's face was impassive. He'd made dozens of trips in this guise, yet, for the first time he felt nervous. It wasn't a feeling he was in the habit of ignoring.

'What denomination?' The eyes were razor-sharp, thinly veiled with politeness.

Thulatu sighed. The information was all there. But he wouldn't be allowed to escape as quickly as usual. 'Methodist. I attended a seminar in London.' The answer sufficiently long to be informative, sufficiently short not to antagonise.

'What was that? This seminar?' The white nail-tips drummed in rhythmic succession on passport, permit, life book. All as legal as the other sets of documents back in his flat in Durban. As a lawyer, he had seen to that. For those educated blacks who possessed the means, every kind of subterfuge was within financial range. Nor, in all the years he'd maintained his several identities, had anything ever gone wrong. Yet his collar felt uncomfortably tight and sweat was beading his upper lip below the neat line of the false moustache. He resisted the urge to wriggle as he answered. 'The relevance of the Bible in the modern world.' That should please him. He'd never yet met an Afrikaner who didn't profess to be a true-blue bible Christian.

The young clerk hesitated. His first day on duty. He'd been warned to keep his eyes peeled. The documents were in order, there was no doubt of that. He knew he was over-doing things. Already, several people had left his queue to join the neighbouring one which was rippling far more briskly. Okay, a last look at the papers and he'd let the hottnot through. He slammed his stamp down, then pushed the papers towards Thulatu, nodding his dismissal. Relieved, Thulatu moved away, glancing at his watch. Customs had yet to be dealt with, and the banks would only be open for another hour. Timol would be waiting in the car park. Half an hour to get to Anglo-American, arrange the cosmetics under which the money his mother had raised would disappear miraculously into church funds.

Twenty minutes later, he was finally out in the foyer, striding towards the exit. When the tall, wiry man stepped into his path, Thulatu had difficulty recognising him as Timol.

'Trouble.' The lips were a grim, iron line in the pewter face. Timol gripped his arm, keeping him moving towards the exit. Thulatu felt a coldness somewhere in his chest. 'Kind?'

'Sadness.'

He stopped dead, his heart lurching. 'Thabo?'

Timol nodded, gripping his arm tighter to try to get him moving.

'Detention?'

'He's out.'

'How bad?'

'Bad. Quick. Come.'

Before Timol had finished speaking, Thulatu was running, his body a coiled spring as he shouldered a path through the small crowd glutting the exit. For a moment Timol stood, his eyes bleak as he watched Thulatu run. Then he, too, dove into the throng at the exit. Lord of Africa, he prayed, let the boy live until his father's face is before him.

In the car, Timol drove as though possessed. Beside him, Thulatu sat, a column of granite, his hands cupping the one photo of his son that he hadn't given to Sophie. She'd kept all the others, poring over them hungrily, delighted that he had at last brought her a picture of his white daughter. But she'd had no love for this photo of Thabo, fist raised in a clenched protest. Thulatu stared down at the firm, boyish mouth, willing it to breathe, something solidifying to ice under his scalp as he sensed the hopelessness in Timol. If Thabo should ... his beloved ... flesh ... how he would tear the world asunder, disembowel it with his raw hands, nothing would ever rest, be at ease again until he smeared the obscenity that was South Africa over the farthest reaches of the earth, until the earth herself hove molten vomit from her womb to burn every parasite that leeched and suckled at her breast!

Chapter Two

Together they strolled the track skirting the forest of sugar cane, the ground shrill with the rasp of crickets in the fading light.

'Any sign of gumming?' Piet watched his father tap the solid green stalks.

'Clean as a whistle,' Claus said, his tone pleased. Affectionately, he rustled the graceful swords drooping above his head.'No sign of leaf scald, either. Zo, we have a fine crop, ja?'

Simultaneously, they sighed. Piet smiled, savouring it. Their love for the land was mutual, a thing keenly felt, communicated through a series of subtle noises that, translated into speech, would have made them both cringe. In such moments as this, he felt a sense of being ....properly aligned, the quiet pleasure of some need being sated.

'Van Meerden is going for overall spraying this season,' he said, still hoping to persuade his father to change his mind.

'Forget it maan. His yield was down by 10% last time. You think he's going to do any better this year?' Pulling a small, heavy machete from his belt, Claus bent low, a web of grey hair on his tanned arms. In one swipe, he had cut clean through an inch-thick stalk, just above ground level. 'And you can forget about band spraying,' he said, topping the cane above the uppermost joint. 'Too many complications. That fool Verwoerd can handle the workers, but when it comes to calculating dose rates, onnosel!' Peeling off the rough bark, he bit hard into the stalk. The flesh tore unevenly, fibrous tendrils trailing from his mouth, so that he became a sharp-eyed civet, chewing. Squeezing his eyes shut, he concentrated on the taste.

'Coming. It's coming.' He nodded vigorously, holding out the stalk. Piet took it, breaking a piece in a twisting motion that snapped through the fibres. A familiar, sweet moisture filled his mouth as he sank his teeth into the toughness.

'Good.' He nodded, spitting out the mesh of fibres.

'Come.' Claus slapped his son's shoulder as they turned back towards the jeep at the end of the track. 'Let's go see if the new crop from Modderbee is any good.'

'That's if they'll come, Papa. Most of them know what parole means now and they're refusing it. They'd prefer to stay in jail. Like it or not, some day there isn't going to be the manpower for hand weeding, we're going to have to turn to herbicides.' Ahead, the gun-metal grey of the jeep brooded bulky as an elephant.

'Ach maan, you don't know Riviers like I do. There never was a chief warden to equal him. Ja, even his own men are afraid of him.' Hoisting himself into the driver's seat, Claus laughed. 'A man who knows his job. A few more like him in the cabinet and—.' He paused as the engine rumbled to life. 'He'll ... persuade them. He had better ...' his voice was hard. '... he's being paid enough. Besides, I told Verwoerd to pick them himself, or he's out of a job.' He glanced at his son as he turned the jeep northwards towards the kraals that housed the farmhands. 'Listen, we're running a business, we make the most of cheap labour while it lasts, zo? Now tell me what you found out about the new Rotopicker. I hear it cuts deep.'

'300mm. Leaves the ground in seedbed condition.' Piet's answer was automatic. It wasn't his father's refusal to spray that bothered him. Plots hand-weeded when the crop was in the vital emergence stages showed no loss of yield, it was true. What got him was the pleasure that bastard Verwoerd derived from beating the parolees.

'... pure as a virgin, ja?' His father was laughing loudly.

'You think it'll rain?' Piet asked, to cover his lack of amusement. For no reason he could divine, his father's jokes always left him ill at ease. No light shone from the farmhouse as they passed, its dark bulk silhouetted against the livid sky. At this hour, Samuel would be in the kitchen preparing Claus' supper. No light. It was Babo who, in the first months after their mother's death, had pointed to it. Returning one evening from a ride together, she had reined in tightly, causing his own horse to buck.

'See, Pietie,' she had whispered. 'No light in the farmhouse.'

He'd looked at her, puzzled. 'Yes, Papa's probably still—.'

'I didn't mean that.' She'd leaned forward, her blond hair screening her face as she patted the horse's neck. 'No light. Don't you think that's the most ... grief-making way of being missed?'

Awkwardly, he had reached out to stroke her bare arm, trying to ignore her soft snuffles. The intensity of her love for the quiet, self-effacing woman whose presence, at times, he'd hardly been aware of, made him uncomfortable, as though it pointed to some lack in himself. But he'd grown up outdoors, in his father's world. Besides, he had his own home to return to, Mia and Jan waiting dinner for him each evening, whereas she and Claus, even then, before she'd moved out on her own, were at loggerheads.

He sighed as the jeep turned onto the rutted track leading to the compound. The memory had sparked his old fondness for her. He'd invited her for dinner this evening. But she didn't know Papa would be there too. Else, she wouldn't have agreed to come. He was ashamed suddenly of the way he and Papa were deceiving her.

'Come. Let's get this over with.' His father ground the jeep to a halt before the low concrete shed built specially to house the parolees. Verwoerd, his large, veined face a rupture in the pink sunset, was leaning against the shed door, waiting. He held a quirt in his right hand, the long braid of rhinoceros hide oscillating as he swung it idly. Piet gritted his teeth. Bloody sadist. Inside the hut, he knew, Verwoerd's men were fleecing the parolees of anything they possessed.

Afraid his father would beckon him to follow, he didn't watch Claus move towards the farm manager. In the distance, a haze of blue smoke was suspended over the low huts of the kraal, an odour of fried mealies threading the air from the makeshift braziers. A woman's laugh rang out in the stillness, a warm, vibrant sound rising defiantly from the kraals, flinging itself against the iron grimness of the compound, finally released above the vast undulating fields of cane in some celebration, mysterious, yet familiar, that eluded him.

Then he recalled it. Those long, blistering days when he'd played with the tiny, native children among the cane stalks while their parents worked nearby, his own childish delight in imitating their strange clicks, the ululating chants.

Until his father found out. He winced, pushing the memory aside.

Staring now through the windscreen at the two men deep in discussion, Piet moved his tongue experimentally to form a Xhosa word, the sharp click an integral part of it. He grinned, wondering if Babo could still manage it. Although he was a gangly adolescent by the time she was born, some perverse sense had driven him to teach it to her. Their secret, he'd told her, knowing it was instead an ugly curiosity to see her punished as he had been, to see how someone other than himself would bend under the brunt of his father's rage. At the time, it had never dawned on him that she might reveal his complicity. But young as she was, she had never ratted. And now he was throwing her in at the deep end once more. Again, he felt ashamed. She hadn't seen Papa since the row she'd had with him. The dinner this evening wouldn't be pleasant for any of them, not once Babo and Papa got going. And Mia wouldn't thank him for it either. He sighed. He could forget about having sex, all she'd want would be to bitch at him in bed tonight. Christ, if only Papa hadn't asked him to do it.

As Verwoerd opened the compound, mouthing orders to the men inside, Piet repeated the clicks until the sounds grew more confident. By the time the parolees were hustled into yard, he had perfected them, the clicks alive with the fury of snapping castanets. Ahead, the men stood, a quiet, cumbersome lot. Christ, it was depressing knowing what was coming: Verwoerd's initiation ceremony, 'Warm te maken,' those he designated his henchmen only too willing to turn on their own kind with knobkerries and donkie piels, rather than be beaten themselves. These were the human herbicides used to weed the plantation. But first they had to be moulded, else they'd never tolerate the long back-breaking hours. The practice had gone on for years.

Piet closed his eyes, blotting it out. Out of his hands. Always had been. For a moment he wondered whether it was the beating of the men or Verwoerd's pleasure in it, he found more distasteful. The question disturbed him, as though the answer might suggest something corrupt in himself. He pushed the notion aside, wishing his father would hurry. All he wanted was to get home to Mia. He leaned against the headrest, the tension suddenly draining from his taut limbs.

Outside, Verwoerd was shouting at the men to line up for inspection. It was not for nothing Claus had employed the former policeman: a small, iron-grey boulder of granite, eyes the colour of flint, the speed and power with which he moved instilling hatred and fear in farmhands and parolees alike. A wise move, Claus thought, the way the men were watching Verwoerd, their eyes shifting. Neither Piet nor a string of ineffectual managers had ever proved equal to the task. Too soft, all of them, his son the worst marshmallow. Claus nodded absently. Ja, zo. It was good he no longer had to waste his time and energy on such mundane matters.

He moved along the line of men, observing each while Verwoerd bawled a litany of regulations interspersed liberally with bursts of invective. A mixed bag. He glanced through the sheaf of papers. Between the fifty of them, a cross section of tribes, Zulu, Sotho, Xhosa, Bhaca, Swazi, Pondo, for the most part, large, shambling brutes, bemused and docile as sheep. Malleable. He sighed deeply, the sight as always, giving him a sharp kick of pleasure: a sense of how far and fast he had climbed, a sense of his place, his inalienable place, the glorious, dizzying height of it defined, reinforced even, by the submissive presence of such baboons.

If only one among his family could appreciate it, understand it as he did. But neither of his children were made of the same stuff.

'When things were not good for us.' The phrase, simple, grossly understated, set his stomach churning. His parents' way of referring to their past. The coldness of their anger when as a child he complained, the mad glitter in his mother's eyes. 'You think this is hunger to miss a meal? Jong, verdomme, verdomme, you don't know what hunger is! Ask your father, go on, ask him when he comes, you'll feel the strength of his belt. Ask him to tell you what hunger is, when your body is too tired, too weak to shake off the rats that gnaw your feet; your eyes, half-open, half-alive, half-dead, something in you so weak, so strong, you are not able to be the one thing or the other so that you are forced to watch those rats. You watch them and you watch them and you watch them!' She had struck his face, the blow taking him by surprise so that he fell backwards onto the stone floor of the little kitchen. She stood above him, trembling in the long, drab skirt that seemed to him part of her very skin. He could never remember her in anything else.

Hardly aware of his stinging cheek, he had stared at her, the sickening pictures that had come from the crooked tilt of her mouth. He wanted to gag it. Yet in the same breath, he wished to tear it to shreds, release all the pictures to feed his own terrible appetite. He pressed his hands against the cramps in his empty stomach. Something dark and slimy and fearful in the pit of him wanted to escape. He leaned over, retching a couple of times, but apart from a bad taste in his mouth, nothing happened. His mother pulled him to his feet, telling him to sweep the floor. Unable to contain it, he asked her to tell him what had happened next. He had really wanted to ask her to take off her old boots, show him her feet, but he sensed it would make her angry again.

She sat on a small stool, using the last trickle of daylight staining the window, to sew a tear in his father's shirt. His father was out, searching for work. She didn't answer him, her face so close to the shirt that she had to lift it away every time she pulled the needle clear. Knowing it would please her, he dragged the clump of switches slowly, keeping the dust to a minimum. Then he asked her again. An old ouma, she said, weak with starvation herself, had cried and called until she roused some of the mothers from their stupor. To beat the rats off.

Her answer left him vaguely deflated, as though he had expected some dramatic conclusion which would horrify him all the more. Both his parents had been interned in Kitchener's camps at the turn of the century. Although the camps had been set up to imprison the women and children of the Boer commando units, his father's father had died several years before the war had started, while his mother was merely a slip of a girl fresh from Holland. He chewed savagely at the corner of his bottom lip. The English had made no distinctions.

He looked now at these bantus before him, his bantus, he thought, revelling in the straight, invisible line that divided him from them. This was what he had escaped. Neither Piet nor Babo, born into privilege, would ever see it. Ja, talk was cheap, it did not cost you your next meal. He sighed. His son's finicky distaste. His daughter's crusades. Silk worms spawned in cocoons. As for that daughter-in-law of his, an empty-headed mannequin. He could have borne it better if she hadn't been English. Would his children ever realise it? Everything relative to what you'd undergone, to who had made you undergo it, everything judged by the yardstick of previous experience, so that, for his mother, it was better to eke out an existence forever hovering on the brink of madness and despair, than to die of typhus in the camps. He no longer hated these blacks as intensely as he once had done. They were now mere units of labour, the cheapest in the world and ja, a highly treasured commodity, the very stuff which cashed his dreams into reality. But he feared the sheer scale of their numbers, the smell of their poverty reaching from the stench of his own childhood.

He nodded, satisfied with the expression he found in most faces. Riviers had not made prison comfortable for them. But the two on the end bothered him, one, a small, tattered branch who looked as though the first breath of wind would blow him out. Underfed. They'd end up burying it. But the larger one with the angry eyes interested him. Trouble. Plain as the flat, wide nostrils on his face. Ugly motherfucker, all lips and ears, and the stupid bovine angry eyes. Yes, this one'd need a tight rein, the five star spurs, if they were to hold him. And he was strong, worth breaking in.

'Jou naam, kaffir?' Claus stood back a little, unable to stand the stink of stale sweat and urine emanating from all of them. The bantu stared back, his gaze hostile. 'Murphy Mphela,' he said, the tone civil enough.

'Murphy?' Claus grinned, raising his voice. 'Ja, Verwoerd! You hear this? We got ourselves a kaffir here who claims he's Irish.'

Immediately, Verwoerd was by his side, peering at the African. 'Sir! You don't say? I could have sworn he was a munt.' The two men laughed. The African ignored them, staring over their heads.

'Zo. We'd better re-name him.' Claus looked at his manager, his gaze speculative. 'Call him James,' he said. 'A good, God-fearing name.'

Verwoerd's mouth thinned. 'A pleasure, sir.' He turned to stare at the African. 'Jou naam, swartgat?' The quirt tapped briskly against Verwoerd's thigh, the pale, fuzzy flesh bulging below the tight-fitting khaki shorts.

The African stared past them. 'Murphy Mphela.'

Hardly had he finished speaking when the quirt struck. Instinctively he'd flinched as he heard the whirring sound, so that the lash was deflected, catching him about the throat. Instantly, the skin caved under the impact, the raw flesh glaring for a moment before the wound began to ooze. He stood rooted, his body a shivering fist as he fought the pain. But no sound passed his lips.

'You made three mistakes, you fucking commie.' Verwoerd's gaze lingered on the wound before returning to the man's shocked face. He smiled lazily, his voice grinding. 'First, you lied about your name. Second, you forgot to say "baas", and third, you never look higher than your balls when a white man speaks to you. Now, what's your name?'

The African closed his eyes. For a moment he fought it, but the pain drove the words struggling through his teeth. 'James, baas.' He breathed deeply, clamping down on his anger. Not now, he thought. But some day. Some dark day or night.

Claus turned to Verwoerd. 'Make it James the meek.' Turning back to the African he laughed, the sound gravel-edged. 'He could use some Bible instruction, verstaan?' He jerked the question at Verwoerd as he turned back towards the jeep.

'Yes, sir, and perhaps a few ... sermons?'

Without looking back, Claus raised his hand in a mock salute. 'Verwoerd!' he roared. 'You made one mistake. Send the bones beside him back! And hose the bastards down!'

Ahead, through the windscreen, he saw his son. Asleep, his mouth slack, accentuating the weak line of his jaw. Claus snorted in disgust.

II

Mia lay on the bed, fists clenched, her face pressed into the pillow. Stay, she thought, stay thus till the heart heaves into darkness, till lungs shrivel for lack of air, till eyes are sightless ears deaf to the words that'd stabbed, stay till the blood freezes never never never could it be true, he was lying lying this dark devil who had come to her house to destroy her, who was downstairs now with Babo waiting waiting oh sweet Jesus, Babo how could you how could you bring him to poison my eyes, to pour his acid into my ears, sweet Jesus I'm burning burning, tell me it's not true not true, make it yesterday again so I can flee before he comes his demon-dark filth spreading in my blood, oozing through my skin heart bone skin heart bone blood hair teeth flesh all ... fouled!

She jerked upwards from the pillow, her lungs screaming for air, mocking her will: you will breathe, you will live to see it crumble about you, you will suffocate in the ruins.

'M-my dear? Are you ...?' The cold white fish hand patting her bare arm. The fish had made her roll up her sleeve for ... something, what? She peered up at the beaded eyes. Yes, an injection, that was it the fish was a doctor, already she could feel it in her system the coldness invading her veins like ... black blood ... oh she wanted to tear the scales from his fish eyes tell him how much she hated him, gut him, make of his blood a river to drown his fishness to leave him lying on the black sea bed where no light shone where all was darkness and shark.

'... looking a little better, c-colour's back in your cheeks, y-you just lie there t-till you feel ....'

She turned away from the fish face and stared at the row of wardrobe doors opposite. The fish was not her father. All her life he'd been her father, clammy to the touch, swimming out of reach at every opportunity but her father nevertheless. Until today. Today she'd been reborn in a swamp of black tar, black as bitumen. Someone was laughing in her bedroom, really she couldn't blame them it was funny so funny why it was hilarious, almost as funny as a fish named Paul, a cold fat fillet who pretended to be her father who had lied through his gills all her life really it was a relief who wanted a fish for a father she'd rather be dead than own either of them sweet Jesus strike them dead make it not true before Piet came home before he kissed her white cheek glutted her body with his white sperm thank God she couldn't have children thank God Jan was not hers the boy was blessed not to share her blood not to have oozed from the black sludge of her womb when Claus heard oh sweet Jesus when his ears pricked to the words his jaws would snap her neck he was coming today Piet was bringing him she was lost get the demon out of her house before they came out they mustn't find him here when they came then maybe she could think what to do they mustn't find out they mustn't she must bury it deep in her bones in the roots of her hair in the raw flesh under her skin trap it there snare it calm calm now cold heart slowing to a chill dark place where she could not feel. Yes her mind was a tomb. She gazed through the wall of the tomb at the fat fish flapping his fins as he floated about the bedroom, let him drown in the oxygen, let him drown in it, the dirt of it, oh the filth!

* * *

Paul wandered about the room, his feet shuffling in the carpet as he waited for the injection to take effect. He stared across at the rigid line of Mia's back on the bed. Already, her breathing was easier. Going to her dressing-table he pulled a tissue from the box, mopping his forehead. In the mirror he could see the sweat gleaming through his sparse white hair. He pressed the tissue down on his crown to soak the moisture. The hairs stayed plastered to his head, making him look balder than ever. He started, watching as she raised herself up in the glass. When he turned, she was staring towards the window, unblinking in the strong sunlight.

'My father is a fish,' she said, her tone chilling him. He turned away, back to the glass.

'How? How could you bring me up—?' Her voice broke. 'Why didn't you tell me before?' She swung, hurling the words at his back. 'Look at me, I'm talking to you! See! See! My mouth is moving!' In the mirror her hand lifted, pointing at him. 'I'm not a reflection, I'm not in there, don't you put me in there!'

He turned, his gaze sheering away from her face. 'W-we were young ... students together in England.' He gritted his teeth, forcing the words. 'She ... y-your mother ... didn't ... love me. It was ... him ....' He jerked his head at the floor, unable to bring himself to mention Thulatu's name. '... she wanted. When she discovered she w-was ... pregnant ... we agreed it.' He moved about, her stillness unnerving him. 'If y-you were ... if the baby were ... too d-dark to pass for a white, she'd remain in England. If not ... she'd marry me ....' He clenched his fists, remembering how he'd felt about her, willing to take any crumbs she'd offered him. 'If not, she'd marry me ... we'd return here as soon as we'd both qualified. He ...' He paused, fighting the bile that rose to choke him. '... still had another year to do in England, he didn't return till later, by which time, your mother was ... had gone.' Paul turned away, hiding his face from her as the anger rose. How willing, gullible, he'd been, too blind in his infatuation to see what a disaster it would be, willing to have her on any terms, her ... lap-dog, nothing more, how could he have had so little pride when she'd preferred that ... thing ... downstairs, to him, him, a respectable white, one of her own, and then, then ... she'd died ... died! Leaving him with the fruits of what she'd done, leaving him with it to stare him down all his days, every minute of every day, her rejection of him mocking from the child's eyes. Oh he should have given her up all those years ago when Thulatu had come to ask for her after her mother's funeral.

'Why didn't you tell me? Why!' Her voice was a screech.

He stared towards the door, longing to escape. The room was stifling. 'It was what she w-wanted for you. I, I only did as she asked. I ... th-thought the world of her.'

'What if I'd had a child? When I think—!'

He loosened his tie. 'I was s-sick when you married Piet. But you were so h-happy. How could I spoil that?' He swallowed hard. Much as he'd resented her, he'd never begrudged her her happiness, she'd never had much of a life with him, he'd been glad when she married Piet. Hadn't he? Maybe he'd done the wrong thing, yes, maybe he shouldn't have kept it from her, but he wasn't a monster, he had meant her no harm: if he'd given her to Thulatu after her mother died, why, what kind of a life would she have had? She was white for all intents and purposes, for the sake of her mother he'd seen to it that she was brought up as a white, that she'd never lacked the privilege of that.

'Sweet Jesus, oh sweet Jesus!'

He went across to her, his gaze averted, his hand flapping at her shoulder, ineffectual as a broken wing. 'Please, my dear, don't ... upset yourself .... I, I can't bear to see you ....'

But she was beyond him, the pillow gripped to her breasts, her body curled foetus-like about it as she howled into its satin smoothness. He stood, wincing at her pain, the doctor in him acknowledging the necessity of such a release. Shambling across to the dressing-table, he picked up another tissue.

* * *

Downstairs, Babo sat on the edge of one of the couches in the large, high-ceilinged drawing room. She tried to listen, catch any sound which might filter through from Mia and Paul in the bedroom above, but the rustle of Thulatu's suit, as he paced, was thunderous in the silence.

'For God's sake, sit down, will you? You're making me worse.'

Thulatu turned. His eyes, the livid glitter of torment, made her sorry she'd spoken. Ashamed, she stared at the Persian carpet, her gaze circling the intricate pattern. But her words had some impact. He went to stand by the French windows overlooking the gardens.

For a while, Babo managed to clamp down on it, but in the end she couldn't resist. 'We shouldn't have.'

Thulatu swivelled, still blinded by it. 'What is she? Sacred?'

'She wasn't able for it.'

'She had to be told.' His lips twisted as he looked around the room, the classic regency cabinets of inlaid mahogany, the gleam of cut-glass, leather book-spines, the finest porcelains, silverware, displayed in a manner he found at once tasteful and obscene. Expensive reproductions, all of them imported by these pampered Europeans suckling the endless wellspring of Bantu sweat. 'This gilded cage,' he said. 'Why should she escape? You saw her! She couldn't stand the sight of me!' He began pacing again. 'Well, I've had enough, enough! I've kept silent for thirty-odd years. Where's it got me, may I ask? I've lost my children. What've I got left now? Thabo, cold-eyed as a dead bird, a, a, mulch for worms, and, and that ....' His finger stabbed towards the ceiling. '... that silk madonna in her ivory tower, a gewgaw living in another world, worse, a shifty little chameleon, how well she's adapted, how well suited she is to this ...' his face was a sneer as he looked around the room. 'You saw her, the stink in her eyes when she looked at me!'

Babo kept her head down, the fair swathes of hair screening her expression. She couldn't bear to look at him. When she did, she was again sucked into his anger, unable to think clearly.

She scratched nervously at the freckles on her arm. 'Mia's never been strong.'

Heaving for breath, he stared down at the silky strands, the thick ridge of lashes, lowered now to mask her eyes. She would have been beautiful except for the pale red birthmark staining her left cheek like an exclamation. It gave her a look of perpetual bewilderment he had found oddly moving when he'd first arranged to meet her through the Black Sash. God strike him if he hurt her after all she'd done for him. Swiftly he moved, hunkering down before her, taking her limp hands in his. 'When I looked at Thabo ....' His voice broke. '... his ... twisted stillness in that box, all I felt was shame, the shame of silence worn like a hairshirt all these years. What kind of man have I been, timid as a sheep on the edge of your white world, getting you to spy on her for me, allowing myself to be shackled by my own tongue! A ... a ... servile mind, Babo ... where's the ... grace in that? I might as well have been her mother's slave instead of her—.' He shook his head.

Babo's sudden laugh was mirthless. 'God's truth, if someone walked up to me in the street and said, "Claus is not your father," I'd be thrilled, you know that?'

He lifted his head, looking at her. 'Even if your real father turned out to be black?'

'You're not black.'

'Oh, and you think she noticed the difference?' He rose, pacing again, thrusting his hands deep in his trouser pockets. 'You seriously think you'd sing for joy?'

'I'm not a racist.'

'I'm not sure what you are, Babo.' He paused, suddenly hating her, hating everything, the plush, well-fed room, the manicured grass outside, luxuriant in the muted hiss of lawn sprinklers. The greedy white suburbs of Durban, bloated gardens, overripe parks, his daughter's world, never his, even in England he had to hide himself. Never his, never Thabo's. His son's name, a knife twisting in his gut. He closed his eyes against it.

Babo stared up at the ceiling. 'They've been gone ages. I never saw her so—. The way she slobbered her drink, her hands shaking, spilling it everywhere! Then using the lace to wipe it up as though it were a floor cloth! She's so ... tidy, normally! And then ... that silence. Her eyes, just staring ... weird. Poor Paul. Did you see his face when she laid into him?'

Thulatu strode to the drinks cabinet in the far corner, his gaze skimming over the squad of bottles lining the rosewood counter. He tried to concentrate on what she'd just said, but it was like having a conversation long distance, like the connection was bad and there was some kind of ... time lapse. He splashed some whiskey in a glass, gulping it in one go. He hadn't eaten properly in days, not since that moment at the airport. Immediately, he felt the impact: the heat in his stomach radiating outwards, a warm numbness, reaching into his very fingertips. The best scotch. His lips clamped. What else did he expect to find in the house of a Boer? He turned to Babo. 'You'd better call them. I have to go soon.'

'Just go then.'

'I've something else I want to say to her. She has to tell them. She has to tell your family.'

Babo leapt up, the words jerking from her mouth. 'No! D'you want to destroy her altogether?'

He stared at her, unmoved. 'You agreed to it.'

'Not all in one go!'

He slammed his fist on the counter, glass shivering in a medley of sound. 'I swore it over Thabo's body. You took my hand!'

Babo held out her hands. 'Thulatu, listen. She's my sister-in-law, we've been close for years, I know her! I'm telling you, she won't be able to handle it.' She drew a deep breath. 'For God's sake, she's just learned you're her father, isn't it enough for one day?'

'I should've taken her after her mother died. Her place was with me, growing up in the townships with her black brother, a spear in her hand!'

'Ending up dead like him too.' Babo's laugh was bitter. 'You and Papa might be brothers!'

He stared, unable to believe it. 'How is it you dare! All those blank years — I starved for news of her! Coward that I was — an obedient spaniel would've had more guts!' He moved away from the bar. 'Whenever I tried to see her, I lay down, let Paul stand with his boot upon my neck! Oh he had cunning enough for that, he knew my limits, every shameful chip inflicted on my shoulder! Our, our ... scalded lives!' He jabbed the air before her face. 'We've been crippled by servility. Well, no more!' His arm swung in a wide arc, dismissing her. 'It took Thabo's death to make me see it!'

Babo dropped onto the couch, the cushions squeaking under the impact of her weight. Jesus, she couldn't deal with any of it, he was like an anti-Christ. And Mia, Mia, a wooden puppet with her strings cut. What had Thabo's death unleashed? What had she and Thulatu done? Was it enough that it was right, that her sister-in-law had a right to know? Was it? Jesus, was it?

Suddenly Thulatu was kneeling before her, gripping her shoulders. 'I, I need her, Babo. I can't go on if ....' He shook his head, his voice leaden. 'Dead. What a dull thud it wakes in the heart.' His grip tightened, the words whispered. 'Don't fail me now.'

She wriggled free of his grasp, jumping up, moving away from him as she spoke. 'They've been gone ages. What's keeping them?'

Unable to speak, he watched her, a caged cat prowling the room, dragging him back from the grave. She stopped, her face raised towards the chandelier, listening. 'Did you hear? I thought I heard—. What's keeping them? An injection doesn't take that long—.'

He took a deep breath. 'The protest's fixed for next month.' He waited, sensing she'd try to back out of it.

'I, I can't face this dinner tonight if Mia isn't here, not with Papa—.'

Rising, he went to pour himself another drink. The future. Only that. Concentrate. Become relentless. The only way he could hang on. To look back would be to invite the nightmare in again. He grimaced. He ought to know better, face it now. But he couldn't. His son was gone. Thabo. The struggle. Sophie. All that ever mattered. Without Thabo, what was there to struggle for? But he was not yet defeated. There was his daughter. He closed his eyes against her whiteness. His daughter, only that, he thought, grasping at the sense of identity it gave him.

'Open Day,' he said. 'There'll be lots of visiting government officials. We'll take over the campus. A twenty-four-hour sit-in. The first of many, co-ordinated throughout the country, every month, the same day, culminating in a massive—.'

'Pour me a rum, will you? I haven't seen Papa since the row.' She went to the miniature battle displayed on the large table to the right of the window, began fiddling, upsetting the small leaden figures.

Thulatu moved across to her, holding out the glass. 'We might even be lucky enough to get reports of it to the outside world. Well, eventually.' He kept his voice even. 'There's a woman, she's with Dick now in Rhaums, a journalist, seems she wants to write about racism.' His short laugh was contemptuous. 'She's come to the right place.' He jiggled the glass. 'Well? You'll do it? I have to let the UDF know, give them—.'

'Listen!' Babo whipped around, facing the door leading to the hall. 'They're coming! You hear?'

But it was the servant, the door already open before he had finished knocking.

Babo stared, her face a mixture of relief and disappointment.

'Oh, Elijah.'

The man stood, a squat, black trunk, his eyes rooted on Babo. 'Excuse, Miss Babo, but I must to talk to Madam.'

'Mia? She's up—. What is it, Elijah?'

'Madam, she not say how much ....' He broke off, glancing pointedly at Thulatu. '... persons for the dinner.'

'Dinner? Dinner, yes, yes. How many? Oh, I'll find out in a minute. It'll do in a minute, won't it? She's just gone—. She'll be down in a minute.'

'Very good, Miss Babo.' Elijah withdrew, casting a baleful look in Thulatu's direction.

'Well?' Thulatu pushed the drink into her hand. 'You'll make the speech?'

'Speech?' Babo stared into the glass as though she weren't quite sure what it was. Absently, she swilled the liquid, watched it splash out across her hand. Spilling, she thought. Too fast. All of it. Moving too fast.

Thulatu looked at her, irked. He'd never seen her so nervous, vague, even. But then, he'd never seen her in this house before. The heart's core of Afrikanerdom. He could smell it in the walls, the very air about him. Yes. Easier when he focused on this. 'Next month,' he said. 'The sit-in.'

'I, I've never done anything so risky.'

'Risky. You, the great white liberal. A family with influence, power. What odds are you facing? May I ask? A few hours in a first-class cell until your Papa comes to bail you out?'

'I'd never ask for his help. You know that.'

'So they all say. Till they're detained.' He drained his glass.

'You should know.' Her voice was bitter. 'You seem to specialise in white women.' She stared at the large, finely-modelled features below the graceful wings of grey-black hair, a perfection that never failed to startle her. An avenging angel, she thought, Thabo's death filling him with the intensity of a zealot. Her legs shook as she went to the bar, placing her glass down. 'We shouldn't have told her!'

He struggled for a moment, his voice thick with it. 'After the way Thabo died? Nothing could have stopped me!'

'D'you have any idea what it'll do to her? Do you? Married into this family, for God's sake!'

'Will you make the speech?'

'You're hard. Just like Papa. What, what is it with me, no matter which way I run I keep hitting into the same ... block of stone.'

'Well?'

Babo turned away, her gaze speculative. 'But even Papa. Maybe there's a way to get to him.'

'Will you?' he roared.

'I'll ... see, I'll think about it.' She swung to face him. 'But only if you promise me you'll say nothing more to her today.'

'Agreed. But it won't end here.' The door opened, startling them both. Mia. Paul ushering her gently into the room. Thulatu had the feeling that she would have stood there indefinitely, framed in the doorway, had not Paul prodded her to enter. She looked calmer. More controlled. But he saw the way she had drawn herself inwards to a rigid stillness, a small, exquisite desert mouse, senses tuned to ward off the next attack. Yet his own pain left no room for ... what? Pity? He'd be damned if he'd pity her. Her horror upon discovering he was her father was based solely upon the mixture of his blood. Nothing more. He had seen it clearly: the slow, ugly birth of it as the full impact was realised, the bloody demon-child of racism glittering in her eyes.

Babo took a few steps towards her, hesitated. 'There you are!' Her voice was breathless. She stared at Mia's white face, the tousled black hair, the wide, dark, red-rimmed eyes shifting, shifting. What had they done?

For a moment, nobody spoke. The silence seemed to build into something solid, tense with the absence of sound. Babo couldn't bear it. 'Paul?' she said, eyes beseeching the elderly white man who stood by Mia's side.

He responded as though somebody had pushed a button on his well-rounded paunch. 'Yes, yes, she's feeling b-better. I've given her a shot.'

'Mia?' Babo moved quickly to her, reaching out. 'You okay?' Tentatively, she touched the other woman's arm. 'God, I'm sorry—.'

She jumped as Mia sprang past her to pick up the antimacassar lying in a heap on the floor, eyes fixed, as though nothing else mattered.

Mia held it to her nose, sniffing the stink of whiskey, her lips twisting in distaste. 'Babo! How could you!' She held out the cloth. 'The finest Irish lace. And the couch! The carpet!' Her hand shook as she pointed.

'But you spilled—. You wiped ....' Babo trailed off. 'I'm sorry.'

Mia swung on Paul, the words erupting with a low intensity. 'How? How could it happen?' Just as suddenly, she wilted.

'My dear, I ...' He led her to sit on the couch, his arm dwarfing her slim shoulders. 'I, I've been telling you upstairs, don't you remember?' He looked down at his feet. 'Y-you remember? How I t-told you? How your mother...? How w-we agreed it?'

Thulatu snorted. '*You* agreed it!'

Paul shifted uneasily, his hand brushing the silk dress covering Mia's knee, before scuttling back to the safe, tight gap between his thighs.

'Sweet Jesus!' Mia's words shivered in the air. Swiftly, Babo went to the couch, crouching down. 'God, I'm sorry, Mia. It's such a mess.'

Mia didn't seem to hear. She lifted the gold watch on the chain about her neck. Piet had given it to her on their last wedding anniversary. She stared at the inscription on the back, the words now hideously mocked by the ticking beneath, the race towards a future she could not control, its shape mapped out long ago, despite her. Despite. The thought jarred. She pulled the watch until the chain was taut, biting into the nape of her neck. Slowly she began to grind the link along the chain, the sound droning in her ears.

'I'm a pendulum,' she said, knowing it was true, but not why.

Watching his daughter's stupefied face, Thulatu turned on Paul. 'You reared her like an ostrich.'

'Get out!' Mia spat the words at Thulatu.

'You had to be told.' He tried to keep his voice even.

'Get out!' Her hands were curled into fists.

Fighting, he thought. But not for freedom. Never for that. She had her freedom. Her white world of privilege. Not like Thabo-.

'When I looked at his body ...' he said deliberately, '... a congested mass in the coffin—.'

'Stop it!' Swiftly Mia covered her ears.

Babo's eyes pleaded. 'You said-.'

'— I said, your sister will know of this.' He breathed deeply, trying to regain his calm.

'D'you still want me to make that speech?' Babo's eyes flared. Mia stood, moving about jerkily. 'They'll be back from the farm soon. If they find—.' She stopped abruptly, facing Paul, her hands fitful. 'Take ... take him away. Sweet Jesus, what'll happen?' She moved again, knocking against the coffee table. 'I have to talk to Elijah about dinner. Maybe he has a remedy for cleaning lace. He can be quite good that way. Though I don't think it will ever be the same.' She frowned. 'Ever.'

'Thembalethu,' Thulatu said. He paused for a moment. 'His name's Thembalethu. Not Elijah.'

Mia swivelled. 'What're you saying? What is he—?'

'They've a right to their own names!'

'— my uncle, or something?' Her lips curled. 'Maybe your whole tribe's waiting outside to be introduced?' She bowed, mocking him. 'Well, bring them in, go on, all of them. What's a few more black faces between family?'

'It's all they own in this country.' Thulatu's voice was quiet.

Babo jerked her arm towards the door. 'Just go, will you?'

Seeing his chance, Paul struggled to rise. 'I-I'm afraid I'll have to go too. I'm on duty at four—.' He shuffled over to Mia. 'M-my dear, I ...' She turned away quickly. He pressed a bottle of pills into her hand. 'Take two of these when you ... you feel ... I'll see you in the morning.' He looked at Babo. 'You'll s-stay?'

Thulatu hesitated as Paul moved toward the door. He stared at his daughter's ramrod back, the slender line of her body in the elegant dress. He would have liked to say something to her, something that would retrieve him in her eyes. But it was pointless, he knew. Her white mind. He would need to give her time. Then, perhaps, together, they could begin to salvage the lost years. The thought gave him hope. Perhaps Babo had been right after all. It was enough. For one day. He lifted his fingers to the blond head, a light, fleeting touch as he passed her on his way out. But, staring at Mia, she didn't seem to notice him.

'There. They've gone.' She went to Mia, hugging her swiftly. 'You poor thing,' she murmured, stroking the untidy hair. 'Come and sit down.' Together, they moved to the couch. Mia laid her head against Babo's shoulder. 'When he said the words ... a mallet crashing in my chest.'

'I know ... it's been an awful shock.'

Mia sat up straight. 'Oh, if only it were a dream! Why me? Sweet Jesus, what'd I do to deserve this? Thank God you're here. This dinner. How'm I going to get through it? How?' She drew a deep breath. 'You mustn't talk politics. Whatever happens, Babo. Promise me!'

'Y'might as well ask the grass to stop growing. Damnit, Papa and me in the same room? I wish it were over.'

Mia gripped her hand. 'You won't tell? Promise, swear to me!'

'I won't tell them.'

'How, how do I deal with this?' Mia pressed her hands against her cheeks. 'No, no. I mustn't think of it now. After the dinner. Then I'll—. Yes, then.' She turned to Babo. 'But you knew! How long've you known—? Oh, why didn't you tell me?'

Babo looked away. 'A while. He got Paul to—. Paul introduced us. Then I met him again through the Black Sash, he ... Thulatu's a lawyer, he works—.'

'Don't mention his name! This dinner—.' Mia laughed, the sound quivering out of control. 'Imagine! I was planning a nice reunion. The family together. Like old times.'

'What old times?' Babo tried to keep the bitterness out of her voice.

'And just when Claus had finally accepted me—.'

'Papa?' Babo gazed at her, wide-eyed. 'Are you kidding? How can you forget the way he treated you when you and Piet first married? He almost disowned Piet for remarrying so soon after Yolande's death. To say nothing of your being English.'

'Three years isn't so soon. And Piet never loved that woman.'

Babo grimaced. 'Papa thought the world of her. That was enough to make Piet marry a woman he didn't love. And look at how they're influencing Jan. It was Papa who decided where he should go to school, who his friends should be. He'll never look on you as that child's mother.'

Mia clicked her shoes together in a furious, staccato rhythm. 'I love Jan as though he were mine.'

Swiftly Babo put an arm about her shoulders.

'Even Claus realises that now, I know he does! And now this!'

'Mia, listen. Papa doesn't make a U-turn without good reason. Yolande's dead. Mama's dead. I'm a lost cause. He's willing to include you because Piet and Jan are all he has left. Surely you see that?'

'Piet's much happier. He thinks the world of Papa.' Mia stared at her white knuckles. White, she thought. So white. By squeezing harder, she could make them even whiter. But for the rest, she'd need to drain the blood from her veins.

Babo sighed. 'Unfortunately, he's never learned to stand up to him.'

'He married me!' Mia struck her breasts.

'Behind Papa's back.'

'Oh, just when everything was going right—. When Papa finds out—.'

'It's a bit much calling him "Papa". How come you've never called Paul "Papa"?'

'That cold fish!' Mia hissed. 'He can't even bear me to touch him.'

Babo's eyes were bleak. 'I can't bear to touch Claus.'

'What'll I do?'

'Let's just concentrate on getting through this dinner.' Babo held out her hands. 'Look at me! I'm sweating already. Why was I invited? Why'd I come?' Her laugh was harsh. 'Need I ask? A moth to a flame.'

Mia stared towards the window, her eyes blank as the glass. 'It's unreal, that's what it is.'

'Papa's up to something.'

Mia jumped up. 'Please, please! Don't make it any worse than it's going to be. Oh, give me yesterday!'

Babo stood, struggling between the pity she felt for her sister-in-law, and a familiar sense of fear. It wasn't only that she was afraid of her father. She was afraid too, of what he provoked her into becoming. Jesus, her whole body was thick with sweat. She hugged Mia. 'Don't worry, I haven't seen Papa in over a year. Things'll have cooled. Look, can I take a quick shower? I'm filthy.' She picked up her hold-all, rummaging in it to cover her own unease. 'You should see the plumbing in my new flat,' she said brightly. 'Works every other day if I'm lucky! View's great, though.' She looked at Mia. 'We'll have a long talk later, sort it all out, I promise.'

'This won't sort. It's worse than dirty washing.' Mia pushed distractedly at her hair. 'Oh, what'll happen? What'll I do? No, no. You go on,' she said as Babo stepped towards her again. 'Have your shower. I've got to finish packing for Jan. His scouting trip—. They'll be back soon.'

'Sure?' Babo searched her face.

Mia nodded, her expression calm.

'I won't be long, I promise.'

Again Mia nodded, even managing a half-smile as Babo left the room. For a moment she listened, then, sure she could not be overheard, she roamed about, saying it aloud. 'I know what'll happen. I know,' the words dropping dully in the emptiness, like stones flung far into the depths of a well, never landing, never arriving, always falling, the thrower held there, listening, unable to leave until the well surrendered the faint echo of something striking the dark, dripping floor, the completion of the action. Cause and effect. But the stones would never land. Neither would she ever know the effect. The thought, vague, diffuse, like an image in a dream, confused her, its sly innuendo only partially grasped.

When she opened her eyes, she was standing on the couch, the heels of her stilettos stabbing the soft fabric as she tried to wipe her feet. Frightened, she leapt down, landing awkwardly. The room was a mess. A pigsty. She rushed about, straightening cushions, clearing glasses. A real pigsty. What would Claus and Piet think?

'A sow would be cleaner, they'll say.' She broke off, the words crackling in the quiet room. No no stop it! She mustn't think like that. Jan's packing. Finish Jan's packing. One foot in front of the other, that was all that mattered. She moved towards the door.

III

Piet stood with his son, arranging the final scenes in the miniature battle display. Absorbed, he kept an automatic ear on his son's excited talk of the proposed scouting trip. 'There!' he said suddenly, stepping back to admire his handiwork. 'What do you think, Jan?'

His son fiddled with the woggle on his scout's neckerchief. 'Great, Papa. I wish I could take it to school, show the others—.'

'Impressive, hey?'

Jan leaned forward, his gaze sweeping the entire length. 'Ten thousand Zulus against a few Boers! And they only got three of us.'

'Only wounded, mind.' Piet re-positioned one of the smaller wagons forming the laager. 'And for each one of the three, we killed a thousand of them. God was on our side.'

Jan lifted an imaginary weapon to his shoulder, aimed it, one eye squinting as he narrowed his focus. 'They should've had muskets and cannons like us. Stupid using only spears and sticks.'

'Savages.' Piet's lips narrowed. 'God helped us avenge the murder of Piet Retief and his men.'

'The Battle of Blood River. My favourite story.'

Piet turned, pointing an admonishing finger. 'It's no story! That's why you've no school today. All over South Africa the promise the Boers gave God before the battle is being made again, just as we did at the service this morning. Remember the words of the Covenant?'

Jan stiffened. 'Of course! Here we stand before God the most Holy in the highest Heaven to make a vow unto Him that if he shall protect us, deliver our enemy unto us, henceforth this day shall be a day of thanksgiving as the Sabbath brings even unto our children in all future generations so that his name may be honoured and the glory of victory be his now and forever.'

'Splendid. A true Afrikaner.' Piet smiled, suddenly realising how high he had to raise his arm in order to rest it on his son's shoulder. Like looking at a mirror image, he thought, though his own fair hair was now well flecked with grey. 'We must never forget that promise, Jan. If we do, we'll forget who we are, we'll be destroyed. We're a tiny country with very few friends. Most of the world is against us now. We've got to be strong, look after ourselves.'

Jan pulled the tails of the neckerchief, watching the woggle slide upwards towards his throat. 'Papa, can I borrow your scouting knife? Oupa promised me his, but—'

'You're not listening!'

'I am! But I'll be late if ...' He broke off as the voices carried from the hall. His grandfather. Just in time!

'Did you remember the knife?' he called to the muscular, silver-haired man who entered the room.

'Jan!' Mia's voice was brittle as she stood in the open door. 'Where're your manners?'

Claus held out the Swiss army knife. 'Anything for my favourite grandson.'

Holding up a glass, Piet looked at his father. 'Join me?' Without taking his eyes from Claus, he spoke to his wife. 'Sherry, Mia?' He released his breath as Claus looked at him, nodding imperceptibly.

'Brandy.'

'Brandy?' Piet turned to his wife. 'You never drink brandy.'

Jan examined the knife. 'Your *only* grandson. Great! It's much sharper than Papa's. The boys'll be here any second. When we cross the Drakensberg, we're camping out for two nights.'

Piet carried the drinks to the coffee table as they sat.

Claus leaned back, loosening his tie. 'Ah, to be young enough to retrace the Great Trek! To pull ox and wagon over miles of bedrock. What an epic journey it was!'

Jan pressed one of the knife blades against the palm of his hand, testing its sharpness. 'Harder for us! We've no slaves now to push the wagons.'

Mia cut in on the men's laughter. 'Jan! Don't talk like that!'

Claus held up his glass, smiling. 'More's the pity.' He paused. 'Isn't Babo here?'

Piet looked at his wife. There was something odd about her, something he couldn't quite define. 'You okay?' he asked.

But she was looking at Claus. 'She's having a shower.'

Perhaps it was his imagination. 'When they get to the camp site ...' he said to his father, '... they put on a play ...'

Jan looked up from the knife. 'We all put our names in a hat.' He snorted in disgust. 'I got stuck with playing a girl.'

Claus leaned forward. 'Which one?'

'Anna Steenkamp,' Mia said, when Jan didn't answer.

'Ah zo. You have the most important lines in the play.' Claus smiled at his grandson.

'Lucky for me she's only in it at the beginning. I'm playing one of the trekboers as well. Nobody wanted to be the slaves, so we decided to leave them out.'

'Hah! Sensible man. Ja, tell me what Anna has to say.'

Mia shifted uneasily. 'Oh, he hasn't time. Go check you've everything packed, dear.'

Jan slotted the small steel clippers back in its groove. 'I have everything,' he said in a martyred tone.

Piet reached out, tapping his shoulder. 'Come on, Jan. Let's hear you.'

Mia felt a sudden sense of panic. 'You might've forgotten something.'

Piet turned to her. 'What's the matter with you? You spent hours teaching him his lines. I thought you'd jump at the chance—.'

Claus' voice was coaxing. 'You wouldn't want to disappoint your old grandfather, would you?'

'Oh, all right.' Rising, Jan looked about for a place to stand. Spying the lace antimacassar on the back of the couch, he grabbed it, placing it on his head. He sniffed. 'Yikes! It stinks!'

'Jan!' Mia reached out. 'Take it off! He really won't have time—.'

'Let him.' Claus was smiling at the comical appearance of his grandson.

'He's improvising.' Piet grinned.

The boy stood, pointing at the three adults. 'You're the British.' Hands on hips, he began in a solemn, accusatory tone, 'You ask us why we are willing to give up everything we know and love? Why we are prepared to endure much hardship and misery trekking across the impenetrable vastness of this land? We wish to go where we can be free to live by our own guiding principles, free to find a new home where we can preserve proper relations between master and servant.'

Fully into the part now, his voice took on a sonorous note. 'By emancipating our slaves you have placed them on an equal footing with Christians. This is contrary to the laws of God, the natural distinctions of race and religion. It is intolerable for any decent Christian to bow down beneath such a yoke. Wherefore we will withdraw in order to preserve our doctrines in purity.' Bending, he mimed lifting a great weight on his back, and began a slow, painful trudge across the room toward the window.

'Uitstekend!' Claus clapped enthusiastically.

Mia reached out swiftly as Jan passed her, grabbing the antimacassar.

'A chip off the old block, eh, Papa?' Piet was smiling.

'I just wish your mother had lived to—.' Claus swallowed, staring into his glass.

The door opened, Elijah still tapping its surface politely. 'Excuse, Madam.' A shrill horn sounded outside.

'Great!' Jan leapt up, pushing past Elijah as he rushed out.

'Jan!' Mia hurried after him. 'You haven't said goodbye—.'

'Oh, leave him.' Piet looked at Elijah. 'Help them load his gear.'

Mumbling, Elijah turned to leave.

'What's that?' Piet strained to catch his reply.

Elijah paused, half-turned, eyes averted. 'Said yes, Baas.' Quickly he left, the door closing behind him.

'He needs a tight rein, that kaffir. Your mother'd turn in her grave—.'

'You've news?' Piet leaned forward.

Claus grinned, stretching his arms across the back of the couch. 'Ja-ja. Approved by all the branches. Had it straight from the horse's mouth. He phoned just after you left.'

'Then I'm in?'

'Was there ever any doubt? A man with nothing to hide—.'

'Ah, it's splendid, Papa!' Rising, he gulped his drink.

'You won't tell Mia. What your mother never knew—.'

Moving to the drinks cabinet, Piet shook his head. 'When—?' he asked, refilling his glass.

'You'll be sworn into the Westeinder cell at Friday's meeting, replacing van der Meer.'

'Then he's out?'

'On his arse.' Claus' smile was satisfied. He lifted his glass from the table. 'Here's to Section 50A. The police'll hold him long enough to prevent his university contract being renewed.' He nodded, the shaft of sunlight from the window rippling in his hair. 'And then some. The bastard. Lobbying openly for radical change. D'you know he's been saying our Christian version of national history is prejudiced?'

'We'd better be careful with Babo.' Lifting his drink, Piet returned to the smaller couch opposite his father. 'If she ever suspected you'd used what she told me—.'

Claus waved his hand in a dismissive gesture. 'The Broederbond's skilful at covering its tracks. But watch your tongue. She's a proper little ferret. And from what I hear, she's started to mix with some questionable types on the campus.'

'That won't go against me?'

Claus shook his head. 'We need all the information we can get.'

'But Babo'd never tell us—.'

'When you wind her up, zo, amazing what she lets slip.' Claus made a circular motion, the gesture oddly graceful despite the large, square hand.

'That's why you wanted us to invite her today?'

'Ja, worth a try. The unrest is working itself up to a fever pitch.'

'If Rachel Mokoena hadn't been killed in detention—.'

'Watch what you say, man! She became ill after being arrested, died while in police custody.'

'Still, it's a pity. It's stirred up such anger in the townships.'

Claus shrugged. 'The Vaal's given us trouble for years. Security will handle it the way they always do. A couple of Zulu impis let loose with spears and sticks. Black against black. Not a white policeman in sight as they hack each other to death. The cameras there to record it all for world-wide consumption. It held the worst of the sanctions back in '76, it'll do the same now. It's all a question of cosmetics—.' He leaned forward. 'Now, what'd Jan say about the Windhoek woman?'

Piet nodded. 'It's true. She's been telling them Apartheid's never been the"Policy of Good Neighbourliness," that the whites are treating the blacks unfairly.'

'Who the hell vetted her? Those teachers are hand-picked.'

'Jan has a crush on her. I'd quite a job convincing him what she said was lies.'

Claus slammed his open hand on the dark wood of the table. 'You see the damage a bloody Marxist can do? Undermining the whole educational structure.'

'It's only one teacher, Papa.'

'Use your head, maan. Twenty, thirty boys, year in, year out. How many Afrikanerised children d'you think we'll have ten years from now? I'll wipe her name off the board if—.' He broke off as the door opened.

Mia stood, hovering, reluctant to step into the room. 'I hope he has enough sweaters. It's so cold in those mountains at night.'

'You're a worrier. Come and finish your drink.' Piet stared past her as his sister entered. He glanced at his father, but the older man's face was masked. Rising, Piet moved to the bar, his ears tuned. He'd keep quiet, leave it to his father. He preferred to stay out of it, anyway.

'Papa.' For a moment Babo stood, her face expressionless as Claus scrutinised her frayed tee shirt and jeans. Ja, she'd wanted to offend him by not dressing for dinner. The thought amused him. Zo. She was still fighting him. Good. He'd get more out of her that way. 'You look well,' he said evenly.

'Never better.'

'Come and sit here with me, Babo.' Mia's hand danced on the smaller couch.

Eyes narrowed, Claus watched her join Mia. 'How is ... everything?'

The pause was deliberate, his way, Babo knew, of slotting insinuation into even the most innocent of remarks. She looked at him. Time had wrought no change in the subtle, hawk-like features: countless years of cruelty and arrogance carved in the dark eyes.

'Such a vague word,' she said as Piet handed her a glass. 'What can you possibly mean? My love-life? My studies? Perhaps my new flat? Or the organisation I've joined? Which kind of everything d'you wish to know about, Papa?' She was afraid to sip the drink, afraid he'd see the tremor in her hand.

'Ah, zo, you thought to surprise me? I heard you'd joined the Black Sash.'

'Only heard? I'd have thought one of your spies would've confirmed it by now.'

'Babo, please—.' Mia's hand was tight on her wrist. 'Piet?' She glanced up at her husband, eyes pleading, but he placed a warning finger to his lips. No help there. Had there ever been? she thought bitterly.

Claus lifted his shoulders casually. 'If it's in the national interest ....'

'My foot. Everything you do is for the Volk, Papa, your precious nation of Afrikaners. And to hell with the blacks!'

Mia leaned forward, her voice rising. 'I should've given him more socks. If his feet get wet .... He could catch pneumonia ....'

Piet came to sit by his father. 'Jan will be fine.' His glance was irritated. 'What's the matter with you?'

Claus watched Babo, choosing his words. 'The blacks have their homelands, their independence—'

'Stuff! Dumping grounds!' Babo drew a deep breath, holding on to it.

'And? And? Don't stop now! Tell me how we've uprooted millions of blacks, forced them to live in tin huts—.'

'It won't work, Papa.'

'—without even a decent water supply. No? Perhaps we've converted you?'

Babo was jubilant. 'You'll never trick me that way again!' Rising, she began to move about. So he wanted to play one of his games. Well, she had a game for him all right. 'This time it's my turn. Hm, now let's see.... How about a little rhyme?'

Mia looked up at her. 'Please,' she whispered.

But Babo was beyond it, her gaze fixed on her father. 'Miss Babo,' she began in a sing-song voice, 'had a golly who was sick, sick, sick, so she sent for the doctor to be quick, quick, quick—'

Claus hissed in disgust. 'You've never left the nursery.'

'But the doctor never came ....' She clenched the muscles in her throat, swallowing hard as she turned to Mia. 'Did Paul ever tell you about Doctor Khumalo?'

Her father's eyes narrowed. 'Paul? What would he know?'

'Khumalo,' Babo said. She went to stare out the window, her eyes held wide to contain it. Whatever happened, she must not show any sign of weakness. Outside, Elijah was moving among the cluster of fruit trees, looking for the ripest mangos and lichees, placing them carefully in the old basket to prevent their bruising. Fruit salad for dessert? The ordinariness of the thought calmed her. 'He used to run a clinic in Mamelodi. For blacks who'd been tortured in detention.'

'What would Paul know?' Her father's voice, a steel probe.

'Until he was detained himself. A week after they released him, four men shot Dr Khumalo and his mother in their kitchen.' Eyes fixed on Elijah, his skin dappled as he gazed upwards among the laden branches, she fought to keep her voice steady. 'Having supper. They were having supper. Afterwards ... there were stains ... even on the ceiling.' She paused. When she spoke again, her voice was deliberate, cold. 'The licence number of one of the cars spotted outside their house—.'

Claus snorted. 'She's always had a wild imagination.'

'—at the time of the murder, was traced right to the commanding officer of the Pretoria Security Police.'

'Paranoid!'

She almost smiled at the fury of the accusation flung at her back. So. It was getting to him. 'The government banned all news reports of the so-called investigation into—.'

'Ja-ja! You think the quack's scummy neighbours wouldn't lie through their teeth if there were a chance of getting a policeman in trouble? We're not barbarians! We uphold the supreme principle of justice: innocent until—.'

Babo turned swiftly, facing him. '—killed in police custody!'

Claus raised a hand mockingly. 'Show me the policeman who was convicted of this crime. Where is he? Zo.'

Babo stood, hands on hips. 'Out on the streets, continuing his filthy, murderous work.'

His face darkened. 'Is it my fault they're not long enough out of the trees? They have to be controlled—'

He broke off as Mia's harsh laugh sliced the air. They all stared as she began to grunt and snuffle, scratching under her arms. Piet looked at her, shocked. 'Cut it out, will you? Have you been drinking?' Embarrassed, he turned quickly to Babo. 'Last week I doled out a hundred bars of soap to the farmhands. Y'know what I found out yesterday? They'd gone and sold the bloody lot!'

'You can't eat soap!'

'Christ!' Piet ran his fingers through his close-cropped hair. What the hell was Mia playing at? He forgot his earlier intention to keep out of it. 'It was our sweat!' He raised a hand, encompassing the room. 'We earned this! Babo, I try with them, believe me! That rainstorm we had. I even gave them a full day off to re-build the huts in the kraal, for all the thanks I got. They're not like us. Look at the squalor they live in. They're like animals.'

At his words Mia leapt to her feet, began moving agitatedly about the room. He tried to ignore her, looking instead at Babo as she came to sit opposite him. 'I've nothing against them, believe me. But don't ask me to share the beaches. Surely it's better they've their own areas and we've ours?'

'Animals!' Mia stood, staring at Babo. 'I've used that word myself.' She leaned forward. 'See? See?'

Piet breathed when she didn't say anything else. She was acting so strangely, he hadn't been sure what thing she might come out with next.

Babo didn't seem to have heard her. 'Oh, Piet.' Her voice was low. 'You sound just like Papa.'

'He's my son.'

'Yes, I mark it,' Babo snapped.

'Babo, don't do this!' Mia stared at the marks her nails had made in the palms of her hands. There seemed to be no sensation, although the welts were livid, ugly.

Claus' smile was thin, his eyes on Babo. 'And you're my daughter.'

'No law says I have to like it.' Babo stood, moving to the cabinet to top up her drink. But the glass was full. 'Still,' she said. 'I'm sure you can get your friends in the Justice Department to change that overnight. A mere drop in the ocean compared with the stinking injustice of the laws we have at present.' She took several gulps.

'Ja-ja. You should spend your mornings at your lectures instead of shooting your mouth off about the government with your kaffir friends.'

'Hah!' Returning to the couch, her eyes were bright. 'Thanks for the warning. I'll be more careful in future.'

Claus leaned forward. 'You're careful enough to be discreet in other ways.'

'You don't say!'

His mouth was a hard line. 'You think I don't know your coffee mornings are a blind—?'

'Secrets? How exciting!'

'Mixing with political agitators, terrorists, is a—.'

'Chancing your arm, Papa? Careful! You might break your—.'

Mia's tone broke in, high-pitched. 'Jan has a cold. His sinuses. He always gets an attack in summertime. Hay fever, the doctor says. I hope he's—.'

'Christ, Mia!' Piet glared at her. 'What the hell's the matter with you!' Swiftly, he turned to Babo. 'Y'think I didn't feel the same at college? Look, is that, I'm not saying we haven't made mistakes, but you can't change the country overnight. Unless you want a war—.'

Babo spread her hands, palms upwards. 'Listen to Rip van Winkle! We have a war!'

'We got rid of the Pass laws—.'

Babo's voice was icy. 'The police and Section 29. That's all it takes. What's worse, the children've become their targets. D'you know how many've been detained in the last six months? Tortured?'

'Stop it!' Mia stood, her hands over her ears. She stared at the three of them. So wrapped up in it, she might not exist. The thought chilled her. She searched the familiar rows of sturdy books lining the bookcase for some relief, but Claus' voice pulled her back to it.

'... nonsense! Some children of known black agitators are simply detained for questioning. Zo.'

Babo gritted her teeth. 'More than 8,000, a lot of them under twelve!'

Mia stared, hating her. She had promised, sworn she wouldn't do this. The thing was escalating, she could see it in Babo's eyes. Escalating. Soon it would be out of control. And then, then, anything could happen. Anything could be said. Panic-stricken, she turned to Piet, but he was just as embroiled as the rest of them, his eyes fixed on Babo. 'You should see some of those so-called kids in action in the townships,' he was saying, '... they'd buy and sell most of our soldiers—.'

'Little bastards.' Claus spat the words.

'As for the rest,' Piet shrugged, '... if they're innocent ....'

'They're black, they've everything to fear.' Babo's mouth set in a stubborn line.

Claus drained his glass. 'You've always had a talent for melodrama.' Quickly, he turned to Mia, startling her. 'Now, my dear, any chance of us eating soon? I still have some things to see to on the farm before I turn in.'

'Getting a new batch of parolees, Papa?' Babo raised her eyebrows.

Mia screamed at her. 'Shut up!'

Claus slammed his glass down. 'You push me too far.'

Babo's smile was taunting. 'It was a simple question.'

'Don't smart-ass me!'

Shaking now, Babo hid her hands between her knees. 'You wouldn't be so livid if you weren't still using slave labour to harvest your crops. God help them, they'd be better off in their overcrowded cells, being beaten by the police—.'

Claus was on his feet. 'How dare you—!'

Babo shrank as the thick hands curled into fists.

'But for your mother I'd—!' He stepped towards her, anger clenched in the line of his jaw.

'Excuse, Madam? Dinner is to serve.'

Startled, they all turned to face the voice. Elijah, sensing the tension, backed out hurriedly.

'Yes, yes.' Mia took her father-in-law's arm, began moving towards the door. Her voice was brittle. 'Your favourite hors d'oeuvres, Papa. Fresh salmon, with just a hint of lemon—.'

'Christ, Babo——.' Piet's mouth opened and closed as he followed the others from the room.

For a few moments, she sat, her breathing ragged, a pulse drumming in her ears. What was between them still lay, festering. There in the first moments when his eyes had rested on her as she came into the room, a delayed explosion of calculated loathing. What'd she expected? That he'd called her here for some kind of reconciliation? In the intervening year, he'd changed miraculously? Wished to make amends? The stuff of fairy tales, she was hardly naive enough to have believed it. Yet, still she was shocked by the savage strength of his antipathy, unmasked now that she was no longer living with him.

When he's near me, she thought, the world seems to tilt. He had never loved any of them. But why had she become his enemy? Even their strongly divergent political views could not explain the depth of that hatred. She shivered. No, it was a lie. He hated her because he sensed she knew what he was, exactly what he was.

Better keep away. She was ashamed of what she had again become in his presence, the two of them locking into the old familial roles, circling warily, jaws snapping, teeth bared, as they sniffed out any weakness, a brute instinct to strip each other to the marrow. So much for civilisation. Except this time she'd survived without giving him any information. The thought sustained her as she rose, heading towards the dining room.

IV

Piet sighed as he pressed the remote control, the car engine hardly audible as he paused for the gates to swing inwards. He hoped Elijah had remembered to keep Brutus tied up till he got back. Bloody dog liked nothing better than to leg it any time he got the chance. Great security guard he was proving to be. But there was no sign of the dog as he drove through the gates. He glanced at the clock in the dashboard. Late. The bedroom light was out. Mia was probably asleep. He didn't know whether to be glad or sorry. If she didn't bitch at him tonight, she'd do it in the morning, over break- fast. And he couldn't blame her. She was fond of his sister, she'd seen how Papa and he had set Babo up. No wonder she'd been jittery, the bloody dinner'd been more like a battlefield, Babo and Papa throwing daggers' looks, Mia giving them all a detailed history of Jan's hay fever from the time he was a tot, Papa drinking himself into a stony silence, ending up having to be driven home, no wonder Babo'd gone off smirking. For once she seemed to have got the upper hand. The only information Papa'd ever managed to elicit from her had been done by skilful outmanoeuvring. He grinned.

Now she was beating him at his own game. Didn't Papa realise it? She'd never rat if she could help it, that was one thing about her, when she believed in something. Undeviating, no, even more than that ... honourable. The word filled him with a strange yearning for something he couldn't crystallise. He eased the car to a halt beside the double garage, the dog barking as the gravel spat at the metal hubs. Suddenly he hoped Mia wasn't asleep. He wanted her to hold him, to wrap himself in her skin until he forgot Papa and Babo and the vague sense of guilt that'd been plaguing him all day. Stepping from the car into the warm dark, he paused for a moment, the garden bathing him in a night-scented fragrance that reminded him of his wife. And the Broederbond! With all that'd happened, he'd almost forgotten. Wait till he told her the good news!

* * *

Mia poured herself another drink. She wandered about the drawing room, her hand seeking old familiarities in the graceful lines of furniture she and Piet had chosen together. But the room seemed to shut her out, the impassive sheen of wood, porcelain, even fabric, offering no reassurances. She tried to concentrate on the paintings and lithographs carefully arranged over the marble mantel, but the vast panorama of the high veld, karoo, savanna, forest, grassland, desert, stared back, their secrets locked in a conspiracy of dark brush-strokes, defying interpretation.

The brandy burned her throat, small trickles trailing from the corners of her mouth to her chin. On her own. She was on her own. No different really, to the way it'd always been, not when you'd lived with a fish. Sweet Jesus, what was she going to do? In the fury of her pacing, the room seemed to shrink, the antimacassar leering at her from the back of the couch. Swiping it, she placed it on her head, her hand raised, accusing the door opposite.

'By emancipating our slaves, you have placed them on an equal footing with—. This is contrary to the laws of God. The laws of God!'

Contaminated. The word shrieked in her head. She clamped her lips to stop it escaping. Shaking, she jerked the cloth off, rubbing at her face, her arms. The silk stockings hissed a static snake dance as she rubbed it against her legs. She stood, nostrils flaring as she fought for breath. About her, the air was heavy with the sour odour of whiskey. She sniffed the cloth. Stinking! How could she have! Flinging it across the room, she crawled onto the couch. Curled, foetus-like, she lay for a long time, watching the light drain from the window as the room slowly gathered the darkness into itself. When it was no longer possible to define which was room, which darkness, which Mia, she closed her eyes, seeing only its paralysis pressing against her eyelids.

'Hey, beautiful lady! You asleep?' Piet snapped the switch, infusing the room with light. 'I went straight up, I thought you'd be in bed by now.'

A blinding flash exploded the dark, warm womb. Mia started, the words spilling out of control. 'What, it's not true!' Still dazed, she winced against the glare. 'Wh-who is it?'

Piet leaned over her. 'You okay? You look—.'

Reaching out, she clutched him, her eyes beseeching. 'Was it a dream, oh, was it?'

Frowning, he put a hand to her brow. 'Hey, up! You're shivering. Feverish too.'

Swiftly she climbed from the couch, wrapping her arms about him. 'Tell me I dreamed it,' she whispered.

'Y'mean Babo? She's a bloody terror when she gets going—.'

Her eyes burned as she looked up at him. 'That silence all through dinner, I thought I'd never fill it! I could've strangled her!'

'From the time she was knee-high, if Papa said yes, she'd say no.' Gently, he lifted the untidy strands of hair from her face. 'It's worse since Mama died. She's had her knife in him—.'

Mia groaned. 'Oh, give me yesterday!'

'Listen!' He smacked a kiss on her lips. 'The Broederbond. I'm in. Can y'believe it?' His grin almost reached his ears. When she didn't respond, he studied her wan appearance, the scorched hollows of her eyes. 'You could do with a brandy.' Releasing her, he went to the bar. 'What's got you drinking brandy?' He poured generous measures for them both. When he spoke again, his voice was a low warning. 'Only, don't let on you know to Papa—.'

Mia swivelled, her skin bristling. 'No, no, you mustn't tell Papa. You must keep it a secret.' Her voice shook. 'Is that possible?' She ignored the glass he held out to her.

He frowned. 'Aren't you going to congratulate me?' He raised his own, slivers of light sparking in the amber liquid. 'The Broederbond!' he said, and drank.

'Babo says they're fanatics.' Mia dragged her red nails along the fabric of the couch. The sound, she thought, a match being struck. Or a fuse. That was it. Already lit when they handed it to her. And it was short. So short.

'Babo doesn't know her ass—.'

'She knows about politics.'

His eyes narrowed. 'Has she been getting at you? Is that, she'd do anything to get at Papa. You should—.'

'D'you have to join? You don't have to, do you?' She gestured around her. 'We're fine as we are.'

Piet stared. 'You can't be serious! You know how much I've wanted—.'

Mia stood, arms folded tightly across her breasts. 'A bunch of fanatics!'

'The word according to Babo!'

'Babo didn't say it. I said it.'

'You just said—.'

'I said it!' Her tone was a childish shriek.

Silently, he held out the glass to her again. What was up with her? She'd been just as eager as he to be accepted by the broeders. 'What's the matter with you? It's the lifetime ambition of most Afrikaners.'

'Did they check you out?' She moved about restlessly, slopping her drink. 'Did they? They didn't dig deep enough.'

'Listen,' he sipped his drink. 'It's the best thing that could've happened. Think of Jan. His future's assured. I'm telling you, farming'll become just a sideline.'

Turning, she faced him, her knuckles white as she held the glass. 'What's it all for? Answer me that! We've got enough, haven't we enough? Why d'you always have to reach for more?' She paused. When she spoke again, her voice was a whisper. 'They're evil. Sweet Jesus, how'll I cope with it!'

'For Jan,' he said deliberately. 'This is for Jan.'

'For your father.' The words were scornful.

He breathed deeply to control it. 'I want this, Mia. I want it.' He spread his hands. 'It can mean a career in anything: banking, politics, industry, you name it.'

'You're a farmer!'

'Did I have a choice? You're always moaning at how tied to Papa I've been.'

She watched him stride back to the bar, his long, girlish arms dun-coloured as the short-sleeved khaki shirt he wore. Everything he did. Half-assed. Even his tan.

'All I ever get from you is promises.' Her voice was weary.

He frowned. 'You're in a filthy mood.'

'Yes, filthy.' Nervously, she rubbed her hands across her face. 'I'm filthy. Don't join, Piet.' The words, barely audible, leaked between her fingers.

'Are you crazy? It's my one chance to be ...' he paused awkwardly '... my own man. I'll have power, influence—.'

'And how'll you use it? To keep the blacks down?' Every time she moved, the furniture seemed to get in her way. Her shins were bruised from the coffee table. Had Elijah been moving it? Either that, or she was going blind. Blind. That was it. They had blindfolded her. For thirty-five years. And she'd never noticed. A peculiar quivering began deep in her gut and she wrapped her arms about her stomach, struggling against the urge to laugh loudly, endlessly.

Piet dropped a hissing ice cube into his brandy glass, then fished it out with his fingers. She didn't even give him time to think straight, she was so bloody hyper. Every time he turned from the bar to face her, she was standing in a different part of the room.

'Listen,' he said patiently. 'If anything's to be changed in this country, the Broederbond must have new blood, younger men like me, willing to adapt, move towards ... democracy.'

'Democracy?' She stared, wide-eyed. 'You mean, one man, one vote?'

'Well—.'

'Will you do that? Will you, Piet?' Something surged through her, exploding in a sense of release. 'Then we'd all be equal!'

'Well—.'

'If you joined for that—.' She held out her hands, the gesture almost supplicating. 'Y'think it'll come? Big changes like that? Oh, when? How soon? Then everything'd be all right! I could—.'

'It's not that simple—.'

'I could help!' She moved towards him, eyes bright with it. 'I could do something! Join the Black Sash, it hasn't been banned like those others, yes, be like Babo, chain myself to railings like those women—.'

'Hey up!' Piet was startled by her sudden switch.

'Yes, yes, you're right, you should join. Oh, I needn't've been afraid!' Reaching out, she hugged him fiercely. 'You're not Claus. It'll be okay. It's time we did—. We were wrong to do nothing. We've been so lazy, but we'll change. We'll do it together, Piet. We'll make things happen—.'

He tried to release himself. 'Wait a—.'

'I'll phone Babo in the morning. She'll know—.'

'Hold on—'

'—what I should do. Oh, Pietie, I can't wait!' She lifted her head from his shoulder to look up at him. 'How soon do you join? I can't wait for—.'

'Now just hold on!' Finally, he managed to pull her arms free. 'It'll take a lifetime to bring about changes like that—.'

'A lifetime?' She searched his face.

'All we can try to do is—.'

'You said we'd have a democracy.' Her voice was cold.

'That's you all over, you twist things—.'

'My lifetime.' She stared at the dense triangle of hairs in the open neck of his shirt. They did not extend below the second button. The first time he'd made love to her, she'd felt cheated, as though he had deliberately misled her. Now he was cheating her again.

'My lifetime.'

Piet was sorry he'd told her. Papa was right, he thought. He should have kept his mouth shut. 'You say nothing to Babo, mind.' He nudged her chin to make sure she heard. She was staring dully at his chest.

'You mean not in my lifetime.' Her arms dropped to her sides.

'What's it matter to us?' Exasperated, he watched her drag across to the couch. 'Where the hell're you getting this sudden interest in politics?'

'Yes. A pipedream.' She sat, her body sagging. 'To imagine it could happen. But the other's a real ... nightmare.'

'You don't want to mind Babo, she makes it out to be worse than it is.' Piet put his glass down, taking in her pale, woebegone face. 'Come on, you should be in bed.' He sighed. She wouldn't be fit for anything tonight, that was for sure. He glanced about. 'Any idea where my book is? Y'know, the one on Antarctica?' He began searching the shelves, pulling out a couple of misplaced books, slotting them into their correct positions. Elijah, he'd put a bet on it. 'What time did Babo leave?' He spoke over his shoulder. 'Papa was fuming all evening.'

Vaguely, Mia was aware of his muttering as he searched. A family, she thought. Was it too much to ask? Like a fire on a winter evening, heating the cold inside. She had fanned it so ... elegantly. Sweet Jesus, was it really too much to ask? What chance had she got now? When Claus, when he found out .... He would stop her holding on to Piet. 'I'm so cold,' she said, the words lifeless.

Piet turned. 'A warm bed's what you need.'

She stared across at the battle display. History. The relentless scourge of it mapping her future. She shivered. 'No one. I've no one. Cold. Like a—.'

Piet's brow furrowed. She sounded weird. He crossed to the couch. 'You look as though you've seen a ghost,' he joked.

Mia laughed, the sound clanging. 'You're close. Oh, you're close.' She stood quickly, arms outstretched. 'Hold me, Piet!'

Again he put his hand to her brow. She was hot! 'Maybe I should call the doctor. You must've caught a bug. I've never seen you so—.'

She leaned heavily against him. 'Yes, I'm ... infected. It's been a terrible day, Piet, terrible! That black man! I've had the strangest feeling, it—.'

'Black man?'

'—won't go away.'

'What black man?'

'Eh?'

'You said, "black man".'

Frightened, she looked up at him. 'No! No! Did I? I didn't.'

'But you—.'

'Wait!' Her face cleared. 'Yes. In the shops today. He served me. So rude! Don't you find they can be rude?' Her voice pleaded.

Worried now, he tried to keep his expression bland. She was obviously delirious. 'The Day of the Covenant?' he said gently. 'Don't you remember, the shops weren't open—.'

Clutching him, she began to tremble. 'I'm cold.'

'Your hands are freezing.' He began chafing them vigorously.

'On the inside. So cold—.'

'Come on.' He put his arm about her shoulders. 'I'm putting you to bed.'

She stood rooted as he tried to draw her towards the door. 'The strangest feeling. I was looking through the wedding album. The negatives, in the pocket, you remember, inside the cover?'

He nodded, half-listening. Perhaps it would be better to phone the doctor. Though de Villiers wouldn't appreciate being summoned at this hour.

'... they fell out across the floor ... all those negatives.' Again, she clutched his shirt, the cold from her hand, seeping through the twilled cotton. 'And, Piet, I could see through them, the tight weave of the carpet. They were so ... transparent. Like we weren't real, like I'd dreamed it all, the wedding, us. And when I picked one up, the only part of me that was white ... my hair. The rest was .... Since I looked at them, I, I can see through me.' She stared, her dark eyes flickering, the brilliant spectre of burnt-out stars. 'And Piet, there's nothing, there's nothing there!'

Firmly, he began to draw her towards the door. 'You're running a temperature, I'd swear. I'll get you some aspirin, then I'll phone—.'

Looking up at him, she tried to resist, her voice low, intense. 'D'you hear ... me? Nothing! A cold, empty space.'

He patted her, his voice soothing. 'You're ill. You're not yourself.'

Mia laughed, a high-pitched sound that shattered in his ears. 'Then who am I? Who am I?' she whispered as he hustled her through the open door, the words fading into the quiet vacuum of the room.

Chapter Three

I

Emma squinted at the tiny, flat-bodied insect staggering in the crevice between her nail and finger-flesh. Lice. The realisation fanned a uniform bristling over the surface of her scalp, where before the itchiness had been restricted to isolated pockets. How long had she been scratching? A week? Longer? Christ. In the labyrinth of body-aching days since her arrival, she couldn't remember.

Here, in the spillage of misery and violence, an idle hour could not be accommodated: time was honed to incorporate only what was essential to the maintenance of life in its most basic form.

The murmurs and shuffles outside told her the hour. Four a.m. Without looking through the cabin window, she visualised the scene in the chilly dawn. The line of squatters passing cardboard pallets, plastic sheeting, jagged pieces of rusty zinc, wooden planks, the odd, makeshift table, packing cases, bundles of clothing, small parcels of food, cooking pots, the wrapped intimacies of family life, a rippling chain stretching from the street, down the side of the church and cabin, across the rubble-strewn ridge, through the yellow grass of the highveld to the clump of black acacia thorns some two hundred yards distant, there to be buried until the whole process was reversed after the police raids. She sighed. How, how in hell could they tolerate it?

She slid from the sleeping bag and stretched, the gesture a mere semblance of the luxury sufficient rest would have induced. She'd had four hours. Normally Dick didn't call her till six, but the thought of the lice made her uncomfortable. This way, at least for one night, she was saved from the dreams. Sneaking into the office, she located the scissors on a shelf, returning to her own room to cut her hair, the dark strands scratching as they slid into the plastic bag she used as a bin. It didn't take long. When she felt what she hoped was a rough inch of growth over most of her scalp, she stopped.

Taking the tiny mirror from her bag, she tried to judge the effect over several sections, but it was impossible. Smoothing it down, she went to make some coffee. Already, Dick was stirring. A subdued fart rumbled through the thin wall and she grinned, knowing he wouldn't expect her to be up at this hour. Somehow it compensated for the embarrassment she felt at the thought of having to confess to being lice-infested.

Thrust together in the small confines of the cabin, they studiously ignored the subtle grumblings, the intimate growls of body language each was forced to foist upon the other. When it came to asking him where she might get tampons, she hadn't hesitated, had known only relief when he told her of the one hardware shop in the main street which sold a hotch-potch of everything.

But lice. How could she not have noticed? Tight-lipped, she poured the steaming water over the few coffee grains in each cup. He'd enjoy her discomfort, she was sure of it. They'd reached an uneasy state of truce, mostly because she began to ignore his sardonic manner, or, more often lately, she was simply too tired to respond. But it didn't make either of them like each other any better.

Sipping her drink, she reached for the sugar packet as the door opened.

'I've made some coffee.' She spooned sugar into his cup. When he didn't answer, she turned. He stood open-mouthed in the doorway, eyes rooted to her head, a leashed bull in his priest's collar.

'I ... cut it,' she said. 'Here's your coffee.' She carried it to the desk, wishing he'd stop staring. There was something so dumbfounded in his look, it was positively insulting. She patted the spikes of hair, resisting the urge to scratch.

He moved forward to pick up the coffee, his mouth working, trying not to laugh. The bastard!

'So what's the idea? You decided on going native?' He blew on the steaming liquid before tasting it.

'Very funny.' Without realising it, she began to scratch. 'As a matter of fact, I have ... things ... lice.' Aloud, the word made her wince.

'So?'

Christ, he couldn't even let her have the satisfaction of shocking him. 'What d'you mean, "so"?'

'Why the Afro hair-cut?'

'It's not an Afro hair-cut!'

His eyes narrowed as he cocked his head. 'No? Couldda fooled me.' Pausing, he sipped his coffee. 'Sides. Won't do any good cutting it. They live on the scalp. Where they lay their eggs too. Scalp's the thing you gotta treat.'

'How?'

He went to the corner where they kept the cleaning fluid and soap. Lifting a small, plastic drum, he carried it back.

'Capful a this. Massaged into the scalp. Be sure you wash your hands well afterwards. Leave it on for twenty-four hours. It'll do the trick.'

Unscrewing the lid, she sniffed, her nostrils quivering, a poisonous odour invading her lungs as he shouted.

'Don't do that!'

She wiped the water from her eyes. 'What is it?'

'Weedkiller.'

'Weedkiller?'

'No need to look so shocked. It's what most a them preparations contain, only more concentrated. It's what's used to kill the weeds round the privies, stop the women from using them for stews.' He grinned. 'And speaking from personal experience, it works fine.' He didn't know why he had tagged on that admission, except perhaps, something about the way she looked almost made him feel sorry for her. Standing there, the dark bruised skin under her eyes lent her a fragile quality, accentuated in the thin line of her body, the spiky wisps of hair. She'd lost weight, the faded jeans sagging about her waist. The only part of her that seemed unaffected were her breasts. He looked away quickly.

'Does it have to be for twenty-four hours? I'll stink to high heaven.'

'No one'll notice, unless St Peter's on gate-duty.' The joke fell flat. He didn't even know why he said it, the kind of trade remark which made it hard for him to crack his lips in a smile when others said such things to him. 'No one'll notice,' he repeated, a sudden tiredness seeping through his limbs, spawned in his efforts to be natural with her.

'Pull the other one.' She scowled at his thick, blunt hands reaching for the prayer missal.

'Today's shit collection.' Tying a wooden cross about his neck with a piece of twine, he moved towards the door. 'It's not a smell that's easily outclassed. Keep the door and windows closed, otherwise we'll suffocate tonight.' He hesitated, nodding at her head. 'It isn't dyed, by any chance, is it?'

'No, it's not!'

'Good. The Black Sash lady ended up with an orange mop.' His lips twitched. 'Really was quite something. But she never forgave me.'

As soon as he opened the door the smell hit her, a vile stench that made her heave in revulsion.

'Sweet, huh?' The door closed on his grimace.

Night soil collection had a big advantage, she discovered. It was the one day the security forces were likely to keep out of the township.

'How often is it collected?' she asked when he returned from the church where, every morning he kept the squatters in the guise of a devout congregation at worship under the razor eyes of the raiding police and soldiers.

'Supposedly once a week. But once in two or three, if we're lucky. Same goes for the garbage.' He was digging in heartily to the grey sludge of cornmeal porridge she had boiled in water. 'You wash your hands well?' He nodded at her greased head.

'In six drops of water, a bar of soap and a bucket of disinfectant, yes.' She held out her hands, the skin raw. 'I suppose I'm lucky I still have fingers.'

'The redness'll die down, just don't touch your head, we got a clinic to run, though it won't be much of a one today, you'll find yourself with almost nothing to do. Most a the women stay cooped up in the huts once they carry the shit pails out in the yards.'

He was right about the clinic. By the time the sun was overhead, blistering the corrugated roof, the church was empty, the few mothers who'd ventured out with sick children having scuttled back to their huts. Even the two nurses, off-duty from the hospital in the official section of the township, had departed by now, their cheerful help having speeded up the process. She'd had little to do all morning except watch his hands assume a sudden deftness as he probed distended stomachs, or pass him lint and gauze as he dressed a foul wound. A trained paramedic, Dick worked as swiftly as the nurses, nothing of the awkward priest about him as he utilised his meagre medical supplies to the full.

Once, as she leaned to pass him the antiseptic spray across the large black woman whose foot he was treating, she sensed a sudden shift in the woman, an almost imperceptible tilting away of her body on the bench, her nostrils flaring as she cast a sideways glance at Emma's hair. Quickly Emma moved away, her lips twisting, the woman's small gesture of distaste stabbing at her pride. To this colony of social lepers she had come, hugging her standards of personal hygiene, only to find herself relegated to the bottom of the pile, Christ, she should be laughing herself sick at the irony of it.

As if to spite her further, the urge to scratch was becoming intolerable. Above them, the roof groaned, buckling under the sun's onslaught. She prowled the heat, staring at the children's drawings of the stations of the cross Dick had used to adorn the walls, clenching her teeth against the unfamiliar warmth in his tone as he chatted with the woman. So she was afraid of catching lice, was she, just who the hell did she think she was, being so pernickety? Was that what it had been about earlier too, when the women had been laughing with Dick, bringing the colour to the great wedges of his cheeks, their teasing tones crossing the language barrier as they cast knowing glances in her direction?

When she'd asked what they were saying, he'd looked flustered, then grinned. 'Oh, they were just commenting on your hairstyle.'

Disbelieving, she had thrown a withering look, utterly lost on him as he returned his attention to the women, easing back into their language, his accent strange, un-American.

So he'd been telling her the truth, all of them having a good laugh about her lice. Now, as the woman limped from the church, her bandaged foot encased in a plastic bag, Emma could barely manage a stiff nod in her general direction.

The church door stood wide, a gaping mouth flushing the hot stink of outside air into the dusty interior. The minutes crawled as they waited, but no one else arrived to be treated.

Emma dragged about, her limbs leaden. 'Can't we close it?' She gestured at the door, desperation in her voice.

'Nope. Church stays open. What's good enough for them's good enough for us. If you don't like it, there's always Jo'burg.' His voice was hard as he squinted to measure the remains of a bottle of greyish liquid. But then of course, what did she expect, she wasn't one of his precious patients!

'You hope!' She scratched, forgetting the weedkiller, its strong odour buried in the fumes of excrement. 'Nobody else in the street has their door open. What're you trying to prove? That you're some kind of saint?'

He slammed the bottle down, his face darkening to liver. 'They might as well be living in the open air. Y'think those patches a zinc, those pallets and plastic sheeting can keep the smell out when they can't keep the rats out?'

'I've got to get out of here. It's got to be better outside.' Emma wiped the sweat from her forehead.

'Wanna bet?' He began stacking the last of the worm tablets in the cardboard box. There'd been no demand for them this morning. Even worms were preferable to being caught on the street when the truck showed up.

'I have to get out of here!' She moved quickly towards the door, her voice strangled.

'They'll be here any second. What d'you wanna do, throw up? Add the strength of your own filth to what's already out there?'

She stared at him, shocked at the venom in his tone. But he wasn't finished. 'You come here to punish yourself, that's one thing.' He paused, grey eyes narrowed to chips of ice. 'Fine by me, whatever turns you on ... mam.' The last word was stretched in a southern drawl. 'But the vermin here got enough puke and crap to feed on without you giving them a free meal. So go on in back.' He jerked his head in the direction of the cabin. 'I'll hold on here awhile, case anyone else shows.'

The muscles of her stomach contracted and she heaved, fighting the rising nausea. So. He had sniffed out her guilt, sniffed it out like some cunning beast, like a ... a warthog, that's what he was, a frigging warthog, Christ, imagine waking up with that beside you in the morning, the thick red crew-cut an animal's bristle, the palpable coarseness of the features, the apish paws, how she hated him.

'Fuck you!' Her jaw twitched as she fought for control. 'I've tried, I've really tried to ignore your gross manners, your stupid jokes, but you're worse than a ... a pig in a poke! All your years here've certainly paid dividends. You haven't risen above this hell-hole, you're wallowing in it! So don't tell me what I am, it's none of your frigging business.' She marched back and forth in front of the concrete altar, the sweat sticky in her armpits as she pointed at the gaping door. 'Now I'm going out there whether you like it or not, you hear me? And if I throw my guts up, I'll clean it up. I'm not here to hide in that cabin and sniff delicately, I'm here to do a job.' Her lips curled. 'It may not be as sanctified as yours, but it'll speak a lot louder than pious platitudes and superstitious mumbo-jumbo. Where's your God right now, just where the fuck is he, tell me that!' Her gaze lit on one of the benches standing askew. She moved to shove it back into position, the wood screaming on the concrete, cumbersome as the whining liability she saw herself becoming. The thought spiked a sudden rage. 'Tell me something,' her voice was thick with insinuation, 'just tell me something, will you, d'you hate all women, or is it just me in particular?'

She turned to confront him, the snarl suffocating in her throat as she caught a flicker of pain in his eyes. Instantly, he dropped his gaze to the items he was packing, a studied expression masking the large features as the dull stain spread upwards from his neck.

Pain. Somehow, she hadn't thought about what might lie under the gruff armour. She'd been too busy bleeding herself. No! — the dream-voice taunted, don't give me that crap, that ... subterfuge. See that furrow there upon his brow, that ridge like a garden fork as he feigns concentration, you put that there, you, you bitch, you wanted to make him bleed! The pump's been broken since you arrived - he's had to share his measly water rations, even his food because of the boycotts, he's a big man, muscular, he works hard, harder than you've ever seen anyone work, these people love him, he'd die for them, you can see that in his eyes, no guile there, he holds out his hand and gives, there's no resentment in his face, not even a glimmer, the only time his voice is harsh is when you complain and you, you stab him first chance you get, so look at him now, watch him squirm in his tight collar as he squints, re-reading labels because he doesn't know where to look, this is your fucking handiwork.

She stood ashamed, the silence weighing awkwardly between them. Only when the need to heave reflexively asserted itself, did she realise she was crying. She turned her back, not wanting him to witness it.

Suddenly, he was beside her, a small blur of cotton wool in his hand. 'Stuff your nostrils, it'll help some.' His voice was quiet.

Still heaving, she managed a nod as she took it and hurried to the door.

Outside, the light was blinding, the midday sun stalking the parched ground. The air was brick-heavy. She stuffed the wool into her nostrils but it did little to alleviate the putrid stench that seemed to rise from the very depth of her being, as much in and of her as it was in the arid air, thick as the stench of her own spitefulness.

Nothing moved. Not even one of the numerous mangy dogs was in sight to slink and sniff about the clusters of overflowing buckets set down at the regular entrances to the row of communal yards.

But in the distance she heard the rumbling, knew instinctively as the smell thickened, gained the momentum of waves swifting toward a shoreline, it was the shit truck trundling over the rutted tracks that laced the township. It was this place, she thought as it lurched into the street, the sun leering in its steel cylinder so that she had to look away until its angle aligned itself more favourably: this place stripped away the niceties, the pretence, here there was only room for the truth of what she was, what she'd done, the truth of a thousand buckets of crusting slime, teeming insect life, scarabs, chafers, dung-beetles mining the gold and quartz sandstones of effluence while their human counterparts burrowed into the dripping, gold-particled rock-beds of the Witwatersrand, their subterranean sweat converted into the few Rands that would buy the service of the shit truck, the cycle unrelenting as the children passing and spewing worms.

To this sewage pit she had come, seeking to redeem herself. But the filth, the uncompromising stare of her own neutralised waste appalled, weakened her resolve.

She didn't want to be here, didn't want to witness it. In those moments she stood watching the bleak eyes of the Bhacas, the 'bachelors' contracted from the desolation of the bantustans to perform the task not even the squatters would contemplate undertaking, her sense of shame magnified. If only Sipho would come, make the task she had set herself bearable!

From the church door, Dick watched her hunched stance. As usual, he'd been answering the same question all morning, those of his people who'd heard rumours of her presence, seeking clarification as to who his visitor was. He grinned. Always a little questioning of their priest so that he'd been forced to pass Emma off as his cousin in order for them to accept the situation. Now he wondered again what guilt had driven her here, what made her cry out in her sleep each night, what her connection with Thulatu was, an indefinable something in her eyes, haunting, solitary, that had touched his compassion as she waited for his friend to come.

But her rage, an ability to wound as unerring as his mother's. He grimaced, knowing if she complained again, he would continue to needle her, living here only became bearable when you accepted it, when you kept your nose in the dung, forced yourself to forget there was fine, sweet air to be breathed somewhere above the veil of paraffin smog smudging the sky, but out of reach, always out of reach.

On a personal basis he just didn't know how to treat her, nor had her outburst surprised him — he'd seen the distaste in her eyes from the moment she'd arrived. The fact that women found him unattractive was nothing new, he'd been living with it all his life, the lesson stressed first at his mother's knee. Yet in terms of working together, this woman was different. For all her frail appearance, she was made of sterner metal than the finicky do-gooders who descended on him from time to time, only to disappear at the first whiff of shit. He sighed. She would stay ... to torment. The thought disturbed him but he refused to analyse it. The manacled grasp of the collar about his neck was suddenly stifling. He pulled it loose, massaging the groove branded in his flesh. For however long she lasted, he might as well make the best of it. Already he noticed her presence in the clinic, the workload a shade less heavy than it usually was.

In the short time since she'd arrived, the sun had washed the pastiness of her skin to a light amber, but if she stayed out much longer, she'd burn. Still, he was loathe to call her in, witness again the misery in her face that had moved him earlier. What would happen when Thulatu arrived at the weekend? Well, his friend would have to deal with it, he had enough on his own plate without taking on a lamed samango monkey. One with lice at that. He grinned, eyeing the stunted hair plastered in weedkiller, the dark stains soaking her tee-shirt, her lack of vanity pleasing him. Right now, she looked no more appetising than the shit men, flies buzzing in their wake as they handed the heavy-duty buckets to the man in stained overalls on the platform at the rear of the truck, his face carefully averted as he slopped the contents into the circular opening in the steel cylinder, each bucket replaced in the metal frame on the side, re-cycled as they were emptied.

When they had moved further up the street towards the heart of the township, he went to join her. 'C'mon. You'll fry out here.'

Staring after the truck, she hardly seemed aware of him, her dark eyes trapped in some punishing image of her own making. He tapped her shoulder once, his finger stiff as a wooden peg, lest she misinterpret the gesture. 'Let's go get some coffee.'

Wordlessly she turned as he pointed, forcing a laugh. 'Bloody little pests, will you look at them! If one a them's caught, they'll have their heads shoved in a bucket, nothing puts them off.'

A group of barefoot children had appeared to dance and chant at the shit men from the relative safety of one of the yards, their voices raised in jeering tones that defied language barriers. Even from this distance, Emma saw the fury it spiked in the faces of the men. She held her breath as one of the workers leapt forward, his face scarified from some past ritual of tribal decoration. As he gave chase, the children scattered, disappearing into the infested gap between two groups of huts, shrieking as they leaped the rubbish-strewn dongas at the rear to scale the ridge to the open veld.

'Most kids here'd never behave like that, they got too much respect. But that tough little shower a tsotis are hard as nails. Y'don't have to worry about them, they'll make it.' Dick's voice was confident at her side, but she didn't breathe again until the man gave up, heading towards the latrines, his rubber boots sinking into the delta spanning the four toilets meant to serve six hundred people. She closed her eyes against it, concentrating on what Dick was saying.

'... far enough away. Y'don't interfere, unless you want the same treatment yourself.' His voice held some kind of warning but she couldn't register it. The inside of her throat was fur-lined. 'I'd love some iced tea,' she said wistfully.

'Or a can of cold beer?' He grinned down at her as they made their way back to the cabin.

'A juicy wedge of watermelon, dipped in crushed ice.' She smiled, savouring it. 'Fresh fruit salad, peaches and cream, cold cream.' She began to laugh, her rising voice tinged with hysteria. 'Did you hear that, cold cream?' she gasped. 'I've got some in my handbag, I wonder how it'd taste?'

He stared at her face. Feverish. Too much sun? 'Y'can start with a long drink of water,' he said, trying to keep the edge from his voice.

'Then the pump's fixed? I'll be able to wash?'

He shook his head as they entered the cabin, closing the door quickly. 'Like stepping into a sauna, huh?'

'Or a sewer.' She dropped panting onto the chair before the desk, wishing she'd remembered to hang the sleeping bag over the window. By noon, the cabin took the brunt of the sun, the metal window frames hot enough to burn the skin.

'You try going into one a them tin huts this time a day,' he'd said when she'd complained.

She stared now at the window, wishing she had the energy to fetch the blanket, but it was all she could do to breathe, scratch feebly at the clogged skin all over her body, even her ass was itchy, the cotton gusset of her underpants soaked, a continuous dribble of sweat running from the base of her spine into the groove between her buttocks, every inch of her a seething prickle of discomfort, her skin a brick wall hemming her in. And in this heat women worked: in this heat ten times magnified under corrugated roofs all over the township. Christ. Whoever'd invented the notion of hellfire must have been born in South Africa.

She tried to scratch surreptitiously between her legs as Dick concentrated on measuring two cups of water from the plastic container, his finger held to catch the inevitable drip when he finished.

Between her legs. The small triangle of dark hair. She stared at the purifying tablets he slipped into the cups. Could she have transferred the lice...? 'Shite, oh shite!' Her voice was a whine.

Startled, he turned to look at her. 'What's that? Irish for it? Still.' Stirring slowly, he laughed. 'Just about sums this place up. Here, drink.' Reaching out, he handed her the larger of the cups, watched her drain it while he sipped. When she'd finished, he leaned over, pouring some of his own into her cup, despite her protests.

'Look,' he said suddenly. 'I've got something here'll put hairs on your chest.' Going to the desk, he took a bottle from the bottom drawer.

'What is it?' She watched as he poured generous measures into both cups.

'Don't ask.' He grinned. 'Genuine home-brew, compliments of the local shebeen queen. Guaranteed to curdle the blood.'

For a while they were silent, drinking. It was hard to distinguish the alcohol in the brackish taste the purifiers lent the water, but it was hitting her empty stomach in pleasant waves.

'I'm sorry about earlier.' Her glance sheered off his left shoulder. 'I'm not in the habit of ... of—.' She gulped to hide her embarrassment.

The apology warmed him. 'Forget it.' He took a sip, savouring it. 'Y'wanna know something, there're more family rows on night soil collection—.'

'Shite,' she said, feeling suddenly happy. 'Night shite. Has a grand ring to it, doesn't it?' Feeling light-headed, she leaned forward, the desk a warm shelf taking the weight of her breasts. 'I'll tell you something about day shite.' She lowered her voice to a whisper. 'The sun turns it to gold, pure, liquid gold. This town's rich, this must be the richest town in all of South Africa, there's enough shite in this town to buy us ten thousand toilets apiece, Christ, what's wrong with me, I can't breathe.' She hiccuped, her breath coming in a peculiar snort. He stared at her, bemused. At last he spotted it. 'You still got that stuff up your nose,' he said, pointing.

Focussing on his finger, it took her a moment to realise what he meant. She drained the cup, wishing it were a river. 'Then you'll pardon me while I pick it?' Giggling, she stood, the blood rushing to her head as she moved to the plastic bag in the corner.

Eyes narrowed, he watched her swaying slightly over the bin as she cleared her nostrils. 'You eat breakfast this morning?'

'Couldn't stomach it.' She straightened. 'Can I have another drop of that stuff?' Moving back to the desk, she tilted her head at the bottle.

'Provided you eat the mealie meal first,' he said quietly.

She opened her mouth to protest, then closed it again. He was right. Their diet was sparse enough without her skipping food.

'Join me?' she said hopefully, dishing the remains of the porridge from the pot.

'You know I don't eat midday. 'Sides, it's your share.'

Returning to the desk with a bowl, she made a face. 'Like trying to swallow sand wrapped in luke-warm rubber,' she said but she forced herself to eat quickly as he prepared more water and added the alcohol.

'That's more than my share of water. Is the pump fixed or what?'

Relieved to be finished, she put the dish down, trying to ignore the stodgy mass in her stomach.

'Nope.' He swilled the liquid in his cup as she drank. 'Black Beauty's supposed to bring the part we need. We're gonna work on the borehole this afternoon. I'm banking on having it going by evening.'

'Great.' Her eyes shone. 'Then I can finally have a decent wash?'

He nodded. 'Providing we get it working. But even if we do, you'll be waiting till midnight, queue'll be a mile long soon's they see us at it.' Glancing out the window, he smiled, raising a hand in greeting. 'Here's Modise now.' Even as he spoke the door opened and the boy entered soundlessly, a plastic bag in his hand.

'Comrade Father, you are ready?' The words were low, devoid of any expression.

'You got the part?' Dick stood and stretched. The boy nodded, lifting the bag.

'You're a wizard, Modise,' Emma said from the surge of alcohol in her veins. The boy cast a glance in her direction, somewhere a little above her head, a flicker of cool acknowledgement in his eyes. Immediately she felt the colour mount in her cheeks at her own effusiveness. Pushy, she thought, over-familiar, that's what he's thinking, we've met briefly a couple of times and now she acts like we're bosom buddies.

As Dick gathered some tools, Modise turned to step outside. Unable to resist, Emma looked at him again, boy beautiful, the blackest child she'd ever seen. No, not child, never child, a seventeen-year-old sculpture of exquisite form, the dark intelligent eyes fathomless, registering neither warmth nor cold nor any kind of emotion she could comprehend except perhaps a sense of listening stillness, of something being awaited in the certainty that it would come. No wonder they called him Black Beauty, his coltish grace, the healthy blue-black gloss of the skin stretched across the narrow bones, a dignity about him that was unselfconscious.

'Why don't you stretch out, get some rest? It'll be a while before you get another day easy as this, leastways not till next collection.' Dick moved to step out behind Modise, his own words surprising him. Did he really expect her to be here as long as that? He felt a small, inexplicable twinge of pain, like someone had made a fool of him publicly.

'Good luck,' Emma said, her voice intense.

'You could try a prayer, that fervent tone might have some influence.'

She made a face at the door as it closed behind them, already the smell of shit permeating the small interior, as though the walls were daubed with the warm thick slobber of it, oozing like sweat through porous skin. She closed her eyes. If only a decent breeze would stir, lift the smell and the heat hanging like a pall over the township. But there would be no relief till after sunset.

Wearily she moved about, tidying. She stared longingly at the half-empty bottle, tempted to pour another drink, increase the sensation of numbness that already invaded her mind, but it would only prove effective in the short-term. Reaching out, she grabbed it quickly, the cork squealing as she forced it into the narrow neck. Replacing it in the drawer, something glinted, half-hidden under an untidy pile of papers. A heavy gold cross and chain. She stared at it in the palm of her hand, wondering why he didn't wear it. Shrugging, she replaced it, but finding it'd spiked her curiosity, she moved to the door of his room, then hesitated. An invasion of his privacy, yet was not her total lack of interest in him since she'd arrived more odd? Besides, she wasn't going to rifle through anything personal, merely take a quick peek.

Inside, the room was flooded with light, dust beams dancing as the sun slowly circled the cabin. Squinting, it took her a few moments to register it; sleeping bag on the floor, a battered, leather hold-all, underwear spilling from its frayed jaws, a cardboard box with dirty clothing, some grubby books stacked beside it, overhead, a piece of twine decorated with two stiff pairs of underpants. No bed.

She stood, staring.

He had given her his bed. His bed. What was he, a frigging saint, determined to prove no hardship was too much for him, what the hell was he trying to prove? Whatever it was, she couldn't tolerate it, everywhere she turned, it was there, a silent generosity of spirit that stifled, nobody could live with it. Well, he could have his stinking bed back, probably where she picked up the lice anyhow, she ought to tell him about the abortion, see how that sat with him, see if he'd still feel so almighty big-hearted then, a wonder he hadn't managed by some miraculous stroke to grow breasts to feed the half-starved kids playing in the gutter of the streets, Christ, what a sight that would be!

She laughed aloud, the sound harsh and ugly, sobering her instantly.

Yes, the voice niggled, go on, hate, resent him for being what you can't, being what you can't even bring yourself to feign, being it as naturally as breathing, every gesture he makes holding a mirror to your own shortcomings, you'd prefer to see his meanness outstrip yours, that would cast you in a more reasonable light, you didn't come here to make reparation, you came to lay your ghost, instead of which it has risen off the dung-heap to greet you, it screams at you from every listless piece of flesh, hair and bone, it leers from the hungry mouths, from the festering sores of the children, it sniffs you out in the sweat and pus and excrement, it knows you, accuses you from the paltriness of this room.

'There's always Jo'burg.' The words were a drumbeat in her head. She sucked the hot air into her lungs, sorely tempted to give in. In the golden city there would still be a story to tell, she could still write the truth. She bit her lower lip. Truth without integrity, a one-sided view showing only the small core of middle-class blacks whom the regime cultivated as a buffer against the monstrous ocean of townships threatening to engulf them. If you had a stake in the system, you were less likely to oppose it, the cunning logic of those in power, the Hottentot dyke, system-built to impress the world, yes, she could write about that.

Coward! the voice screamed in her throat, a small choking sound escaping through her teeth as she fought to hold it back. She moaned, knocking her head against the cabin wall, welcoming the pain as she cursed what was in her, this vicious stripping which plagued her every thought, this relentless sniffing out her own deceit, her own willingness to dissemble.

But there was no room for compromise. She stood for a long time, watching the sun fade in the flickering dust. At some stage, the cities would have to be visited, but if the articles were to be written with full historical accuracy, she had to stay, witness, in and through this township, the subjugation of a population of twenty-eight million people, scrupulously record the misery of their existence. That much she owed. But to whom? These people, insects, scratching out their days in the earth's underbelly? Or the half-formed child scraped as debris from her womb before it too, could be sucked into the maw of racism? Did it matter which? The end would be the same. Wouldn't it? Reparation. In that act lay the possibility of peace. She had no choice.

Turning, she staggered to her own room, her feet cumbersome as swollen marrows. The alternative was terrifying — to cut and run, return to the London bed-sit, a future writing vacuously about principles of justice and equality and brotherhood, the words and phrases sharpening their claws on the lodestone of guilt, until one night she would put an end to it.

She sank onto the bed. Would that she possessed the cold purpose of Modise! Gelding, she thought, his youth, his childhood gelded. She clamped her eyes shut, trying to blot out what Dick had told her, but the image gnawed; the boy, naked, wrists manacled to the grid high on the wall of the torture room, the rusty wire being tightened on his penis, countless hours of eating into flesh, the inflammation, the swelling, the bleeding, the disgorge, until finally the gangrenous odour had driven his tormentors to fling his unconscious body in the hospital prison. That was how Modise became a eunuch, Dick had said, a savagery in his tone as he cut the rough fabric of a mealie bag into bandage strips late one evening.

Unwilling to grasp what he was saying, she had scuttled about her mind for some distraction.

'Why did they call him Black Beauty? Was it—?' She had stopped, the rasping jaws of the large scissors making her shiver.

'There y'go ...' Dick threw her a couple of strips to roll up. 'Apart from his looks, there's a price on his head. Unofficially, of course. If the SP ever get their hands on him again, he's had it.'

'So?' Uncomprehending, Emma stretched a piece of cloth, snapping it taut to release the fine cloud of mealie dust clogging the weave.

'Used to be a story going round that the censorship board'd banned *Black Beauty*, y'know, the book?' He grinned. 'Without ever reading it. Seems they thought from the title it was a story about a black prostitute. Day they released Modise, he was served with a five-year banning order. He's supposed to be in the Transkei right now, slowly starving with all the other poor unfortunates.'

Emma stared at him. 'But he moves around here quite openly. Don't people know? Won't he be caught—?'

'Eventually.' Dick's voice was grim.

Eventually. Programmed for death, the solitary, waiting stillness in those dark eyes, the knowledge of the pattern he had mapped out, simply a question of the precise timing, how had it come to this for a seventeen-year-old boy who should've had his eyes full of hot dreams and desires?

Lying now on the bed she stared at a few tiny red ants scurrying across the cabin wall, the structure of their movement ordered, programmed to reproduce the pattern endlessly. Programmed. But perhaps it was more than that, how could she know? — perhaps even trees could weep. Locked in the confines of her own being, what could she ever know? Of Modise? Of these ants? Or they of her? Did they sense the beast of her presence here on the bed as she had sensed it in herself: the savage instrument of unnatural selection that had deleted a life as so much unnecessary code, that had kept thought and emotion suspended, garnered in a storehouse of dreams to drive her screaming from the vengeance of her own sleep, the furtive butchery behind the wall of her womb a legal act more insidious in its execution than any crime of infanticide.

Christ, it was always with her. She'd thought to escape it here only to find it thrust more fully in her face, the rough generosity, the guileless eyes of the priest anathema to her guilt. Only in the cold, ruthless calm of Modise, could she forget herself. And Sipho. The ants blurred to flecks of blood as her eyes closed. He must come soon.

II

She was not wrong about Modise. The following night she caught a glimpse of his power at the squatters' meeting held in the church.

'Pity we can't draw these kinda numbers when we preach,' Dick joked with the other two ministers present, an Anglican and a Methodist, both of whose churches were in the official section of the township. The three of them smiled at the solid mass of bodies, wall-to-wall, a steamy heat glutting the choked interior as a couple of hundred pairs of lungs fought for air space. Emma, seated with him to the left of the altar, looked around with interest. Already, there were certain faces she recognised, here and there a woman waving gaily to her from the sea of bobbing heads. The festive air did not surprise her. The pump was fixed, a miraculous thing which again made their lives bearable. Unable to resist the impulse, she pulled casually at the neck of her tee-shirt, the warm, clean odour of her skin rising faintly to please her nostrils. Lovely. She closed her eyes, savouring it. Even her hair was clean, a sharp whiff of carbolic soap whenever she turned her head quickly. As long as there was water, the sweet dignity of it. She smiled, glancing at Dick. Even he smelled approachable.

'It's as though we've all come to see a film show, or a circus.' She aimed the words at his ear to make herself heard above the hum of conversation and laughter. Before he could reply, there was a sudden, almost sanctified hush as six youths entered the church. One of them was Modise. Emma watched in disbelief as the crowd assumed an air of reverence she had never seen them accord their priest. The wall of people filling the central aisle suddenly crumbled, allowing the youths to make their way to the altar.

'This is the action committee?'

'That's it. Apart from me. But my side's mostly the paperwork.'

'They're so young!' She watched the youths, calm, self-assured, group about the altar, the crowd unnaturally quiet. Modise sat on one of the cabin chairs, a little distanced from the altar to the right. For several minutes there was silence as the youths scanned the crowd. Emma watched Modise, his flickering gaze combing every face. Searching. For what? Suddenly one of the youths spoke in English, a tall fellow, hard and brown as an almond, with an unruly mop of brownish-black hair.

'Rhaumsfontein Squatters' Meeting.' He looked at Modise. Modise threw his head back, his dark gaze roaming the corrugated roof.

The boy turned back to the crowd. 'This meeting is for squatters only.' His voice was glacial.

Emma started guiltily.

'Not you.' Dick's words were little more than a breath released from the corner of his mouth. Emma wasn't the only one the boy's tone disturbed. The crowd rippled uneasily, people staring about, or leaning to peer openly into the faces about them. No one got up.

Slowly the shuffles, the whisperings subsided, the silence a palpable thing ringing in her ears.

'Squatters only.' The words were the metallic ring of iron on stone. Still Modise stared at the ceiling.

There was a subtle shift in the centre of the crowd, a movement no less slight than a leaf stirred by a breeze. In that moment she knew, sensed the leashed anger radiating from every direction to focus on one man sitting ramrod stiff between two old women about half-way down the church, left of the aisle. The man stared at some fixed point above the altar, his grey head hunched with the stillness of a stone on the thin outcrop of his shoulders as they came for him, two youths crashing swiftly from either end of the row through the yielding throng of bodies.

Unconsciously she grabbed Dick's arm as they dragged the man out into the aisle, a spidery wisp of flailing limbs.

'Awu, comrades, Solomon has yet to learn what is wisdom.' It was Modise, his dark face impassive as he flicked his head in conspiracy at the youths, the threat tangible as the heat. All he lacked was a mane, she thought, stupefied.

'What'll they do?' Her hand nagged at Dick's arm as the man was asked to leave the church under the rigid stare of the crowd. He shuffled out, the youths accompanying him.

Dick shrugged. 'He'll be taught a lesson.'

Once, watching the news back in England she'd seen how two informers had been necklaced. She closed her eyes, remembering: charred sticks of tinderwood bearing some resemblance to the human form as they lay in the scorched veld on the edge of the township. 'They're not going to ... kill him?'

He passed a hand over his face, his hesitation chilling her. It was one thing to witness a deed after it had been committed, another to be part of the process, the act of commission.

When he didn't answer, she shook his arm, the rigid muscles unyielding under the rough grey cotton. 'Are they?'

'A warning, that's all.'

'A warning? You mean they'll ...? Why don't you and ...' she pointed to the other ministers, '... stop it?' She stared at his face, suddenly seeing it: while he and the other ministers were not powerless, working as they did as a body, while they were respected and listened to because of their track records, yet they did not have control. So even Dick was no more than any man with feet of clay after all. The thought pleased her, then immediately, thinking of the cost to the old man, she was ashamed, her own greedy ego fed by someone else's pain.

'He's a suspected informer. This is the second warning he's had — if they find out anything for sure, then they'll—.'

'Butcher him,' she said flatly, thinking how wizened, how helpless the man had looked as he sat defying his accusers. He was innocent, surely he was innocent, he wouldn't have dared to sit there alone against the hostility of the crowd if he were guilty.

'Burn his house, beat him up.' His tone was quiet, the words hardly distinguishable above the murmurs of the crowd as they waited for the youths to return.

'Same difference.'

'These people are at war.'

'And what if they're wrong about this man Solomon?'

'His name's not Solomon, it's Moagi, Solomon's just—.'

'What if they're wrong—?'

'D'you realise what'll happen if they're right?' His voice was a low snarl. 'People'll disappear overnight, just vanish like they never existed — some a them'll be shunted back to the homelands to starve, some a them'll never see their kids again, or if they do, they'll be sorry they aren't dead, I'll be burying the ones who get shot trying to run away ....' His voice was swallowed in a surge of cheers greeting the return of the youths. Emma stared at the smooth faces as they made their way back to the altar. Unruffled, she thought, as though they'd just been outside admiring the glorious star-pricked southern sky.

To her surprise, the meeting was conducted for the most part in English, with several of the youths acting as interpreters, relaying the information in Sotho and Zulu for the benefit of the older people.

The almond youth seemed to be in charge, reminding them of the whistle from one of the youths at the church door, which would give warning of an impending police raid.

'But they raided this morning, surely that's it for today?' Emma whispered.

Dick rubbed his eyes. 'Y'never can tell. Been times lately, when they've shown up three times in as many hours.'

'... no panic,' the youth was saying. 'Just everybody down on their knees and Comrade Father will lead us in a hymn.' Grinning at Dick, he mentioned the water pump, his words bringing a stampede of applause drumming on concrete as the crowd showed their appreciation. Clapping fervently, Emma turned to smile at him, remembering the sweaty, grease-stained hulk that had hauled his way into the cabin the previous evening just after dark, his hands blistered from the sun. Impulsively, she leaned across, smacking a kiss on his rough cheek. He did not acknowledge it, but as he looked at the crowd, his hand raised in a brief salute, his skin was the flush of a beef tomato.

Turning to include Modise in her applause, she found him staring implacably over the heads of the crowd.

The first half of the evening was taken up with a heated discussion on how best the squatters could cope with police and paramilitary raids in order to avoid being caught. A list of names was read out, squatters whom the police had detained, or forcibly driven to the bantustans. Suddenly a gleeful shriek erupted from the back of the church, flowing swiftly into waves of mirth that engulfed the whole crowd as they twisted to see. A woman's voice was ringing out stridently in Zulu, punctuated by much hand-clapping and laughter.

The gaiety was infectious. Smiling, Emma turned to Dick. 'What is it?'

His lips were stretched in a grin that exposed a shrivelled triangle of gum jutting between his upper teeth.

'It's Mimi Mutambirwa,' he said, almost crowing as he told her. 'Her husband's got a job in a factory in Vanderbijlpark, he's living here in one of the single men's hostels since the police endorsed Mimi out. They were squatting on the edge of Rhaums, when she was caught, y'know what she did?' He laughed, watching the fuss being made as those who knew her well climbed over bodies to greet her. 'When the soldiers came to take her, she and her kids'd wrapped some large stones in a few blankets. When they dumped her in Stutterheim, she dropped the stones, folded up the blankets, 'n she and the kids walked all the way back here.' He looked at Mimi, his eyes bright. 'Walked. It took them ten days, I tell you, these people are really something else.' He raised his arm. 'Look at them enjoying it, she's the best thing that's happened round here all week.' He grinned again. 'It's called beating the system, her man doesn't even know she's back yet, he's working shift.'

She looked at the laughing, defiant eyes of the woman being kissed and embraced, her presence celebrated as though they had all gathered for some kind of feast, like a wedding. Or a funeral. Seeming to come from nowhere, the thought made Emma uneasy. What if this woman were caught again? She would have liked to ask Dick but knew the question would sap his pleasure.

The youths stood for several minutes, until the excitement had died to the odd ripple of laughter among the crowd.

Finally, the almond youth spoke again, drawing them back to the issues which needed to be discussed. Two of the youths were from residents' associations within the official and unofficial sections of the township, street numbers being bandied about, leaving Emma confused.

There followed street patrol and committee reports on the boycotts, school raids, detentions, and deaths. In the previous fortnight, twelve children had been shot by the police while attending a funeral. Dick had buried two of them. Two old women, a middle-aged man and two sixteen-year-old youths had been stabbed by the tsotsis, the marauding thugs who, ignored and sometimes even encouraged by the police, often went on the rampage at night in the unlit streets, before they'd been 'neutralised' by the Comrades. 'Neutralised,' she discovered, meant being visited and talked to, in an effort to curb their effectiveness, just as, in the mid-eighties, the Comrades had frisked and disarmed people in an effort to make the streets safe for the innocent. Mentally she stored it up, the stuff of journalism.

But as the second half of the meeting unravelled, she was sucked into the nightmare of the squatters' lives.

Story after story unfolded as people competed to air their grievances and yet, always it was the same story: they had jobs, but the police were harassing landlords in the town to prevent the latter giving them accommodation. That way, they couldn't apply for housing permits, or, where a few landlords were willing to rent, the town councillors were leaning on them to charge exorbitant rents, taking a cut for themselves, or the regional service council officials had to be bribed and if someone came along with more money than you had and wanted your house, all he had to do was pay the white lekhowa at the regional office who would demand what little money you had and when you couldn't pay, he'd send the kitskonstabels to your house to break the door down, confiscate your furniture and in the end they'd drag you to the rent office where the white lekhowa insisted you hadn't paid all your rent, that you'd tampered with your rent book and you had twenty-four hours to clear out else he'd have you jailed for fraud. And in twenty-four hours he comes in a police van or a municipal pick-up truck, very bad-tempered with a couple of his black underlings and stands by raving at them to throw what remains of your stuff out into the street as fast as they can and when it's done, he puts a padlock on the door and off he goes and the next day someone else is in your house and now you've lost your housing permit and they say because you've no housing permit you must go to the Ciskei, or the Transkei or Venda, that is where your tribe belongs though you were born here, you've never been to the Ciskei or the Transkei or Venda in your life. But now they say you are an alien. The soldiers come with the Government Garage trucks to take you. No matter how you try to explain to them, you're packed off. But there's nothing there except drought, pieces of waste ground. All around people just sit, their eyes locked on the next breath, holding out their hands when the sun drives a shadow on them because they think maybe it is someone who might give them something. And the ones who were evicted from the black spots are given a pittance in compensation and a piece of ground where even a hen could not scratch out one day's living. The police there are more brutal than here because they too are trying to survive and if you want to go back to look again for work in Soweto where you had a job, they will give you a working permit only for a lot of money, so you sneak back here, this is where you had a life, a house, your children went to school, you have water most of the time, it is better to be a squatter here where you were born, burying and resurrecting your possessions in the bush every day, better to risk your children being detained or enticed into the youth camps to be re-educated than to die slowly in that graveyard, too tired, too weak to attend the funeral of the old neighbour who gave you grains of sugar for your sick child while you were there.

The cunning of it, the premeditated dispassion with which it was carried out, appalled her: the government's low profile a stroke of genius, state machinery superbly disguised in a labyrinth of military and bureaucratic controls which forced the black landlords and town counsellors into the vanguard, surely they, as they each stood in turn to rant against the cruelty of the landlords, would not lose sight of it?

Finally, Modise spoke, his low voice compelling everyone to be still to catch his words. What had she expected from him? Catch-phrases, slogans, political rhetoric? A cold, hard anger? She was not sure, but in the half-hour which followed, she was staggered by the simplicity of his approach.

From somewhere, a blackboard had been produced. The chalk squealed against the dark slate as he stripped away the facades of the local authorities, the town and regional service councils, laid bare the vast underlying network which forced them out of their houses, out of their jobs, into the bantustans. Beginning with the local authorities and the councils which fed the joint management committees, he took them step-by-step through the insidious structure that led directly to the State Security Council, the warlords who deployed police and soldiers with their Hippos, Casspirs, Olifants, their tearsmoke, sjamboks, their guns and hand grenades. As he finished, the voice of one of the interpreters continued to rise and fall, punctuated by the sharp castanet of his clicking tongue, translating the final points. Had he managed to keep it as simple as Modise? She looked at the older people in the crowd and knew even here the message had been clear, some indefinable difference in the warm, stale air, a kind of focussed stillness she could not analyse. She watched it grow in the dark faces before her, not a vast flame certainly, but a slow smouldering fanned by Modise's words, growing stronger, eyes bitter-bright with the dawn of awareness, a sense, finally, of who to blame. In that moment, Modise raised his arm in a rigid salute, his clenched fist a small cannonball. 'Amandla!'

The swift reaction, everyone instantly on their feet, the chanting, ululating, the ripple of raised fists exploding in a tide of fury, the pulse of feet on concrete, made her skin bristle so that she too, wanted to stand and join them, become part of this huge beast of power that overrode thought or logic or any reasonable emotion, that made the walls quake as though the church stood on ground that threatened to engulf it. If they marched on Pretoria this instant, neither tanks nor guns could stay them!

She shivered. The stuff of dreams, threatening to overwhelm them all. Dangerous, too dangerous, the blind heartspawn of passion, the birth of a struggle, a revolution whose time had arrived. This is what he does, she thought, how he channels it, how he ... recruits.

But can he control it? She wiped the sweat of her palms across the roughness of her jeans. Another moment would take them out into the streets to run amok, to find stones and bricks and bottles, to march on the rent offices, the town councillors, the police station on the far side of town. She closed her eyes against it: the bladed walls of wire fencing the station, the fortified windows and doors, the concrete walls that housed a conspiracy of weapons while a soft, bloodied mound thickened on the perimeters like so many gutted sandbags.

It didn't happen. Just when she expected him to fuel it, the thing was suddenly defused. Modise stepped back. Instantly, the almond-skinned boy held a loudhailer, the youths bursting into song, their high, clear voices carrying relentlessly into the crowd, penetrating whatever chinks of silence they managed to find, so that gradually people stiffened, joined with them in singing their own national anthem, a haunting wistfulness in their tone every time they came to 'Nkosi Sikelel' iAfrika,' Dick's pleasant baritone beside her as fraught as the rest.

'That hymn's the closest we'll get to a prayer this evening.' His lips twisted as the song finished.

'What does it mean?'

'Lord bless Africa.' Gathering the bundle of papers littered with his scribbles, he whispered with the other ministers as they tried to agree on a date for the next meeting. It wasn't something they'd publicise to the crowd filing out: if there were any further informers among them, there was no sense in giving the police foreknowledge of their plans. Modise and his friends were barely visible in the midst of a group of chattering, eager-eyed teenagers, some of whom couldn't have been aged more than twelve or thirteen. Emma didn't have to move closer to know what it was they were talking about.

III

Later, when they were alone in the church, she watched Dick, one small lamp guiding him as he hid the papers behind the loose concrete block in the altar. Behind them, the bulk of the church crouched in shadow.

'Modise comes looking for this stuff 'n I'm not here, you give him the bunch a keys.' He spoke over his shoulder, his eyes never leaving the block as he aligned it carefully.

'What time'll you be back tomorrow? I hope I can manage the clinic.' Emma rubbed her bare arms, suddenly cold in the night air seeping under the corrugated roof, drenched with the fumes of paraffin lamps, the hot wax of a myriad candles.

'You'll be fine. Modise promised he'd send a couple of his buddies to help out. And don't forget to wear that nun's outfit when you go into the official section to help Vusi tomorrow.' He stood, his shadow flung against one of the walls, wavering across the children's drawings. It was almost midnight. In about four hours he would leave for Johannesburg, catching the first mini-bus with the squatters who worked in the city.

The thought of his absence irritated her. 'Friends of Modise?' She moved about restlessly, her arms a shield across her chest. 'No thanks. If the police come round, I don't want to be caught with two ANC cadres holding bandages for me.'

She glanced at him swiftly. Had she surprised him? But his eyes, bleared from lack of sleep, registered nothing.

'What makes you think that?'

'Isn't Modise?'

'What?' He stretched.

'ANC?'

'What of it?' He was suddenly hostile. 'You seriously think Modise'd take a chance like that? He doesn't know you from Adam. The two boys who're coming are just kids, that's all, schoolkids.'

'I don't understand it, on the one hand he's ordering everyone to boycott the Putco buses and the white shops in the cities, yet he's quite willing for me to go with this man to the regional service office tomorrow, kow-tow to see if we can get him a housing permit—.'

'Vusi has a wife and six children. He has a job. And an offer of a house at rent he can afford. The only thing between him and security is the fact he's got no housing permit. If he's to make any kind of life for his family, he's got to try and get that permit, no matter how vicious the system is, otherwise, he and his family'll be endorsed out. He's got no choice, even Modise knows that.'

'Then why rouse them all the way he did tonight? Surely it's harder on them if—.'

He held the lamp high, a small arc of light embracing them both. 'Know your enemy. That's all he's asking.' He almost added 'at present,' as he nodded for her to follow him into the blackness of the central aisle, the echo of their footsteps devoured by the dark. The fact she had guessed that Modise was ANC did not matter. Long before Modise had joined, the police had tortured him to admit to it anyway. But there was no point enlightening her. If she were ever detained, the less she knew the better. By the time Modise and the thousands of youths like him throughout the country were given the instruction to mobilise the townships, she would be long gone. Perhaps one day, light years away, someone would unearth her series of articles, discovering in the minutiae of township life the storehouse of grief and despair that seeded a revolution. Meantime, Modise invested his dream in the people. And men like Vusi stockpiled.

* * *

The following day, one of Vusi's sons came for her at about two o'clock. Hopping on one bare foot, the heel of the other tucked into his buttocks, he told her Vusi was near the head of the queue.

'Go! Go!' one of the youths Modise had sent said to her, as she washed her hands in a small chipped enamel basin. 'We will manage it, there are few left to tend ...' he looked at the four remaining people sitting chatting on the first pew, '... and we enjoy. It is better than school.' They both smiled, nodding their heads eagerly. They would be in total charge, since the two nurses had already left.

'Okay. You'd better have a look at that one too.' Emma jerked her elbow at the boy's bloodied foot as she dried her hands. The car that Modise was supposed to arrange to take her hadn't shown up. She'd have to go on foot, no matter what kind of attention she drew. Luckily, she wouldn't have to contend with the police. Normally they were everywhere, roaming the streets in their Casspirs, but today, most of them were over in Vanderbijlpark where there was rioting. Just as well, since there was no time to don the nun's habit or brush her hair. Running her fingers through it, she grimaced. What there was of it.

'How do I look?' she called back as she hurried down the central aisle.

'White,' one of them shouted. 'Yes, nice and white.' Their laughter followed her outside into the swarming heat.

Very funny, she thought, squinting against the sun as she picked her way through the rutted street. All right for them, they didn't have to face some boorish civil servant who, because of her whiteness, would expect certain standards of her, no sense in prejudicing them against Vusi before he even had a chance to plead his case. She moved warily around a pack of mongrels snarling over something rancid in the rubbish piled at a gap between two rows of tin shacks, the sweat trickling between her breasts. If only Dick were back. The one time she had been to the regional service office before, that time to produce her identity documents, he'd been with her to verify her status as a member of a religious order. That way, she didn't need a permit to be in the township. The few trips in the nun's habit she had made to the shop in the main street, he'd always been with her.

'Your face isn't well enough known yet in the main part of town, better play it safe,' he'd said.

A group of youths, kicking a ball against the crumbling, blackened wall of what had once been a primary school, stopped and stared hard at her as she passed. She heard laughter, then footsteps behind. If she ran, she'd look guilty. Or afraid. Were they following her? She sucked in air, but it didn't seem to reach her lungs. Christ, would she ever make it? At last she turned into the main street. At least the man in the hardware shop knew she was with the mission clinic. Here there was a footpath of sorts, the same level as the dirt street, outlined by small rocks, the dusty surface less potholed than the road.

From the far side of the street, someone called a greeting.

'Awu, Sisi!'

A large black woman, two toddlers dragging from her skirts, waved at her. A plastic bag encased one of her feet. The woman who'd been afraid of catching lice. Emma breathed. Turning, she saw the youths watching from the corner, small clouds of dust about their feet as they scuffed at the sand. If she delayed now, she'd ensure her own safety, but Vusi might miss his chance.

Waving gaily, she called to the woman, loud enough for the youths to hear. 'Don't forget to come to the clinic tomorrow about that foot. See you then.' She began to run.

At the end of the main street, she swerved right, running past the burnt-out husks of two cars, past the large groups of children sitting in the fenced yard of the primary school, their lessons taken under the relentless sun because the concrete building was already bursting at the seams as it tried to cope with the massive numbers. A few scrawny hens, eyeballing the middle of the road, scattered in squawking protest as she raced toward them. Lathered in sweat, she began to slow as a small, pretentious church spire whizzed past. Looking back, she registered it dizzily. The church Dick had mentioned, its coat of whitewash dazzling in the sun.

'Rich, independent evangelist,' he'd said, his voice contemptuous as they'd passed it. 'A true blue Bible fanatic, giving with one hand 'n fleecing the poor with the other. He buys converts with a couple a bags of mealie meal, you want to leave, first you gotta give the flour back, he's got a pump out back, size of a small windmill, but you want water, first you gotta be a member, he wastes more water on baptisms than what he allows the poor, the creep!'

'But he's doing God's work,' she had teased him. 'Just like you.'

'I have no God. I have a religion. That's all anybody has, belief, not faith.' He had strode on, his massive legs uprooted tree trunks, easily outstripping her. She'd had to run to keep up, but that day had been cooler than it was now.

Turning left at the end of the street, she almost collided with the queue snaking towards the grey outline of the regional office in the distance. People stared. Again she ran, her throat raw, sweat blurring her vision, her body a pulse propelling her quivering limbs. Faces floated by, dark curious eyes set in a rippling rainbow of skin tones, low murmurs, growls, snippets of strange languages and laughter, the whine of children zipping past as though she were flicking the tuning dial on a radio. Perhaps that's all she was doing here, running backwards and forwards past their lives, catching glimpses of it, never stopping long enough to become entangled, knowing at any moment she could say, enough! — abandon all of them, walk out, just walk away. How then could she say 'I know what they feel, I've lived with them in the townships?'

Mumbling her excuses, she squeezed past the throng at the open gate, making her way across the tarmacadamed yard to the concrete steps of the entrance. A young municipal guard, arms folded, stood in the shade of the porch, calling people on as the queue within the building diminished.

Emma saw the struggle in his face as she approached: he wanted to ask her what business she had, yet her whiteness made him reluctant. Afraid of being delayed, she nodded arrogantly and moved through the open glass doors, cringing inwardly at the sweat-soaked state of her body under his eyes.

Inside, there were several queues leading to different corridors and doors. She stared about but couldn't locate Vusi. Christ, if she were too late, she'd scream. A couple of black women sat behind a counter at the back of the crowded reception area, scribbling in the face of two tired queues waiting their turn.

Quickly, Emma moved to the counter, asking where she might locate Vusi. One of the black women looked up with annoyance, her expression masked when she saw Emma.

'For what is he applying?' The pink-tipped fingers flicked through the register book.

'Housing permit.'

The woman pointed with a pen. 'D corridor. Both queues are for housing.'

'Thank you.' As Emma moved away, the woman spoke in Zulu to the next man in the queue, her voice a staccato of spite as she rapped at his papers, his mumbling apologetic tone fading in Emma's ears as she turned into the corridor.

'Vusi!' Her voice was a shriek when she found him. He was second from the top of the queue, thin face beaming at the sight of her.

'You have come, Madam. I thank you. Maybe now I am getting the permit.'

'Don't call me "Madam," my name is Emma.'

'But I am having to ...' he nodded his small grey head at the door in front of them, '... in there, for I must showing respect, you understand Vusi?'

Emma raised her hands and let them fall to slap against her thighs. 'I'm not much to look at right now, never mind "respect".'

His gaze slid from her tee-shirt and she glanced down, grimacing at the stains seeping from her underarms. Even if she pinned her hands to her sides, it would still be noticeable, to say nothing of the dark patchy line dividing her breasts. Wonderful, just fucking wonderful. What the hell was she doing here anyway, immersing herself in this ugliness, why, why the hell did she have to come, why couldn't she be like anyone else, marry a nice man, there had been men, nice, pleasant men who would have loved her, cherished her if she'd let them, angelic men who wouldn't harm a spider, refined, educated men who liked sailing and fishing, who would have wrapped her life in lustrous, well-fed children, blond and blue-eyed, and white. A safe, sanitised oblivion until death do us oblite-rate, why, why couldn't she have chosen it?

'You are very hot, your face? Please, you are using this to wipe?' Vusi's eyes were apologetic as he pulled a faded khaki shirt from the plastic bag he was carrying. 'It is old, but clean, very clean, it is for my work, I going there after here ...' again he nodded at the closed door, '... for here I wearing my best shirt.' He coughed, a trembling hand patting his tie, as the woman in front of them was called into the office.

Emma pounced on the shirt as though it were a liferaft. 'Listen, we're about the same size, if anything, you're thinner, can I wear it? I ran all the way, as you can see, I'm a mess, I can't go in there looking like this, I'll wash it out for you, I ...' Already, she was struggling into it.

Vusi stared, eyebrows touching the furrowed ridge of his brow. 'You want wearing? But it is—.'

'Clean,' she said, smiling. She rolled the long sleeves up and buttoned the shirt to just below her neck. 'There, terrific, thanks a lot, Vusi, now I look almost as respectable as you.'

The elderly man shook his head. 'You are not minding to wear this? Never have I seen this, my wife, she will not believe, hau!'

He broke off as the door opened abruptly and the woman shuffled out, her grey lips as tightly clenched as the papers held in her hands.

'Kom, vinnig! Phakisa, monna!' It was the authoritative voice of one of the young blacks acting as interpreters for those who couldn't speak Afrikaans and therefore couldn't understand the white official who sat behind the large desk. When the interpreter realised Emma was with Vusi, he spoke rapidly to the white man. The man looked up, startled, his faded eyes raking Emma's appearance as he spoke to Vusi.

'Jou naam?'

Vusi bowed his head. 'Vusi Sontonga, baas.'

'Wat doen jy hier bij die kaffir?' Without taking his eyes from her, the man jerked his head in Vusi's direction. Her recall of Afrikaans was sufficient enough to know what he'd asked. How he had asked it was also clear. He held her in almost as much contempt as he held Vusi, simply because she was with him. Please, she thought, let it go well.

She smiled. 'Could you please speak in English? I'm afraid I don't speak Afrikaans. I'm a nun from the Catholic mission clinic. Vusi is hoping you'll be kind enough to grant him a housing permit. He asked me to come here with him as he doesn't speak more than a few words of English or Afrikaans,' she lied. No one trusted the interpreters, Vusi had told her, if you had no money to cross their palms, you couldn't be sure of anything they translated in Afrikaans about your case.

His mouth twisted, a line of crooked teeth leaning drunkenly against one another. 'Won't speak it you mean, they like nothing better than to make as much work for us as they can, haven't you learned that by now? There was no need for you to come, yes? My interpreter here speaks enough tribal languages to translate for him.' The man was bristling as he snapped his fingers for Vusi's file.

Was he dismissing her? She stared stupidly at the small fan whirring overhead. Beside her, Vusi stood, head bowed, eyes on the tiled floor, the abject yes-baas-no-baas-stance blacks were forced to take before such whites. So strong was the man's antipathy towards them, his expression of repugnance so compelling, that she felt herself, like Vusi, bowing under the weight of it. Christ, was it this easy to submit, to be convinced, even worse, to accept the defiled image of yourself in another's eye, to passively don the hairshirt of victim, the threat of power sufficient to render you powerless?

It wasn't going well for Vusi, she sensed it in the flick of the man's wrist as he rustled through the file. If only Dick were here instead of giving evidence in some bloody courthouse in Jo'burg! 'Charm him ...' he had said grinning when she'd asked how she should act, '... flattery will get you everywhere.' Charm. She'd about as much chance of charming an ant as this cold-eyed ape.

'You had a meeting in your church last night?'

The question caught her like a blow to the stomach. 'A meeting?' she echoed foolishly. The pale gaze settled on her face and waited.

What should she say? What would Dick say? He hadn't prepared her for this. But the psychiatrist had, role-playing her through every type of police tactic for eliciting information. Except this was no policeman, this was merely a civil servant. Then, in an instant, she remembered what Modise had said: '... comrades, I tell you, if your dog pisses, they'll make it their business to know, there's enough poverty in every township to keep them with a supply of informers for every day of the year, so be careful, all incidents, information, rumours are assessed, divided between what is considered welfare and security, if it's a welfare problem, you'll be treated like a common law criminal, every piece of paper you lack, your housing permit, your working permit, your life book, or your passport if they say you are an alien because you belong in the bantustan, every one of those pieces of paper, either not having them or not having them stamped can mean prison, but if it's a security problem, and this meeting is a security problem for them, then beware, talk to no one, if someone asks were you at the meeting on such-and-such, say "what meeting?" because if you are picked up for security reasons, comrades, you can wish you had never been born.'

Still the pale eyes waited.

'I'm afraid you are mistaken. There was no meeting,' she said, trying to smile. Her lips seemed to tremble with a will of their own, and she knew she'd merely managed to bare her teeth at him.

'Then your church is haunted, yes?' His open hand slammed on the desk, making her jump.

'Haunted?'

'A big number of people were seen leaving it around midnight last night. Spooks, were they?'

'Around midnight?' She shook her head, frowning in an effort to look puzzled. 'But the church is always locked before dark to comply with the regulations. Perhaps I should report it to the police?'

It was the wrong tactic, she saw it the moment the words were out, his face bellicose, suffused with fury. None of it would help Vusi. Unless she could retract.

'Oh, wait!' She smacked her palm against her brow. 'Yes, yes, now I remember, yes there were people in the church last night, Father Carruthers, you know he's very religious, he held a prayer service.'

'Kom?'

'A ... a thanksgiving service, you know, the pump wasn't working, the water pump? Father fixed it, people were delighted to have water again and Father said it was not his doing, his hands were merely the Lord's instrument, we must give thanks to God. We also prayed for rain, oh, and for the government and Father Carruthers said we must not forget the soldiers, the brave soldiers who are guarding our borders, willing to die to defend South Africa.' Too pious? He was staring at her, his eyes slits of suspicion. She rushed on before he could make up his mind.

'When you said "a meeting," just now, I didn't realise it was the prayer service you were talking about.' She smiled warmly.

He was not appeased. "Meeting" is an English word, is it not, yes? You asked me to speak in English which I have done though it is not my native language.'

They hate being forced to speak in English, Dick had told her.

'Nor is it mine. I'm not English, I'm Irish actually. Have you ever been to Ireland?' She paused briefly, but he didn't answer as he stabbed the sharp tip of his pencil against Vusi's file.

'It's very small of course, tiny, in comparison to the size of South Africa.' She forced a laugh, nausea rising from the pit of her stomach. 'You know, it wasn't till I came here I realised we really have no mountains in Ireland, just small hills actually. When I saw the Drakensberg! Now they are mountains, your country is really so beautiful!' Christ, she was going to be sick, puke all over his desk, but his eyes had lost their searching look, the rigid line of his shoulders suddenly more flexible.

'Perhaps you could give a visitor advice on which are the nicest parts to see?'

It worked. She breathed deeply as he leaned forward, the pale eyes instantly approachable.

'You been to Kruger National Park yet? Maan, now there is something you won't find anywhere else in ....'

He was launched. She heaved inwardly, nodding, smiling, raising her eyebrows with clockwork precision as he talked of vast herds of wildebeest, springbok and eland roaming freely in the glorious panoramic landscape of his beloved country.

She even got him to write down the name of a few landmarks he felt it would be a crime for her to miss. Human, utterly human, she thought, who'd have believed him five minutes previously, or the despicable role she had played, licking ass to get what she wanted, the need to be adaptable, to weed out truth, to culture deceit, no different from any wild thing grubbing for survival.

And it worked. He even went as far as being nice to Vusi to impress this visitor to his native land. When they left his office half an hour later, Vusi's nervous hand gripped a shivering white form stamped and starched with officialdom. Half-way down the corridor, still trying to thank her, he collapsed, pitching sideways into the queue he had earlier stood in. The wall of bodies broke his fall, an octopus of arms rising to support him. Emma stood rooted, staring at the leaden skin, the grey lips, the network of veins emeshed in the staring eyes. Dead? How, how could he be dead, it just wasn't possible, after all she'd been through, all she'd done for him, all, all of it for nothing, how could he go and die on her just like that, how dare he do this to her!

But Vusi wasn't dead. A fainting fit, that was all. As he came round, a plastic bottle of water was produced, eager hands propping it to his lips. The woman who'd tapped his cheeks to revive him, said, 'It is hunger and thirst, you see how he drinks, and the standing, not good for the legs, I know this, sisi, I am with the queue since six o'clock this morning.'

Six o'clock. And Vusi had been before her. Emma glanced at her watch. It was now four. More than ten hours, most of it in the grinding heat of the sun.

Her arm linked through his to lend him support on the way out, she asked him why he hadn't eaten all day.

'I was being too nervous for the permit,' he said, not looking at her.

In their uneven progress towards the door, her elbow rode up and down his ribs, a child's stick snapping along a railing. She wanted to weep.

Outside, a young black kitskonstabel in a bottle-green uniform was trying to talk to an old woman sitting on the steps, a small bundle of papers and money in the crater of her skirt, her arms trailing like lopped branches.

'It's Mambo Lithuli,' Vusi said, extricating himself from her grasp. Emma kept her eyes on him as he went to bend over the old woman. If he fell again, he was likely to smash his skull on the steps.

There followed a rapid exchange of words between Vusi and the guard. The old woman didn't seem to notice any of them. She was staring towards the crowd at the open gate, her face bleak, her round black eyes strange ... extinguished, Emma thought, as though she were already dead.

Then she recognised her — the old woman who'd spoken at the meeting the previous night, her story no worse than anybody else's: two of her sons in detention, a third having fled to Botswana to avoid the same fate, a daughter killed by police in the Sharpeville massacre, then, several weeks ago, her husband's employer had died. His son had closed the firm down, saying his father had been operating a charity, not a business. He paid the employees one week's wages and fired them. The day his employer was buried, Mambo's husband went to the Dutch Reform church in Jo'burg for the funeral service. He had liked his white employer, had worked for him for over thirty years and he wanted to pay his respects. When he came home, Mambo said, he was very upset. The white people in the church had whispered and stared and then the minister had come to him privately and asked him to leave. The next morning he got up and left the house very early, without telling her. For three days she waited for him to come home to her. Then the police came. His body had been found floating in the Vaal. Now, because the house was registered in his name, the white lekhowa said she would have to move out. She had begged him to let her stay, all her papers were in order, she'd find work so that she could pay her rent. But the lekhowa was like a piece of stone, he had another family waiting to move in and besides she was a woman, so the house could not be registered in her name. She would be endorsed out, sent to one of the bantustans. What would she do there? All her life had been lived here. Even now, with no family, she had her neighbours to help her, but she knew nobody there, who would help her there? She had heard from a neighbour that this particular white official could be bribed. But she had no money.

A collection had been made for her, Emma wanting to contribute a lot more than Dick would allow.

'Two Rand, that's the limit,' he'd murmured, placing his large hand over her wallet as she tried to extract more.

'But why? — I've got tons—.'

'You'll offend them. It's more than pride, they have to feel they can manage it themselves.'

She had shrugged, disgusted with how little the collection raised: thirty Rand in all. Her donation, plus one from Dick, could have made such a difference.

Now, as she looked at the old woman, she felt detached, unfeeling. It shocked her how quickly her sense of outrage had begun to adjust, the stories, so many the same, already fused in her mind, so much fodder in a tedious repertoire as if somehow she'd become de-sensitised, each case of hardship needing to be more gruesome than the last if it were to win her sympathy. The more frantic people had become with the need to speak, the more she had distanced herself, just as she'd done with Vusi today, cursing the inconvenience, even in the possibility of his death. Charming.

She did not care about these people, did not care one jot. Ashamed, she couldn't look at the old woman, finding relief in concentrating on the argument heating up between Vusi and the guard.

She tugged Vusi's arm. 'What's going on?' Nodding at the guard, she said, 'Can you get him to speak in English, Vusi? What's wrong with Mambo? Is she sick? Couldn't he get her a chair to sit on till it's her turn?'

Vusi looked at her, confused. 'You must speaking more slow for Vusi. It is the end for Mambo, she will not move, she will not speak. In the office of the lekhowa, she is sitting on the floor, the lekhowa is calling this kitskonstabel.' Vusi pointed to the young guard scratching the back of his neck, his peaked cap tilted on his brow, shielding his eyes from the low sun.

'When this boy is coming in the office Mambo is on the floor, and money is, I want to say, spreading on the floor and the lekhowa is screaming at him to getting her out but Mambo is saying I will not leaving until the lekhowa is picking up what he has put on the floor, so the boy is picking up her money and bringing her outside so now she is sitting and saying she will not move, they have taking away her house, she has money they must giving her another.' Vusi drew a deep breath, wiping a layer of sweat from his forehead. Shaking the moisture from his hand, a couple of drops fell, the dark stains drying on the hot stone. He wiped his hand on the seat of his trousers.

The three of them stood, watching Mambo. She didn't seem aware of them. Emma went to the old woman, hunkering down before her. She took the two listless hands in her own, surprised to find how cool and rough they were, the coarse skin of granite. The black eyes stared ahead, curiously calm, indomitable, even now, at the very end, the peaked scarecrow face lined with the scars of struggle and grief. She would not submit, she would not lie down. Emma swallowed, her throat thickening. To come to this, to come through all those years to this exact moment, eyes anchored to the next indignity, the next breath.

There was nothing for it. She sighed, a long, deep sigh that was strangely satisfying. Later, when she looked back she would know that this was the moment when she capitulated, when she stepped into an arena whose outline she now only vaguely sensed. With Vusi translating, it took her a while to convince the old woman.

But in the end, they managed it. She took Mambo home.

'You sleep here,' she said, using signs as she pointed at the camp bed. Thinking of Vusi, she made Mambo eat some porridge, then together they went to her house to empty it before the truck could arrive to dump all her things in the street.

Though the house was in the official part of the township, built of concrete with a corrugated roof, there was so little in it, Emma could have wept. It seemed since her husband's death, Mambo had been making and selling beer as well as most of her possessions, to meet the rent. With the neighbours' help, in ten minutes they had everything out in the communal yard, the old bedstead with no mattress, some frayed blankets, the oil drum that had served as a coal brazier and cooking stove, a small table with one leg missing, a stool, some cooking utensils and dishes, several candles, the flour sack that had covered the one small window, and a startlingly beautiful porcelain chamber pot with half a handle, the setting sun a benediction in its smooth glaze. Every neighbour took something to mind for her until, they told her with forced cheerfulness, she could have a place of her own again. A place of her own, six foot deep. The thought chilled Emma as she rolled the bundle of grey blankets they were taking with them. As they left, the women stood tight-knit and silent watching them go.

Later, while the old woman got ready for bed, Emma went to check out the church. The youths who'd helped her with the clinic that morning had left the cardboard boxes sitting on the altar, the medical supplies neatly packed inside. Pleased, she locked the church and blundered around its side, her eyes raised to the flickering sky. In the darkness she grunted, colliding with something, someone, a body, thick, hard, a pleasant musky odour, that odour, was it possible ...?

'Emma?'

Dick's voice, the word a warm breath on her forehead as he put a hand on her shoulder to steady her. She stood, eyes closed, savouring it.

'I was coming to find you,' he said, stepping back, his arm still tingling with the impact of her breast as she had crushed against it. Would she think he'd run into her deliberately?

'Emma? You okay?' He spoke sharply to cover the way he was breathing.

Emma opened her eyes. Stupid, she thought. Stupid to believe it possible, merely the suddenness, the darkness, the maleness, but the smell .... She sniffed again. Yes. That she had not mistaken.

'You're wearing aftershave,' she said.

'Y'make it sound like a crime. C'mon, it's cold.'

Inside, a pot of water was beginning to boil on the little stove. 'You want some tea? I got some tea from—.'

'Wait, I'll just see—.' Emma had tiptoed to the door of her room. If the old woman were awake she might take a drink too. She stared, horrified. The room was empty, the light from the office strealing across the floor onto the bed, the door to the chemical toilet hanging wide. She turned to Dick, incredulous. 'She's gone! Where the hell is she gone? I just left her for a few minutes, that's all, check your room, will you?' Without waiting for him to do it, she rushed past, his gaping face wreathed in steam as he held the pot. But his room was empty.

Turning, she stared at him, agonised. 'D'you think she might have gone outside? — but I showed her the toilet, Christ, if she's gone wandering the streets this time of—.'

'What on God's earth are you—?'

But already Emma had opened the cabin door. 'Mambo!' she called into the well of darkness. She listened to the shrill of the crickets, wringing her fingers together. It had never dawned on her that the old woman might leave, Christ, there were enough murders in the streets to—. 'Mambo!' she shrieked, jumping down the step.

'Emma!' Dick's voice coming from inside the cabin, was muffled. 'You hear me? Get in here!'

Turning, she looked inwards, but couldn't see him. In one bound she was back inside. Dick was standing, scratching his head as he looked towards her room. Her gaze followed his to Mambo, standing in the doorway, one of the old blankets draped about her shoulders.

'Where were you?' Emma moved towards her. 'I couldn't find you anywhere, I, I thought ....'

Mambo shook her head, her eyes questioning.

'She was under the bed,' Dick said. 'I almost had a heart attack.'

Mambo spoke to him rapidly.

'She says you told her to take your bed, but she doesn't want to, she'd rather sleep on the floor.'

'But why?' Emma's eyes were wide.

'She's afraid of a police raid.'

'But we've never been—.'

Dick snorted, then was sorry when he saw the way she was watching him. He couldn't face talking about the last time, not tonight. 'It's always a possibility, you been warned about that before you came. The collar doesn't make me immune.' He turned to make the tea as she began to gesture to Mambo to use the bed.

But nothing she could say or do would change the old lady's mind. Eventually, Mambo lifted the blanket she'd draped over the bed and crawled back under into her makeshift tent.

'Stubborn, eh?' Dick grinned at Emma as she returned to the office.

'Aren't you going to ask me why she's here? You don't even look surprised.' She sat on the edge of the desk.

He shrugged, handing her a mug of tea. 'She wouldn't be here if she didn't need a roof over her head. Happens often enough. Some a them've even slept in the church, although it's a dicey refuge.' He grinned, stretching. 'Speaking from a temporal point of view, of course. I've had it, if I don't turn in, I'm liable to drop. Lock up, will you?'

Emma nodded. 'How'd it go in court?'

'Piece a cake. They've all been released. The youngest one couldn't even see over the rail in the witness box.' He paused, looking at her steadily. 'Thulatu made a meal of it.'

'That's the lawyer?' Emma sipped the tea.

So. She didn't know him by his name. He nodded. 'Yeah, you'll get to meet him in a couple a days. He's coming with the doctors from Lenasia for the monthly clinic — Thulatu gives free legal advice to anyone who needs it.'

He watched her as she moved about, tidying up. Curious as he was, he hadn't asked his friend any questions. Thulatu was still burning with Thabo's death, unable to focus on anything else. And time had been short, the day in court one of the longest, most tedious he'd ever participated in. Still. He grinned. The shower in the tiny flat Thulatu kept in Riverlea had made up for everything, though perhaps he'd been a little self-indulgent with his friend's aftershave. He drained his cup. 'I'm off. 'Night, then.'

''Night.' Emma watched him stagger to his room, a familiar muskiness lingering in his wake. Sipho, she thought. Sipho. How completely the scent conjured him up. If only he'd come!

Chapter Four

I

Long after they'd left the tropical air of Durban, Thulatu still wore the peaked cap as he drove the jeep. Babo sat in the back, the classic picture of any white madam being driven by her coloured chauffeur. He'd picked her up just before dawn, the city angles coming into their own behind them as they headed towards the dense coastal forests, the white holiday resorts, Scottburgh, Margate and others, nestling southwards in foliate good taste. The habitual detour had been made absent-mindedly, and he was annoyed when he discovered he'd done so. A waste of bloody time, he thought as he finally headed north-east, skirting the Sugar Way, the ocean of green cane gradually fading in the rear-view mirror. If they were stopped, he had, as always on these trips with Babo, enough papers to legitimise his existence ten times over.

They didn't speak. The tape deck in the jeep issued forth the mutinous strains of Gustav Holst: Mars, god of war, the avenging tread of feet towards retribution.

Babo shifted to glance at his profile, a determination in the line of his jaw that matched the music. She could tell a lot about him from the music he played. Her memories of the times they'd spent together were littered with musical interludes bound with the way he'd been; love-making she would always associate with Vivaldi, talk of Thabo and Sophie steeped in Chopin nocturnes, his political rhetoric rising on tides of Beethoven, the well-heeled, educated South African male. Except he was coloured.

Once, only, there'd been no music: the night he'd come to her, crazed with Thabo's death, his shirt smeared with the blood of his son. He'd made hate to her then, in the dark hours before the sun climbed to the window of her flat, skin against skin, the fury of grief sucking them into a dark whorl of brute release. Primordial. Starless. As though man had never stood straight, nor talked, nor dreamed, nor made music to still words.

Afterwards, they'd both been ashamed. While Thulatu had lain on the bed, crying, she'd sat by the window, unable to shed a tear. She'd only been glad that nothing would come of it, no child could have seeded in her womb from the stem of such cruelty. Claus' example had made her see to that as soon as she was old enough to sign herself into a hospital.

Sterile. She stared out the window. Barren as the Karoo sandstone and lava peaks that swooped towards them above the foothills of the Drakensberg. Nor did she regret it.

They were nearing Van Reenen's Pass, the tarred road quiet at this hour, snaking towards them with mute abandon. They'd never speak again, not properly, she sensed it. That last time together, something had withered, something different in each, a need, mutual only in its desire to be sated. Nor had it withered in the destruction each of their bodies had wrought upon the other, but in the promise she'd given him before they'd begun: that she would lead him to Mia.

She sighed, finding no relief in the dry air conditioning blasting the jeep's interior. The silence between them wasn't a thing of tension, merely that of acquaintances who might never have contemplated becoming, let alone become, lovers.

Now, only their politics held them together. And Mia. Oh why did she ever have to complicate things by going to bed with him? Zachius, that was why. Lying with Thulatu, staring at his skin through half-closed eyes, she could almost pretend Zach hadn't been detained .... She swallowed. Someday she was going to have to face the real word for what had happened him, face the fact that he wasn't coming back. Face the loneliness.

Being with Thulatu hadn't helped her deal with any of it. Jesus, if Mia ever found out, she'd never be able to look her in the face again. God, how could she have done it, so wrapped up in her own loss, she didn't give a damn who she might hurt? Well, it was over. She searched the sunlight bleeding the familiar red oat grass of the lower slopes as they began to descend from the cut, but could find no comfort. The music came to an end in a crescendo of orchestrated chaos, the whine of the tape dropping featherweight in the sudden vacuum. She waited for him to turn the cassette, but his hand didn't leave the steering wheel.

His voice, when it came, startled her.

'Have you seen ... her ... recently?'

'Yes.' She wouldn't make it easy for him.

Thulatu glanced in the rear-view mirror. Still she blamed him, it was there in the set of her jaw. Would she ever realise that she, too, had used him? His hands tightened on the wheel. He didn't know why, but she had. He'd always been honest with her, always. From the very beginning he'd told her who he was, he'd never lied about that. She'd been his passport to Mia, his way of by-passing the wall of silence about his daughter's life that Paul had built over the years. Being close to her allowed him a kind of vicarious closeness to his daughter. And he'd grown fond of Babo, something in her marked face that made him think of a starling with a shattered wing. An unexpected pleasure to find something more than sex again at his age.

But she didn't feel as he did, though she'd tried to. She'd had an appetite for his body, his politics, merely that. His lips curled. The body politic where the body was flesh, the spirit politic. Well, it was a bit late for recrimination, a bit too bloody late. Nor would he tolerate it from her. The women in his life had done nothing but dictate from the strength of their whiteness, what they'd felt for him, not even skin-deep, he'd be damned if he'd allow Babo to add to that list. He sighed. The irony of it: the only black woman he'd ever made love to had given him a son, no strings attached. He still hadn't told her of Thabo's death. She was living in King William's Town, happily married with a brood of six, or was it seven? He couldn't face going there yet, seeing Thabo's eyes staring at him from the face of his only half-sister.

Too soft, that's what he'd been, a jackal without teeth, well then, that day was past. Dead, earth-cold as his son. What was a man without his children? What was a man who allowed others to decide the fate of his children? A man without roots. Impotent.

Well, no more! From the moment Thabo's breath had stuttered in a snarl of pain, a drum had beat in his veins, a reckless staccato finally to be reckoned with, as though he were charmed, now, when it mattered least. He gritted his teeth. And it was true. He'd nothing to lose now, nothing, unless Mia—.

'Has she told them, then?' He slung the words across his shoulder, swerving to avoid a young Blesbok crashing across the tarred motorway, dark eyes stunned in the white blaze of its face. Lost, he thought. Alone, what chance did it have? No more than his son, blundering into the predatory arms of the SAP. His beloved ... beloved .... What they'd done to him .... His heart jarred, the pain instant, as though he'd been struck in the chest. He stiffened, fighting it, his breath a soft hiss between his teeth. Channel it, he thought, channel and gather till it churns, bursts its banks!

Babo stared at the animal plunging into the sweet grass on the far side of the road. It might be Mia, she thought, the necessity to seek cover instinctive.

'Well?' Thulatu's voice when it came, was hard.

'No, she hasn't told them.'

Air whistled in his nostrils. 'I might have known.'

'Lay off, will you? You don't know what it's like for her—.'

'Yes, really tough, isn't it, South Africa of all countries, the genetic throwback coming to stare you in the face, a Boer's vision of hell, that.'

'A Boer? Ask Claus if she's a Boer. To him, her being English is almost as bad as if she were ....'

'Black? Well, it's six of one at this stage, isn't it?'

'It's making her ill. She's not well—.'

'Oh? What's wrong with her? May I ask? It couldn't possibly be grief at the untimely death of her younger brother now—.'

'Stop it!' Leaning forward, she gripped his shoulder, the flesh through the safari jacket hard as bone under her fingers. For a while there was silence. Eventually she released him, her fingers fluttering.

'How did it get to this?'

He snorted. 'It was always this. For you.'

'We would have gone on, if Thabo hadn't—.'

'But Thabo did.' His voice was flat. They were out now on the open veld, lush savanna undulating towards the black pall on the horizon that heralded the townships. 'She had to be told.'

'It's driving her crazy.'

'The sooner she tells them—.'

'It'll wreck everything.'

'What makes you so sure? Perhaps—.'

'I know my father. And Piet.' She tried to keep the bitterness out of her voice.

'But perhaps you don't know Mia as well as you think.'

Her laughter made them both wince. 'Listen, if there's one thing I know, it's my family.' But it was no longer true, she thought. The Mia she knew now was Thulatu's daughter, eyes glittering in the same secretive way, shutting her out. She searched the dark line of hair above the jacket collar in front of her for a way she could make him understand. But he spoke before she could think of how to couch it.

'I'm going to see her again.'

'With or without my help.' Her words were drops of acid.

'Precisely.'

'Then at least leave it till after the demonstration. At least that should give her time to ... adjust.'

The demonstration. Emma. Another traitor. But he forced himself to relax, loosening his grip on the steering wheel. It was a good opportunity to redirect the conversation. He didn't want Babo to glean what was in his mind. 'This woman in Rhaumsfontein, it might be worth our while taking her back. She could cover the demonstration for us.' As soon as he returned to Durban, he was fully intent on seeing his daughter again, whatever the outcome. But if he told Babo, she'd try to persuade him otherwise.

Babo glared at the set of his shoulders, a bulwark against any plea she might make. Diplomacy was not one of her strong points but if she forced it, they'd have a full scale row, then he'd tell her nothing of his plans. She sighed. Thabo's death had opened a chasm. If she were to protect Mia, she'd better let it go. For now.

'Just exactly who is this woman?' she asked eventually.

'I told you, a journalist. I met her in London.' He kept his voice neutral.

'What brought her here?'

'She edits a magazine called *Focal Point*. She's been writing about racism for years. She was born here, somewhere near old Sophiatown apparently. Perhaps that accounts for it.' He shrugged, the gesture deliberately casual. 'I met her through the Institute of Race Relations. Max introduced us.' Smooth, he thought, keep it smooth. But despite himself, now that he'd begun to talk of Emma, he found he was bristling. Rounding a curve in the road, the jeep lurched a little as he braked to avoid a mini-bus, its cargo of bobbing heads and dark bleary faces fixed on the freeway stretching like a lifeline to the city. Babo gasped as she was thrown sideways and he muttered an apology, reminding her she should have worn her belt.

'You want me to put her up?'

'Would you mind?' His hand lifted momentarily from the wheel, a graceful question mark.

'Do I have a choice?' she said dryly. 'Hm, well, I suppose she'll be better than the last lot you sent me. Four hungry men on the run from the police isn't exactly my idea of fun.'

'You've got nice hands, nice clean white hands. Safer with you than anyone else.'

'Not for much longer, I think.'

'You think they're on to you?' He glanced back at her swiftly. She was staring out at the hills rolling past, her mouth a taut line.

'Claus is having me watched. I'm not sure about the flat, but he knows about the student meetings.'

'Kids' stuff. A typical father keeping an eye on his errant daughter.'

Babo snorted. 'He doesn't know how to be typical. Anyway, it's not me he's concerned with. He doesn't think I have the guts to be a real rebel. But he is interested in who I might know. You, for instance.'

'I've been careful.'

'So far.'

He nodded, dropping the shield to screen his eyes as the sun emerged from a cloud. For a while they were silent, the memory of those nights between them awkward now with the weight of what he'd left unacknowledged. He wouldn't come to her flat to lie with her again, they both knew it.

Eventually she spoke. 'Anyway, it's a bit soon to bring her back. Demonstration's not till next week.'

'She'll need a legitimate reason to be on the campus in case she's picked up. I thought you might sign her in for one of those extra mural courses. She needs to be shown how the other half live.'

'What's she like?'

The question hit him in the gut. After a while, when he didn't answer, she asked him again. He stared at the arid plains unfolding through the windscreen, the odd tree or thorn bush brooding in the tall, sour bunch grass of the highveld. A butterfly, he thought, gauze wings blading the air efficiently as any cleaver.

'Thulatu? You hear me?'

'What?'

'This woman. Emma-what's-her-name, what's she like?'

He'd better make an effort or she'd pester him. 'Oh, so-so. She's good at her job.' His lips narrowed. 'Handles words as a surgeon does a knife, she's written some scathing stuff. We're getting close. You've got those permits ready?'

Babo patted her handbag. 'All doctored and correct, sir.' She grinned. He wasn't a lawyer for nothing.

Already they'd left the freeway for the labyrinth of roads serving the townships, rutted tracks she'd never managed to find on any map. Here, even the sky was different, splodges of gunge solidifying in the air above the smoke that rose from the coal stoves huddled amid clumps of metal and brick. With a bit of luck they wouldn't need the permits at this hour, she thought, clinging to the hand grip above the window as the jeep negotiated the track that led to Rhaumsfontein.

But they did. As they approached the small, scrapyard town, tongues of corrugate flickering in sunshine, a sudden flash blinded her.

'Police,' she hissed.

'Soldiers,' Thulatu murmured. He inserted another tape in the machine, the music frivolous as he slowed the jeep. Some distance ahead a Casspir squatted, its jaundiced hulk blocking the track near where it had been widened to a makeshift terminus for the mini-buses. Two khaki figures in fatigues leaned against the steel carrier watching them approach. Behind them the police, a swarm of blue-bottles on the track, herding prisoners towards a waiting kwela van.

'How many?'

'Seven, no eight.' Thulatu squinted. 'All children, three girls and—.'

'Modise?'

'Too far away. Madam is ready?' His voice was a sneer as the jeep trundled slowly towards the Casspir.

'Madam's ready.' Babo leaned back, tossing her head in a conscious gesture of arrogance. Even before they'd stopped, one of the soldiers was moving towards them, hand raised authoritatively. They sat waiting, the dust stirred by the wheels drifting in the windows as they wound them down.

The soldier, assault rifle cradled in his right arm, stopped by the driver's door, eyes raking the chauffeur's appearance before he glanced towards the back seat. Babo leaned towards the window, smiling. 'Goeie more.'

Briefly the young soldier touched his helmet, his pink face twitching in the semblance of a smile. Just as he began to speak, Thulatu, staring through the windscreen, suddenly pulled the hand-brake lever, its defiant shriek overriding the soldier's greeting. Thulatu made a sound, low, muffled, something about it almost suggesting amusement. Babo stared. Jesus, the selfish bastard, this was no time to be provocative. The soldier looked at him sharply, his outstretched hand stiff as a shovel as he thrust it in Thulatu's face, an imperceptible shift in the angle of the gun that redefined its nondescript bulk, shaped it into something menacing. 'Ek wil jou identiteits dokumente sien.'

Thulatu took an infinity of time, long fingers sliding into the inside pocket of his jacket to remove his identity document. He stared at the Casspir, its yellow flank blocking his view of the kwela van as he handed his life book to the soldier. Babo glared at the back of his head, wishing she could sink an axe in it. For Jesus' sake, what was he up to? Sweat trickled on the nape of her neck, plastering the heavy hair to her skin. He'd never behaved like this before, never. How could he sit there, cool as a breeze, baiting the soldier? Asking for it, his head rocklike, in spite of the thick barrel inches from his ear, the glossy strip of flesh between hairline and collar, smooth as marble — no sweat. She stared, her breath caught in her throat. He had no fear. Normally, it was she who had to be restrained from making biting comments to every figure of authority she came in contact with. Childish, he'd always called such behaviour, her whiteness a privilege that allowed of such games.

Now, for the first time she couldn't predict how he would react, something in him that was iron, something that reminded her of Claus, as the soldier scrutinised his documents. Nor was it for herself she was afraid. She thought of Zach, his dark skinny face fading in a labyrinth of police cells. She swallowed, the action painful, as though a nut were lodged in her throat. Despite their efforts to locate him, he had vanished utterly into the jaws of state machinery, as though he'd never existed. If Thulatu were detained, she might never see him again, he would follow Zach's tortuous path. And all Mia's problems would be solved. Neither Claus nor Piet would ever have to know. The thought, shocking, spiked a sudden fury, a self-loathing that she could neither focus nor analyse.

The soldier tossed the identity documents through the window onto Thulatu's lap before turning back to her.

'Ek het jou papiere nodig. Wat doen julle hier?'

Babo handed him their permits, explaining the outreach services the group from Lenasia offered to the townships on a rotating basis.

She wanted to ask him if the mobile clinic had arrived yet, but the tightness of his lips put her off.

'You will wait until police business is finished,' he barked in Afrikaans.

She fought an urge to make a scathing remark about what he so euphemistically called 'police business.' Instead she asked him how long it would take. He shrugged, his shoulders snapping to attention.

'As long as it takes,' he said, boots grinding the rusty soil as he swivelled and walked away.

* * *

In the church, Emma and Dick were sitting it out with the squatters, those lucky enough to have jobs having long departed for the cities. Mambo was hiding in the cabin under Emma's bed. Nothing either of them had said would persuade her to join them in the church. Out among the acacia thorns on the veld, in a deep pit, one of many dug at regular intervals, lay the bits and pieces of the squatters' lives, buried under a makeshift roof of wooden slats loosely thatched with yellowed clumps of sour grass. Amplified by the corrugated roof, the sounds of the police Hippos filtered in, engines whinging as they sought to negotiate the craterous streets, the sporadic whine of sirens rising to a death wail before falling away in a confusion of directions. Shouts. Screams. Snarls of pain, of rage. The rhythm of running feet. The smell of burning rubber, petrol fumes. A faint whiff of tearsmoke. The staccato beat of birdshot, buckshot, the thud of rubber bullets, the pneumatic drill of live ammunition singing in bricks, the splintering notes of ricochet on corrugate, a crazed medley of sound striking the hour with savagery.

Inside the church, all was quiet. Save for the eyes, Emma thought, all those eyes, focussed only on what was happening outside, the dread tumbling inwards, the wary gaze of sentries banished to some forgotten outpost in the hostile wasteland of an alien species. You could tell which mother had a child out on the streets, tell it in her special stillness, the flickering fear that never left her face. Emma began to count: ten of them, at least. She rubbed her bare arms. At this hour, the air was cool. Or perhaps they were the ones who were cold, numb with it. The couple of rangy dogs that had managed to slink in with the crowd were crouched, silent and trembling under the front pew. Watching the slack jaws inches from the stick legs of an old woman, Emma shivered.

The raid had come later than they'd expected, late enough for them to hope it wouldn't come at all, some of the children already on their way to school when the police struck. A few of the squatters collecting their belongings from the open veld, ears tuned to the rumble in the ground, threw their possessions back again, jumping in after them, unmindful of the jagged edge of corrugate, the spiteful point of rusted nail clawing tender skin as they fought for space among the whole rotting paraphernalia that confirmed their existence.

A little distance from her, Dick sat in front of the altar, his large body enveloping the child in his lap. In the face of the noise from outside he'd given up trying to coax his congregation to pray. Pity, he thought, nothing like its small familiar ritual for binding them against the scourge of panic. His gaze scanned the crowd, searching for the particular face that would give him forewarning, one face where the eyes might suddenly widen, leap like things possessed, the frenzy that would follow, unleashing the floodgates. They were all close to it, eyes fever-bright as they gazed fixedly at him. A lot depended on how calm he could keep his appearance. For the rest, he'd have to rely on luck, masses of it. And the ability of Modise to distract.

Some day, he knew, when the rifle butt slammed against the little door of his church, when the police marched up and down the aisles scanning the squatters as they sang their hymns, there would be no Modise to protect his flock, no young comrades hurling rocks and taunts through the windows to draw the police out again into the streets, Modise would be lying in a donga, eyes quenched, more lead in his body than bone. When he'd said as much to Modise, the boy had shaken his head. Another will be called after me, and another. Yes, Dick thought, but for his small community, one hour's police work would make it too late. Lord, let it not be today. His heart thundered as he jogged the child on his lap. He prayed then, his wish as full as though he believed in God, standard patterns of prayer, a habit that had long outlasted faith.

Watching him from where she sat to the left of the altar, hands stuffed between the coarse denim hugging her thighs, Emma wanted to speak, break the barrier of silence that amplified the outside noise, but something in the set of his face stopped her, his head a gleaming monstrance bent to the dark woolly halo of the child as he rocked her continuously, whatever words he was whispering bringing a smile to her round mouth. Suffer little children, she thought, but there was no malice in it. Like a rock he sat, solid, stoic, his garish vestments the flow of lava rippling to his feet. Blood bright. But she wasn't afraid, something about his presence radiating an oasis of calm.

Nor, if she were honest, could she feel what these women felt as they waited in terror of detection, their children exposed as raw meat in the streets while she nestled in the assurance of her own whiteness, a slough of armour that couldn't be shed, the epidermal yardstick, pink as a flushed, ecstatic pig. Yet if she could choose to shed it, she wouldn't have the guts. She sighed, sickened by her own duplicity, seeking relief from the thought as she tried to surmise what would happen if the rule of the squatters were broken, if one of those unfortunate enough to be caught on the streets or dragged from their hiding places when the raiding began, managed to break free, running in panic towards the church, the wrath of the police hard on his heels. It had happened before, Dick had told her, his face grim as he recounted the random violence of the police seeking to pin down their man burying himself in the thickness of bodies. Christ. Let it not happen today.

II

'It's over,' Babo said. She and Thulatu watched the clouds of dust settle in the wake of the Casspir as it drove back through the township behind the kwela van.

'We'll be needed today,' Thulatu's voice was bitter as he started the jeep, the engine truculent in the silence.

Babo gripped the front seat as the wheels spun, singing their way forward on the track leading into the town. She stared at the human havoc the security forces had created, people clustered in stunned groups, seeking comfort in one another's arms, women, children, old men weeping openly as they sought for their own. A woman hung lifeless across a thick strand of wire fencing one of the yards, the bright tapestry of her skirt a limp carpet waiting to be pounded. A baby rode its mother's back as she lay face down in the dirt, his fat fingers entwined in the reins of her hair, spittle trailing from his chin as he gurgled with delight, never had he found his mother more amenable to play. At the pump, children's faces were being pushed under the water to relieve stinging eyes and inflamed skin from the effect of tearsmoke. Two women were using stones to beat off a dog licking the bloodied corpse of a small boy.

'For Jesus' sake,' Babo whispered but Thulatu did not respond. He drove as though blinkered. He'd seen it all before, many times, some worse, much worse than this — underlying it, the other silent atrocity that would take days to become apparent — how many had been detained, how many would manage to survive that detention? Well, that was his province. He sighed. It didn't look like he'd get back to Durban tonight, much as he wished to keep any contact with Emma to a minimum. But perhaps he could persuade Babo to take her back.

When they pulled up in the small, bare space before the church, he got out quickly, leaving Babo staring after him as he made his way to the open door.

* * *

Inside, Emma and Dick had been working furiously to divide the church into makeshift sections that would accommodate the various clinics. Soon the first casualties would arrive to create bedlam in the emergency section they'd cordoned off to the left of the door.

Now Dick was stringing a length of twine across the width of the church on which to hang the signs Emma was making. She stood at the altar, the black felt-tip squeaking as she wrote the various words, 'Psychiatrist,' 'Medical,' 'Lawyer'. Saves time, Dick had said, even with the signs, people often queued for hours in the wrong lane, it drove everyone crazy. Everyone crazy. Crazy, crazy. Her hand froze, the signs blurring in a confusion of ink, the hairs on the nape of her neck bristling, truth slamming home in a subtle shift of mood that left her breathless. She stood rooted, knowing he was there, sensing his presence somewhere behind her in the dusky well of the church. Even as she swivelled, his voice filled her ears, Dick's awkward response bumping like driftwood into Sipho's words.

'This is Thulatu,' he rushed on, but she wasn't aware of him, her gaze riveted on his friend, the joy in her face, like nothing he had ever seen. Or known. Something thudded like a dead bird in the depth of his stomach. So much for being curious about such a moment, he had no part in this. Without looking at them, he turned and strode from the church. Babo had to be somewhere outside. Perhaps it would be better if she, too, didn't witness it. He paused briefly at the church door, registering the solidity of the silence within as he drew it closed. Outside, Babo was stacking boxes of legal forms on the ground beside the jeep, applications for permission to breathe, Thulatu had once called them.

Dick blundered towards her, a sudden need for physical contact asserting itself.

'How's my gal?' His voice shook, a pain somewhere in his gut that he didn't want to analyse.

'Dick!' Babo jerked upright, twisting around to greet him. He gathered her to him, her warmth, her softness, balm to a wound that bewildered him.

'What's this? A welcome for the return of the prodigal? It's only been a month. What d'you want to do, make Thulatu jealous?' She smiled up at him, her eyes teasing with the comfortable, sexless familiarity of old friends.

'How've you been?' He searched her face, his large thumb tracing the exclamation mark on her cheek.

Her eyes clouded. 'So-so.' She shrugged, her shoulders twitching under his hands. 'He's told Mia.'

'Your sister-in-law? When?'

'Dick, I brought him to her.'

Dick's hands slid from her shoulders. 'He never said.'

Babo snorted. 'Doesn't surprise me. Since Thabo, he's been ... different ... secretive ... he's beginning to take risks you'd never believe, a little while ago, on the road, look, you've got to talk to him, and if that isn't enough, he's going to try seeing her again, Dick, he's threatening to tell Claus and Piet if Mia doesn't, you've got to talk to him, if you saw Mia, she's half out of her mind with worry, Jesus, why'd I ever agree to helping him do it?'

'He'd have done it anyway, better that you were there to cushion it.' He lifted a long tendril of hair back from her cheek.

Her lips twisted. 'That's what I keep trying to tell myself.'

Dick's gaze followed hers to the street as he took the gold cross and chain from his pocket. A few moments longer, that's all he'd be able to give them. Already a group of people were making towards the church, their progress hindered by the wounded they half-dragged, half-carried to his doorstep, God in heaven, where was the mobile clinic, they were out of antibiotics again. He rubbed his eyes, the slight stinging a warning that the air was still threaded with tearsmoke. Another few seconds, then he'd have to go back in.

'Do the same with this, will you?' He pressed the cross into her hand.

'Another gift from your lady friend?' She tried to smile. 'Even heavier than the last one, what d'you want me to use the money for?'

'Same as last time, medicines, I've made out a list. C'mon, let's move it.' He lifted some of the boxes, unwilling, even now, to go back inside and face them.

* * *

In the dusty interior they stood facing each other, long moments stretching the space between them into a desert, trackless and barren.

Shocked by what she saw, the speech she'd rehearsed died still-born on her lips. His eyes, she thought, a bush fire spending itself, did I do this?

'Why'd you come? Tell me.' The words jerked from the hard rim of his mouth.

'I, I ... you said if ever I wanted to contact you ... that is—.'

'That was a long time ago.' His mouth worked, tongue flickering between the strong, white teeth. 'Things change.'

She struggled, trying to keep the fear out. 'We can talk, can't we?'

'It's too late, Emma.'

The words dropped with the weight of lead. The tired way he spoke, no anger, she thought, no feeling. Nothing. And his eyes. Beyond her, beyond anything they'd ever been together. Irretrievable.

'Yes,' she said and something crumbled inside. Dazed, she turned again to the signs, her hands spread in a flapping sacrifice on the altar. She peered at the large words but couldn't make sense of what she saw. Stupid, stupid to think it could ever have been otherwise, Christ, what a fool she was. But why, why then had he let her come? She closed her eyes, even yet willing him to break, a yearning, thick, powerful, for the life that had once been his voice.

But no words reached to rescue her. Instead, the rhythm of feet snapping at concrete as he crossed towards one of the windows. She stood, marooned, unable to stem the sludge of despair rising to swallow her. Irretrievable. Only one chance at it, one stab, but her stab had been vicious, a child gouged out, a piece of his flesh, the piece that was heart, this was what she had done. Well, then, get it over with, the thing that had to be voiced.

She turned swiftly, her mouth trembling with it. 'I was wrong.'

The words rang out, their faint, tinny echo trapped in folds of corrugate. He stood, a black silhouette framed by the outside day, her voice dredging, prodding the pain he'd managed to bury in the laughing eyes of Thabo. He'd been insane to let her come, insane to think he was immune.

'You came all the way here just to tell me that?'

'Yes!' she screamed.

'Oh, and what good is that to either of us, may I ask?' He stepped forward, the darkness releasing him. 'Don't you think it's a bit late to find you have a conscience after all? Why do you come here to rake up the past? Just what is it you're up to?' He moved towards her, dust exploding under the impact of his feet.

'You ... you always said you wanted me to write about racism here.'

'What's this? A noble gesture?' His eyes narrowed. 'Well, it won't wash, Emma, you're incapable of doing anyone a service without an ulterior motive.'

The words cut deeply. She was silent, almost welcoming them. If she couldn't have his love again, then she needed his hate, the punishment of it, anything rather than his indifference.

Eventually, she managed to speak. 'Then why'd you let me come? You could have stopped me, it was through the contacts you gave me—!'

He shrugged, hands sunk in his trouser pockets, the boredom in his face making her wince. 'Does it matter? It seems neither of us is immune to ulterior motives — I saw a way of using you, your skill as a journalist, that's all.' His upper lip curled. 'I knew this was at least one area in which you were to be trusted.' He wouldn't admit to his curiosity, or the need he had to exorcise the degradation of that last time with her — when he'd got down on his knees, his knees! — and begged for the child's life. He passed a hand across his eyes to blot it out.

Her gaze searched his face. A closed door. No more than she deserved.

'I'll do whatever you want me to,' she said quietly.

'I ask no more than you promised my mother.'

'Your mother?'

'You met her at Holbrook Hall.'

'Y'mean ... Sophie? Sophie Chamberlain?' She stared at him, eyes wide, answers slotting into place. She'd been too preoccupied to see it.

'Precisely.' His dark head flicked in acknowledgement. 'All we ask is that you write the truth, that alone is sufficient to help our struggle.'

She stiffened at the 'we' and 'our,' the distance it implied between them.

'You never told me.' She turned back to the altar, to keep her face hidden. He'd always been secretive, always. Knowing that, it hadn't surprised her to discover that here he had a different name.

'What?'

'About her, your mother. Or your name. I mean—. When we were ... together.'

'No.' The word stabbed at her back. 'By the time I knew you were to be trusted, it seems you'd decided that I couldn't be.'

She turned. 'I couldn't trust myself.'

He laughed, the sound crashing in her ears. 'Oh, and is that why you put your faith in the pin-striped quack in Harvey Street with his gilt-edged clinic and his—!'

'Fuck you, it was easy for you, wasn't it, it wasn't your life—!'

A sudden commotion at the door distracted them.

Dick stood, his voice roaring above Emma's, drowning her out. Arms cradling two cardboard boxes, he strode inwards, his head a great flushed peach above the load he carried. Behind him, Babo entered, moving more leisurely in his wake.

'... you hear me? Clinic's here. C'mon you two, it's gonna be a helluva day.' He slammed the boxes on the altar, his mouth forced in the semblance of a grin. Emma stood, struggling for breath, the signs shielding her chest. Dick nodded to her. 'You not got those blessed things up yet?'

Emma didn't seem to hear. Her eyes were full of the young, tanned woman in dun-coloured shorts who'd moved to Thulatu's side, touching his arm briefly, questioningly, as though she'd always had the right to question. So. There was more to it than he'd said. This woman knew him, knew him intimately, had traced her fingers over the small map of scars on his thigh, the mole hidden in the dark line of hair descending from his navel. Trembling, a weak smile plastered to her lips, she held out her hand as Dick made the introductions.

Babo looked at the scrawny creature before her, trying to hide her surprise. Jesus, that haircut, the weirdest she'd ever seen, and those heavy jeans, several sizes too big, a clown wearing a fur coat to the beach in high summer, the woman'd hardly come from England looking like that, had she? A journalist? She looked about as literate as an urchin in the street. Then she sensed it, a thickness in the air between the woman and the two men, an awkwardness in the silence that was almost palpable. What was going on? She looked from Dick to Thulatu but couldn't decipher it.

Outside, a horn blasted, making Emma jump. The small group fractured in relief as the team from Lenasia hailed from the door, bearing down on them with the first casualties.

It was a long day, longer than Emma had ever thought imaginable. She and Mambo spent their time scurrying between the sections until the distinctions became blurred, so that at times Dick, or one of the gentle-faced doctors, had to remind her where she was or what it was she was supposed to be doing. The only section she didn't go near was Thulatu's, not that he needed her help, Babo's blonde head bent close to his whenever she managed to steal a glance in their direction.

By the time the sun was overhead, the church was crammed with the hot stink of sweat and blood, the unrelenting babble of shock and grief pierced here and there by the bladed squeal of a child's terror as the two Indian doctors plucked at skins laced with bird and buckshot, cutting, lancing, stitching, dressing, a conveyor belt rhythm in the movement of their hands.

The psychiatrist, a tall, spare, elderly white woman, had taken the worst of the injured to Baragwanath Hospital in Soweto. One young man, half-crazed with pain, hands clutching the livid glare of his own intestines, had begged them not to take him as Emma helped drag him into the large recreational vehicle that served as the mobile clinic.

'Whiskey, give whiskey, then the pain, I can manage,' he begged.

The psychiatrist shook her head as they laid him on a small bunk. 'You need a general anaesthetic, a doctor will have to operate, there's a bullet lodged—.'

'Whiskey? I stay here?' The man's feverish eyes pleaded as he lay, too weak to resist their efforts to keep him still. Again, the woman shook her head.

'Then I will die.'

'I promise you you won't die.' The psychiatrist's tone was firm.

'The polisie will be waiting, there inside the door of the casualty, they do it all the time, you do not understand ...' his voice rose screaming on a wave of pain ... 'if you are shot, you are guilty!'

The woman swabbed his soaked skin, her voice soothing as she assured him her whiteness would be enough to protect him. Emma saw the crease of worry on her brow, realising the dilemma she faced. Here, without proper facilities the man would die, if not of his injuries, of the shock and pain the meagre supply of anaesthetic sprays could not alleviate. Yet, at the hospital, she'd be effectively handing him into the waiting arms of police who would refuse to believe he was innocent, hadn't he been shot? — he wouldn't have been shot by police or soldiers if he wasn't guilty of something, besides, hadn't he been running away? — people only ran when they were guilty of something. The treadmill of state butchery: if you stood still on the street in the middle of a raid, you were shot, if you ran away, you were shot, if you were caught, you were detained, interrogated, tortured, if you were tortured too much, sometimes you died, always, always by committing suicide in the most magical ways, you jumped from the eighth floor through the barred window of your cell, you beat yourself senseless and from the depths of your own unconsciousness, managed a last, bone-shattering blow that crushed your skull, you died of food poisoning when you were on a hunger strike, and sometimes, though they wouldn't allow you to wash, you slipped on a cake of soap while manacled to the window grid high on the wall of your cell. And sometimes you hanged, the rope woven by your own imagination from the dank, solitary air in the cell at the farthest end of the segregation section, your voice stifled in your throat.

It was all there, in this man's eyes, the same despair of the mothers whom Dick accompanied to the police station each day in the hope of gleaning some information about their missing children. But Dick, white and priest as he was, couldn't work miracles. Emma turned from the man, unable to bear his accusing eyes. Modise was standing on the step, a small girl draped across his arms. Wordlessly, he held the child out to her.

'Is she—?'

He gave a slight nod. 'Her mother is injured, her home was destroyed by a hand grenade. She asks that you keep the body here until she is treated and can go to Kuali to arrange for a box. It is upsetting there in the church for the other children.'

Deftly, he slid the child onto her shaking arms. She lay, a perfection of features and limbs, a small dribble of blood drying below her left ear, an epiphany of death in the limpness, the warm fusion of flesh and bone. Emma swallowed. Such a child could have been hers, such a child come to such an end. And the grief, then. Killing. She clenched her teeth, fighting an instinct to howl. There's no life here, she thought, no God, God hadn't survived the process of selection, a new breed had emerged, a savage divinity of warlords, alive and thrashing, their white skins smelted to the armour of tyrants.

When she lifted her gaze to share her anger with Modise, he was gone.

Later, much later, when the clinic was cleared, when they slouched on the disordered pews, conversing dully, a fiery exhaustion in their faces as the low sun splintered the windows, Emma again remembered the little girl, the stillness she'd harboured in her arms for those few moments. She glanced at Thulatu, wondering if he'd seen the child. He was bent over a bundle of forms, stacking them neatly into several piles as he chatted to Dick. Mambo, the long dark wings of her skirt flapping against the stick-legs, was hobbling about, tidying what no one else had the energy for. They'd finally eaten a little while previously, although none of them proved to have an appetite for the hamper of cold food and drinks the psychiatrist had brought. Emma hoped she'd offer to leave some of it behind — the chicken and tomatoes would keep them from needing to resort to mealie meal for days. The thought shamed her, the minute trivia of life asserting itself amidst the day's horrors.

'Tired?' Babo had come to sit beside her, her face creased in a smile.

Despite the jealousy she felt, Emma nodded, smiling back. There was something so warm and open in the younger woman's face that she couldn't dislike her. She shifted a little, afraid Babo would smell the stale sweat.

'God, it's hot.' Babo pulled the loose cotton blouse she wore till it stood out in a tent from her small breasts. She flapped it, fanning herself. 'Hm, a cool shower, now there's something to look forward to when we get back.'

The 'we' was lead in Emma's stomach. She sighed. What had she expected? That he'd have become celibate as she? Sipho liked women too much. No, not Sipho. Thulatu. He hadn't even trusted her with his name.

'... perhaps? You could come with me this evening, if you like?'

'I'm sorry?' Emma tried to concentrate on what the younger woman had said.

'Didn't Thulatu mention it?' Babo's eyebrows arched.

'What?'

Babo looked across the pews which divided them from Thulatu and Dick. As she raised her voice, the Indian doctors from Lenasia, engaged in a conversation with the psychiatrist on the far side of the aisle, turned their heads for a moment to listen.

'Didn't you tell her this morning?'

Thulatu glanced at them, raising his hand to forestall Babo as he finished saying something to Dick. Together the two men climbed over the benches to where the women were sitting. Thulatu, straddling the pew in front of them, sat opposite Babo.

'You never told her,' Babo accused him.

Emma looked at his closed face, suddenly afraid. He was sending her back, well, she wouldn't go, she'd be ....

'Oh, and when was I to find the time, may I ask? It hasn't exactly been a public holiday since we arrived.' The tone was mild, sardonic, the hint of boredom in the slight shrug of his shoulders, something Emma was beginning to hate.

Babo turned to her. 'We were wondering if you'd like to come back with us for a while? You're welcome to stay at my place. There's a really big demonstration planned for ....'

Emma bent down to keep her expression hidden as Babo's voice wound on. So. They didn't live together. She fiddled with the strap on her sandal. In Durban, she'd be able to see more of him, perhaps, perhaps then ... 'I'd love to come,' she said, her voice muffled. 'It'd be terrific to have a break from—.' She straightened, her gaze catching Dick's, something wounded in his face at her heartfelt tone.

'What I mean is, I ...' She gestured awkwardly. 'I wouldn't say no to a decent bath ...' her voice petered out and she avoided looking at Dick.

'You take the jeep, I'll collect it from you when I need it.' Thulatu looked at Babo. 'There's enough to keep me here for most of tomorrow as well, it seems. I'll come back with the others.' His head jerked in the direction of the three doctors as he glanced at Emma, dark eyes hostile. 'Babo'll look after you, I've told her what to do.'

Emma stared at her sandals, trying to analyse it. So much for hope. She'd have to face it. He didn't want her anywhere near him, hence his willingness to foist her on Babo. Well, fuck him, yes, she was wrong, guilty, whatever word he wanted to put on it, but then the alternative he'd offered her was his alternative, the one that suited his life, that overrode hers as though it were something of no consequence, oh yes it'd been easy for him. But what if he hadn't wanted the child, what then? — easy to choose the good when the good was what you wanted to choose, no danger of putting yourself to the test and finding yourself wanting there, well, she'd do what he wanted, but when it was done, she wouldn't leave, wouldn't meekly pack her bag and go back to England, she'd stay, stay to the bitter end and finish the job, despite how he felt about her, if that didn't go some way towards making reparation, if that didn't give her some kind of peace then she'd be better off being fished out of the Thames.

She tried to adjust her face before she raised her head to look at Dick, wishing she were somewhere on her own, somewhere dark and quiet and empty. 'I'll be back.' Her eyes held a question as she forced her lips in a jerky grin, '... that's if you'll have me. As soon as Siph—, Thulatu, as soon as I've finished what—.'

'Bed's here any time you want.' He smiled, eyes warm in the mountainous contour of cheeks.

Thankyou, she thought, thankyou, thankyou, thankyou.

As though he sensed her need to step out of the limelight, he turned to Thulatu. 'This demo, now the UDF's banned, how you gonna get round the legalities?'

'That, my friend, is the least of our problems.' Thulatu stretched, hands linked behind his head, the vee of his bare arms supple as wings jutting from the back of his neck. He grinned. 'We've got a new organisation now, it'll take the government time to ban this one.' He brought his hands forward to slap his thighs. 'Universal

Human Rights Union ... UHURU! to those of us who know better.'
His belly-laugh resonated against the corrugated roof, filling the
little church, the kind of laugh it was impossible to resist. Despite
herself, Emma began to smile.

'You're kidding!' Dick and Babo were laughing with him.

Babo tossed her head, the golden strands flickering in the low
light. 'He's not, he means it, he's already setting it up—.'

Thulatu's face became mock-serious. 'Tell me, don't you think
they'll find it difficult to ban another organisation that has the words
"Human rights" in the title, they'll look pretty tyrannical in the eyes
of the world when they—.'

'They found a way with Tutu.' Dick's voice was decisive.

'Tutu's no lawyer, don't forget.'

'But why is it funny?' Emma looked from Dick to Babo, avoiding
Thulatu's face.

'It's the word.' Babo smiled. ' "Uhuru" is Swahili, it means freedom, so it's a double-edged title.'

Dick looked up suddenly. 'Here's Modise now, time for the night
vigil.' He stood. 'C'mon, move it, I've four more to attend tonight.'

Babo groaned as she rose, flexing her arms to shake the stiffness
from them. 'How long do we have to stay? I've to be up at the crack
tomorrow and I've still got to drive—.'

'An hour should do it. It's just a question of paying your respects.'

But it was more than that. The house, a two-roomed shack of
brick and corrugate, belonged to mKulie, one of Mambo's neighbours, whose son had died in the mobile clinic en route to the
hospital. His body was already laid out in a rough deal box placed
on top of the only mattress that dressed the bedroom floor. Emma
stared at the waxen peace of the face, recognising the young man
who'd pleaded with them, could it really only have been a few hours
earlier? Well, he was safe now, safe from the police, safe from the
refusal in her eyes, safe in death as the child she'd held, safe as the
half-formed infant she'd driven from her womb. The room smelled
strongly of incense. Was it part of some special ritual? Or a cover
for the faint odour emanating from the body? The cheap polyester
suit he wore, several sizes too big, gave no evidence of the gaping
labyrinth of his intestines, perhaps somebody had bound the
wound, perhaps too that was why she could no longer smell the
rankness that'd choked her nostrils in the recreational vehicle earlier. She turned, feeling strangely detached, squeezing through the
throng of bodies glutting the room. There was no space left in her
mind to take those pleading eyes on board.

In the other room, a number of black people, including Modise
and his friends, the doctors, Dick, Thulatu and Babo were squatting

on the floor, listening to mKulie's tearful account in halting English of the events that led to her son being shot by the police. Her tale was punctuated by comments from friends and neighbours eager to fill in the details she was leaving out. Emma didn't want to hear it, there'd been enough today to last her forever.

Deliberately, she pushed mKulie's voice aside, staring about for some trivial thing on which she could focus. Was it really possible to fit so many people in one tiny room? Apart from an ancient metal range and a small laden table in one of the corners, presided over by Mambo and several elderly black women, there was no other furniture. She picked her way through the wad of bodies, squeezing down between Dick and one of Modise's friends as she tried not to look in Thulatu's direction. The room was like an oven, yet now that the sun had set, the concrete beneath her buttocks was already icy. Overhead, a bare bulb hung suspended from a nail in the roof.

Mambo came to her, handing her something in a cracked blue mug. Emma smiled up at her. It was because of Mambo they had come, the old woman insisting they all honour her neighbour. Emma sipped the drink, recognising the acrid flavour of the alcohol Dick kept in the bottom drawer of his desk. She bit on one of the small hard biscuits that had been passed around, chewing forever on the woody splinter before it became soft enough for her to risk swallowing.

'You must take it,' Dick'd murmured under the keening wail of mKulie's voice. 'They'll be offended if you don't.'

She made several dummy runs around her mouth before she worked up sufficient courage to try swallowing it. For a moment it seemed to lodge in her throat and she gulped the drink, forcing it down, her eyes watering. When she could see again she found Thulatu watching, his gaze cold and mocking. See, his eyes said, see how uncomfortable you are here, you come here to play your selfish little games, you try to pretend you are part of this but you don't fit in here, this is my world. She looked away quickly. When Mambo filled her mug again, she drained it almost before the old woman had refilled Dick's.

'Easy on that stuff. It's pretty lethal.' Dick's voice was the scratch of gravel beneath the general hub of conversation. 'You okay?' He was watching her carefully. Too carefully.

She nodded, forcing a smile that seemed to crack her cheeks. 'Fine.'

'You sure?'

'Really.' She looked around the room, anything to avoid those eagle eyes. 'Quite a crowd, now I know what a sardine feels like.'

'You ever wanna talk, I'm here.'

'You'd like to hear my confession?' She kept her tone light.

'Nope. But maybe you would.'

'I've nothing to confess.'

'We all got something to confess.'

'Then maybe I should re-phrase that.' Thinking of Thulatu, his coldness towards her, the words tripped off her tongue. 'I've nothing to confess to you.' Turning, she caught the dull flush rising from the white collar, suffusing his face. Instantly, she was sorry. Why, why, did she have to be such a bitch to him? She laid her hand on his bare arm and he flinched as though she'd burned him. Embarrassed, she withdrew it, wishing his shirt sleeve'd been rolled down. 'I'm sorry.'

'Forget it.' His hand was dismissive. 'Maybe a break from each other'll do us no harm.'

If his words were meant to console, they failed. Perhaps he was sorry he'd made her that offer today? Nor could she blame him. She stared at the blank bottom of her mug, wishing Mambo would offer her more, anything to relieve the ache inside, the feeling of misery which threatened to overwhelm her. She couldn't cry here, she mustn't.

Suddenly, someone was calling her name, worse, drawing everyone's attention to her. Vusi stood at the bedroom door, speaking animatedly, a beaming woman by his side, her tight curls peppered with grey. Everyone turned to listen to him recount the saga of how he'd managed to get his housing permit. He should have been an actor, she thought, mortified, as he embellished the part she'd played, rolling his eyes in a provocative way to indicate how she'd managed to extract the permit from the boorish Afrikaner clerk. There was much laughter as he flitted through the various roles, sparing neither himself, head bowed obsequiously in the age-old grip of oppression, nor the hard-faced lekhowa flouting his power, nor finally Emma in the role of virtual seductress. By the time he'd finished, the little room vibrated with mirth, tears rolling freely down the faces of some of mKulie's neighbours, mKulie herself distracted from the dark truth of her son in the next room. Emma was dumbfounded. In the midst of grief they'd managed to find laughter: Vusi had taken their shame, poked fun in its face, transforming it into a triumph.

Emma found herself laughing with the rest, an edge to her laughter that wavered on a tightrope, tinged, she knew, with the faint undertone of hysteria, the day's brute passage branded in memory, a kaleidoscope of livid trails leading to her own darkness within, the need for release intense as the need for the next breath. So it was for all of them, she felt it in a sudden fusion, a yearning to reach one another, to find comfort in the solidarity woven from the patchwork of tin, brick and rubble in which they scratched out their lives. She swallowed, her throat hurting. For the first time she was part of it.

Somebody began to sing, the tune, nostalgic, a lament seeping through the strangeness of the words. She closed her eyes, her head spinning with the alcohol, giving herself up to the voice, not quite aware when it died away and Dick's pleasant baritone took over, a ritualised rhythm to the words that defined its hymnal tone, a defiant celebration of life in the midst of hardship.

Somebody was calling her name, shaking her. She opened her eyes to find Mambo pointing at her, the young student grinning as he spoke. 'Grandma says you have the voice, she has heard you, you must sing for us, something of your country.'

She stared at him, stupefied, shaking her head, her heart skipping as she registered the sudden quiet, the expectant faces smiling about her.

'C'mon, it's an honour to be asked, make a stab at something, otherwise you'll offend them.' Dick's voice was a warning in her ear.

'I, I can't,' she said, 'I'm a lousy singer. Please explain to them—.'

'Oh, she can sing, I'll vouch for that.' Thulatu's voice carried across the small space, cruelty carved in the glitter of his eyes. 'But perhaps she'd prefer more auspicious surroundings in which to air her vocal chords?' He laughed, the sound exploding in her ears. 'It seems she doesn't care to honour us with her voice.'

The bastard! She gritted her teeth, knowing he'd trapped her. He knew her well, too well, knew what she liked, what she most hated, worse, he knew what she feared. So much for thinking he was indifferent to her, he was out to punish her any way he could, no dirty tricks spared. She turned to Dick, trying to keep her voice calm. 'Wha— what'll I sing?'

He grinned. 'How should I know? The only Irish song I know is "It's a long way to Tipperary."'

'Irish?' She stared at him.

'Sure.' His eyes narrowed. 'You drank any more a that stuff?' He nodded at her empty cup.

'I'm not drunk!' She spat the words in a low whisper, aware of the waiting eyes.

'Glad to hear it. Well, what d'you wanna sing?' He grinned again. 'I'll announce you if you like.'

'Terrific.' She threw him a filthy look, her mind searching feverishly. Irish, her passport, that was a laugh, and Thulatu knew it, he knew it, he was deliberately putting her on the spot, Christ, she could kill him, the closest she'd ever been to Ireland was her Irish mother, the stories she used to tell, the song she used to — no, not song, verse, a poem, a poem she'd taught Emma by singing it to her, she hadn't sung it in years, could she remember it? Her mind flew over the words, enough snatches slotting into place to make her think she could get by.

'I, I'll sing something, not a song, it's a poem actually.' She stared into a crevice in the bricks above the watching faces, stuffing her hands between her thighs to hide their shaking. 'My, my mother taught it to me a long time ago, I may not remember all of it.' She grimaced, her apology flung upwards at the concrete wall, its every crevice exposed in the pitiless light.

Closing her eyes, she began, her voice tentative against the breathing mass of air that filled the room. Halfway through the first line, she faltered, realising too late she had forgotten to give them the name of the piece. She staggered on, her voice gaining momentum as she reached the second line, and the next and the next, surprised to find how suddenly fitting the words seemed, a song of yearning for a lake isle, for a wattle and daub home you'd find in any kraal, for peace, for freedom, it could have been South Africa she was singing of, the keening of shattered lives that longed to be healed, the keening of her own heart for the thing she'd destroyed, her voice sharp with loss as she reached the final lines,

> '... and whether on the roadway,
> or on the pavement grey, I
> hear it in the deep heart's core.'

When the last note faded on her lips, she struggled for control, her eyes tightly shut against the awful stillness in which even the warm, stale air was devoid of a single breath. She had to get out, before she made a complete fool of herself. Daring to look at no one, she jumped up, peering at her feet as she stepped over the bodies lining the stone floor, an eternity passing before she finally made it to the door, oh he would enjoy it, how he would enjoy it.

Outside at last in the darkness of the dusty communal yard she heaved, the stars chaotic explosions through the thickness of the tears she held her eyes wide to contain. Behind her the door opened, light streaking to hold her in its track. She moved out further past its punishing beam, the smell of mouldering refuse invading her nostrils.

'Congratulations.' Thulatu, the word whipping her back. 'That was quite a show you put on. Even managed to move the natives to tears.' His outline merged with the darkness as someone closed the door.

She laughed, a queer, jerky little sound, glad he couldn't see her face.

'You find something amusing?'

She stayed silent, knowing anything she said would fuel it. Far above, a meteorite streaked across the sky, bright as hope, dying as though it had never been born, the sky more intensely black, the stars paler in its wake. She shivered. Somewhere, a dog snarled.

'It seems in the small time you've been here, you've managed to ingratiate yourself, I'm amazed how easily people can be fooled, I thought at least Modise had—.'

'Modise?' As the word left her tongue, a cricket shrilled, drawing her voice into its high-pitched chirp. She turned, peering up at him, unable to make out more than the faint luminescence of his skin. 'What has Modise got to do with anything?'

'I'm warning you, I want you out of here, out of my hair, just as soon as this job is done, the next plane out, I've enough on my mind with Thabo's death—.'

'Thabo?' She pictured the small photo of his son he'd often shown her, the warmth in his voice. It didn't seem possible. 'Dead?'

'I want you out of here.'

'But he was only a kid, how, how could he—?'

'How?' He laughed, the sound filling the darkness. 'Like a dog, that's how. Tortured. Beaten to the point of death, then left to rot in the gutter, no different to the piece of black trash lying in there.' His arm moved swiftly, air smacking her face and she knew he was pointing back towards the hut. The singing had begun again, a low sad sound that spoke of pain.

'Christ, I'm sorry, Sipho.' Instinctively she reached out, her hand tentative, stopping short before it reached him.

'Shock treatment, bones crushed—.'

She winced. 'Don't.'

'Don't, don't don't.' His voice mimicked. 'What's this, you're developing some sensitivity?'

'I'm not a monster,' she said quietly. 'What happened your son is terrible, it's—.'

'Oh? And is it any more terrible than what you did?'

Her stomach caved.

'That was different—.'

'How, how different? Do tell me.' His breath scorched her face.

'You can't compare somebody being tortured to me having an, an—.'

'Why not? Tell me. Who are you to decide which living thing feels pain and which doesn't?' His hands gripped her shoulders, the fingers biting deeply. He shook her, her head snapping back and forth before the rasping onslaught of his voice.

'Who are you to decide anything? You're a murderer, a cold-blooded whore, you took my child and destroyed it as coldly, as clinically as those bastards destroyed Thabo, you're no better than they are, you're—.'

'Don't, oh don't!' Her voice was a low howl as she struggled to get away from him.

'Don't, oh don't,' he mocked. 'It seems I've heard those words before, only the last time I was the one uttering them! Well, this is what you came here for, I'm not blind, you wanted this, you wanted me to punish you, whatever it might cost me!'

'You let me come!'

'Yes.' His breathing was ragged as he fought to hold back the words. He'd thought he could handle it, thought there was enough distance, but he couldn't punish her without reliving it, nor could he disentangle it from the cold truth of Thabo, a truth echoed now in the young man lying in the bedroom of the hut. How many thousands more would echo it before the tide would turn? With a low snarl he threw her from him. She reeled backwards a few paces before managing to steady herself.

'Yes. It seems my motives were as base as yours.' His voice was thick with disgust.

She stared at the vague outline of his presence in the dark, wondering what he meant. They were silent for a long time, the song rising against the walls of the hut, voices tinkling in the confines of a music box.

'What's evil, what's really evil, is that you used me. When you became ... when the whole thing became an inconvenience, you just—.' He broke off, his breathing harsh.

'Well, now it's the other way around, that must give you some—.'

'I don't want revenge, Emma, not any more.' His voice was tired. 'All that matters now is the struggle. That and my—.' He stopped. She knew nothing of Mia. 'After this demonstration, I want you to leave, you've had a taste of township life, Durban will give you another slant, you'll have enough material to fill a newspaper, the very next plane, that's all I want of you.' Turning, he strode back towards the hut, leaving her under a sky smeared with the dust of a myriad stars.

She stood, frozen with it. Calm, even. Empty. She couldn't deal with it, not now, not yet. It would fester in memory, her mind skirting it, his words snapping at her heels as she ran from it. Though he'd said nothing she hadn't already faced. But it was one thing to accuse herself, another to stand and be accused. Between the two, a darkness yawned, speechless, terrifying.

Her calmness lasted right through the drive to Durban with Babo, the younger woman's chatter affording her a strange sense of relief. The road sped under the wheels, devouring the miles as the conversation finally turned to Thulatu. For no reason she could fathom, except perhaps the other woman's friendliness, the warmth of her smile a sudden lifeline, Emma found herself pouring it out as she'd done to no other, all, all of it in one huge spillage from the beginning in London to this exact moment, reluctant even to cease speaking when she had finished, so great was her sense of release. In the silence which followed, the drone of the engine asserted itself. She knows, Emma thought, none of this has come as a surprise. 'He told you? About ... us?' She tried to keep the jealousy from her voice.

'No.' Babo dipped the headlights as the jeep rounded a curve. At this hour the freeway was virtually deserted. 'I guessed it.' She laughed wryly. 'Eventually. I'd a lot on my mind today. My family—. But the vigil tonight, the way he spoke, I thought, there's more to this.' She shrugged. 'I wish I could say something helpful, but—.'

'You really don't mind?'

'I told you, we're finished, that way at least.' She pressed a switch, spraying water on the windscreen, the wipers moving to clean the gunge of dead insects smearing the glass. When they could see clearly again, the headlights picked out a large moth trapped flickering in its beam. It was then Babo told her of Mia. Emma stared at the dark mass of the Drakensberg gliding towards them, utterly confounded. A daughter almost her own age. White! At least to all appearances. White as the driven snow. White, white, white. Christ. The child she had .... Could have been white, white enough to live in a white world, to pass for a white. She needn't have killed .... The thought stabbed her.

'... I'm really worried about her.' Babo's voice impinged. 'That's why ... I was wondering if perhaps you wouldn't mind coming with me, to see her, I mean. Might cheer her up, meeting you. She's always had a soft spot for England, still keeps in touch with her mother's relatives, although that was before she found out—. Anyway, maybe knowing you're writing about racism, it might give her a boost, she has a strange way of looking at things ever since we, Thulatu told her, it might help, I don't know. Would you?'

There was a jerkiness in Babo's tone, the last words almost a plea.

Sipho's daughter, the living embodiment of the potential she'd destroyed. Too much to face. More rope with which to lash herself. She was tired, so tired of it. Babo had no idea what she was asking. She closed her eyes. 'Yes, I'll come.' She heard her own voice speak the words, calm and distanced as a greeting uttered to a stranger. Babo glanced at her quickly. 'Thanks, I appreciate it.' Her tone was heartfelt. She didn't seem to sense there'd be anything difficult about it from Emma's point of view, but then, why should she? — she had nothing to reproach herself with. Emma gazed at the blur of winking lights clustered on the skyline. Durban. Without Sipho. No, she mustn't think of him as Sipho again, that which was Sipho lay with his son in the earth. With the life she had taken. Only Thulatu remained, his eyes livid with broken dreams, a fearless defiance in their depths which made her afraid.

'There's one thing,' she said a long time later, her voice apologetic. She opened her eyes, surprised to find they were already in the city. 'I'm a poor sleeper, what I mean is, I, I dream a lot, nightmares, sometimes I think I shout out, I hope I don't disturb you too—.'

'Poor Dick.' Babo laughed. 'How'd he cope, cotton wool in his ears? Or did he make it an excuse to come and comfort you?'

'I don't know, he never said anything, you know, we never talked about it, isn't that strange?' She stared at Babo's profile flickering in the street lights as they cruised through the silent suburbs.

'Dick never asks questions. With him, people usually volunteer.' Babo slowed for a traffic light although nobody was about. 'I speak from experience. He's a good friend. If you ever need to talk to someone. Well, here we are.' She veered left into a driveway that had been converted from a small garden. Emma squinted at the two-storey house squatting in the dark, its beige stone facade just discernible in the glow from the street light.

'It's not much I'm afraid, especially in this light, but it's home, I can't afford anything better on the size of my grant. I'm on the top floor, the view's a sight for sore eyes, you'll see in the morning.'

What Babo termed morning turned out to be early afternoon. Emma was sitting on the balcony, sick of sipping coffee when Babo finally surfaced, her face still flushed with sleep.

'You like it?' She yawned, waving at the spread of rooftop suburbs half-concealed in exotic growth, beyond which the sea glistened in postcard glory. The air was warm, humid.

'I must warn you, it's the best thing about the place, the water doesn't work half the time, seems the pipes are ancient. Landlord wants to pull it down, re-build something stylish to fit in with these plush apartments around us, what he means is, something lucrative.' She grinned. 'He's having a hard time getting us out, thanks to Thulatu. You slept okay? I must admit after that drive last night, it'd have taken more than your dreams are worth to wake me. You up long?'

Emma nodded. 'A while. I thought you'd have lectures this morning—.'

Babo made a face. 'I did. Plato: The Theory of Ideal Forms. When I decided to study politics, I wasn't expecting them to sidetrack with so much unnecessary junk.' She hesitated, pushing back the tousled mop of hair. 'I thought perhaps we'd ... go see Mia, that is, if you don't mind being foisted on her so soon?'

Emma, stared down at her feet, stalling.

'It's a bit late to get you signed up for something today. The registrar's office closes at four. And I'd like to see Mia, I haven't seen her for a few days, not since—.' Babo turned away, squinting against the water's glare. She wouldn't tell Emma how weirdly Mia had been acting. It'd be a relief to see what a stranger might make of her, perhaps she herself was over-reacting, perhaps the worry she'd felt ever since Mia had been told had more to do with her own role in the affair than any real need for concern.

'Fine by me.' Emma tried to mean the words as she rose, following Babo inside. It was strange to be in a house again, to wake to a room littered with furniture, her feet shuffling in the thick pile of carpet. Disorientating. Stranger still, not to have dreamed. Could it be that her outpouring to Babo had broken the cycle? Please let it be true. She rubbed the sweat of her palms against her thighs, trying not to think about Thulatu's daughter as Babo went to see if the shower was working.

III

For the third time that day, Mia stood in front of the bedroom mirror, changing. She mustn't go back to the same places she'd visited this morning, particularly, most particularly the shops where the assistants were beginning to know her browsing face, it would be most embarrassing if, no, really, she ought to keep a list, that way at least a day could elapse before she returned to the same place. Oberholzers on West Street was the most dangerous temptation, the fine gold jewellery drawing her like a magnet.

She stared at her reflection, eyes critical as she tried to remember if she'd been shopping. What had she worn? That would give her some clue. Her gaze rifled the clothing tossed on the bed; linen trouser suit, yellow sun-dress, the beach, the golden, golden mile, and, yes, the Rand Exhibition. Dairy Beach, a wide-brimmed straw hat shielding her skin, she'd watched the surfers, early, very early, before the sun could burn, before even the fun fairs and Sea World and the paddling pools could burgeon with life. She'd begun to avoid the sun, all those white skins toasting, lunacy, sheer lunacy. Like trying to be, to be ... something you weren't.

How long had she stood staring at the sign? 'Slegs Blankes.' Or was it 'Net Blankes?' Had it been there at all? Had it? Had it? Maybe someone had come and taken it away? Maybe she'd only seen it there, in the mind's eye of memory? Maybe it was changed, all of it? Maybe blacks could vote? Oh she should've had her camera, taken a picture of it, then she'd remember, then she wouldn't forget. 'By order of Durban Beach By-Law, Section 37, this bathing area is reserved for the sole and exclusive use of members of the white race group.' How many home movies did they have with that thing in the sunny background of sandcastle days? Net Blankes. Net Blankes. This bathing area is reserved, reserved. Note, bathing. If you were one of ... them, you could walk on the beach, let the sand trickle gold-dust between your toes, but you couldn't paddle, you couldn't swim, you couldn't surf, that water was pure, silk on sanctified skin, that water was consecrated, South Africa had extended its territorial rights to include the Indian Ocean, a bad name that, better re-name it. Then where? Yes, later she had driven north towards St Lucy's Estuary, or was it south, Port Shepstone way. Oh what did it matter, those glutted dunes, luscious hilly shrubs, the casuarina trees, she'd wanted to lie among the wild fig creepers, wreathed over by the fleshy leaves, the bright pink blossoms, a safe, sweet bower of oblivion. Instead she'd plucked a green fig pod, bitten through its tough new skin to taste the sweetness inside, standing there among the wild banana clusters, the lichees, flamboyants, mangos, avocados, the cachous, standing there, juice dribbling down her chin as she sucked — like a wild monkey, like a native, naked and savage, no, this dress wouldn't do, not in Oberholzers, the assistants would expect something more of her, something more quietly lavish. She stripped to her bra and underpants, flinging the green dress as she moved again to the bulging wardrobe. All that black, Piet's fault, little cocktail numbers, lounging pyjamas, evening gowns, too much of it, far too much, she'd pandered too long to his taste.

Thumbing through the clothing she pulled out a pale floral creation. It swished across her skin as she immersed herself in its silky folds. Yes. Perfect for Oberholzers. And the belt she normally wore with it? Shoes, bag, credit cards, keys, with any luck she'd slip out before Elijah realised it, she was sick of his mundane questions, really, he was the cook, he ought to know by now what he had to buy to plan the menus.

Tripping down the stairs, she held her breath. No sign. No sound in the quiet house. Perhaps he was in his shed at the bottom of the garden? Or picking fruit for this evening's dessert? Looking neither right nor left, she glided across the hall, past the open doors of both dining and drawing rooms, stiletto heels infinitesimally raised above the thick trap of carpet. And out. She gulped in the warm air.

She was already easing the Mercedes down the long drive when she saw the hall door open, Elijah reduced to a ridiculous puppet gesticulating from the rear-view mirror. Too late, too late. She eased her foot down on the accelerator and the car leaped forward, wheels spraying gravel against the hub-caps, a child's effort to elicit a drum-roll from the rattle of a biscuit tin.

And out the gates. Free. Where to, now? Where? Sweet Jesus, let her not forget again, think, where had she been this morning, the clothes on the bed, the green dress in a heap on the floor, the green dress? Green dress, green dress, green dress, oh, where had she been? Not good, not good not to remember that, wait, wait, take it easy, easy now, red lights, slow down or you'll crash, aren't the cannas wonderful, the tree ferns, or maybe they're palms, shame, shame not to be able to tell them apart, you know this, you know it, think fern, think palm, decide which, a small thing, a small simple thing, those green tight strips whipping mother bark, those deep, deep leaves, green green green, green dress. Where was she now, yes, those fat sleek hotels smirking in sunlight, but cannot pass this part of the sea front, Lower Marine Parade all pedestrian now, then turn round, do not stop at the green light, do not run over blue-haired crone with the rhinestone poodle, do not run over rhinestone crone with the blue-haired poodle, do not laugh, do not cry, drive, drive, drive inland, uphill, away from the beach and the surfers and the figs and the sand dunes. Figs. Linen suit soiled with fig-juice, linen suit on bed, beside it, yellow dress, Rand Exhibition, the relief! — no shops visited so far today, nothing bought, yes something, something bought, the exhibition, all those weapons pinned with rosettes, howitzers, darter missiles, rocket launchers, limpet mines, quiet as well-trained pets at an animal show. And the trophies, dazzling. Armscor with the biggest, a crystal punch-bowl big as a small jacuzzi, well, they would, they would, the biggest arms pro-ducers and state owned, what could one expect, the stand mobbed by drooling delegations from Israel, Argentina, Chile, Sri Lanka, Morocco, she'd stood giggling as Iran and Iraq, working through the exhibit from opposite ends, avoided each other like the plague, all to the tune of riot soundtracks played out endlessly on back-ground videos, and the young soldier wrapping her purchase, telling her they had enough artillery on display to wipe every township off the face of South Africa, his pink fingers wrapping the little model SAP Casspir she'd bought for Jan's collection, how she'd stood with it in her hands outside on the pavement, seeing again the large video screens flashing 'simulation' every ten seconds, (she had counted, yes she had counted) as the SADF rolled into the townships to show how their wares could be plied, to convince their customers of the viability of South African artillery, the industry of war at its most mongering. And then Babo's voice out of a blue smoke there on the pavement, saying there's nothing simulated about it, nothing, so she had thrown the little yellow Casspir into the nearest refuse bin and come home to change. Again. There, that was all of it, nicely fixed in her memory, the relief, perhaps she wouldn't go to Oberholzers after all, perhaps she would treat herself to 'The La Lucia Mall', it didn't feel as though she'd been there for a few days, and the new jewellers there only admitted customers one at a time, sacrosanct, the thrill of that.

Calm at last. Tomorrow she'd make a list of what she wore and where she wore it, yes a list would keep her calm, keep her memory in order, she'd find new places to visit, Snake Park, or the zoo perhaps? No, too many baboons there to stare at her through the bars. She switched on the radio, something light, a mindless pop tune drifting with her all the way through the tree-lined white suburbs, the well-groomed gardens bursting dark with growth, until she reached the mall, was this the right mall, think, think, oh what did it matter, here was the new jewellers.

And inside, stilettos ringing on mosaic tiles, past the bronze children bathing in the wishing pool, the waterfall a prism of incandescence harnessing the sun through the blue dome high in the vaulted roof, nature re-made, man-made, a cool cathedral of scientific light to titillate the well-bred shopper.

At the jewellers, she rang the bell but wasn't admitted immediately: another customer must already be in the inner sanctum, she'd have to wait, she didn't want to wait, perhaps she should leave, go to Oberholzers, that amethyst bar pin she'd seen the other day, really most attractive, she should have bought it, perhaps it was gone by now, if she drove all the way back and it was gone, perhaps she should wait, have a drink in the bar, have her nails done, that nail artistes, hadn't she had them done there before, didn't last three days without chipping, what were they promising now, silk nails, gold and silver, instant, no, she wouldn't be caught dead in those, the real thing or nothing, the real thing, real thing real thing, dangerous ground, change tack, examine the windows, displays weren't what they used to be, in the furriers, a single, small mink stole screaming from a dais of white satin, the opticians, a pair of diamante-studded frames, as though each shop existed for the sole purpose of selling this single item, there, her name being paged over the intercom system, hurry to the steel door now ushering the previous customer out, a small slim Indian, Indian? — it wasn't possible, an assistant perhaps, though all the staff she'd seen were white, this was after all the La Lucia Mall, or was it? — perhaps she cleaned the jewellery?

And in: subdued lighting, the music straining through the speakers more suited to the waiting room of her gynaecologist. But the seal, beautiful, the purest City Deep gold mounted on a rope chain, an exact replica of the seventeenth century seal of the British High Commissioner, yes, she'd take it, no, she'd wear it, no, there was nothing else she was interested in today, thank-you, yes, certainly she'd be back, she would be back, and out again into the main thoroughfare, deceptive as a street with its indoor trees, hothouse proteas, or were they wax effigies? — in bloom, dense, overblown clusters of extravagance, she didn't know why really they kept being chosen as tree of the year, too blowsy, down in the elevator to the underground, the car, cool, dark, responsive to the lightest touch of her foot, and the seal, snug in the hollow of her throat and she knew where she'd been all day, could account for every moment, but now time to go back, soon time for Elijah to start preparing dinner, the thought of food made her queasy, food and Piet and Jan to deal with, perhaps she should say she's ill again, slip away to her room, have something sent up on a tray, how many times had she done that lately? — don't know, don't remember, mustn't do it too often, must act normal, whatever normal is, must hurry home, get upstairs before Elijah can pounce, yes, lock the door and sit in bed with the hand-mirror, admiring the seal on her throat, her white, white throat, mirages on the road big enough to drown in, the cars skimming the surface like silver birds and all around, all around, streets hemmed in by oases of gardens pulsating with foliate growth. Stifling-dark.

Then home, gates open — why? — who was expecting her? — Elijah? Just happening to glance up at the screen at the precise moment she came into view at the gate? — yes, that was it, that must be it, no need for this tightness in her chest, the gravel gorging the tires, then rounding the curve and Babo, the guard dog bounding towards her playfully, the jeep, sweet Jesus, who was in the jeep, let it not be, no, breathe again, steady heart, a strange pale golliwog stiff with terror as it gazed at the slobbering dog, the dog? — what could a white skin find so terrible in a Rottweiler's face?

Chapter Five

I

Perched on the edge of the couch opposite Babo, Emma stared at the beautiful woman, a dazed cat prowling the confines of the drawing room. Thulatu's daughter, a fusion of races in the dark, tormented eyes, the gossamer skin, a perfection of features on which the eye dwelt, unable to drink its fill. She swallowed hard, wishing she hadn't come. Fuck Babo dragging her into this, there was enough pain without this, she didn't want her dreams haunted by the fruit of what might have been, stupid to come, stupid to think she could escape unscathed.

She bit her lip, resisting the urge to tap her fingers against the glass, the other woman's inability to be still, infectious. Even on the most desultory level, the going hadn't been easy, though she'd been relieved when Babo avoided mentioning Thulatu.

The small talk about England was suddenly fraught as Babo revealed the nature of Emma's visit to South Africa.

'Emma's written heaps about racism, perhaps you two could ... have a chat ....' Babo's last words dropped like bricks.

Mia, fidgeting with a chunk of gold at her throat, acted like she hadn't heard. 'Another drink?' The dark eyes glazed, her voice wistful. 'We almost went there, once, a long time ago. London, that's where I wanted—. I love cities. I wish—.' She broke off, gaze jerking from Emma to Babo, her face accusing. 'What has that to do with me?' She swiped her hand along a washboard row of book-spines, the sound slapping like wet linen.

Babo's shoulders twitched, her face sheepish as she searched for something to say.

She knows, Emma thought, she knows Babo told me. Christ, what am I doing here, what possessed me, like a frigging peeping tom, that's what she's thinking, what right have I to intrude like this, the contempt in her eyes, her father's eyes, her father's contempt? Well, salvage something, anything, then get out, run from this room, the smugness of its ass-cloying cushions.

'Perhaps you could recommend a hairdresser?' She patted her hair self-consciously. 'I'm afraid I made rather a mess of—.'

'Butchered,' Mia said, 'you butchered it.' Her tone carried no more inflection than if she'd said 'trimmed,' but the word drifted on the air, a wreath of smoke that wouldn't dissipate.

Babo tried to laugh. 'That's what I told her, she'll have to—.'

'Butchered.' The tonelessness was chilling.

'Yes.' Emma swallowed. 'I'm afraid I didn't have a decent mirror, I couldn't see what I—.' She stiffened, slopping her drink as Mia leapt forward.

'Oh, let me style it, will you? — I'm very good at it, ask Babo.' Her eyes glittering, she crossed the thick carpet, hands outstretched, a cat about to pounce on its prey.

Emma almost choked as she drank to cover her confusion. She looked swiftly at Babo. Was it some kind of joke, or was she actually serious? She couldn't be serious.

'We'd better hurry, Piet'll be home soon and I don't want to-. But it'll only take a couple of minutes.' Mia's hand pecked at the stubs of hair. 'There's so little of it, come up to the bedroom, come, c'mon, I've a very sharp scissors ....' Already she was out the door, the lingering scent of sandalwood trailing in her wake as she headed across the hall towards the stairs. Emma looked at Babo, her mouth gaping.

Babo gave a small embarrassed shrug. 'I know it's ... a bit weird.' She gestured after Mia, her eyebrows a pleading arc. 'But would you ... please?'

Weird was not the word for it, Emma thought, sitting before Mia's dressing-table, a fleecy towel draped across her shoulders, the scissors snapping at her scalp, Mia's voice teetering as she squealed with mirth about the old days when Babo had been a gawky teenager, the fun they'd had experimenting on Babo's blond, silky mop. Emma crouched, teeth clenched, hands gripping the towel like a shield as she willed it to be over, the minutes stretching into hours as the scissors grazed her ear. Would it ever end, like being shaved by a jittery Jack the Ripper. She should never have come, never have poked her nose in. She had aborted this, aborted it before it could grow to be this wild-eyed thing that made you want to weep at its torment, her own could-have-been, this child's sister-or-brother-in-flesh, Christ she was going crazy.

'There ...' Babo was saying, her eyes an apology from the mirror. '... I have to agree, it makes all the difference in ....' The mouth in the glass worked hard for a moment, but couldn't find a way to finish the words.

In the jeep, she apologised to Emma. 'I'll treat you to having it done, I promise. It's, it's kind of ... punkish.' Her gaze sheered away.

'What's left of it.' Emma's lips twitched as she tried to grin. She raised her hand to flip down the sunshield, then changed her mind. Better not to witness Mia's handiwork in the cosmetic mirror.

'I thought your visit might help, cheer her up—. I didn't expect you to have to go through—.'

'Such a close shave?' Emma's laugh was feeble. She couldn't blame Babo for what she'd willingly agreed to. 'Seriously, she needs to see someone.'

Babo nodded, her voice miserable as she manoeuvered the jeep through the gates. 'I've tried to tell her that, but she just wants to pretend it never happened. Jesus, and Thulatu wants her to tell Piet and my father.'

'Have you told him how she is?'

'Hah!' Unconsciously Babo eased her foot down on the accelerator and the jeep lurched forward through the empty streets. In another ten minutes, the rush-hour traffic would begin to stream from the city centre towards the low hills that hid a myriad architect-designed homes among their green folds. 'I've tried to talk to him but since Thabo's death—.'

'D'you want me to have a bash?' As soon as the words were out, she wished she could take them back. He'd no more listen to what she ... worse, he'd be angry at her having the nerve to interfere ... the vicious accusations he'd made yesterday, she'd have to take the same from him again, she'd no strength to fight that, Christ, what was she, a masochist? Was this what guilt did? Had she been whipping herself for so long she could no longer do without it? One thing was sure — if there were a prize for self-flagellation, the way she was heading, she'd win it hands-down—.

'Would you?' Babo's voice was careful as she shifted gear to negotiate a steep street. 'Look, after that little scene, I wouldn't blame you ... I mean, you have your own problems with Thulatu ....' the engine shrieked as she tried to ram the stick into top gear. 'Damnit, I can never drive this thing without that happening.'

Emma had to smile. Babo didn't drive the jeep, she attacked it with a fierce determination, as though it were some monstrous animal that deliberately set out to thwart her.

They got stuck behind a delivery truck unloading crates at a fruit and vegetable shop. Outside, under a wide canopy, a bright carnage of sub-tropical fruit lounged in artistic splendour, harvested, she thought, by starving hands — some of the women in the township travelled every day to the distant fruit farms, glad to break their backs for the few Rands that would help them pay the school fees the government insisted on. Her mouth twisted. While the white schools were free, while white children had a choice of paw-paws, guavas, lichees, papayas, mangoes, pineapples, bananas, others she couldn't even begin to guess the names of, fruits bloated with their juices, their ripe scents begging to be tasted.

'Hey, wake up! What d'you think?' Babo's nails danced a staccato on the steering wheel as she waited for the truck to move.

It would mean she'd see Thulatu. She pushed the thought back, ashamed. Why, why couldn't she make an offer without it being stained? If that were her only reason then there was time to take the words back, forget she'd ever met his daughter, his flesh, part of the same flesh she'd grown in her womb, part of what she'd destroyed.

She sighed: because Mia was his daughter, because she'd seen the fragility in those beautiful eyes, but mostly, mostly, because she'd destroyed the child. Enough reasons. And this young woman who sat beside her, struggling now to manoeuvre the large jeep in the wake of the trundling van, this woman into whose ear she'd poured the misery of months as though they'd known each other all their lives, the unexpected balm of friendship, the comfort of it wrapping her in a warm cloak.

'I'll try. I don't think it'll do much good, but—.'

'Thank you.' Babo's tone was odd. Emma looked at her, surprised. Was it possible she was crying?

'You're funny, y'know that?' Babo's laugh was muffled. 'You take ages to answer a question, me, I speak off the top of my head. Mia ... matters a lot to me, more than—. I'm grateful.' She turned the jeep towards the sea, a vast expanse of stippled ore in the low sun. Or night soil, Emma suddenly thought, pure liquid night soil lapping at the white city, all it would take was one storm, a tidal wave that would savage the shark nets, the sand booster stations, smothering stuccoed lives as it had smothered townships, the remorseless urge of chaos, deaf-mute and godless. And vengeful. Treat me like a jackal, and someday, when I'm weary of scratching in a lean desert, I will devour you.

'When'll he be back?'

'Tonight, I'd imagine — the clinic'll be moving on, he can get a lift part-way. He has a car here as well, he mayn't need the jeep immediately, he often leaves it with me for a few days, I'll try phoning him when we get back.'

'You think he'll come, what I mean is, he knows I'm here, I don't think—.'

'Are you kidding? If it's about Mia, wild horses won't keep him away.'

'Then get him to come as soon as possible, I, I'd rather get it over with.' Emma pulled on her fingers the way she'd often done as a child, cracking them one by one. The sooner the better. Coming from her, she couldn't see it making any difference, but then, Babo had failed also. She at least had to try, that much she owed him.

II

But they were too late. Thulatu didn't return until two days later, early enough in the morning for him to consider going directly to see his daughter. He glanced at his watch. Ten o'clock. Late enough to ensure she'd be alone, early enough to catch her at home, Babo had said she never went out before eleven. He stopped long enough at his apartment to shower and change, then, checking neither his post nor his answering service, he collected his car keys from the writing bureau in the hall and took the elevator to the basement car park. The last time, using Babo as cover had been sufficient to offset the problems of the guard dog and the heavy iron gates. This time, if Mia refused to see him, he'd climb the gates and brave the Rottweiler.

He had more luck than he bargained on. The gates were open. As though he were expected. He drove in without pausing to ring the bell, the heavy scent of cut grass filtering through the air vents.

He frowned. Perhaps she'd just gone out, Babo hadn't seen her all that much recently, perhaps her habits had changed? Rounding the curve, the car skidded slightly, the left wheel shuddering against the grass verge. Just in time. He hissed with relief, his gaze registering the slim blue outline of his daughter beside a sports Mercedes, her hand arrested in mid-motion as it stretched towards the door handle. She stood transfixed, a small, marble statue as he swung his car to a halt in front of hers. For a moment he sat, unable to move. This creature, this skin changeling, spawn of his blood, his child, his now to be claimed as he should have done all those years ago. By the time he felt calm enough to climb out, she was already rushing to the hall door. He followed her quickly, the dark panelling thudding against the pastel wall as she hurried inwards. She stopped suddenly, throwing open the door to the room he'd been in before. 'In there!' The words were bitten off, flung across her shoulder as she hurried to the end of the long hall.

He strode across the carpet into the drawing room, her voice carrying back to him as she told Elijah she wasn't to be disturbed.

He wandered the room, nervous despite himself, turning to face her as she entered, the door slamming shut behind her.

'Why're you doing this? Why? Why've you come?' She stared at him, wishing she'd stayed at the fashion show, if only she hadn't come home again to change, sweet Jesus she'd run straight into his little trap, he must have known her movements, known the gate would be open, he was watching her, people would notice him hanging round, begin to ask questions.

'If you were seen—.' She raised her arm in a sweeping gesture. 'This is a white area. A black spot for—.'

'Blacks? Coloureds?' Thulatu snorted. 'Ironic, isn't it?'

'It's against the law.'

Looking at her, the wide eyes flashing, he couldn't help himself. 'You're beautiful,' he said quietly. 'Like your mother.'

'It's against the law.'

'Law? With racism written in every line?' He paused, struggling for control. 'Looking at you it's as though she never died.'

Mia stared at him. Why, why was he doing this? She watched him reach inside his jacket.

'I've got an old photograph—.'

Raising her hands, she fended him off. 'I don't want to see it!'

'Your mother—.'

'She's dead. Dead! I don't want to know.' Turning, she moved to the window. 'Please go now.'

Thulatu stared at the rigid tilt of her back. 'We have to talk.'

'No!' She hurled the word across her shoulder. 'You've said all there was, the last time.'

'I'd like to ... to know you.'

She turned swiftly. 'You're insane!'

'We're father and—.'

Her hands flew to cover her ears, pressing painfully against the small gold studs. 'We're nothing!' She gulped for air, suddenly seeing it. 'An old photograph? What's this? Money? Is that what you're after?'

'You insult me.'

'You expect me to believe you have feelings?'

'I want to get to know you.'

'I want to forget you, don't you know that?'

'You've had time to ... adjust—.'

'Photograph.' She laughed, the sound ringing in the silence. 'And I'm the negative.' She roamed about, seeking some way she could escape. But the room hemmed her in, the walls tight with conspiracy.

'I've lost my son.' Thulatu's voice was hard.

'I'll lose mine!'

'You're all I have—.'

She swivelled, burning. 'How dare you, dare you say that! You've ignored me for thirty-six years, if your son hadn't died—.'

'It was wrong, I know.' Thulatu passed a hand across his eyes, surprised to find it trembling. 'But your mother married Paul. It was all arranged. You were swaddled in a white cradle, behind my back,

145

need I say it?' He paused a moment, fighting for control. 'I loved her, despite what she did. I, I couldn't speak out, it would have destroyed her.' He moved to the window, not wanting her to see how the humiliation still moved in him. 'In the end, I agreed to the deception. Oh, she knew I would, knew me too well!' He screwed up his eyes against the glare of the lawn, unwilling to lay himself bare. How could he speak of the pulp he'd been in her mother's hands? He grimaced at the swaying palms outside. The thwarted bole of a baobab tree would've had more steel in its tender core. No, he couldn't be that scrupulous with her, she despised him enough already. 'I kept in touch, though. When I saw Paul at the clinic, I'd ask about you, I even tried to see you. Many times.' He made a short disgusted noise. 'He always fobbed me off. Eventually, I ...' He raised a hand, the gesture futile. 'I gave up, it was too ... awkward between us.' He paused again, breathing deeply. Now he had come to it. 'I want you to tell them.'

Her face didn't change as she played with the heavy gold nugget at her throat. Had she heard him?

'What clinic?' Her voice was mild, curious, even.

'Hm?' Turning, his eyes narrowed. She was playing games.

'You said, clinic.'

'For blacks.'

'Blacks?' The painted mouth sagged, a vivid wound against the pale skin.

'Torture victims. When they're released from detention—.' He broke off, seeing again the body of his son, a broken sparrow lying in a ditch, too late for any clinic to help him. 'Like Thabo.' His voice was cold, filled with fury. 'Your black brother.'

'Paul runs this clinic?' The dark, pencil-thin brows arched, her expression that of a stunned clown.

'Funds it. He hasn't the guts—. He keeps a low profile.'

'Sweet Jesus, have I ever been told the truth! He said he was helping poor whites.'

'That too.'

She looked away from him towards the bookcase as she spoke. 'What'd you mean, you want me to tell them?'

So. She'd heard him after all. 'Your family.'

'What? What? About Paul?'

He heard the fear in her voice, steeled himself against it. 'About you.'

She moved like a blind thing towards the couch and he felt a moment's remorse.

'I, I can't tell them about Paul. A clinic for blacks? Claus would—.' She sat abruptly, as though her legs had given way.

'I want you to accept who you are.'

'No, no, I can't do it.' She shook her head, the long hair whipping her cheeks. 'Piet loves me, he loves me.'

'Then there's no problem.'

'But Claus ... Claus—. Never! It's impossible!'

He moved to sit opposite her, twisting down to catch a glimpse of her face between the swathes of hair. How could he make her understand? She mustn't turn him away, she mustn't, the last of his children, his only hope! Pleading, he held out his hands. 'I want to be able to come and see you—.'

'See me!' Her head jerked up, her mouth an ugly twist. 'You're never to set foot inside this house—.'

He rose swiftly, wincing at the hatred in her face. 'If you don't tell them, I'll have no choice—.'

There was a long pause, the room filled with the savagery of their breathing. Mia stared at her white knuckles. So that's what it was. She knew, really, deep, deep down, these last weeks, she'd had a ... dread ... chilling ... she couldn't sleep for it, and the days, fractured, running, always running from it ... from him, the snaking rustle of his suit now as he paced the room.

'It's wrong, wrong!' Thulatu turned to look down at her hunched body. 'All these years, denying my own flesh because of a promise I made to her! I want to put things right—!'

'Your son is dead, you want to use me!'

Locked in the bitterness of his memories, Thulatu hardly heard her. 'She was stubborn, so anxious to cover it up. She didn't think I knew ....' His jaw worked as he sought to get the words out, she would have no illusions about the white woman who had borne her, not by the time he had finished. 'The look on her face when she found out about you! Revulsion! Pure revulsion! I was good enough to screw around with but not good enough to father—.'

'Stop it!'

'It's time I set things right!'

'You'll destroy me!' Her voice was little more than a whisper, but Thulatu didn't hear, his own thoughts rooting in hope. 'We'll take time, get to know each other. What are any of us without our children?' Vaguely, he registered her low voice pleading, but the hope grew, even as the words burst from his lips, it would come right, he had wish enough for both of them, his need would make it possible, she'd see, in time, she'd see.

He came and hunkered down before her, his voice gentle. 'It's a godsend! I'm not saying it won't be hard on you in particular. You'll have to face your feelings about me, deal with them, but think of what we can achieve together! In the end you'll be—.'

She raised her head wearily. 'Please! Leave me alone. You'll ruin everything I have, everything I've built up—.'

'If they can't accept you as you are, then you're better off—.'

'You're doing this for spite!'

He stood abruptly. 'Oh, is that it? It seems you haven't heard a word—.'

'It's cruel, cruel.' Her eyes were wild.

'Is it any more cruel than what happened to me? May I ask? I don't want to hurt you, but—.'

'You'll do more than that.'

Her stubbornness made him angry. 'All your life you've been living a lie. So've I. So's Paul.' He moved about, his eyes sweeping the bookcases as he sought for words with which to convince her. 'It's time we stopped creeping around like guilty children. Otherwise, we've no future, this country has no future. What did Thabo die for?' He swallowed hard, his son's name alive, stirring on his lips. 'He died fighting for the right to be human. He never denied who he was, he was never afraid to face it. You're an ... an impostor in this family. If you can't face who you are, tell them who you are, then what hope have we of ever wiping out racism?'

'You'll kill me.'

'Talk to Babo. You'll see I'm right.'

'Babo.' Her voice centred on the only word she could relate to.

'She's very fond of you.'

No longer able to concentrate, she echoed him foolishly. 'Fond of you?'

'I'm rather more than fond of her myself.' He hesitated. She looked ... punished. There was so much more he wanted to say, convince her of. But it was enough for one day. If he pushed too hard, he might lose her altogether. Little by little, that was the way. 'I must go.' He waited, but she said nothing. 'You'll tell them, then?'

'You're killing me.' She stared somewhere beyond him, her tone flat, expressionless.

He sighed. Give her time, Babo had said, and he had, but it didn't seem to have made much difference. If he were to wait a year, she'd still manage to have that crucified look. He spoke stiffly. 'I'm sorry you feel like that. I don't want to ... hurt you. But you'll thank me in the end.'

'In the end.'

The words were balm. 'Good girl. Look, I'll be here, if you like. Babo, even.'

She leapt up, her eyes scorching. 'Stay away! You, you ... scum!'

He flinched, hating her. So that was the depth of it, well, he'd show her another depth, a depth she'd never dreamed of, thrust its

148

foul entrails in her face: so he was scum, was he, his son was scum, well let her see what her kind of scum did, how they devoured!

'He died ten hours after the police slung him on the side of the road!' His voice was thick with it.

Moving to the window, she kept her back to him. 'I won't listen.'

'Your black brother.'

'You're nothing to me, nothing, d'you hear?'

'Standing on a block of cement for six days, six nights.'

'Stop it!' The palms of her hands pressed against her head, the gold spikes puncturing the skin behind the lobes.

'Whenever he fell, they whipped him. When his feet became swollen, they tied him to the wall.' His voice was relentless as she whimpered.

'They worked in shifts, seven, eight hours each.'

She turned to face him, eyes beseeching. 'Please, please!'

But he was past caring, he was in a dark tunnel, no light at either end. 'Round the clock, like this.' His hand had begun to make a circular motion, slow, hypnotic. Her gaze was riveted to it as he continued. 'Just like this.'

'Just like this,' she echoed.

'Lashed with a sjambok till his skin opened.'

'... till his skin ....'

Still the hand moved. 'Wires attached to his fingertips, tongue, balls, toes—.'

She moaned. 'No more—.'

'Sprayed in the face with teargas, his face a mass of open sores—.'

'No!' She couldn't bear it, the low, dead voice, and his eyes, locked in some dark place, eaten by it.

'Thulatu's son. Born on a Monday, oppressed on a Tuesday, detained on a Wednesday, tortured on a Thursday, tortured on a Friday, tortured on a Saturday, died on a—.'

'Stop it!' Her voice was a thin scream, piercing him. Dazed, he came out of it, vaguely registering her slim shape blundering into the furniture. For a long time there was silence, the grandfather clock in the hall stabbing the hour with relentless spite. At last the final echo died, the house shrill with the absence of sound.

It was a while before he could trust himself to speak. 'I'll call next week.'

'You won't.' She stood with her back to the window, her dark outline framed in brilliance. 'I won't be here.'

He frowned. He couldn't see her face clearly, but there was something odd about her voice. Calm, he thought, it was the first time she sounded calm, almost ... detached. For some reason, it worried him more than her anger had done. He moved forward, arms instinctively outstretched. 'Try to—.'

She recoiled as though he'd struck her. 'Don't touch me! Just ... go! Go!' Her hand had closed on something soft, malleable, crushing it in the ball of her fist, if only it were his heart, she thought, the life squeezed out of it, sweet Jesus, let him leave, now, before she .... She stared down at the bunched velvet in her hand, one of the drapes, yes, the drapes, that was what she held, its rich dye blood-heavy against her skin.

It was over, over, finally. She saw it in the sudden slump, the lopped branches of his arms as they fell to his sides. For a moment he hesitated. Go! — she screamed silently turning again to the blinding eyes of the outside day. The thick whisper of his step on the carpet began to recede, an eternity of moments before she heard the door open, his voice, backwashing, lapping at her ears in a quiet rhythm. Unremitting. 'Until next week, then.'

She waited, lungs screaming for the breath snared in her throat: the self-possessed click of the door, a moment later, the small slam of the outer one, the chatter of gravel, a car starting up, wheels crunching slowly into the distance.

She breathed, her lungs drowning in the luxury of air. The velvet was ruined, creased in a random series of silver stab wounds where the thick pile had been flattened. She moved about uneasily, peering at objects, furniture that seemed different. Suddenly she stopped, eyes wild, her scalp prickling. Of course. The room was not hers! He'd taken it away from her, his dirty brown hands touching everything, infecting, it belonged to him now. Well, he couldn't have it, it was hers, hers! Elijah must clean it, everything, everything that he'd touched, but there, where he'd sat, disgusting, the mark of his buttocks, his filthy buttocks, pound the cushions, yes pound them, no, not enough, it's not enough, Elijah must have them cleaned, drag them out, out, and fling them, where was Elijah, he must do it now, now, wait, she must breathe slowly, more slowly or he wouldn't hear the words screaming in her head, then a shower, wash, wash, scrub it off before Piet could notice, or, no, no, mustn't think of Papa Claus, he could, no, mustn't think of what he could do, throw the dress away, the dirt of her hands smeared on its silk folds, Babo, Babo, she must talk to Babo, Babo would help her, talk to him, make him stop, stop him, make him stop, make him stop!

III

'He's been to see her!' Babo shook Emma awake. 'Emma? D'you hear me? He's been, the bastard, I'll kill him. Emma? For God's sake, wake up, please!'

Emma groaned, her head throbbing as though someone were lobbing cacti on the inside of her brain. Never had she been so hungover, the slightest flicker of movement excruciating. Opening her eyes took all the strength of an act of faith, nor was it rewarded. She moaned again, her parched tongue coated in fungus. 'Fuck it, never again, I swear it,' she muttered.

'Look, take these, it'll help. I'm going to try his number again. He left Mia's about half an hour ago. If he were going back to the flat, he should be there by now.' Babo held out two pills and a glass of water. Emma clutched at the glass gratefully.

'He went to see her this morning, told her if she didn't tell Piet and Claus, he'd do it, she's in bits, I could hardly get any sense out of her. The only thing which seemed to calm her down was when I promised I'd talk to him, I don't know what to do, maybe I should talk to Piet, we were close once, I don't know.'

Emma's eyes watered as she struggled to force the pills through the fur in her throat, right now, getting rid of the beast raging in her head was all she could focus on. She closed her eyes against Babo's pacing. 'I'll get up,' she said, her whole body shrieking against it as she swung her bare legs over the side of the bed. The small mesh of thread veins that had burst on her leg in the early weeks she'd carried the child, became a livid network of writhing worms. She heaved reflexively, the taste of bile in her mouth as she fought the nausea.

'You okay?' Babo's hands were on her shoulders, supporting her as she stood to make her way to the bathroom.

'Never again!' Emma whinged. 'Never, never again.' Somehow, with Babo's help, she staggered blindly out of the room, the bathroom door a tantalising smirk at the end of the long passage, each dizzying step taking her further away from it, she was walking backwards, she'd never make it, the fucking thing had moved to the other side of the world, Christ, her legs had vanished in a haze of black spots, somefuckingbody had stolen her legs, she was on her knees now, crawling, when she got her hands on that door, she'd frigging kill it, there'd be blood on the sun.

'Emma? For Jesus' sake! Answer me, will you?'

Someone was slapping her face, and water, warm thin streams of it prodding her skin. She opened her eyes. A disembodied head was talking to her. She closed them, opened them again. The head was still there. She blinked. No body. Strange, that. Another dream, there were times now when she dreamed dreams, knowing she was dreaming them.

'Emma!'

The word was a roar, exploding in her head, an urgency that cut through the vague thoughts. She opened her eyes, squeezed them tight to release the water. The shower, she was sitting on the floor of the shower, the nightshirt Babo had loaned her glued to her skin, lukewarm water raining fitfully on her sodden scalp. The head belonged to Babo, stuck through a gap in the pink curtains as the younger woman tried to keep herself dry.

' I thought you'd never come round. You okay?'

Emma nodded, wincing as the pain resounded in her head. Better to make the effort to speak.

'Look, can you manage? I've got to try Thulatu's number again, I promised Mia—.'

'Go on. I'll be fine.' She'd become a mouse, the words little more than a series of squeaks.

'Sure?'

She almost nodded again. 'Yes, honest. Go ahead.' She brought her lips back slowly, hoping it resembled a smile. Babo's head vanished. For a few moments she stared at the steamy tiles, afraid to move, her stomach churning with the gluttonous excesses of last night's binge. She dared not think about the wealth of what she'd eaten. Or drunk. Reaching, she gripped the chrome handrail, gingerly easing her body up the wet tiles until she finally stood. She began soaping herself, then realised the peculiar feel of her skin was Babo's nightshirt. Peeling it off seemed to take forever. The shower spluttered moodily. Let it last, just long enough for her to finish, the pain between her eyes was finally easing to a dull ache. She reached up to soap her head but found nothing only hard, thick stubble, a man's evening jaw-line. Her fingers scrabbled frantically. No hair.

Her hair was gone. She stared stupefied at the dew-laden roses sprouting on the steamy tiles. Christ, what'd happened last night, you couldn't lose hair the way you did a handbag, where had she been, what'd she been frigging doing?

She pressed her shaking fingers against her temples. Think, concentrate. Babo had taken her out to dinner in one of the posh, esplanade hotels and then, then, it seemed like they'd had a drink in every five-star hotel lounge in the city. Fragments of memory began to surface, a crazy patchwork of images she could make no sense of so that she was forced to go right back to the beginning, to the hotel dining-room, its succulent smells, its damasked tables precisely arranged under minute, crystal chandeliers, the prisms of light splashing on twilled linen and silver, the tanned faces of the diners, couples, young and old, some family groups, a troupe of high-spirited holiday-makers, landed Afrikaners, Babo said, from the Free State, small clusters of businessmen, jovial penguins in their dark dinner jackets, cheeks here and there spattered with the coarse flush of alcohol. 'You think we can afford this?' She'd been incredulous as they'd waited for the head waiter. Shivering too, the conditioned air piercing the silk shift Babo had loaned her.

'Sure. Since we're not paying for any of it, ah, Claude, it's good to see you again!' Babo had held out her hand regally to the tall, lean Indian holding a leather-bound wine list. 'Can you manage it?' her voice low as he bowed formally.

'Miss Babo, it's a pleasure to have you here again.' He'd winked, his own voice equally low. 'I'll do my best.' Then, louder, 'I'm afraid you're a little early, perhaps you'd both enjoy an aperitif in the bar while you browse the menu?'

And the brazen smile on Babo's face. They hadn't even booked.

All through dinner, she'd refused to answer Emma's questions. 'Eat! Eat!' she kept saying, 'you look half-starved, anything you want.'

The menu had no prices. Babo had grinned. 'Normally he gets the priced one, she, the unpriced. But since we're two ladies, that solves one problem, after all, how can we be expected to pay in such chauvinistic circumstances, stop frowning, Jesus, you're such a worrier, I'm not planning on doing a bunk, eat and enjoy!'

'Nor us ending up in the kitchen doing the dishes?'

Babo laughed. 'That neither.' She held up her hand. 'Scout's honour.'

They ate with gusto, the food alone enough to make Emma drunk, meats marinated, flambeed, or braised in alcohol, sauces spiced with burgundies, twelve-year-old malts, liquors she never knew existed.

Later, over dessert, Babo explained it.

'But won't your father mind?' Mentally Emma wrestled with converting the rand to sterling. 'That bottle of wine cost twice our ages put together.'

'Mouton-Rothschild, mark it, this one's only a child, and, as Papa would say, already the connoisseurs are rating it a prodigy,' Babo held the crystal glass up to the light, the wine blood-dark. Deliberately, she tilted it, dribbling the contents over the half-eaten chocolate souffle.

Emma was shocked.

'Oh he'll mind, yes he'll mind, but there isn't a damn thing he'll do about it, not a damn thing, I'm telling you.' She laughed, her breath caught on a sudden hiccup that stretched the sound into a nervous bleat.

Emma kept her eyes on the inches of sediment in the wine bottle as several heads turned.

'Claude'll make a point of telling him this particular bottle is gone from the cellar, he'll mind a lot more about that, he was saving that, not for himself, mark it, but he's been dying to see who's actually going to blow six hundred rand on it, that, my friend, is one of his favourite little games.'

'You come here with him often?'

'Never! That is, not since ... since Mama died.' Babo stirred the wine into the souffle, the mixture a congealed mess.

'He used to take us here about once a month, Mama, me, Piet, that was in the days when all the staff was white. But even now, he still dines here occasionally.' She tossed her hair back, trying to shake off the image of her mother, meek eyes slowly glazing to the opaqueness of wine, the exaggerated care of her mincing steps as she made her way to the powder room. The tattered dignity of it: heart-crushing. 'We'd sit all evening while he pointed out every cabinet minister, every government official, every police commissioner, who was with his wife, who wasn't, who was paying, who was on perks, who was overstepping his expenses, whose political career was about to be shredded, who knew it, who didn't, who the new pet boys were in the State Security Council, just how long they were likely to last, the Diatribe Dinners, Piet and I used to call them.'

Emma stared around at the well-fed, sun-boiled faces. 'You make this place sound like a session of parliament.'

Babo laughed. 'That's exactly what it is, a House of Assembly dining-room, only, unlike the real one, this place doesn't even pretend to admit Africans, except as employees of course, their rightful place, as Papa would say, that, mark it, isn't surprising coming from a man who—.' She broke off as a slim coloured waiter bore down on them with coffee.

Just as well, she thought, there were some things that lay too deep for dinner-table revelations. She liked Emma, liked her a lot, there was something about those big wounded eyes that was reminiscent of Mama. But the way she felt about Papa, the darkness, the incoherence of it couldn't be dredged up painlessly, and this, she determined as she told the waiter to bring her the bill, was going to be a painless evening, tomorrow, when the haze of alcohol had faded, she'd go back to worrying about Mia.

As the waiter left, she found Emma looking at her expectantly. What, what had she been saying? Yes, yes, something about her father, keep it simple, what Papa was on the outside, it'd be sufficient. She leaned forward, pouring the coffee for both of them. 'Look, the kind of man my father is ....' She frowned at the gleaming silver pot, her face a soft blur through the ornamental carvings. 'When the House of Assembly dining room opened its doors to non-whites, that is, members of the Indian and Coloured tri-cameral—.' She snorted. 'Parliament! — a euphemism, if ever there was one. Anyway. Papa ensured that the first Indian daring to cross those doors, walked out an hour later with the same empty stomach on which he'd entered. My father, need I say it, is what's commonly known as a racist.' Her tone was bitter.

'Your father's in the government?' Emma swirled the last of her wine.

Babo blew on the steaming coffee. 'My father's a chameleon, the face any president wears, Botha, de Klerk, it doesn't matter which, he's the pen between their fingers, he and Steyn—.' She made a small slurping sound as she sipped. 'Thick as murdering thieves, if you'll pardon the truth. Weird, isn't it, the way most cliches, hackneyed though they be, happen to be truths?'

'What happens now?' Emma eyed the folded bill and pen on the plate the waiter had discreetly placed at Babo's elbow.

Babo picked up the pen. 'Nothing to worry about, I'm telling you.' Her eyes skidded over the charges to the total. Emma watched the tight little smile about her lips as she signed her name with a flourish.

'I haven't done this in a long time, it should get right up Papa's nose, all the way to the back of his head.' Babo laughed.

'Why do you hate him?'

'Hate?' Babo chewed on the word, her gaze searching the ornate frieze decorating the high-ceilinged room. 'Hm, I'm not sure that's the right word.' She looked at Emma. 'Listen.' Her eyes darkened, hard slivers of sapphire in the cold setting of her face. 'I'm not sure there's a word for the way I feel about Papa.' She jumped up, almost overturning the Jacobean chair. 'Come on, this place gives me the creeps, besides,' she made a face, her mouth a small sickle curving downwards, 'there's lots more I want to show you.'

Emma rose. 'Where're we going now?' The words were fuzzed with alcohol.

'Slumming.' Babo grinned.

'What if Thulatu comes back?'

'Even if he does, it's too late for him to go anywhere tonight. And once he gets my message, he'll come see me first, probably in the morning. We're safe enough.' She grinned, patting her bloated stomach. 'Pure piggery, c'mon, let's walk some of it off.'

On their way through the bustling foyer, they again passed the large sign prominently displayed inside the revolving doors. Babo bowed at the classic script, her hands joined in an obsequious gesture. 'You know best, oh great white father,' she told the sign, her tone loud and solemn. Several heads turned. Emma didn't know whether to be embarrassed or laugh. She took Babo's arm, pulling her away. 'We're blocking the entrance, come on.'

'Don't y'think we should thank the management first? I wonder how many skin tones they reserved the right to turn away tonight because so many of us little white monkeys just had to be fed? Y'know, that sign went up the day before the government announced that five-star monstrosities would be open to all races, mark it, the day before. You ever read the small print on some of the tourist information brochures? Well, don't forget to. It'll give you plenty of warnings about small or out of the way hotels where you'll find "entrance may be reserved"!' She raised her voice even more, pointing at the sign. 'Imagine all of them ... having the nerve to print it ... in black and white!' She hooted with laughter, making a great show of dabbing her eyes.

'Go on.' Emma pushed her firmly into one of the slowly revolving spaces, anxious to be out of range of the frowns and scowls they were attracting. Christ, she should have been an actress, she thought, or perhaps it was the drink, or her youth, or both, she had to be at least a good ten years younger, what had she been like herself then? — it seemed light years away. Irretrievable.

When they emerged on the steps leading to the pavement, she shivered, glad of the light jacket Babo had loaned her, the sea-breeze an invigorating tang in her nostrils. A limousine was parked directly below them, the chauffeur a wizened dwarf in its monstrous shadow as he watched the entrance, his eyes black pools of boredom, patience, a submission that was old as the slow haul of centuries in the dark inalienable face. Beyond him, people were strolling through the beachfront gardens, the spray of fountains molten in the low sun before the murmuring quiet of the pedestrianised promenade.

'Let's go, we've a lot of ground to cover.' Babo danced down the steps, Emma moving more slowly in her wake. 'Hah, wait, there's something I want to show you first.' Taking Emma's arm, she propelled her along the stuccoed facade. They turned into a narrow dusky alley flanking the hotel.

'Now then, mark it, this is how people like Claude used to enter and leave their place of employment not so long ago, sweet, hah? Nowadays, it's a real collector's piece.'

Emma stared at the faded sign over the service entrance. 'For natives and dogs only,' she translated the words, thinking suddenly of Modise, the solitary vigil in his eyes. And Mambo, under-the-bed Mambo hugging the broken-handled chamber pot she'd rescued long ago from a white rubbish tip. What the fuck was she doing here on these laundered streets, stiletto-strutting in a hothouse jungle?

Her place was in the township, away from the savage calculation of that sign, the mind behind it steeped in a fetid swamp of its own making. Power-crazed. More rancid than the shit of any township privy.

'Somebody should deface it, isn't there any grafitti in this fucking city, someone ought to put the writing on the wall for them.'

Babo squeezed her arm. 'Not so loud.' She looked up into the gathering gloom. 'In one of those windows, count two across, no, three I think it is, you see that harmless pane of glass, well, smile, say cheese, or better still, Marietjie van der Merwe has dirty knickers.' She pulled Emma back towards the acute rectangle of sunset enshrining the entrance to the alley. 'The whole place is bugged, every room.'

Emma stopped abruptly as they arrived on the street, her mind racing. 'The dining room?' What had they talked about?

Babo shook her head, loose hair swathes of rippling corn in the low light. 'Claude,' she said, sliding her arm through Emma's. 'He's not there for nothing.' She laughed. 'C'mon, let me show you some other places.' She wouldn't say anything more about Claude as they clattered along the pavement saluting statuesque doormen who eyed them politely, seeing no more before they looked away than two slightly drunken white women out for a good time.

Instead she talked of the debate raging in the newspapers about whether the federated group of hotels should continue allowing the security police carte blanche in placing bugging devices in hotel rooms. She snorted. 'They're worried about the damage it's doing their business, particularly in the tourist and extra-marital lines.'

The next hotel they visited had four stars and a well-dressed 'coloured' couple brazening it out at the bar among the whites who studiously ignored them, the free leather-topped stools either side of the couple indicative of the wide berth they were receiving.

Hoisting herself up on one of the high stools, Babo was soon chatting to them, Emma smiling and nodding, wishing her tongue would stop behaving like a wedge of blubber in her mouth.

'We make a point of coming in at least once a week,' the husband was saying, 'normally, they are glad of our custom, but now, the peak season, they have no need of us ....' he shrugged, '... it's not our idea of fun, but ... we force ourselves, yes, Douvi?' He looked at his wife, a dark, pretty woman in her early forties. She smiled, strain showing in the tight lines about her painted lips as she formed the words carefully in English. 'We have children, for their sake we feel we must come, we do not want the people here should say, look, nobody comes, even they prefer to be separate, let us go back to having the law the old way.' She sighed, fingers fidgeting with a thin gold chain about her neck. 'But it is difficult.' Another sigh. 'In the beginning our friends came with us, it was a good support for all of us, but, in the end,' she gestured, her hand fluttering to land on the glass of tomato juice before her, 'it was too difficult for them, so now we come alone.'

'It is something, a step forward, progress,' the husband said, raising his glass in an amber salute to his words, but his eyes were bleak. Is it, is it? — Emma thought, looking around at the rigid postures at the bar, stone effigies with cold, shuttered faces.

Babo took her to other places, a couple of educated hotel discos and bars where it was fashionable for the races to mix, hot, smoky caves of ultra violet light that washed your whites whiter. 'Pseudo stuff,' Babo roared into Emma's ear above the blare of music. "The Lib-Lab," some of my African friends call this place, where the whites come to argue politics, to show how liberal they are, but when the bar closes, they all head back to their own areas, blacks, coloureds, Indians back in their boxes in Isipingo, Kwa Mashu and Lamontville while the whites scuttle to their Fort Knoxes, their Bereas and their nice end of Overport. Look at her, you can tell it's the first time, she'll go home telling herself what a good, brave little liberal she is, but there's no fear of her inviting him to lunch with Mama and Papa.' Babo's mouth was an ugly twist as she pointed to a white woman being led onto the minute square of dance-floor by a black, the flare of fear and excitement in her eyes as her hand fluttered to rest on his bare arm, the spice of danger, exhilarating when it was only that, when it needed no form of commitment other than this one dance in this place at this moment.

Babo stared into the flat beer already warmed by the clenched grip of her hand about the glass. She lifted it to her mouth, the texture of the glass strange against the numbness in her lips. No different to herself, since when had she become any better than that woman, Thulatu sneaking into her apartment late at night, out again before dawn, before anyone spotted and reported him? Why'd she brought Emma here? To boost her own opinion of herself? Even when she'd stayed on the farm for that awful while after Mama's death she'd never dared to invite her coloured friends from the university back for dinner. She was no better a liberal than this crowd of thrill-seekers. And now Thulatu was asking for more. Commitment. She didn't know if she had the courage to take the final step across the line.

'Le's go.' She jostled Emma's arm, spilling some of the wine Emma was holding. 'This place gives me the creeps.'

Emma peered into the blue eyes glazed as her own. 'Maybe we should call it a day, night.' She enunciated the words carefully. A wreath of smoke from somebody's cigarette drifted into her eyes and she winced against its sting.

'Jus' one more place,' Babo said, pulling her towards the exit.

The 'one more place' seemed odd for Durban, a kind of working man's pub, dark, smoky and dimly-lit, on the edge of a white area, not too far from the Indian township of Phoenix. Close enough for several Indians to come in while they were there, only to be refused service at the bar, no matter what they asked for, beer, wine, whiskey. At first the owlish bartender muttered something about not having permission, then he kept saying he was out of stock, turning away even when there was no one else to serve.

'And they say apartheid is dead,' Babo sneered, slamming her glass down on the counter as she pointed to the squad of bottles lining the bar shelves. Emma placed a warning hand on her arm. 'Keep your voice down, will you?' She glanced nervously at the group of rowdy drinkers playing darts in the corner, some of them with the close-cropped look of policemen or soldiers out of uniform. The big man who seemed to be winning was watching them, a huge, round barrel, his belt hitched under his bloated belly like a metal hoop, his open shirt strealing to his flanks, something about his demeanour disturbing, rousing her from the soporific effect of too much alcohol. She didn't know if they were being watched because of what Babo had said, or because they were women. Since they'd entered, several looks had been cast in their direction, accompanied by much sniggering, remarks in Afrikaans, the coarseness of tone defying translation.

Now, as the big man dropped the darts on the table, ignoring his friends' vociferous complaints, Emma, aware he was heading toward the bar, the thick fumes of his cigar preceding him, felt distinctly uneasy. Fuck it, they shouldn't have come here, not on their own, if they'd had less to drink, they would have seen it. If only Dick would walk in the door!

But perhaps it would be okay. She breathed again as the man sat three stools away on the curve of the counter, scratching his red beard in the mirror behind the bar, a gold Krugerrand glinting on the writhing mass of snakes tattooed on his chest. The only other customer at the counter, an elderly bald man with a pink mottled scalp, got up and left.

Babo was staring into the beer she'd just ordered. Emma nudged her. 'I think we'd better go, I've seen more'n enough.'

'Hm, think you're right, this place was one too many.' She rubbed her watering eyes. 'God, the smoke in here—.' She broke off as a thin, gangling Indian strode up to the bar, his companion, a stocky youth somewhere in his twenties, trailing him nervously.

'Two beers please,' he called after a few moments as the bartender continued wiping some glasses. The usual ritual established itself: the games' corner reduced to the soft spit of dart into elm, tsick, tsick, tsick, the relentless march of a clock; the mouse-squeak of polished glass in the bartender's hands. Otherwise, silence.

'Two beers please.' This time the voice was a little shakier, though still determined. Spidery fingers placed some money on the bar, enough, more than enough, Emma thought, suddenly depressed, all the laws in the world couldn't change this.

'Got a thirst that's cutting my throat, give me a beer, will you, maan? — more dust on the road today than I've ever seen.' The glasses jiggled on the counter as a large hand slammed against its surface. With sideways glances the two women watched: the clouded beer swirling into the glass under the pump, the steady pink hand of the barman as he waited for the snowy head to emerge, settle, the reaching of the mallet-hand for the glass, the natter of coins on the formica counter, the smug ring of the metal register, the slamming home of the drawer. Again, there was silence.

The younger of the two Indians tugged at his friend's shirt-sleeve. 'We'll go, I told you they wouldn't ....' The words were low.

But his friend stiffened, his voice louder. 'Two beers, please.'

The barman glanced towards the sound, his face feigning surprise to find the Indian still there.

'Out of beer.' He turned away.

'Wine then. Two wines.'

'No wine left.' The remark was slung across the bartender's shoulder. A hail of darts thudded simultaneously in the wood.

Emma held her breath as a sound escaped the Indian's lips, hissing in the silence. His friend tugged again at his arm. 'We'll go, it's no use—.'

'We'll have two whiskies please.' The man stared rigidly at the glass colonnade of whiskey and spirits on the shelves behind the bar.

'Out of whiskey.'

Silence. No darts, nothing. Still the man hesitated. He didn't look at the bartender. Instead, he gazed at his own whipped image in the mirror. Emma swallowed, pity stifled in the anger that surged in the sudden clenching of her fists, if she were a man, she'd ... what would she do? — she didn't have the guts to do anything. She closed her eyes, fighting the sludge of her complicity, her own shame.

'Take this, if you like, I haven't touched it.' Babo smiled, holding out her brimming glass of beer towards the man. His jaw dropped to reveal small glossy teeth nestling in the pink oyster of his mouth.

Emma saw the suspicion in his face, the quick sweep of his gaze over both of them as he tried to gauge whether it might be a trick.

'I've had more than enough, take it,' she repeated quietly. It was then Emma felt it, Babo's words devoured in the sudden thickness of silence, a pressure that seemed to grow out of the very vacuum of air in the bar, that condensed, settled like a living thing on her head, her shoulders, a living thing that breathed hatred — surely Babo too, could feel it? Emma sat petrified, her limbs dangling from the stool. How, how could Babo do it, it was madness, pure—.

'I pay for it,' the Indian said, picking up his money from the bar. 'Certainly, it cost—.'

A sudden clatter made them swivel. The long barrel of an automatic rifle leaned smirking on the counter in the subdued orbs of light over the bar, the tattooed heap tapping it briskly with one stout finger as he said to the barman, 'When thine eye offends thee, wipe out what offends thine eye, ja maan, this is your answer when you find your own place overrun by vermin.'

The younger Indian turned and fled, the bar door crashing in his wake.

'You'd better leave too,' Babo's lips hardly moved as she kept her eyes on the gun.

'And you?' The Indian was backing away, his eyes carefully averted from the two men at the bar.

Babo shook her head and turned back to Emma, her voice the merest whisper. 'Trouble.'

'Now she notices, let's get out.' Emma rubbed her sweaty palms against the cool silk on her thighs, her eyes rooted on Babo as the door rattled. The Indian was gone. About them the silence gathered, the menace tangible as Babo's stale, garlic-laced breath on her face.

'No. If we go too, they're likely to kill the Indian. As for us,' she grimaced and Emma felt something cave in her stomach. 'Don't worry, I'll sort it.' She reached, squeezing Emma's fingers in a bone-crushing grip, her eyes flicking towards the door marked 'Toilets'.

'See if there's any way out through there, then come back.'

The utter calm in Babo's face did little to reassure her.

Trembling, she slid from the stool, the floor a tightrope under her wavering feet. She made her way towards the door, eyes riveted to its scarred wooden surface, heels tick-tacking on the stone tiles. Unconsciously, under the eyes of the silent men, she fell back into an old habit, raising her hand to push back her hair in a contrived gesture of carelessness, the urge to appear unruffled, age-old, instinctual. But her fingers met only the blunt offering of Mia's handiwork. 'Butchered.' She shivered, dropping her hand quickly to turn the handle. Behind her, Babo watched. As soon as Emma had disappeared, she swung towards the big man, meeting and matching the fury in his face with her own.

'You could at least have given me the satisfaction of pouring the beer down his filthy shirt!' Her glass slammed, beer spraying in all directions.

She might as well have shot him, his mouth a wet wound beneath the bulging eyes.

'Jesus, you've no sense of timing, either of you.' She affected a yawn, then stretched slowly, deliberately, back arched, breasts straining against the silk bodice. He'd noticed her as soon as she'd stepped into the bar, she'd been aware of it, as aware of Emma's fear as her own lack of it, weird, the way she sought it out, the need to test her power against this brute, the hatred wreathing from his eyes savage as the venom in her father's veins.

'That's not the way it looked to me.' The snakes writhed a little as he adjusted his large rump on the bar stool. The eyes were still suspicious.

'Then maybe you need glasses.' Her gaze flicked to the bartender. 'That koelie was breathing over my glass, give me a fresh beer, will you?' Delicately prodding the glass with the tip of her nail, she screwed up her face. The barman nodded, eyes sympathetic as he reached automatically for a clean glass.

'That yours?' She pointed to the rifle brooding on the counter. Grasping the pump handle, the barman nodded again.

'You should use those darts, dip them in poison or something, bullets are too quick.' She laughed, turning to include the big man in her smile. He frowned, uncertain, but she saw the appetite in the narrowed eyes raking her body. Behind her, voices mumbled, gradually increasing in pitch until a desultory level of ease was reinstated, the darts once more punishing the elm.

'Are they dangerous?' Her gaze wandered the labyrinth of serpents breathing in his skin. Her laugh was low, husky. 'Someone ought to suck the poison out, seems to be enough there for a couple of hundred darts ...' you turd, she thought, you cankerous, self-serving blight. She smiled lazily, looking at him through half-closed lids, the heat spiking from her groin in radials as she saw it flare in his eyes, the carnality, the urge to violate that which she'd offered in the moist flick of her tongue across her lips.

When Emma opened the door and stepped back into the bar, she stood for a couple of moments, astounded. The tattooed ape was rubbing knees with Babo at the counter, both of them laughing uproariously, their noise drowning the dart game in progress. Emma blinked, unable to take it in, the fraught mood a nightmare she might have dreamed. The barman smiled across at her, holding up a glass half-filled with whiskey. Babo turned, grinning as she spoke in Afrikaans. 'Hey, Emma, meet Hennie, he's just bought you a double, come 'n join us.' Her hand slapped the seat of the bar stool beside her own.

'Dankie.' Emma tried a smile as she walked slowly towards the bar.

'Plesier.' The man waved an arm in a wide arc, dismissing her thanks.

'You can come back to my place,' he was saying, 'I got a big place, big enough for three of us, I can tell you, maan.' He laughed bawdily, his other arm drooped on Babo's shoulder, thick fingers proprietorially kneading the flesh that flowed into the swelling of her breast.

'Sure,' Babo said. 'But let's have one for the road.'

Emma stared at his broad hand, mesmerised. Now, she thought, now, get out of this, how the fuck do we get out of this? — he's big and mean enough to frigging kill us.

'Well?' The word was a taut whisper, Babo's brows arching as the man leaned forward to order more drinks, the stool tilting with his weight, as though it were rammed up his ass.

Emma stared at the mounds of flesh draping the stool, her voice a squeak.

'There's a dog ... big.' She shivered, seeing again the alert face of the Rottweiler padding the concrete yard. 'We'd never get past him.'

'Phone?'

'Broken.'

Babo grimaced. 'No window in the toilet?'

'Skylight, a pigeon wouldn't fit.'

Babo squeezed her hand. 'Don't worry. It's a lot better than it was.'

Oh is it, Emma thought as the tattoo turned to call one of his friends to join them.

Behind her, uneven steps approached across the tiles. Wonderful, just fucking wonderful.

The man was half-way to the bar when it happened. They seemed to come from all directions: pouring silently in the bar door, flowing through the door marked 'Toilets,' fanning out so quickly they were everywhere, some of them carrying sticks, machetes, others holding Molotov cocktails, a large group carrying lighted candles. Candles! Above the flames, something sacred quenched in the dark eyes that flickered, the silence icy as movement finally ceased, a grim, funereal procession that had reached the grave they wanted, the air choked with the scent of wax.

Emma stared. All over her body, skin stretched, rigid with a thousand tiny spines, a helpless barbican in the face of such an army.

Behind the counter, the barman was frozen, a spear pressed hard against his double chin. Then hands, dark, firm, on her shoulders, her back, her head, pushing, passing, spinning her along the line of illuminated eyes, the sting of wax congealing on her skin, the warmth of breath on her face, the sour odour of food and tobacco in unwashed mouths, here and there the pungence of after-shave, toothpaste, and out, out into the warm air, the dark sky a dishevellment of stars in the blind eyes of the dog lying contorted on the pavement. Planting her feet some distance apart, Emma tried to steady herself. There had been no time for fear. Still blinking, she heard the voice, low, urgent.

'Go, go quickly, we have no fight with you.'

Turning, she saw Babo, eyes dazed as she stared up into the face of the Indian she'd offered her beer to earlier. They stood, staring stupidly as he mouthed words, his face exasperated.

'Off! Off! Go on!' He pushed them roughly. 'Is no place to be.' He jerked his head towards the door of the bar. Suddenly, Babo's hand was on her arm and they were running, stilettos breaking into an uneven canter that echoed in the deserted street. When they got to the corner, Emma looked back. She screeched, the sound ripping through the stillness towards the dog draped across the neon sign outside the bar, his whole carcass a garish, luminescent glow, another weight to add to the nightmare, to enmesh her deeper, she would never escape it, never.

She ran blindly past shuttered shops with silent, winking signs, the begrimed windows of late-night cafes staring into the night, the pulse of music from a basement humming in the concrete beneath her feet, Babo's voice somewhere behind, a protest in her ears as she fought to keep up. Then, miraculously, a taxi, a glossy beetle foraging in the nocturnal streets, the cool sane whiff of leather as she leaned her hot face against the upholstery in the back, the cruising comfort of it lulling her fear, Babo in the front directing him. Finally, in the distance, the floodlit facades of the hotels on Marine Parade, the hotel they'd dined in, was it really only a few hours ago? — the luxury holiday apartments folded snug as buds in dark clusters of sub-tropical growth, then away from the sea, inland, past the racecourse, through the quiet, well-behaved streets she was beginning to recognise close to Babo's apartment.

Back in the flat they were silent for a while, sipping the brandy Babo had poured, the warmth eating into their limbs, the lamplight skirting the shadows in the cluttered living room.

'I'm sorry,' Babo said eventually, 'I seem to have done nothing but get you into my messes.' She laughed, the sound toneless as she topped up their drinks. The pain in her eyes made Emma look away. All the pent-up fury she felt at the younger woman's foolishness died on her lips. Instead, she found herself saying, 'You have courage.' The words, tinged with admiration, surprised her almost as much as they did Babo.

'You've got to be kidding!'

Emma shook her head, seeing again the men in the bar: in her unwillingness to help the Indian, she'd been only one step behind those men, hugging her shame like a second skin. She raised her glass. 'To courage.' She hiccupped, half-choking on the burning liquid, some of it backfiring into her nose. Babo threw her a box of tissues.

'That wasn't courage, Emma, it was sheer lunacy.' The words drifted uneasily about the quiet room.

'You got any cigarettes?' Emma had a sudden craving.

Babo pointed to a shelf above the couch. 'There's some in a pack, matches too, but they've been there ... a long time.' She watched Emma drag herself from the depths of the couch, her arm swinging like a scythe, narrowly missing the large framed photo of her mother as she reached for the packet.

'They belong to ... a friend of mine.' She swilled the brandy in her glass, her knuckles white. 'He was detained.'

Emma, cigarette half-way to her lips, stopped in mid-motion. 'You mean, he's still in prison?'

'I'm not even sure he's still alive.' Babo drained her glass. She nodded at the cigarette packet, her eyes bleak. 'Suppose you could say I keep them in loving memory.' She lifted the brandy bottle. 'Either way.'

Emma stared at the cigarette.

'Smoke it, for God's sake.' Babo topped up both glasses. 'If Thulatu knew, he'd have my guts.'

'Knew what?' Emma lit the cigarette, the smoke wreathing from the tobacco, like a life, she thought, burned up, burned out, dissipating, thinning into the very air that once sustained it. What could she know of his life, this man whose stale cigarette she smoked, or this woman with bitter eyes focussed on a horizon she'd never been forced to contemplate?

'Knew what?' she asked again, a languorous stupor invading her body as she drew deeply on the cigarette.

'About tonight.'

Emma shrugged, draining her glass, her tongue wedging itself between her teeth. 'Whassit to him?'

'He wants you in one piece for the demonstration. Me too.'

Emma sat down abruptly, the answer disappointing her. Leaning over, she reached towards the bottle on the carpet beside Babo, the room oscillating in a confusion of flying books, paintings, orbiting lampshades.

'Ah, sod him, who gives a fuck.' She blinked, focussing carefully on Babo's startled face. Suddenly, they were both laughing, a teetering sound born of the need for release.

'Tell me,' Emma wiped the tears from her eyes, 'just tell me, will you, how you were planning on getting away from, from ... whassisname, "Sssnakes Alive"?'

Babo choked, the brandy spraying in spluttering jets from her sucked-in lips.

Emma doubled up with laughter, and fell off the couch. 'Your mouth,' she gasped, 'puckered ... like a duck's ass.' Her nostrils quivered as she registered something burning. Her hair, her frigging hair, the cigarette was singeing it.

Babo, still heaving for breath, wagged a finger. 'You stop knocking my man, you'd want to've seen the little white monkey that was coming up behind you, no, mark it, it isn't every woman who's given the chance to go to bed with Percy Python.'

'And Adam Adder, and Randy Rattler and—.' Emma giggled, struggling to her knees, dusting away the singed hairs as she peered to find the ashtray.

'You're jus' jealous 'cos he didn't fancy you. Y'want to know what he said when you were outside?' Babo gestured as though the door in the bar marked 'Toilets,' was somewhere just beyond the photo of her mother. 'He said he thought your hairstyle was really freaky.' They collapsed on the floor, unable to stem the tears of mirth that rolled freely, poking fun at the dark underbelly of the night, a conspiracy of silence about that which was uppermost in their minds: what the Indians had done after they'd left the scene, neither of them would mention it ever, neither would look through the next morning's papers, neither needed verification of what they already knew in their bones, the silent witness they'd been to the hatred that stripped civility to its brute core.

Really freaky, all, all of it, Emma thought as she stepped now from the shower into the wreaths of mist swirling in the bathroom. Babo had forgotten to switch on the extractor fan. She flicked the switch and the noise ate into her throbbing head like a greedy vacuum cleaner.

Freaky. She touched her bare scalp, seeing again the drunken hysterics of the night before, both of them vying to put the finishing touches to Mia's handiwork, their laughter squealing with every snap of the scissors, the short hairs dusting her shoulders as each pair of staggering hands tried to match the length of growth remaining on the other side of her head.

Eyes closed, she wiped the steam from the mirror, stepping out of its line of vision. Not yet. She wasn't able to face it yet. Sitting on the edge of the bath, she patted her skin, reluctant to finish, face herself in the glass, face herself in Thulatu's eyes when he arrived.

Raising her shoulders, she dried the underswell of her breasts. Aware of a vague need for comfort, she fondled them, brushing her fingertips across the nipples, watching them peak. Responsive as a leaf to the wind. Yet there was no desire, nothing but the ache of emptiness in watching that response, old as the instinct in a tiny, suckling mouth. What'd she done, what the fuck had she done?

Her breasts wavered, bloating through the tears that wept across the darkened aureoles like the first sweet release of milk. Stupid. Stupid thoughts. She stood, wrapping the towel about her, tucking the corner into the shadowy cleavage. Stupid. Even if she'd kept the child, she'd never have breast-fed, who was she trying to fool, what kind of fucking guilt was she trying to dredge up now to whip herself with, this nostalgic yearning for the fulfillment of a wish she'd never had, the only mouth she'd ever wanted against her breasts had been Thulatu's, Christ, she'd go crazy, think of something else, no, not the night before, too many things there best left unexplored, the jeep, where had they left the jeep, somewhere, at a hotel, or perhaps in one of the university car parks after she'd registered for the series of lectures on Geophysics? She couldn't remember. And still they hadn't managed to contact Thulatu, though now it was too late.

She sidled across to the edge of the mirror, easing her face into its reflection. Opening one eye, she squinted through a blur of lashes, please let it not be as bad as it felt, let touch be deceptive. Difficult to see anything clearly this way, a darkness about the half-moon of her head suggestive of hair, perhaps it would be all right, open your eyes, look properly, move directly in front of the mirror, ah Christ no, let it not be true, an open-mouthed alien gaping from the mirror, a creature she might never've seen before. She stared at the oddly spherical shape of the head, the bluish coating of stubble, no half-measures there: a living, breathing disaster, let it not be real. Bald as a coot, whatever that was. Ludicrous. She stood, the moments stretching into days, her eyes huge dark orbs magnified by the absence of hair. A wig, maybe she could wear a wig — in the township heat? Never.

She stumbled out of the steamy room, the conditioned air in the passage chilly about her head, don't think about it, just don't think, get dressed, be ready in case he comes.

She searched through the bundle of khaki clothing Babo had given her, choosing a light cotton shirt and shorts, as least she'd be cool when she met him. When he came. No sooner was the thought born than she heard him arrive, her skin bristling as his low voice penetrated the bedroom wall. She went to the mirror, her head throbbing viciously at the speed of her movements. Please let it go well, let something be salvaged. Automatically, she reached for the hairbrush, then froze, hand in mid-air. Instead, she applied a little of the lipstick she'd used the previous night, staring hard at her reflection.

Freaky, all her features acutely defined, as though they'd mushroomed to offset the foetal dimensions of her skull. She grimaced, her mouth a scarlet slash in the pallor of her skin — if only she hadn't drunk so much.

IV

She found them in the living room, the walls rigid with their anger as they stood staring through the balcony window towards the distant glare of the sea, the sun prodding spiteful fingers into every dusty niche and corner. So. Babo had had no success. She waited, squinting against the light. They didn't turn round.

'I, I'm here,' she said, feeling stupid.

They both swivelled, the precision-timing of mechanical figurines in a clock that had just struck the hour. Emma tried to swallow, the membrane in her throat a stodgy self-adhesive that sealed off speech. She stood, cracking her fingers, unable to gauge his expression.

He stepped forward, his stunned face emerging swiftly from the light, eyes bulging as he took in her appearance.

'What's this?' he snorted. 'Some kind of joke?' He glanced at Babo. 'Just what're you two up to, may I ask?'

Babo moved across the room, her foot clinking against the empty brandy bottle. It rolled towards a stack of books on the floor beside the couch. Looking at Emma, she lifted her hands in a helpless gesture. 'I can't get through to him.'

'Make some coffee, will you?' Emma's eyes pleaded as she staggered to the couch.

'Isn't anyone going to enlighten me?' Thulatu folded his arms, the dark patina of his skin flexed against the short-sleeved shirt.

'About what?' Emma lowered herself carefully as Babo left the room.

'About what. A couple of days in Durban and you look like a bald-headed ibis, just what are you playing at? If you're trying to get yourself noticed, you're going the right way about it.'

'I hardly did it to make you notice me.'

'Me?' Dark brows arched in a sneer under the wings of hair. 'There's no fear of that. I simply meant you'd stick out like a sore thumb at next week's demonstration.'

'Well, don't worry, I'll wear an Afro wig, I'll blacken my skin with boot polish, I'll—.' She swallowed, trying to control it.

None of this would help Mia.

'I'll think of something, a scarf, maybe,' she said more quietly, resisting the urge to touch her scalp. 'Babo took me to meet ... your daughter.'

'She'd no right, I told her, no right whatsoever.' He prowled the room, lifting ornaments, books at random.

'She's not ... very well ... your daughter, couldn't you—?'

Turning, he pointed at her, his arm a ramrod. 'You stay out of it, it does not concern you!'

'Thulatu, please, listen to me, she—.'

'Stay out of it!' His fist slammed the plate glass of the French window. The view shivered in its frame.

'Please, just give her time to—.'

'I said stay out of it!' His narrowed eyes were shards of flint.

She rose, determined to make him see it. 'What you're doing is wrong.'

'Wrong!' The word spewed, his jaw working as he fought for control. The couch nudged her trembling calves as she swayed and leaned back, glad of its support.

'Oh, and who are you to be the judge of that?' He thrust his hands deep in the pockets of the light slacks.

'She needs to see someone, a—.'

'You dare to talk to me of what is right or wrong, you dare!'

'She's ... it can't be easy in this country, finding out you've got mixed blood, a thing like that takes getting used to ... it must hurt a great—.'

'Hurt? Oh, yes, you'd know all about that, wouldn't you?' He rushed at her so quickly that she shrank.

'Yes, you'd know about that!' His fingers gripped her face, the pressure on her jaw relentless, his musky scent thick in her nostrils. 'You're an expert when it comes to that, when it comes to pain.'

A fine spray of spittle pricked her bottom lip.

'An expert.'

She groaned, pain radiating across her face, fusing with the ache in her head. Was there ever a time when his hands had been gentle, she couldn't recall it, so far had they diverged.

'Don't do it,' she whispered. 'You'll lose her, you'll lose her altogether.'

'And that'd bother you? You cost my child its life and now you want to convince me you care about me, about my children?'

'You'll hurt her, you'll hurt yourself, can't you see?' Eyes wide, she stared up at him, his breath beating her skin.

'Oh, and what about what you did, did that hurt?' His eyes were savage. 'When the butcher cleaves, does the eel bleed? Does it writhe?'

'Nnnnnnn!' She tried to get the word out but it wouldn't leave the distortion of her lips. Instead she was snarling, wrenching her face from the vice of his hand, the sting of torn skin on her jawline as his nail caught her flesh. She swung her arm with all the will she could muster, her fist cracking against his cheek before she sank onto the couch. Where was Babo? — giving her time, too much of it, let her come now, she couldn't deal with this, out, his words must be driven from her mind before the image took root.

She lay panned against the cushions, screaming inwardly for Babo as she tried not to look at the closed eyes in the taut face, a dark welt on his skin where she'd struck, a dribble of blood thickening in the corner of his mouth. Opening his eyes, he turned, striding to the window. Out in the bay, yacht-sails were pinned to the sea like bunting. From the kitchen, spoons tinkled against porcelain. As though all were sane in a civilised world.

He stayed, hands curled by his side, ashamed of his own cruelty. Her pain was big enough. He had seen it, gorging, in her eyes. There was nothing he could inflict that'd not already been self-inflicted. Then let it be. Thabo was dead, he had room only for the pain that was Thabo, hope only for the salvation that might come to him through his daughter. His sights were aligned, there was no room for peripheral vision, for cruel games, he was too full of Thabo to accommodate it. Turning, he said, 'I can't give it to you, the sooner you realise it the better.'

She stared at him, her eyes smudged hollows below the blue-dark dome of her skull. Vaguely, somewhere beyond the pain, she registered the low rhythm of his voice but couldn't make words of what she heard. She passed a hand across her eyes. Let him go away. She needed to crawl to some place, speechless, quiet, a dank covert in which to skulk from his accusing presence.

But his voice forced her back.

'Did you hear me?' He stood, a dark tower hovering above her.

'Go away.' Somehow, the words made it past the stiffness of her lips. 'Please. Just go.'

He looked down at her face, something quenched in her eyes, beyond him, beyond even herself, the high cheekbones stabbing the stretched skin, death grimacing through the fragile mask of flesh. He saw it clearly. As terrifyingly as he had seen the grey waste of Thabo. He knuckled his eyes to blot it out.

Hunkering down, he looked in her eyes. 'There is no absolution, Emma, I have no space for it.'

She stared at him for a long time: every angle and crevice of his face, the wings of grey-black hair shorn above the neat ears pinned to the shapely head, all, all of it so often explored, an indelible map printed on her mind, as familiar a terrain as her own body. Yet he wasn't Sipho. Sipho had died with the child. Irretrievable, as the death of hope. This man in the skin of her lover had been moulded from the death of his son, he wasn't hers, never hers. In that moment, she saw it. There was nothing he could give her. Nothing. Never, never the thing that she wanted. Needed. The thing that she breathed for. Now, the voice sneered, now, look it in the teeth if you have the courage, you and your purblind heart, see it there, in his eyes, he knows it, needle-sharp gaze locked on magnetic north, fuck you, face it!

'I came to be ... forgiven.' She stared at him, shocked.

'Yes, you came for that.' He rose, moving away across the sun-streaked room, his shadow haloed in light, his form insubstantial, fading swiftly as a vision. She blinked to bring him back. But he couldn't deliver her, she couldn't deliver herself. What she had done was beyond propitiation.

'You must take responsibility.' His voice whispered to her out of the spectral light.

'Yes,' she said, the word a dull intonation. She heaved a sigh. It was over, the running, the building of facades around the why of her coming. She'd reached the place that clawed her sleep. Here she'd live in the snarl of her guilt, there could be no flight from it. No exoneration.

Vaguely she was aware of Babo's return, the steaming mug gently pressed into her hands. She sipped, welcoming the punitive scald of liquid across her tongue, on the membrane of her throat, the pain alerting her. She stared at Babo sitting beside her, registering the question-mark in her eyes, the ridges on her brow.

'I'm going back,' she said, the words distant, as though, had Babo's mouth moved, the words might have belonged to her.

Thulatu's hiss streaked across the room. 'No guts, I might have guessed!'

She sat, numbed, unwilling to take her gaze from the rippling outline of Babo through the water in her eyes. Strange that she could speak, weep from such coldness, perhaps it was Babo who wept.

But no, Babo's hand reached out to her face, wiping the wetness from her frozen skin.

'To the township.' In the silence, the air wheeled in and out of her lungs, a relentless cycle she couldn't abrogate.

'Oh, and what about the demonstration?' He turned to stare at her.

'I'll come back for it.' She looked at Babo. 'If you'll have me. There's no ... need for me to stay here in the meantime.'

Babo squeezed her shoulder, relieved to see her eyes waken. 'Of course, but you're—.'

'Very well.' Thulatu crossed his arms, eyes narrowed against the light. 'If that is what you wish. I'll book a flight for—.'

'You'll book nothing! After the demonstration, I'm going back to Rhaumsfontein. I came here to do a job and I'm not going back till it's done!'

'I told you—.'

'Fuck you, I'm done with you telling me!' Her cheeks flushed. 'You've said it all, I'll take no more, d'you hear?'

'I've enough on my mind without—.'

She rose swiftly, her thin frame bristling against his words, her breasts lifting and falling in the effort to dredge air. 'Yes, you've enough on your mind, so leave me out of it, we're finished, you've made that clear, just look on me as another white elephant, I'll keep out of your way, don't you worry on that score!'

'I brought you here, you're my responsibility!' He began pacing, his lean frame flickering through light and shade as though the room itself were shifting with the fever of his movements. It hurt her eyes.

'I came with your help, that's all. And now I'm here, I'll stay as long as I like, as least until my residence permit runs out. You can't stop me, it's a free—. ' She bit her lip.

'Country?' He stopped, his mouth twisting. 'For whites.' The words snarled in the sudden quiet.

'I might as well take advantage of it.'

He laughed, the sound crackling in her ears. 'Oh yes, take advantage of your white privilege.'

Her eyes flared. 'You don't exactly seem to suffer from underprivilege yourself. A museum of a house in England, apartments all over the place, I don't see you spending seven days a week wading through the shit in the townships!'

'You, you ...!' He sprang forward so swiftly that she flinched, grateful when Babo leapt from the couch to shield her.

172

'Enough! It's enough!' Babo's arm was outstretched, pressing against his heaving chest, the vitriol in his eyes centred beyond her, on Emma.

'Both of you, stop it, for God's sake, we're on the same side!' Sandwiched between them, the fair hair swung as she snapped from one to the other. 'On the same side, you hear?'

Emma, unaware of the grip she had on the younger woman's arm, stared past her into the fury she had stoked.

'You were right,' she said, still trembling. 'There's no absolution. But you don't have the right to punish. There's punishment enough without you ....' She dropped her hand from Babo's arm. It slapped limply against her thigh. She moved away to stand blinded in the brilliance cascading through the window. She shivered, keeping her tongue clear of her chattering teeth, the air conditioning working too efficiently, despite the sun's warmth. The sooner she was out of this the better, this cold storage city generated on hate, its gluttonous parks and gardens mulched on fear and greed. There was more grace, more integrity in the corrugated stamp of the townships.

She wouldn't speak of her need to make reparation, the only indemnity against the brute rack of the nights. For him, the thing was done, there was nothing she could do to salvage it.

'Very well. You were given six months. Do as you wish in that time. All I ask is that you cover the demonstration for us, then, if you wish to spend the rest of the time in Rhaumsfontein, Dick won't refuse your help.' The cool words prodded her back. She turned. His face was impassive as he crooked a finger to lift the light safari jacket from the back of a chair.

Babo was sitting again, tangled swathes of hair screening her face. Without looking up, she spoke, her head held in her hands. 'Will you think about what I've said?'

The jacket hooked on his middle finger, he slung it across his shoulder. He looked down at the bent head. 'It's too late for that.' Reaching down, he touched the lustrous hair fleetingly. Emma turned away, the warmth, the gentleness of his gesture spiking old needs, a mindless hatred for them both, gnawing from the slough of her own jealousy. She heard the rustle of his clothing as he left, the door closing behind him. Even as Babo spoke, the outer door banged.

'So much for that.'

Emma hardly heard her. She dug her nails into the soft flesh of her upper arms, fighting the venom that threatened to spill from her lips. Even from the depth of his grief, his rage, he could manage to spare some kindness for this woman, whereas for her, for her, there was nothing. Nothing but the black inscrutable face of—.

'Emma? Did you hear me?'

She swallowed, rearranging her features into a stiff, polite mask before she turned. Even then she wasn't able to look at Babo, staring instead at the bric-a-brac lining the shelf above the blond head.

'I'll have to go.' Babo rose, her teeth doing a jittery tap-dance. She stared at Emma's face, noticing it for the first time that morning: the livid scratch along the line of her jaw ugly as any suture, the shorn insult of the scalp, God they must have been pissed out of their minds to have done it, a zombie'd have more life, except for the ... pain in the eyes.

If she only had time ... but Mia ... if she didn't get to Mia's soon ... she'd sounded mad as a hatter on the phone, Jesus, that high-pitched note in her voice, if Piet and Claus walked in there now, she'd spill it, she wouldn't be able to stop herself, then get there, get there fast, don't leave her to deal with that pair alone, a lamb to the slaughter. She pushed her hair back, her fingers catching in the tangle. She'd better not turn up looking so dishevelled. Where'd she left the hairbrush? C'mon, quick. Where'd she left the jeep last night, think, think, if she had to catch a taxi she'd be all day, God, why didn't Emma say something?

'Listen, I'll have to go, Mia's waiting for me, I'll ... have to let her know he's going to—.' Prowling the room, she found her handbag. She dumped the contents onto a chair, finally locating a comb. 'She'll have a fit when she hears—.' She winced as the comb caught in a mesh of hair. There was a sharp ping, the metal teeth rebounding as she dragged it free.

'Emma? Please. For God's sake snap out of it, will you? I have to go to Mia's.'

Mia. Emma stared at the photo of Babo's mother, the tired eyes fixed on some injury beyond the camera. Mia. In the hateful spillage of his words, she'd forgotten his daughter entirely. Christ. Some help she'd been, feeding on her own misery and spite.

'I'm sorry.' She grimaced. 'I wasn't much use, was I?'

Babo began stuffing everything back in her bag. 'He didn't give you much chance.' She stood straight, the zip droning as she closed it. 'But, thanks for ... for trying .... I appreciated it.' She forced a smile. 'I don't know what time I'll be back, but if you feel like talking then, about ... everything—?' She raised a hand, palm upwards, as though she were testing for rain.

Emma shook her head. 'I'm going.'

'Now?' Babo stood still. 'You sure?' For a few moments she stared at Emma, taking in the line of her jaw. 'Okay.' She dropped her hand, moving to the small rosewood bureau in a corner of the room. 'There's a bus timetable in here somewhere.' Already every drawer was open as she rifled. 'Take a taxi, don't try to bus it into town, the city buses operate on a farcical colour-by-numbers timetable, it's even confusing if you've lived here all your life. From the station in Umgeni Road you'll need to take a bus to Pietermaritzburg, no, wait, there's the Greyhound inter-city, I forgot about that, the phone number's here somewhere, you'll need to change at ....' Her voice wound on as she jotted down instructions. Emma nodded, willing her to finish and go, anything, anything to be on her own, to let her features sag, to let the tears come, to wallow, to lick her wounds, to curse him, curse the feeling she bore for him even in the face of his cruelty.

Much later, when the bus was lurching through Durban, sunlight scavenging among streets thick with gardens of cannas and bougainvillaea, she thought finally of Mia, the dark torment of those eyes, and wondered what the outcome would be.

The interior of the bus was airless as a sauna, the silk scarf she'd borrowed from Babo sticking to her scalp, the urge to scratch reminding her of lice. Christ, if only she were back in Rhaumsfontein, at least then she could remove it. Yes, the voice taunted, it won't matter there will it, it won't matter who sees, who are these people after all, blacks, just blacks and coloureds, who gives a shit what they think of your appearance? Now the nice white clientele on this bus, with their shopping bags, newspapers, their polite smiles, they're the ones, these skin comrades, they're the ones in whose eyes you need to be favourably reflected, so keep your scarf glued to your scalp, tied in a civilised knot under your chin. And sweat.

For a moment she struggled with it. But the voice was conscience, she knew it now. Either she submitted to its natural law, its iron imperative, or she'd wither.

Gingerly, she raised her hand to her chin, untying the knot, the faint whisper of insects scratching in grass as the silk slid from her unshaven scalp to her shoulders. There was little more than a handful of passengers scattered among the neat rows of seats, but she stared hard through the window, wishing she'd taken the cab Babo had suggested, the heat burning in her cheeks as she sensed the sly rustles that spoke of surreptitious glances, curiosity ill-concealed in the garb of courtesy, a hundred practised little manoeuvres endlessly repeated, they'd have done better to stare at her outright, drink their fill in one gulping glance.

She kept her eyes fixed on the street, the car park and shopping centre opposite a begrimed blur through the glass as the bus belched uphill towards a red light.

When the blast came, it seemed to shudder from the ground beneath them. For an instant, everything was frozen, silent. Even the engine had cut out. Then the barrage came as they began to roll backwards, shards of flying glass, slivers of stone, brick, a mad staccato erupting in her face. Instinctively, she swerved from the window's hailstorm, raising her hands to protect her eyes. She tensed, anticipating the stab of glass embedding itself in flesh, but nothing happened. Miraculously, the window held. Still they were rolling downhill, metal bodywork whining under the barrage, the glass at her ear a deafening protest. Somebody was screaming. Two men were hauling simultaneously at the brake lever, a third man climbing over the dazed driver to get to the controls. Suddenly the engine wailed to life, and the bus lurched forward as he rammed the gears. He drove as though demented up the hill, careening to avoid the worst of the debris, tyres chewing glass as the storm eased. Still he didn't stop. At the intersection, the traffic lights loomed dead-eyed through the pall of dust. He drove straight through without pausing to look in either direction. Emma closed her eyes. For the first time since the blast, her mind began to thaw, register the shocked voices around her, the rapid speech defying her limited knowledge of Afrikaans.

'I was going shopping in Overport, I was going shopping there today,' one distraught woman kept repeating.

'Black bastards! Fucking terrorists! They don't care who they kill, it's always the same this time of year, they know they'll hit the tourist trade, d'you know what they're calling this place now? — DurBOOM, fucking animals, they should be ....' The rest was lost on Emma.

A small wiry man with a crew cut was talking above everybody, eyes feverish in his flushed face. 'Did you see those steel girders? — like broken matchsticks. A big one, maan, really big, two hundred pounds at least, I'm in the army, I know these things, you can tell if it's big by the noise, that one ...' he continued talking, hands over his ears, his wincing face a dramatic reconstruction of the decibel level.

Finally the driver stopped the bus. Emma got out, the ground heaving beneath her. She stared at the side of the bus, blinking in disbelief. What had she expected? Twisted metal, raw and exposed in the absence of paintwork? She wasn't sure. But it seemed incredible that the bus, apart from a network of minuscule scars and scratches, should be so totally intact. She shivered. It had been horror enough at this distance. Christ help those who'd been up close.

Chapter Six

I

Propped in bed against a mountain of satin, Mia kept flicking the remote control, the television a kaleidoscope of images returning her always to the scene of the explosion: the gutted shops, the random spillage of flesh among the debris, the keening of ambulance and police sirens, too late, too late.

She looked at the wrecked pram, its wheel still spinning as the cameraman dove through the labyrinth of twisted steel, the picture stumbling with his jerky progress.

She switched it off, taking with her the image of the white woman sitting amidst the rubble and glass, a pool of glossy red apples at her feet as she clasped the limp, blood-smeared child to her breasts, rocking backwards and forwards, her dazed eyes streaked with pain.

And shock. Mia stared at the dead screen, her own image distorted in its depths. Sweet Jesus why didn't Babo come, yes shock, what else could you call it when they sneaked up behind you, thieves in the night, murderers, filthy animals wanting to devour you, click-ticking tongues spitting poison, promising to tear you limb from limb, their wives serving you with a polite smile in the shops while all the time their husbands and sons crawled about the underbelly of your car, planting their blasphemies, clawing with their pink-tipped paws until they'd mauled your life, until there was no life worth its breath, sweet Jesus what was keeping Babo, let her persuade him, please, let him not come again, his words a fuse exploding in her ears, what was that, a noise, someone coming, voices, let it be Babo, please, please, eyes on the panelled door, will it, will it to be true.

She jerked upright, the pillows sliding in an avalanche behind her back as Babo entered the bedroom.

'Well?' The word sprang from her lips before she'd time to register Babo's face.

'I'm sorry I took so long, the bomb, there was a diversion—.'

'What'd he say?' She needn't have asked. It was there in the younger woman's face as she came to sit on the bed.

Babo reached to hold the erratic hands plucking the sheet. 'I talked to him for hours. Hours!' She bit her lower lip, not knowing how to say it.

Mia stared past her, eyes unseeing. Oh she'd known, deep in the brute heart of hearts. 'Mia, you're a fool.' The words were little more than a whisper.

'He wouldn't budge, no matter what I said—. I tried, I really tried—.'

'Deep down, I knew. He wants to destroy me. For spite.'

'Mia, no! Thulatu's not like that. If I thought that—.' Babo shook her head, hair flapping. 'No. It's just Thabo's death has him knocked ... sideways. You don't know what Thabo meant to him.'

Mia wrenched her hands free. 'Does he care what Piet means to me?'

Babo tried to put some conviction in her voice. 'He loves you. He should stick by you.'

Mia's laugh grated. 'What Piet should do and what he's capable of doing—. You, of all people know him.'

'It might be the making of him.'

'It'll break me.' Mia's hands assaulted the sheet. 'Oh where will it end?' She paused, her breathing heavy, uneven. 'I know where. I can feel it coming—.' No, she wouldn't talk, wouldn't think, about that. 'When is he going to—?' She swallowed, unable to bring herself to finish.

'I don't know. The protest's the end of next week. Sometime after that, I suppose.'

'Couldn't we stop him?'

'How? All he's got to do is phone Piet. Or Claus.'

'Claus.' Mia twisted the sheet into a tight knot. 'I'm so afraid, Babo.'

'Look, I'll be here, I promise. I'll stay with you—.'

'Not knowing which day, waiting, waiting, oh, I'll go mad! I really thought there might be a chance, he said he was fond of you.' She started as the door opened, relieved to find it was only Paul, bald patches glistening as he mopped the sweat from his face. For a moment, nobody spoke, the silence between the three of them awkward with the weight of his embarrassment.

'W-what happened?' His gaze sheered away from his daughter's ravaged face.

Babo grimaced. 'No dice.'

Mia leaned forward, hands outstretched, a sudden hope spiking from the familiarity of his presence. 'You must talk to him, you know him a lot longer than Babo, a lot better. He'd listen to you, I know he would.'

Her words panicked him. 'If he wouldn't do it for the woman he's ... for the woman he loves—.'

'Tell him it's really made me ill. Even if he put it off for a while, yes, that's it, put if off, just to give me breathing space, then I can think what to do ....' She trailed off, eyes suddenly widening. 'The woman he loves?' She looked at Babo's hot face, waiting, unwilling to think further than the denial which would surely burst from Babo's lips in the sudden tight silence. Surely?

'We, I ...' Babo felt the colour pulse in her cheeks as she turned to face Paul. Goddamn him, he'd done it deliberately! 'Did you have to say that?'

Paul shuffled his feet, the sound whispering in the thick pile of the carpet. 'I, I thought you'd have told her—.'

'What?' The fear in Mia's voice prodded his anger as he stared at Babo, his eyes cold. 'You've never exactly tried to hide your taste in that ... kind of man.'

'You mean you—. Not him! Please, Babo, not him!' Mia pressed her palms against her face. Sweet Jesus, let it not be true. She waited, stiff with it. But there was no denial in her sister-in-law's shifting eyes. Vile, it was vile. Her mouth twisted. 'How could you! He's ....'

Babo's voice was quiet. 'Old enough to be—.'

'He's nothing to me, nothing! He's black!' The word spat, a deformity on her lips.

'More off-white, I thought.' Babo breathed deeply.

'It's disgusting! How can you, with someone like ....'

Her eyes, Babo thought, rabid as any dyed-in-the-wool racist, as though Thulatu were filth, as though she were filth. Not because he was her father, but because he was black, God it would be funny if it weren't so sick. 'And what about your mother? For God's sake Mia, where d'you think you came from? Under a cabbage plant?' It was as though she'd struck her. Instantly, she was sorry.

'There's n-no need—.' Paul stepped forward.

Babo leapt up. 'You keep out of it! If it wasn't for you—.'

'Go, go away, Babo.'

The tired voice wrenched her back to it. 'Oh Mia, don't. I'm sorry. There's been so much happening, I didn't think about how you might feel—.'

'Just leave me alone.' The face was pinched, a fragile control in the thin crack of the mouth.

Babo stared, the silence between them thickening to a vast forest. Impenetrable. What'd she done? She'd come to help, instead of which she'd driven a wedge between them. She'd better go, now, before she destroyed it altogether, she couldn't bear it, the grim accusal in Mia's eyes, as though somehow she'd betrayed her. Had she betrayed her?

'I'll call you later. We'll talk.' She tried to keep her voice steady.

'I'll be asleep.' Mia's fingers twittered to the seal at her throat as she stared at the crumpled sheet.

Babo hesitated. 'In the morning then.' She paused, her voice crumbling in her own ears. 'I'll ... I'll call in the morning.'

'I'll be asleep.' Still Mia didn't look up.

Babo stretched out her hands. 'Look, I'm—.'

'Just leave it for a while, will you? I need to think.' Mia's arm was raised, a rigid barrier against any kind of intrusion.

'I'll call anyway, see how you are.' She chewed her bottom lip, hardly registering the salty tang in her mouth when she bit too hard. 'You'll call me if you need to talk?' The silence was killing, but she was loathe to leave without some kind of gesture from Mia. 'Promise me?' Her voice was a whispered plea.

Finally, Mia inclined her head, the gesture so slight, had Babo blinked, she might have missed it. But it was enough to raise her hopes.

'I'll come anytime you want.' She hesitated, then moved towards the bed. 'We'll sort things out, don't worry.' Leaning, she pecked the unresponsive cheek. Cold, so cold. She shivered, moving towards the door. What had she done? 'Don't worry, don't worry.' The words jabbered, empty as a parrot's refrain. She stood for a moment, unable to look again at the bed.

Mia stared at the bunched sheet in her fists, willing her to go. The longer Babo stayed, the harder it was to rearrange her mind, erase the vile image she had conjured, oh how she'd been ... betrayed, the blasphemy of it! She held her breath as Babo finally left, the door closing quietly behind her. At last. Mia sagged against the pillows. 'We'll sort it out.' Babo's words drummed in her head.

'Yes,' she said, her eyes fixed on the dark oak panelling. 'I'll sort it out. My way. I should've seen that from the start.'

Paul's gaze followed hers to the door, half-expecting to see someone standing there.

'At least I'll have control over how and when, that's something, isn't it?' She turned, making him jump. He stared into the fever-bright eyes, remorse thudding in the depths of his stomach. He spoke quickly, afraid to analyse it.

'I'll h-help you, I'll be here for you, no matter what happens. God knows, I've done little enough—.'

'That's right.'

Her icy tone cut him. He didn't know what to say.

'Both of you, patting me on the back, telling me not to worry. Avoiding the issue like the plague. Well, it is a plague, I'll grant you. Neither of you have faced what I'm staring at. What'll happen when I tell Piet? Answer me that! I'm telling you, I'll lose it all!' She gripped the sheet, pulling it over her breasts. 'Sweet Jesus, I'm so cold!'

Paul stared at her, his tongue thick in his mouth. 'W-what can I s-say?'

'Nothing! It's what you've been saying all your life. Listen ...' she leaned towards him '... it's a kind of relief knowing you're not my father. All those tepid years! I used to think there was something wrong with me. Well, there was. I wasn't your child. Isn't that it?'

He wrung his hands. 'I, I couldn't help the way I was with you. It wasn't deliberate, y-you mustn't think that.' He stared at his bloodless knuckles. 'I grieved so much for her, I wanted to ... die. Only for the work, I'd've—.' He clamped his lips. He couldn't tell her about that, the nights he'd spent in his study, staring at the gun on his desk. It'd been an abyss he thought he'd never escape from. He frowned, trying to concentrate. 'You were such a ... q-quiet little thing. Always in the kitchen with Rachel. You s-seemed happy.'

Mia snorted. 'How would you know what I was? You were never there! How could you let him come like that? No warning, nothing!'

He started as her arm shot out, pointing to the window. 'You just stood looking out ... separate.'

He leaned towards her. How could he make her understand how the thing had spiralled? 'I couldn't stop him. He went berserk when Thabo—. Those hours it took the boy to die were ....' He shook his head, trying to shake the image from his mind. 'I wanted to give Thabo something to make him sleep, keep the pain at bay, but he refused, he wanted to talk, tell us what they did to him. Thulatu sat through it like a piece of stone.' He rubbed his eyes, wanting to be rid of it.

'You never had a single photo of her in the house.'

'W-what?' He shook his head, confused.

'Not a single one.'

'You mean your mother? I couldn't bear—.'

'You never mentioned her name.'

'It was difficult—.'

'For years you let me think she'd just gone off and left us. I was thirteen when you finally told me she was dead.'

He looked away, unable to bear the accusal in her eyes. 'I loved her so—.'

'Did you really? Eh? Not even a twinge of resentment, of, of hatred, when she didn't choose you?'

The words stabbed him in the gut. 'My God! That's a cruel thing to say. B-but you're distraught—.'

Her laugh made him wince. 'Sweet lord, can y'believe it? I'd've been better off growing up with ... with him!'

She couldn't mean it! 'Him?' He spat the word. 'Why, he's ....'

'Black?' The arched brows mocked him.

'An ... an agitator. You'd've ended up like Thabo.'

'I may yet.'

'Babo too, if she doesn't watch out. It'd serve—.' He took a deep breath, but he couldn't control it. 'She's a d-disgrace! He's not the first one. Why she can't stick to her own kind, I'll—.'

'Why didn't you let him see me? He wanted to.'

He could hardly believe his ears, how naive she was. 'D'you think he'd've stopped at that? I promised your mother—.' He paused, wishing there was some way he could make her understand. 'He was always so c-cocky. I was always the one who was e-embarrassed when we ran into each other.'

Mia shivered. 'Don't you think it's cold?' Wrapping her arms about herself, she nodded at the window. 'Is that window closed? Check it, will you?'

Crossing the room, Paul mopped his brow, his handkerchief sodden. The room was sweltering, but perhaps it was best to humour her. He made a pretence of checking the window. He glanced down as a lawnmower started up. The gardener, a skinny black in a frayed vest and shorts, was pushing the thrumming motor across the lawn, leaving a neat, geometrical track in his wake. Lucky devil, he thought. If only he too were outside, carrying nothing but the warm weight of the sun on his shoulders!

'Is it closed?'

He turned. 'My dear, you're just feeling—.'

'How'd you know what I'm feeling?' Her hair was bitumen against the mound of pillows. And her eyes. The crazed glitter of them. He felt a stab of fear.

'I'm losing myself. D'you hear? Where's this clinic for blacks? I have to be treated, I'm suffering from ... from fugue.' Her hands fluttered above the quilt, small birds unable to find a branch on which to settle. He stared at them, mesmerised, not knowing what to say until the doctor in him surfaced, affording him a way to handle it. 'Did you t-take those pills? Did you get any sleep? You should—.'

'When word gets out, I'll disappear, I won't exist! Already it's begun—' She shivered, her gaze suddenly focussing, as though she were seeing him for the first time. 'How'd you expect me to sleep? Isn't this nightmare enough? There's no safe place to sleep.' She cocked her head, listening. 'Yes, yes, there is. One safe place. I'm saving it till last.' Her harsh laugh drowned out the noise of the lawnmower. 'Like the best sweet.'

The words were flat, toneless, chilling him. The whole business was making her ill, he had to reach her, save her from it, he'd been so wrong, oh if only he'd told her when she was little, when colour meant nothing.

'I need—.' She held out her hands, palms upwards, staring at them as though she'd never seen them before. 'I'm fading.'

He stuffed his handkerchief in his breast pocket. He had to do something, before she—. He had to try and fix it, make amends, that much at least he owed her. Shuffling across to the bed, he spoke. 'Listen, my dear—.' He touched her hands, avoiding her eyes, the way she was peering into his face. As though she were blind.

'All the times I've called them ... I'm not an animal.' Her voice was low.

'Listen, I'll go to him. R-right away. He won't tell Piet. Or Claus. I promise, I swear to you—.'

'You?'

At least she was registering what he was saying. 'Don't worry, I know a way, a little ace up my sleeve.'

'It's too late.'

'I swear to you, i-it'll never come out.'

'Too late.'

If she could only get a grip on it. For all intents and purposes, she was white. 'No one need ever know—.'

The dark eyes flared. 'I! I know! You can't change that! My whole life's been a lie, a filthy, black lie. Y'want to go on with that? Haven't you had enough? Haven't I? Of course it'll come out. If not now, with him, then someday, sometime. Y'think I'd ever be able to relax spending my life looking over my shoulder?'

'I thought you—.'

'What if I ever had to have a skin test?' The painted nails scratched at her arm. 'All those allergies I get in winter.'

He tried to look reassuring. 'The likelihood of that—.'

'Look at this!' Reaching past him, she swiped a newspaper from the nightstand. 'Read it!' She pushed it crackling into his hands, her finger staccato-tapping the printed words under a large photograph of a white baby. 'Out loud!'

He began to read: 'There was w-widespread controversy over racial classification when a ten-day-old baby was found abandoned near Port Elizabeth. In order to classify the infant, named Victoria by the hospital staff caring for her, t-tests were carried out on her skin in a Port Elizabeth police laboratory.' His gaze skipped over

183

the next words, and he paused, unwilling to continue. Mia suddenly grabbed the paper from his hands, the words tumbling from her lips before she'd even glanced at the page. 'As a result, the infant was classified coloured.'

'I know h-how you must feel, but—.'

'That's nothing. That's all nothing. That's a load of ... of crud!' She flung the newspaper, watching it lift on the warm air before it dropped in an untidy heap. Facing it. That's what it was about. She couldn't deal with any of it until she faced it.

Outside, the lawnmower ceased. 'D'you know the awful thing?' Her voice was calm in the sudden vacuum. 'Finding out they're not animals.' That was the worst lie she'd been living, it was ... indefensible. Vaguely, she became aware of laughter in the room, Paul staring at her, his eyes screwed up with what? Prejudice? Pain? It was hard to tell anything anymore. Finally, it dawned on her: the laughter was her own, low, amused, outside her control. Terrifying. She spoke to stop it. 'Shall I tell you a secret, a dirty secret? I've always been black.' The laugh threatened again, trembling on her lips. She clamped her mouth. Whatever happened, it mustn't escape, if it did, it would drag her screaming with it, so speak, speak, cover it, camouflage it in words, any words. 'Oh, it's true, that's true.' What was true? Think, find the pattern in the words, the logic that kept the laughter at bay. Black. Always been black. Only black if you have nothing. "Starvation, that's the stipulation." ' She laughed raucously. 'So that's what a black hole is.' She stared at the flushed face before her, the eyes downcast. As usual. When'd he ever been able to look her in the eye? Oh, she had ... hungered. Who should know it better than he! A medusoid man o' war, all sting and no blood. What was it that spilled in his veins, what kind of arctic sludge? She breathed deeply, fighting it. 'Why d'you think I jumped at the first man who—? Marriage delivered me to a warm bed, a candle-lit table, my very own dumb waiter. Except the lobster bisque was always bitter — too well seasoned by the cook. The cook, y'see, is the waiter's papa.' She stared across at the dressing-table, trying to find some relief in its classic lines. 'D'you suppose they feel it when they're boiled alive? D'you suppose the blacks feel it when they're shot alive? Why d'you suppose the cook hates them so much? The dread of too many mouths, less broth? I've been on a low moral diet for too long. I'm overweight. Look at me!' The words were hurled in his face.

He shook his head, bewildered. 'My dear, I—.'

'D'you suppose I can shed it? As sure as there's a hell for blacks, the cook will sniff it out.' She snorted. 'It's not an appetising smell.'

The door opened suddenly, startling him.

'How's the patient today?' Piet, his face fixed in a let's-humour-the-patient smile. She scowled at him. 'Nauseous.'

Paul struggled to rise, his heavy paunch jigging. 'Oh, eh, fine. Fine. She'll s-soon be on her feet again.' He made a play of searching for his doctor's bag. 'I must be on my way.' Leaning down towards Mia, he brought his lips to within a hair's breadth of her cheek. Turning, he moved quickly towards the door. 'See you tomorrow, my dear.' The words were tossed at her over his shoulder. As they always were. Her hands curled into fists. A scrap to a dog would've had more meat on it. She watched his glance sheer away from her husband as he moved through the open door.

'What's his hurry?' Piet loosened his tie, coming towards the bed. He stood looking down at her, his voice gentle. 'How d'you feel?' Leaning down, his mouth sought hers, but she turned sharply away, his lips brushing her cheek instead.

'Am I so distasteful?'

'I am.' She kept her head down.

'What is it with you lately?' He stroked the glossy crown of her head.

'I thought you were at the farm.'

'I came home to have lunch with you. I thought you'd like—.' Sitting, he took one of her hands.

'I'm trying to diet. I'm not hungry.'

'Good. Neither am I.' He moved closer, his hands sliding over her shoulders, drawing her to him. 'I thought we could .... It's been ages ....'

Instantly, she stiffened, her hands flat against his chest, pushing him from her.

'What the hell's—? If you'd agree to see a doctor—.'

'Paul's a doctor.'

'I didn't mean him, he's your father.'

'My ... father's a lawyer.'

He stared down at her face, the eyes shuttered against him. What the hell was the matter, he couldn't bear to see her this way, it was frightening. He took her hands, surprised to find how cold they were. The room was like a furnace. The bloody air conditioning had packed it in again.

'Mia, you need help. Please. I can't bear to see you—.' He broke off as she pulled her hands free of his. Christ! She just wouldn't give him a chance. 'You look at me. There's hatred in your eyes. What've I done?'

'Not hatred. Not for you.'

'Tell me, what'm I supposed to have done? I'm in the dark. It can't go on.'

He rose, wincing at the way she laughed. 'I'm in the dark!'

'You heard me. Either you get up out of that bed, behave like a normal wife, or you see a doctor. Talk to somebody. I can't take much more—.' He moved across the room, unwilling to let her see his face. But Mia was thinking of Paul.

'The way he kept out of it,' she mused, her voice low, 'Why, he hated her!'

Piet turned, her vacant eyes stabbing him. She didn't seem to hear what he was saying half the time, like she'd walked away from him into a world of her own, a world he couldn't reach. Leaving him behind in a grey, dead place. Why was she punishing him like this?

'Whatever it is you're blaming me for, I'm sick of it.'

Suddenly, her eyes cleared. 'Please let Jan come to see me. I need—.'

'Are you crazy? These last few days, you wouldn't even look at him.'

'I, I wasn't myself.' Her laugh was glass grinding. 'I'm still not.'

She knew, she knew what she was doing. Well, he'd not have his son exposed to this. 'He'd be better off on the farm with Papa at the moment.'

'Don't give him to Claus!' She lifted her hands from the snarl of sheets. 'Please! He's too fond of his cooking already.'

Piet began pacing, the carpet muffling the low groan of a floorboard every time he passed the foot of the bed. 'You're paranoid.'

'I'm afraid of him.'

'Papa?' He stopped.

'A man who always knows what he wants.'

Christ, she wasn't going to start picking at old wounds, was she? 'It's what I admire most about him.'

'He'll destroy me.'

His lips twisted. 'You blame him for the way you are?'

'I'm not Babo. I've no resources.'

'What're you talking about?'

'I won't be able to resist.'

He stared at the array of bottles and jars on the dressing-table, her small white face in the mirror hardly distinguishable from the pasty pillows. But for her hair, he wouldn't have believed she was really in the bed behind him. 'You're living on another planet.'

'Yes. No. A black hole.'

It was more than he could take, this flippant cleverness deriding him at every turn. As though they didn't inhabit the same world anymore. Without a word, he walked out. He was half-way down the stairs when her scream caught him up.

'Piet!'

He hesitated, then turned to climb up again. Back in the bedroom, he stood, silent, just inside the door. He'd slit his throat before he spoke the first word.

'Please. Stay with me.' Her dark eyes were wide.

'So y'can hurl more insults at my father?'

'I, I need you to stay.'

So now she was in the mood to play ball. Well, tough. 'I've a meeting at two in the city. Papa's picking me up.'

'Don't go, please, just this once, stay. Talk to me.'

The nerve of it, she'd had him dancing to her tune for the last hour! 'You've built a wall between us. You're going to have to knock it down yourself.'

'The wall is in me.'

'More riddles? What d'you take me for? A bloody fool?' Distantly, he heard a car horn sound, low but insistent. Papa. 'For Christ's sake, pull yourself together!'

'Don't go!' Mia leaped from the bed as he left, the door thudding behind him, a brick wall, hemming her in. She shivered. A tomb in a room. She stood, listening until she caught the faint slam of the hall door, the slither of gravel under tyres receding into the distance. Now she would look. Define herself. Crossing to the door, she snapped the brass key home in the lock. Elijah would leave the lunch-tray outside on the landing-table, as he'd done so often lately.

The book was under the bed, shoved well in, so it wouldn't be noticed. She dragged it out, straining to lift it onto the bed, the deadweight of all South African law between its hard covers. She climbed up beside it to search the table of contents. Definitions of Race, 240. She flittered the pages, anxious to get it over with. There, the outline definition in bold print, battalions of black ciphers sweeping across the virgin page to tabulate, identify and classify. To pass judgement. Sentence. To annihilate.

She mouthed, repeating the words: a white person is defined as any person who in appearance obviously is, or who generally is accepted as a white person, but does not include any person who, although in appearance obviously a white person, is generally accepted as a coloured person.

She stared at the page for a long time, vaguely aware when Elijah knocked at the door, the polite voice yapping through the wood, lunch Madam lunch Madam must to eat cold ham and chicken fresh very fresh very tasty juice of the grape cool very cool Madam must to come out must to eat eat eat Baas he says Elijah must to make Madam eat.

Suddenly she slammed the book closed, the noise explosive in the quiet room. Lifting it, she felt the strain in her back as she tried to hurl it across the room. It crashed on its page edges about three feet from the bed, its covers splayed like tent flaps to lend it staggering support.

'The wall is bleeding.' She heard the words outside her head but couldn't think where they'd come from. A shaft of sunlight pierced the tomb, making her squint. Bright, overbright. Crossing quickly to the dressing-table, she opened a drawer, rummaging until she found the sunglasses. How dark her skin looked through the polaroid lenses. How ... bituminous. Even the room had changed, the pastel walls embalmed in a dull twilight, no, no, she couldn't have this. Swiftly she opened the jar of cold cream, a large dollop smoothed on the lenses, there, that was better, now nothing positive to be seen, nothing that she could positively identify, just a grey blur through which she found her way to the haze of the bed and climbed in to its snug warmth, its safety net folding about the ashy gunge of her skin that was neither black nor white through the black and white of the glasses, then lie back and pull the cover over your head. Go some place where no light comes. And hide. Hide from Piet, from Papa wolf with his all-seeing, all-knowing eyes.

II

Late that afternoon, when they were driving northwards towards the farm, Piet almost confided in his father. Almost. What stopped him was the fear of what Claus would say, the knowledge that his father would use Mia's illness as a weapon against both of them. When Papa didn't like something, when he smelled weakness, he had a way of bending, shaping everything to his own design. It wasn't a deliberate, conscious process, more a blinkered thing, a way of being that relished courage, power and strength. That despised weakness. Piet sighed. The only time he ever tried to analyse the kind of man his father was, was when he felt threatened. As now. For the moment, he'd stay quiet, all Papa knew was that Mia wasn't very well at present. He'd told him nothing of the glittering eyes, the sudden lapses into a world where he couldn't reach her.

'Zo. A good meeting, ja?' Claus snapped the file on his lap closed. 'If they were all as productive — that Kruger jonge, a good man, efficient, we could do with more like him. Too many relics on the central committee, the blood gets sluggish, worse, the bones go soft.' He whistled through his teeth. 'Old women, the best part of them.'

Gripping the steering wheel, Piet hauled his thoughts free of Mia. Ahead, the tarred surface of the N2 curved away from the ugliness of Kwa-Mashu township. On the freeway, it was possible to pass such blots without the necessity of having to look it in the eye. Nor was he ever tempted to. 'Kruger, he was certainly right about opening the polls early, I'll say that for him. Is that, most of the blacks've voted by now and there's still a few days to go to election. We're home free.'

'Ja, most of the blacks. They can't say they haven't had their municipal elections.' Claus gave an amused snort. 'All one per cent of them.'

'What figure'll the Bureau for Information release?'

Claus shrugged. 'Fourteen, maybe fifteen per cent. In some areas, we'll say as high as thirty percent. A respectable enough turnout for international consumption, more than enough to keep the few friends we have happy. If we can keep our heads above the foreign debt—.'

'Papa, Mia's not well.' Unconsciously, Piet pressed his foot down on the accelerator, streaking into the fast lane to avoid the car in front. A bellicose horn sounded behind them. His teeth clamped. What the hell'd made him open his mouth?

But his father, staring back at some commotion in a lay-by on the far side of the freeway, didn't seem to have heard. 'Take the next exit and turn back, maan.'

'What?' Piet's eyebrows lifted.

'Do as I tell you. There's something back there. Something....' Claus's voice was sharp. He turned back towards the windscreen, eyes narrowing as he pointed at the next exit. 'There! Go for it, you'll make it.'

Piet held his breath, swerving across the lanes of traffic to much blasting of horns. He hated it when his father did this, springing something on him at a moment's notice, demanding an instantaneous response. What was it this time, another test? Or something genuine? Lurching into the exit, he braked hard, a tightness in his stomach as he recalled all the boyhood tests he'd had to undergo, 'to train his reflexes' was how Papa put it.

But this time it was different. Claus, eyes scanning the traffic ahead, seemed hardly aware of him as they headed back south towards Durban.

'What'm I looking for? Papa?' He glanced at his father straining forward against the safety belt.

'Zo!' Claus pointed at the lay-by ahead. 'Pull in behind the truck.'

A Government Garage truck, large and dowdy, one of its wheels punctured, two soldiers jacking the vehicle while another two guarded the small group of blacks who'd been ordered off the truck while the job was being done. Easing the car to a halt a few yards from the huddled group, Piet stared. Well? What was it? A crowd of misfits, undesirables, being transported somewhere for re-settlement, nothing special about that.

'There's nothing here.' He turned, but Claus was already climbing from the car. Well, whatever it was his father wanted, he could get it himself. They looked a dirty bunch, three of the men sucking cigarette butts, the women too lazy to wipe the snot from the children's noses. If they could afford to smoke, surely, between all of them, they could manage a bar of soap? He sniffed. Germ and lice infested. Who knew what diseases they might carry? He had Jan and Mia to think of.

Mia. Christ, what'd tempted him just now to open his mouth? Luckily Papa hadn't noticed. Maybe when he got home this evening, things would've improved. He grimaced at the thick band of gold on his finger. And pigs might fly, as Babo would put it.

Outside, Claus was already in conversation with one of the soldiers. Seeking distraction, Piet opened the window.

'Venda,' the soldier was saying, a note of respect in his voice, 'they've been designated citizens of Venda. That's where we're taking them now, sir.'

Claus nodded, slipping his identification back in his breast pocket. But Piet's gaze had strayed beyond them, his eyes suddenly riveted to the woman sitting with the thing in her arms, its skin and hair blanched beyond possibility of racial classification, as though it might, before the kwashiorkor became advanced, have been any skin shade under the sun. Even white. Like his grandmother when she'd been released from the camp. Fleshless, Papa had always said, starved into near madness. He watched his father move towards the woman, vaguely registering the soldier's voice as he rubbed his neck to ease the tightness in the muscles of his throat.

'... squatting over at Kwa-Mashu with bits of plastic and cardboard, we had to get a bulldozer to clean up all the filth ... and the vermin, sir, big as olifants.'

This, then, was how his grandmother had looked. Papa must see it too, the spectre that even yet, gnawed at his heels. How often Claus had described it: the bird-cage ribs in a translucent caul, the listless eyes anchored to the next breath. All the terrible possibilities of his father's past concentrated now in this, this ... thing whose bones defined its form more acutely than could any flesh. Human. Yes, difficult to admit the word, for so long had he refused it entry. Suddenly Piet was afraid. Closing his eyes, he tried to concentrate instead on Mia.

Ahead, the woman curved protectively over the stillness cradled in her arms as Claus stood looking down.

'You must go to the hospital,' he told her. 'They will help.'

The woman glanced up at him, frightened.

'She doesn't speak Afrikaans, sir, none of these kaffirs do.' The soldier's lips tightened. 'Or won't.'

'English?'

'Very little. Xhosa. I can speak it reasonably, sir, I took a course in tribal languages at the university, if you—.'

'Tell her she must take him to Entabeni. He needs medication ... he is starving.' Claus stared at the child, death leering from every skeletal line.

A Durban hospital? The soldier hesitated. The man was mad. Yet he was an important figure, a member of the State Council, no less — it'd make a great story to tell back in the barracks. But orders were orders, the necessity for blind obedience branded deep. For all he knew, the whole thing could be a trick. The Colonel could be a sadistic bastard. 'With respect sir, our orders are to deliver them across the homeland border. She can bring him to a clinic there. Colonel Kurstijns would blow his top if—.'

'He won't make the journey to Venda, you know it as well as I, maan!'

'I'm sorry sir, orders are orders.'

Claus glanced at the two soldiers fitting the new wheel. Raw recruits, he could smell it without the need to check for stripes. And the other one gaping as he guarded the kaffirs - straight from kindergarten. He sighed. An army of fresh-faced boys deployed between the townships, the homelands and the wars on the borders. The laager was self-destructing, the enemy within and without. Military might, that was what counted now, but ja, one thing was certain, his own grandson would not be robbed of his childhood, he'd make certain of that. When the time came, a nice, safe commission—.

'I'm sorry, sir.' The young soldier shuffled on the hard shoulder. Whichever way he played it, he could end up in trouble. At least if he were polite—.

'You're in command?'

'Yes sir.' The soldier saluted, reddening under Claus' contemptuous glance at his one distinguishing stripe. 'I'm—.'

'You have a radio?' Claus jerked his head at the truck as a car with a faulty exhaust farted past on the freeway. He raised his voice. 'Get your superior on the line. Tell him who I am, you've checked my identification, zo.'

Without a word, the soldier went to the cab. This was one story he wouldn't be able to embellish, the other three were listening too closely. Laughing at him, even, he was sure of it.

While he waited, Claus took out his wallet. Eighty Rand was all he had in cash. Mostly he didn't use money, operating always on credit. Ja, but to her, it'd seem a lot. It'd pay for a deal box. He held it down to her, the bills folded along their length to avoid the possibility of touching her hand. She shook her head, muttering, eyes aflame in the low sun. What was she gibbering about? — he couldn't see her expression. He moved, throwing his shadow to cut her off from the light.

His mouth sagged. Who would believe it? Her hand raised in a shield over her breast, the sweaty pork of the palm facing outwards, a dark groove of pigment pencilling the lifeline. Refusing him, her eyes terrified.

'Take it.' He emphasised the words, shoving the money a little closer to her hand. Instantly, she shrank, the sudden movement forcing a hiss through the child's grey lips.

Verdomme, what'd she think he was trying to do, the stupid munt, couldn't she get it through her dense skull he was offering her help? More than anyone had ever offered his own mother.

'Sir? Colonel Kurstijns.' The soldier called, standing beside the truck, the mouthpiece straining from the coiled wire he held towards Claus. He stood a little aside, his ears pricked, as Claus barked into the mouthpiece. The Colonel's scratchy voice issued clearly enough from the radio in the cabin, once the door stayed open.

'... never had the pleasure of meeting you, sir.' Old Kusty's voice whined over the line with unusual deference. The young soldier turned away to hide his grin. Kusty crawling, maan, there was a story here after all.

Claus explained what he wanted, overriding the Colonel's attempts to punctuate his monologue.

'Perhaps that would be a little unwise, sir?' The tone, for all its half-hearted objection, was wheedling.

'Listen to me, Kurstijns, if that bantu dies in that condition it'll stir up more ill-will. Zo. They go to Entabeni. Never let it be said that the Afrikaner hasn't got a heart. And remember this. Nothing I do is ever unwise. Perhaps your superior was unwise to give you authority in such a sensitive area as forced removals. You don't seem to know your own ass. We're sitting on a powder keg maan, we don't need criticism from within our own ranks.' His voice dropped an octave, the velvet tone thick with innuendo. 'I'd be more careful if I were you, someone might mistake you for a left wing radical — they're breeding like rabbits, I hear.'

There was a long pause. The soldier almost wet himself. He pictured his superior the other end of the wire, face apoplectic as he bit down on his anger. Oh the pleasure of it. The others were straining their ears, but they couldn't catch it all. It'd be his story —

eating and drinking on it for days. He tried to look sombre as Kurstijns found his voice again. Claus shoved the babbling microphone into his hand and strode back towards the squatting woman.

Quickly the soldier climbed into the truck and closed the door. Old Kusty was winding down with some lick-ass phrases in a placating tone. His subordinate blew a swift hard raspberry into the mike and hung up, opening the door and leaping out to run after Claus.

'Tell her to take the money, she'll need it to—.' Claus stopped himself. The soldier didn't look old enough to have learned discretion, no sense in driving her to distraction talking of burials. These bantus were apt to out-shriek a baboon over spilt milk, let alone—.

But the soldier, his voice a mincing parody of Xhosa rhythms, was having no success. The woman stared at them, her eyes popping. She threw a frightened look over her shoulder towards the cluster of eavesdropping bantus. The money might have been a hissing snake as she shrank from the soldier's outstretched hand. Claus winced as her action spiked a prolonged tremor in the child's form. As though the bones were rattling. He turned away. The woman began to babble in a low voice.

'She says she can't take it, people would be suspicious.' The soldier turned to Claus. 'What she means is, sir—.'

'They'll think she's an informer. You don't have to tell me, maan, I've been dealing with these bantus long before you learned how to wipe your ass.'

The soldier's face reddened as Claus jabbed a finger at the money in his hand. 'Give it to her when you drop her at the hospital. And see she takes it. The faster she buries that one the better. Tell Kurstijns I want a report on the outcome of the whole incident ...' he stared hard at the soldier, '... down to every last cent of how she used the money.'

The soldier's face deepened to puce. 'Sir, if you're implying—.'

'I'm not implying anything which hasn't already crossed your mind, zo?' Claus jerked his head at the woman. 'See that my instructions are carried out to the letter.' He walked back towards the parked car, satisfied to catch the faint sniggering of the other soldiers. He nodded. She'd get the money, his friends would watch him like hawks. In his pocket, the wallet, a bulge of credit cards, was reassuring as ever, its deadweight knocking against his chest as he moved. Ja, almost impossible to believe his mother had risen from the ashes of that, humanity skinned from her bones, a frenzy of fear ever afterwards burning in the scorched depths of her eyes. Joyless. Ahead, the low sun dipped into the windshield, the ochre sky framed in its depths. In it, his son's dreamy expression was reflected, a worried orb suspended in the heavens. Claus's lips twisted. Zo, apt for someone who spent most of his time living on the moon.

III

When the mini-bus finally rattled to a halt on the edge of Rhaumsfontein, Emma was exhausted. Eyes bleary from fitful dozing through the long journey, she staggered out with the rest of the passengers. Early afternoon, the dusty heat airless as the bus had been. At least the clinic would have cleared by now. With any luck, she could sidestep Dick's questions by pleading tiredness. Go straight to bed. Oblivion. If the dreams would continue to allow, as they had done the last few nights in Durban.

When she was still standing on the same baked ground beside the bus a couple of minutes later, the small crowd in front of her making no effort to disband, she looked up. There was hardly an eager queue to get into the township, now was there? It wasn't exactly where most people'd choose to come on a holiday. A smile ghosted about her lips and she felt the skin crack. Oh for a drink of water, let the pump be working! Her stomach grumbled, the sound seeming to rise from a bottomless pit. When'd she last eaten? She couldn't remember having had anything since she'd left Durban. When had that been? Christ, what was the hold-up? She stretched on tiptoe, trying to peer over the sea of bobbing heads, but the effort was futile, the people in front straining to see as well. The clothes Babo had given her weighed a ton, if she didn't get something to eat soon, she'd collapse. And she needed to pee. What was it with this place? — soon as she landed back, all she could think of were her bodily needs. Eat, sleep, drink and evacuate. Like nothing else mattered. Was this all poverty left room for?

A woman's scream rang out, high-pitched, curdling her insides. Soldiers? Police? The vicious bastards, what were they up to now? Well, whatever it was, they'd have a white witness to worry about.

She pushed sideways, breaking out of the cluster of passengers to run to the front of the queue, the hold-all a shield mounted on her chest. She pulled up short. A group of black youths, hostile as bristling porcupines. The old woman they held in their midst was still screaming, arms pinned to her sides, the whites of her eyes rearing in her frayed face. One of the youths, a thickset boy with the physique of a mastiff, stood hacking open a box of washing powder with a machete. A sundry collection of groceries were scattered at the woman's feet: some burst packets of sugar and tea, a tin of powdered milk, a plastic tub of cooking fat.

The passengers stood silent, even the men among them, petrified as the youth jerked the opened box of washing powder up to the woman's face. Instantly, her mouth clamped. Another of the youths grasped her hair to still the wild dance of her head as she strained backwards.

Emma shrieked. The youth swivelled, powder spraying from the box, the machete glinting in mid-air, his eyes glacial. Emma flinched.

In the thickness of the silence she became aware of every other pair of eyes in the group fixed on her. On her oddness. Her baldness. Her whiteness. She shivered, trying to look only at the youth with the machete. She licked her cracked lips. Still none of them spoke, the air swollen with the sense of threat. She hugged the hold-all harder, wanting to turn and run. The metal loops at the handles bit into her breasts. Her heart pummelled the bag, its echo in her ears, its faint vibration reaching through the clothing to her clenched hands. A bird prattled, swooping overhead. She jumped. The boy with the machete laughed. Immediately, the others took it up in a jerky chorus.

She stared, suddenly seeing how young they were. No more than fourteen or fifteen, most of them. Mere children holding them all to ransom. Adults who outnumbered them at that. Well, she'd be fucked if she'd let them intimidate her further. She took a deep breath, trying to still the tremors in her legs.

'I, I'm with Father Carruthers in Holy Cross Mission, the Roma church? I only speak English.' She bit her tongue getting the words out, immediately tasting salt. So much for courage. The sickly whine in her voice was hardly likely to impress a mouse.

'I, I'm sure he'd be very upset if he knew what you were doing ....' She lifted a hand, pointing vaguely in the old woman's direction.

'Yes, sisi, he will very anger, Father comrade is good man.' The woman's eyes devoured Emma, fervid with hope.

Emma nodded at her, trying to look reassuring. 'Yes, very good. He, he fixed the pump.' Her gaze flitted over the youths, unable to settle and meet the hostility in any one.

The boy flared. 'That has nothing to do with us here. This woman guilty, she must punished.'

From the corner of her eye, Emma saw people slip away from the edge of the small group who'd made the journey with her. Perhaps one of them would go for Dick? She'd heard a few responsive murmurs when she'd mentioned his name. Surely an encouraging sign? But what if she and the other woman were left finally to face the wrath of the youths alone? As young as they were, most of them were bigger than her. She could end up with a bellyful of powder herself. Christ, it didn't bear thinking about.

'I'm sure whatever's happened, she doesn't deserve—.'

'She was to a white shop, has broken the boycott!' The youth's eyes were hot coals. Emma's mouth dropped. For this they were going to poison the woman? Make her eat what she'd bought?

'I went the city because cheap is price. I have no enough for shop here, old Mdala, he black but big his price.' The woman's sunken eyes pleaded with Emma.

The youth turned to the woman, his voice hard. 'You break the boycott, you are enemy of the liberation struggle. Grandma, it is your rights we fighting for, what you doing is making our work more difficult.'

'A chance, child, please? Again, never!' Her head swerved from side to side.

The boy shook his massive head, lifting the box of powder.

'Can't you give her a chance? Please? That stuff'll eat her insides.'

The boy moved closer to the woman, ignoring Emma's voice. Christ, these weren't children, they were some kind of cold-blooded automatons.

'Then get Modise,' she snapped. 'Don't you dare punish that woman till you get Modise.' She blinked, surprised to discover the voice was her own. The youth turned, his eyebrows raised. It was the first time his expression had altered and instinctively she felt she'd hit the right note. Afraid of losing whatever advantage she'd gained, she rushed on.

'One of you go and get Modise. Does he know you're doing this to a poor woman who didn't have enough money to buy the things she needed here? D'you want her to starve?' She drew a deep breath. Pleading hadn't worked, she might as well go for broke. Either way, it couldn't do the old woman any further harm. 'Don't you think she's a little old for your revolution? Fit you all better go and talk to the shopkeeper here, find out why the prices are so high, do something about that. Then maybe she wouldn't have to go to the city to buy what she needs.'

The rumble of agreement from the remaining few passengers was birdsong in her ears. 'How old are you anyhow?' She paused, deliberately looking each of them in the eye. 'I'd like to know what your mothers'd say if they heard the fine revolutionaries you're turning out to be, terrifying old women, I'd like to hear what Modise'd say.'

In the silence that followed, the two youths who were holding the old woman shuffled a little, glancing at their leader. He stood, grinding the machete against the box in his hands, his knuckles blurring as Emma squinted through a sudden wave of dizziness. Please. Let it work. And quickly. She didn't know how much longer she'd be able to stand upright, the sun a branding iron on her unprotected scalp, the hot sweat trickling in rivulets through the uneven stubble.

'Know your enemy, said Christ!' The words burst from her lips, strident with religious fervour, startling to her own ears as it was to theirs. She blinked rapidly. Christ, she was going crazy. A Bible-thumping harridan. Joan of Arc wasn't in it, not when it came to Emma the Coot. No wonder they were peering at her now as if she had two heads, the mastiff body of the boy pawing the ground as he stepped back a little. She didn't blame him. If she were able, she'd step back from herself, walk away and leave herself standing there, her plucked ostrich scalp baking in the sun as she jabbered and hissed her way into madness.

She sucked deeply on the warm air but it offered no relief. Know your enemy — where the fuck had she dredged that archaic remnant from, words learned by rote in a childhood so distant that some-times she wondered if it had been dreamed rather than lived. Except for the dog. The dog had been so real it had carved a life for itself in her dreams.

No, wait. She tried to stem the thin laugh that trickled through her lips. It wasn't 'know your enemy,' it was 'love him.' And here she was preaching Christ the militant. Dick would thank her. The rest of the words came back swiftly: '... do good to them that hate you, pray for them that persecute and calumniate you ....' Let's hope none of them knew it, they didn't exactly strike her as a crowd of cheek-turners. She looked around the silent group, her eyes bleared. They seemed a little further away, as though they'd stepped back en masse. Or perhaps she had? Why didn't someone say something, do something, release them all from the stalemate of dead clay, the sun's blistering gaze?

Suddenly the ground shifted underfoot. If she didn't move, she'd fall. She peered towards the dark blur she knew to be the woman, and spoke to it. 'We'll walk into town together.' She held her breath, eyes fixed on the blur as she nodded, the ache in her head gathering itself to crash against the confines of her skull. The woman sprang forward into focus, the youths' hands falling furtively away.

'We'll go now.' Her voice shattered in her ears as she grasped the thin arm, pulling the woman towards the huts drifting through the haze. The woman was eyeing the groceries on the ground. Christ, she couldn't be contemplating picking them up after what had happened?

'I'll see you home.' In her panic, Emma tightened her grip and heard a sharp intake of breath.

'I'm sorry, did I hurt you?' Grimly she held on, pulling the woman further away from the youths.

'Don't worry about the food. I'll give you some money,' she hissed in the gnarled maze she hoped was the woman's ear. Afraid to look back, she propelled her forward, stumbling as fast as she dared, hoping it didn't look to the youths as if they were running.

After a while she became aware she was no longer leading, that it was the old woman who dragged her through the grim line of squatter huts, a surprising strength in her tenacious grip. She wasn't sure how or when it happened, coming to notice it only when she tripped over the children playing trains with empty mealie cobs.

The blind leading the blind. She began to laugh as the church floated ahead, washing in and out of her vision like some dead, waterlogged thing adrift on a great ocean that might be her own tears or the pump overflowing or a flood sent by Christ the militant or the tears of all the women in the world who had worn themselves down rearing hot-eyed boys to crush them underfoot.

'Emma?' The voice was hurled in her face, the sharp crack across her cheek bringing instant pain. 'For Chrissakes, snap out of it, will you?'

Concentrating, she focussed on the meaty orb rotating before her face. Dick, his gaze an astonished bulge as he gaped at her head. She rubbed her stinging cheek and looked away, surprised to find herself sitting on a tuft of grass in the yard, the coarse spikes pricking her thighs below the khaki shorts.

The old woman was standing near the church door giving Mambo an earful, Mambo's eyes washed in the excitement of a story being well told. Worth repeating, even. Emma would become the butt of this new tale, to be related, with Mambo's talent for embellishment, at some future night vigil.

She grinned, a sharp jab in her lip as the skin split again. Somehow the bare, dusty yard, the little church, Mambo's eyes popping, even the roughness in Dick's voice, offered her a warmth, a familiarity which was balm. While she remained in this country, this was where she belonged. The word was a lifeline. She grasped it deep inside and held on to it.

'So you're back, huh?' He reached down, hauling her to her feet.

The words were gravel on her dry tongue as she fought to get them out. 'Yes, I, I know you weren't expecting me till after—.'

'I didn't mean here.' He stared down at her. 'I meant, in your mind. For a while there, I thought you'd lost your marbles.' A ridge of lines rippled across his brow making the red hair spike to attention. He lowered his voice. 'God in heaven, what've you been up to?' His tone was gentle. Too gentle. She shook her head, trying to swallow the rock in her throat. 'This old lady—.' She gestured at the two women.

'I didn't mean that. One a the men on the bus came running in here a few minutes ago, telling us what's been going on. Cousin a Vusi's, happens. I was just coming to get you when you showed.' He snorted, his voice grim. 'Showed. Sure is the word for it, an apparition outta hell'd look a whole lot healthier right now.' He grasped the soft flesh of her upper arm, drawing her towards the cabin. She stumbled over the uneven ground, glad of his support.

'I needn't a worried. Way you look, you must've scared those boys crapless.' The word came awkwardly off his lips, as though he'd blasphemed.

Once they'd moved down the side of the church onto more even ground, she thought he'd release her and was surprised when he didn't. He'd never liked it when she brushed against, let alone touched him, there was no need to put himself through this.

'It's all right, I can walk,' she said, but he wouldn't let her go.

In the stored heat of the cabin, she sank onto the chair in front of the desk, her breath expelling in a loud hiss. He stared at her as he lifted the plastic container. What the devil'd happened in Durban to drive her back here in such a state? What'd Thulatu been up to? His lips twisted. He'd have his guts for garters.

'Do we have any water?'

But already he was pouring it. The 'we' pleased him as nothing had done all week. It was good to have her back, he'd missed her help in the clinic. No, if he were honest, it wasn't that but this wasn't the time to analyse it. He turned away to keep his face hidden as he screwed the cap back on the water container.

'I've a fierce headache, d'you have any aspirin?' She sat, panting from the effort of gulping the water, too tired to wipe the trickle from the corner of her mouth.

'You've burned your scalp.' He reached for an antibiotic spray on the shelf. 'You're in luck. The clinic left us couple a these. They're new on the market, supposed to work wonders.' He aimed the aerosol at the crown of her head. 'Close your eyes.'

She howled as he sprayed, reaching out to grip blindly at the edge of the desk, the cool mist worse than the shock of ice on feverish skin.

She began to shake, great shuddering jerks that blanked out thought, leaving her vaguely aware of a dimmed consciousness between the spasms as her body ran out of control. Christ, was she dying?

'... know it's uncomfortable, but it's the quickest way to bring the temperature down,' he was saying, when at last she could hear and see again. '... a shock to the system, works like a dream, long as you don't have a bad heart.' His hands were a vice gripping her shoulders. 'If I'd a given you warning, it'd a felt worse.' The hands tapped briefly, like mallets driving nails home, then withdrew.

'Oh I have a bad heart all right, there's poison in it.' She stared down at the sprawl of papers on the desk, hardly aware she'd spoken.

He stood over her, frowning at the crown of her head, livid through the dark spikes. Oven-fired, like reddish-brown clay with its stubble of straw. Already this country branded on her, deep as any Bhaca would permit in the most sacred rituals of tribal scarification. He was filled with pity. God in heaven, what was she doing to herself? What was it between her and Thulatu that drove her towards such crucifixion? Whatever it was had brought her back here, to him, when he'd thought never to see her again. He grimaced. Her misery was proving to be his gain, a real ... blessing. The word lingered in his mind, making him uneasy. For the clinic, he hastened to remind himself, she was a great help to him in the clinic, only a fool'd deny it.

But first he'd have to straighten her out, lay some firm ground rules. Otherwise, he'd have an invalid on his hands. He went to get her a couple of aspirin.

'Poison,' she said again, the word lingering on the air like an echo.

'Nonsense. Your heart's fine. Anyone that comes here is well vetted,' he said, ignoring what she'd been getting at. She wouldn't have wanted him to hear it anyway.

'When did you last eat?' He poured her some more water.

She gagged on the second pill, finally managing to swallow it, her eyes watering. 'I'm not sure, this morning, I think.' She stood up slowly to minimise the throbbing in her head. The light tone was suspect. He hesitated, knowing she was lying. Better to wait until she'd eaten, she was in no condition for a lecture right now.

'I have to go to the loo,' she said, wriggling a little.

While she was gone, he put some water on the primus to boil and got the food ready.

She came back, ready to plead tiredness from the journey, the need for sleep. She stood in the open doorway, her eyes huge as she took in the food: white bread, slivers of ham, bananas, coffee, black and strong already steaming in the mugs.

'Where'd you get it?' She swallowed the sudden stream of saliva in her mouth.

'Modise.' He grinned. 'Some friends of his blew in from Jo'burg, brought him quite a supply.'

Between the hand grenades, Emma thought, unable to keep her eyes off the spread on the desk. The green skin of the bananas that at home she was used to thinking of as unripe, had never looked so appetising, something glorious in their pale, foliate curves. 'C'mon.' He gestured at her to sit.

Her stomach groaned as she moved across to the chair and she felt the blood pulse furiously in her head.

'Leastways one part of your anatomy refuses to lie. Eat.' He pushed a mug towards her. As she lifted it, she inhaled deeply, the pungent aroma smothering her nostrils.

He sipped his own. 'Great. No half-measures, huh?' He nodded at the coffee. 'We'll get back to rationing it tomorrow.'

'Aren't you going to eat?' She bit deeply into the fresh bread, savouring it.

'I'll wait on Mambo. You keep going, though.' He grinned. 'Give me a chance to preach you a sermon uninterrupted.'

The food in Emma's mouth became sawdust. She might've known. She stared down at the creamy ivory of the peeled banana. If Babo'd sensed something between herself and Thulatu, then, chances were, Dick had too. Perhaps Thulatu had told him, anyway? The thought of him knowing what she'd done filled her with shame.

But he surprised her. 'I wanna make this absolutely clear so we understand each other.' He leaned forward, hands splayed on the littered surface of the desk. 'Thing is, if you want to stay, you gotta eat.'

Was that all? The sawdust changed back to banana. She took another bite to stifle the laugh that welled from the sudden sense of relief. 'I'm eating, I'm eating.' She held up the fruit, her voice muffled through the food.

His face darkened. 'Don't take me for a fool! You been starving yourself since you got here. Look at you, you're a mess! Lips bleeding, bones sticking through your skin, I suppose none of it's your fault?' He lifted his hands and slammed them down on the desk. Some loose papers near the edge rose and floated to the floor. 'As for your head, I suppose you were scalped by a red Indian on the way back? Goddamn it, I don't know what you're up to, Emma ....' He paused to catch his breath, instantly sorry he'd used her name, knowing it pointed to some weakness he didn't want to decipher. He rushed on, hoping she hadn't noticed. '... but I sure won't condone it by providing you with sackcloth and ashes, I got enough on my plate without taking on a penitent who's hell-bent on flailing herself to death.' He stopped, seeing her face suddenly, pale and bunched as a tight fist.

'Thanks,' she said, the word snapping like elastic.

He sighed, reining in his voice. 'I just got no space for it. You want to punish yourself, this isn't the place.' He hesitated, rubbing his eyes. Maybe he was going too far, but it had got to be said, even if it meant driving her away. The thought stabbed at something inside him. 'You can't keep whipping yourself forever, there's nothing you couldda done that can't be forgiven, remember that.'

Her breath hissed. 'Oh yes?'

The derision in her eyes made him grimace.

'But then, you're a priest, you'd have to say that.' She gulped some coffee to steady herself. But Thulatu wouldn't say it. For the rest of her life, his accusations would stare her in the face.

'For Chrissakes, I wasn't talking about God! I came here because I'd lost my faith, not because I'd found it. Y'think I'm any cleaner than you?' He paused, clamping his lips before he said too much. How could he speak of his despair when he realised he'd turned to the priesthood to fill the vacuum in his life? How could he tell her it was his own ugliness that had driven him here to seek refuge? But once he'd come, once he'd seen what was here, there'd been no going back, not if he'd wanted to be able to meet his own eyes in the mirror every morning when he shaved. And keeping faith with his conscience had paid dividends. In this place he'd been able to function as a man, forget about his looks, here, he was wanted, needed as he'd never been by anyone in his life, needing these people in turn as much as they needed him. 'Listen,' he said now. 'We're all guilty of something. I'm here because I can't see no other way of living with myself.'

He looked at her, tempted to ask her what it was she'd done. She was near breaking point, he could see it in the clench of her throat, her hands knuckled about the mug. Ready to burst, disgorge the sludge in his ears.

And if she caved, what then? Lord knew she'd enough resentment towards him, more at times than he could stomach. But if he encouraged her now, she'd resent him all the more afterwards. Working together would become impossible. Finally, she'd leave.

He pressed on his eyes, filled with a sudden yearning. Nothing about him pleased her, never had she once thought well of him. If only once, just once she could look at him with the same warmth in her eyes she reserved for Mambo. Fool, he thought, going soft in his old age. Loneliness, that was all it was, the way he'd felt when she'd run so eagerly to Durban with Babo, he'd gotten used to working with her, used to having someone around he could talk to in his own language, freely, with all the nuances of meaning which were lost when he tried to communicate beyond a certain mundane proficiency in Xhosa or Sotho. That's all it was.

'Well, you got a choice,' he said finally. A movement outside caught his eye. Mambo, heading down the side of the church, having, doubtless, milked the old lady for every last detail. She'd be wanting coffee. He hid a grin as he got up to make some more. Mambo, never having tasted coffee in all her long life for some superstitious reason which he still couldn't quite fathom, was now addicted to it. He spoke quickly as he poured more water into the pot, setting it on the primus, wanting to have done before the old woman walked in the door. 'You can pick up the pieces, build something new outta them, 'n maybe what you build will be something better because this time it'll grow outta what you've learned, that's the kinda forgiveness I'm talking about.' He turned, his smile awkward, but she was staring into the mug in her hands. He didn't even know if she were listening anymore but he said it anyway. 'You wanna do penance, you want punishment, I got plenty of it for you here, helping people exist in this hellhole.' He cocked his head, trying to read her face. 'Look at it this way,' he joked, 'I'm sentencing you to a spell a community work, what any well-heeled society would allow a first-time offender, long as you promise me you'll eat, now what d'you say, mam?' He waited, hearing the shuffles outside, but her face remained closed against him, tight as any book.

'Okay,' he said quietly as the old woman entered. 'But I'd like you to remember something. Your help these past weeks, has been a ... blessing.' He turned from Mambo's animated face to the water on the stove. When he expected to hear them greet each other, there was no sound save a faint rustle of clothing. He stared at the water until the first bubbles began to form. It was unlike Mambo to be so silent. He turned, his mouth dropping open as he took them in, the two women standing close, arms about one another as they swayed gently to and fro. They might've known each other all their lives. Might be mother and daughter, he thought, a sudden tightness in his throat. Hard to imagine his own mother reacting like this. The notion almost made him laugh aloud.

Suddenly, he needed to break it up. 'C'mon, you two. Fresh coffee.' He poured the steaming water from the pot. 'Mambo, you sit in my chair.' He gestured, but the old woman shook her head, muttering so fast that he couldn't translate it. 'Sit!' he barked, pointing at his chair. Still muttering, she collected the coffee tin from the shelf and sat down. As soon as he placed the steaming mug in front of her, she began to spoon in more coffee.

'No, Mambo!' Emma leaned across to stop her, speaking loudly as though that would miraculously make English more intelligible to her. 'Look! See?' She pointed into the mug. 'Coffee's already in there.'

'Might as well be talking to the wall.' Dick's voice was cheerful as he cut more bread. 'She doesn't think it's coffee 'less it's got the consistency of tar.'

Emma watched, shocked, as Mambo counted in three heaped spoonfuls.

'Christ, you'll kill her! How long's she been drinking the stuff like this? I thought she didn't even like it.'

Dick grinned. 'She didn't. Leastways not till I introduced her to the taste yesterday. Beginning to be sorry I did. Never saw anyone become addicted so fast, might be manna from heaven, way she tackles it.'

'Well, the least you could do is stop her, hide it or something.'

He didn't tell her he already had. 'Reckon that's your job, if you decide you're gonna stay.' The grey eyes regarded her steadily.

'I'll stay as long as you'll have me.' Her voice was quiet, but she looked directly at him.

Her answer was a lot more than he'd hoped for. 'Good, good.' He picked up the coffee, turning to hide his face as he replaced it on the shelf. The colour of the tin startled him, he couldn't remember having noticed it before, its cool blue more intense than any ocean. Nuts, but if he lifted his arms right now, he was sure he'd fly, burst through the roof of the cabin to soar and swoop in the sweet air high above the veld.

Emma stared at the broad expanse of his back. What was it with him? The minute she found the courage to look him in the eye, he turned away with a brusqueness that was squashing. She sipped the coffee, wincing as it stung her lips. Yet, despite the unflattering way he'd turned from her ... a blessing, he'd said. She grew a little, rolling the word about her mind, warmed by its presence, the word itself a blessing, a gift he'd unwittingly bestowed on her when she was most in need of it.

The three of them ate in silence, Emma chewing for appearance sake, since she'd already eaten as much as she could stomach. Dick leaned against a corner of the desk, one thigh straddling it like the haunch of a large animal. From time to time he glanced at the food in front of her, checking its diminishing size. The silence was comfortable in the darkening room, the muffled thud and shriek of a football game carrying from the church yard where the children often played when the air cooled towards evening. For a while, none of them seemed anxious to speak. Emma closed her eyes, unaware of how deeply her lungs sucked the air, her body juddering. Mambo muttered something as she stared at the younger woman. Dick shook his head, muttering back. He'd said enough for one day, time to quit while he was ahead. But when Mambo spoke again, her words chilled him. He stared at her dark eyes fixed on some certainty beyond him and felt a rush of icy fluid spreading beneath his skin. He wasn't superstitious, for all that he offered these people the myth of his religion. Yet neither was he dismissive of their sudden intuitions. Too many had proved accurate in the past.

Emma opened her eyes. 'What is it?' She stretched, relieved to find the throbbing in her head had eased.

Dick stood, shaking off his fear. 'You were lucky those tsotsis didn't kill you.' He drained his cup.

'Tsotsis?' She looked from him to Mambo. The old woman nodded, her face grim as she echoed the word.

'Thugs. Louts. Thieves and murderers the lot of them. They go round the township in gangs, creating mayhem. That's why nobody goes out at night, except the very foolhardy.' He rushed on, his voice harsh as he tried to block out Mambo's words. 'That's why people feed their dogs even when they can't afford to feed themselves. That's why so few mornings go by without some poor soul being found in one of the dongas, the rats nibbling his guts.'

Emma shuddered, spilling some of the coffee. Mambo rose and began tidying, shunting him to the other side of the desk to allow her room to manoeuvre.

'Sometimes they're working for their own ends, sometimes for the police, the army.' The heavy shoulders stirred, stout branches lifting in the wind. 'Depends on the profits. Though normally they don't bother us much, there isn't a lot you can steal from squatters.'

'You, you mean they weren't activists?'

'Those hooligans? Hell, no!' His laugh grated. 'You'd a stood a better chance if they had been.'

She stared, open-mouthed. 'But what about Modise? They were afraid when I mentioned—.'

He shook his head, the desk creaking under his weight as he perched on a corner. 'Some a the passengers got away. Reckon they were afraid we'd come back with a crowd.' He grinned. 'Then there was you, bald 'n bloodless as a bat outta hell. Seems from what the old lady said you were spouting in all directions. A real dancing dervish. Musta been quite something, pity I missed it.'

Blood throbbed in her face, spiking the dormant ache in her head. Christ the militant. Her frenetic outburst, the way they'd all stepped back. If Mambo repeated that part for public consumption, for his consumption—. She sucked in her breath. Christ, she'd never be able to live it down.

'God got angry in the temple, didn't he? I mean when those people were selling things, what I mean is, he wasn't all love and forgiveness, was he?' She searched his face, seeing the lines between his brows gathering to the prongs of a garden fork.

'You okay?'

'I'm fine.'

'Then what's with the sudden interest—?'

She avoided the narrowed eyes, turning to watch Mambo as she measured a minuscule drop of water into each mug to rinse it. 'Oh, nothing, nothing, I just wondered, is all. I was just trying to remember something—.'

' "And Jesus entered the temple, and he cast out all those who were selling and buying in the temple, and he overturned the tables of the money-changers and the seats of them that sold the doves." Matthew, 21:12. That it?' He cocked his head. 'That the one you been trying to recall?' The grey eyes were amused.

She stood up, wishing she'd kept her mouth shut. He was watching her too closely. Stretching, she tried to keep her voice off-hand. 'Eh, yes, that's probably it, then. Look, I'm really whacked. If you and Mambo don't mind—.'

His roar of laughter filled the little room. The old woman turned, her gap-toothed smile wide in response to the sound. That she didn't understand the joke was immaterial. It was enough that there was laughter. She nodded, her dark eyes bright as Emma picked up the hold-all.

'Next time you're planning on giving a sermon, lemme know, huh? You're always welcome to borrow my Bible, least that way you might get the quotation straight.'

She gritted her teeth, keeping her face averted as she moved towards the door of her room. 'I don't know what you're on about.'

'Don't you? Well, maybe you're right. Maybe I'm the one's got it wrong.' His voice was a soft drawl catching her up as she moved into the other room. 'But don't you worry about filling me in, I'm sure Mambo'll be only to happy to do that. You go right on and get some sleep.'

The bastard! She banged the door closed on his renewed laughter. For a moment, she stood, ear pressed to the thin gap between door and frame. Mambo murmured in a low voice. The floor beneath her feet vibrated as Dick moved about, his mono-syllabic rumble punctuating whatever it was the old woman was saying. Somehow, the tone of her voice lacked zest. Emma heaved a sigh. At least for now, they weren't discussing the fool she'd made of herself. She stared across at the camp bed in the gathering gloom, the sleeping bag folded as she'd left it, the grey blanket covering the mattress, hanging to the floor to hide where Mambo slept. Why hadn't he taken the bed back while she was away? She frowned, wincing as the skin stretched tightly across her burnt scalp. She put a hand above the crown of her head, the heat rising like a blast from a furnace against her palm. Christ, she'd love to dunk it in ice-cold water, leave it there until it froze.

When she finally lay in the sleeping bag, the faint odour of her own stale sweat embedded in its folds, the perennial odours of unwashed years in Mambo's blanket beneath, she realised why he'd left the bed well alone. Served him right. She grinned, keeping her eyes fixed on the crack of blue light outlining the door, the smell of paraffin seeping into the room. If she concentrated on it very hard, she could keep Thulatu's words at bay. It was good to be back. A blessing, he'd said. The word was balm, drifting with her into the darkness.

* * *

Dick stepped outside the cabin into the night, Mambo's words still clutching at his gut. When he'd tried to draw her out after Emma'd gone to bed, she'd bustled about, talking of other things, her eyes frightened. He stared up at the dusty galaxy of stars, trying to shake his disquiet by teasing out the familiar landmarks in the vast array of sky.

There, to the south, was his little ochre fire, beaming its spectre across centuries, the flickering aftermath of a star that once had been. Like the empty rhetoric of the psalms he sang, the sermons he preached in church. Like the driftwood dreams an old woman had garnered from the storehouse of a race whose myth and magic were more ancient than any religion. No more than that.

In California, any shrink would tell him that Mambo'd made the leap by association. And who could blame her, faced with Emma's spectral appearance? Enough to put the wind up a ghost, let alone an old woman.

Still the words clung to him, as though, like tearsmoke, they threaded the very air: 'I see a skull. It is death I see.'

Nonsense, the very idea was nonsense, simply the skeletal out-lines defined more sharply in the absence of hair, bringing with it the message of mortality. Only that. Nothing a few days' growth and regular meals wouldn't put straight. His mouth set in a hard line. And he'd be the one to see she did it, or know why.

Somewhere close by his feet, a frog belched among a crop of shrilling crickets in the long, dry grass. He smiled. That was one guy who wouldn't starve tonight. Emma could do with taking a leaf out of his book.

IV

Next day, the clinic finished earlier than usual because of the funeral. Dick didn't want Emma to accompany him to it.

Back in the cabin, the three of them finishing off the remainder of the over-ripe fruit which wouldn't last the heat till evening, she stared at him. What the fuck'd she done now, why was he so uptight?

She leaned across the desk towards where he stood looking out the window, her voice placating. 'Honest, I won't get in your way, I promise.'

He shook his head. 'Not this one. Next time.'

'Why the hell not?'

'Because I say so!' He turned to glare at her, a ridge of flesh at his throat bulging against the tight collar.

'May one make so bold as to ask why?' She sniffed. 'Sir?'

'You need more rest. You won't get much of it at this funeral. There's sure to be trouble. The police put a limit of twenty on this one. You ever seen an African family that small? Especially an African family who believe the only reason their boy died was because he'd had his head kicked once too often in detention. The graveyard'll be full to overflowing — ideal target practice if the cops decide they're in the mood.'

'I'm here to observe everything, what kind of journalist would I be if I didn't give a balanced view?'

'A live one. There'll be other funerals. I don't have time to play nursemaid. You ever seen a couple a hundred people stampeding when they panic? Makes a herd a buffalo look like chicken-feed. Have some sense, will you?' The large arms lifted, folding across his chest, a drawbridge closing in her face.

'I may not be here next time. I've got to grab any-.'

'Yeah, you're right. You might not be here, way you're heading, you're more liable to be the guest a honour at the next funeral.'

'What's that supposed to mean?'

'Look at you, look at the state you're in! When you came here first, you were—.' He lifted the black prayer missal from the desk, glad he'd stopped himself in time. 'Gimme a break, will you? Get some rest.' Turning to step outside, he jerked his head towards the other room.

She followed him to the door, her words rising in pitch as he hurried along by the side of the church. 'Christ, just because I'm a bit sunburned and I've lost a little weight doesn't mean I'm—.' But he was gone, disappearing around the corner as though he were seeking to escape the army or police. Her voice hung on the warm air in a nagging echo. Like a wife, she thought, disgusted. Well, fuck him, she was damned if she'd let him dictate to her. She'd go to that funeral or die at the heels of it. The thought made her grin.

It took her some time to persuade Mambo, so well had he drilled her. In the end, Emma tied a scarf over her peeling scalp, indicating she was going, with or without the old woman's help. The bluff worked, but was not without its drawbacks. Mambo kept up a string of invective for the entire half-hour it took them to walk through the deserted streets to the far side of town. Yet she was aware that they were being watched; here and there a mealie sack, a frayed blanket, even a net curtain twitching as those who didn't wish to be caught on the streets, should the police decide to disband the mourners, kept out of sight.

She tried to ignore the abuse Mambo was hurling at her, Christ, where'd she get the energy from at her age? — some words repeated over and over, 'makaka,' 'marete a ntat'ao,' 'kak! kak! kak!' their violence leaving her in no doubt that the old lady had a vocabulary of swearwords to equal the worst in English.

They stumbled along the centre of the cratered street in the official section, the tall lamp-posts lining the route a civic oddity in the absence of any footpath, most of their bulbs smashed, the distance between each one double that which was usual, stretching to an infinity of rubble-strewn dongas, wild yellow grass, the odd hacked thorn-bush, bits of rusting machinery and corrugate, a few dead husks of cars that would never be tolerated in the pampered suburbs of Durban. Yet here at least, the houses resembled houses, concrete walls, some of them painted, some of the roofs even tiled. On the window ledge of one, a dusty plant stirred in limp defiance at the squalor of the yard.

The graveyard was on the outskirts of the official section, Dick had pointed it out to her on a hand-drawn map he'd made of the area, in the absence of any official one. He'd drawn seventeen of them, one for each year he'd been here.

'You don't need to be a journalist or photographer to record history here,' he'd said, his voice bitter. 'Nor do you need to be a general to make it. Modern war's waged on a map, your army's the civil service, your weapon's an armoury of ink-pads and stamps. And your up-and-coming general's a cartographer drawing and re-drawing boundaries. His strategy's to designate: black spot removals, re-settlement areas, bantustans, prescribed areas, non-prescribed areas, closer settlements, relocation, slum clearance, township deproclamation, you name it, he's got a plethora of official titles for it, anything but what it is, a human pendulum driven across the face of South Africa, homes and streets and towns and lives obliterated, re-located in wastelands. In graveyards.'

She had stared down at the wad of maps, flicking through them as she would the pages of a book. The maps sped by, the years running together in spurts of upheaval, of forced migrations, the slow haul of change across the centuries compressed into seconds, lives flung into the wilderness with the stroke of a felt-tipped pen.

Dispossessed, as Mambo had been. She looked now at the old woman hobbling along before her. What chance had she ever stood against technocrats, bureaucrats and map-makers, lethal as any gun?

Suddenly Mambo stopped dead. Emma twisted her body in a sideways contortion to avoid crashing into her, the old woman's stillness frightening after so much volubility.

'Mambo! Christ, what is it?'

But before Mambo could point at her ears, Emma heard it, the chanting, the ululating rising from a low hum in the distance to a dense pitch that reverberated in the quiet street. Grinning, Emma raised her voice above the noise as they moved on. 'Well, at least that's put paid to your swearing.'

The graveyard was located on a piece of flat land bordering a dry river bed outside the town, a sprawling labyrinth of wooden stakes and crosses hardly visible now in the mass of singing bodies that swayed like the branches of a huge forest, dense and black, here and there clenched salutes fisting the sky.

Mambo's elbow poked her ribs. She turned to look as the old woman pointed. Beyond the graveyard, where the land rose towards the crumbling dam, the police watched. Emma shivered.

Mambo mouthed something, tucking Emma's arm through her own, squeezing it to indicate she wanted it kept there as they moved forward towards the crowd. The chanting died away and above its last echoes rose Dick's voice, the words indistinct at this distance, but something in his tone carrying the solemnity of prayer. The crowd hushed finally, straining to hear.

There seemed to be no official entrance except through a gap which had been filled with red clay in the donga surrounding the graveyard. Emma began heading for it but Mambo jerked her back, shaking her head. Taking her hand in a vice-grip, she began to negotiate the uneven hump of rock to the right of the entrance, on which a young black man stood, hands in pockets, surveying the scene. His glance at Emma was curious, a white woman in khaki shorts with a doek tied on her head in the African way, not something he'd expect to see here. He'd have been suspicious if it hadn't been for the old woman, Mambo, wasn't it, who'd been thrown out of her house after her old man killed himself?

Mambo glanced up at him and spoke, her words sharp jabs that made him roll his eyes at Emma as he reached down to help them. Didn't she realise there wasn't room for all three of them up here? — always the same, these aunties, expecting everyone to dance to their tune just because they were old. If it weren't for the young like himself, they'd all still be on their knees to the Boers.

He rolled his eyes again, stepping closer to the edge, his foot scrabbling for a niche in the side of the rock as the two women made it up almost on top of him, the old grandma sandwiched between them, one hand leeching on to his tee-shirt for dear life, the other grasping the shoulder of the white woman. Just as well the three of them were thin. Another inch of flesh and they'd've all ended up at the bottom of the donga.

Emma stared across the rippling heads, straining to see Dick, his beefy complexion pale in the distance, visible in spurts through the cage of swaying limbs as he looked down into the earth, his hand raised in a blessing. Beyond, on the rise, some police in camouflage uniform were playing idly with a bat and ball, their muddied khaki distinguishing them from the polite blue of other policemen lolling against the armoured carriers.

Afterwards, when she thought about the young policeman who'd turned towards the crowd, batting the ball into their midst, she hoped he'd been one of the ones trampled underfoot, so deliberate had been his gesture to provoke.

The ball spun towards the bobbing heads close to Dick, his voice drowned in a sudden scream of pain. Emma strained to see, but in the swift thrash of bodies panicking about him, he was blacked out. The voice came over the loudhailer at the same instant:

'This is an illegal gathering, we have been very patient. You people who do not have permission to be here will leave this place and return quietly to your homes.'

She stared open-mouthed at the sudden swarm on the rise. From one of the armoured carriers, police in riot gear were pouring in rapid succession, the leashed Rottweilers dragging their handlers behind them, a snarling line of savagery straining towards the crowd, soldiers flanking them, assault rifles mounted on their bulky vests.

She froze, vaguely registering the voice of the police commissioner as it droned, cutting through the angry shouts of the mourners, '... I repeat, you are breaking the law. If you have not disbanded in two minutes, we will be forced to fire a warning volley over your heads. For your own safety, we advise you to leave now. If you remain, we cannot guarantee your safety.'

They were never given two minutes. Before Emma could climb down from the rock, the first shot was fired. Afterwards, she discovered it killed a sixteen-year-old girl, a cousin of the boy they were burying. The girl had been standing beside Dick, ready to fling a handful of clay down onto the coffin, when the ball struck her mother's face. She saw the blood ooze from her mother's nose as the voice hailed over the loudspeaker. She reached out as her mother began to stagger back against those pressing behind her. The Boers. The Boers had shot her mother. She screamed as her mother's eyes glazed, the words ripping from her lips in a fury of hatred, 'They are dogs, dogs, they've killed my mother!' Those around her took up her cry, heads swinging wildly as they tried to move away from the grave.

Dick tried to make his voice heard above the screams, but it was futile. If he could calm the girl, there might be some hope of quieting those around her but already she was out of reach, lunging towards her injured mother.

When the shot was fired, it struck the girl on the nape of her neck, severing her spinal cord as she pitched forward into the grave. Dick winced, the thud of her body a death-knell striking the coffin. Thank the Lord he'd made Emma stay at home. Knowing she was safe made it easier to concentrate on what must be done to prevent more bloodshed. If he could get to the police, persuade Badenhorst to let him talk to the crowd himself, the whole thing might be defused. He dug out the white rag he always carried in his pocket, raising it to wave high above the tight weave of heads about him as he turned to beat his way through the heaving crowd towards the police. He'd done it once before, when the Okanga child had died. Pray the lord he'd succeed again today.

* * *

When the first shot was fired, the young man on the rock panicked, his body jerking.

'Makaka!' Mambo spat the word as he clawed her shoulder to steady himself. Quickly, she released her grip on his tee-shirt.

But it was too late. Together, the three of them fell into the donga. They sat, dazed and breathless, as more shots rang out above the screams. Emma drew herself up, the ground trembling as people began to run from the guns. There was blood on Mambo's cheek, otherwise, she appeared to be fine. Please, she thought, hauling her upright, let her be okay, let nothing be broken. If they didn't get out of here, they were liable to be trampled upon, the crowd surging now in all directions as they fled before the batons and the snarls of the dogs. She turned to ask the young man to help, between them they could move Mambo along more quickly. But already he was gone, his heels kicking dust as he sprinted down the track leading back to the township. She gaped after him. A real knight errant.

'Come back here, you frigging coward!' The words were out before she could stop herself.

'Baleka!' Suddenly Mambo was propelling her forward, the word hurled in her ear before the old lady's lips clamped. Hand in hand, they began to run down the track. Already the youth was out of sight among the squat, grey barrack-line of houses ahead. At her side, Mambo ran as though possessed, the air about them raucous with the petrified rasp of the crowd thickening on their heels. Baleka, baleka — the word thundered in the earth underfoot, snapping with the staccato of gunfire, leaving no room for thought or logic as blood, heart and bone fused to a single screaming pulse that was each of them and all of them moving in one great body, a mass exodus hurtling from the graveyard as though the dead had risen.

Suddenly, they were in the township, the houses closing like a blurred forest as the fleetest of the crowd outstripped them, Mambo ducking sideways into the nearest yard, past the refuse stacked in a corner, the gutted innards of an old stove, down by the row of silent houses to the yard at the rear, the line of outside toilets stretching like sentry-boxes on parade, the sun glinting in the zinc roofs.

They hid behind one of the toilets, the thick odours permeating the concrete blocks against which they collapsed. Emma hauled air in, pressing her hands against the scorched heat above her heart. Vaguely, above the air wheeling in her lungs, she was aware of the screams, the shots, the rumble of trucks in the streets. Her nose twitched. Tearsmoke. Distant enough not to suffocate them. If only it would stay that way. What was happening out there? Had Dick got away safely? Most likely he had, he was used to this after all. Christ, let them not be found here, let no one else run into the yard. When her breathing finally slowed, she turned to find Mambo, her face rigid with pain as she clasped the weight of tired breasts to her heart.

'Mambo! Mambo! You okay? Mambo, talk to me!' Emma grasped the thin arm, shaking her. She hardly seemed to be breathing at all, the dark eyes staring with the blank glaze of pebbles out across the open veld to the black snarl of undergrowth in the distance. Emma stared, fear spreading under her skin. Christ, what had she done, she'd killed her, that's what she'd done, tricked her into going to the funeral, knowing it was against her will, knowing it as surely as she'd sensed the threat in the raised arm of the policeman who'd turned to hurl the ball into the crowd.

'Mambo!' In her terror, she screeched in the withered ear. Mambo jerked, air whistling through the gaps in her teeth, her gaze snapping into focus as she turned to look at Emma. She grimaced, her hand patting the pain in her chest.

'Oh, Mambo, I thought you'd, I thought you'd .... Here, let me help.' Quickly Emma knelt before her, undoing the doek Mambo always wore about her neck. 'Now breathe like this.' She cupped the old face between her hands, inhaling deep draughts of warm air through her nose, releasing it through her mouth, nodding at the old woman to follow suit. Oh, why wasn't she a doctor or a nurse, she hadn't a clue what she was doing, please, please let it be the right thing, don't let her die, not now, not now when .... Suddenly, she was weeping, the tears spilling down her cheeks as though a well had sprung in her eyes. She bowed her head trying to check it as the old woman fought for air, a conscious will to breathe imposed on the body's sudden urge to abdicate.

How long they stayed like that, Emma couldn't be sure, but when Mambo finally lifted the cupped hands from her face, the sun was a spatter of veined light trapped in the thorny branches of the distant bush.

'We go. Home.' Mambo patted her shoulder.

Emma peered at the old face, the pewter tinge to the lips bringing her a message she didn't want to read. 'You okay?' Standing, she flexed her aching arms.

Mambo nodded, patting her chest. 'Is okay.'

Emma frowned. Did her voice sound funny, or was it the strangeness of the English words on her tongue? She rubbed her face, the skin itchy with dried sweat and tears. Around them, the noise had died to sporadic bursts of gunfire fading in the distance. If they didn't leave here, it would soon be dark. Tsotsis-time. She shivered, bending down to help Mambo as she struggled to rise.

'Here, lean on me, heavily as you can.' She draped Mambo's arm across her shoulder, slipping her own arm around the thin waist. As she began to head towards the silent houses, the old woman stopped dead, twisting around to point at the open veld. 'Is home. No umboomboom.' She nodded, the wiry hair brushing against Emma's cheek.

No umboomboom. Emma looked at her. Out in the bush somewhere, a baboon barked, making her jump. Maybe snakes in the long grass and who knew what else? Safer than the streets. She nodded. 'Okay.'

Together they headed out onto the veld, the grass hissing underfoot as it pressed around them, Emma's bare legs itchy to the bottom of her shorts, as though a myriad insects scrabbled for a foothold on her skin. Several times she stopped, insisting that Mambo rest, despite the old lady's protests. To their left, the dark line of houses, some larger buildings that were perhaps schools, a community hall, etched themselves against the pinpoints of emerging stars. Here and there a fire burned, tongues of sunset licking the blue-dark sky, the meteoric burst of sparks shooting new stars into the heavens.

Out here, the faint whine of a truck, the ricochet of metal on stone, was amplified, as though they stood wrapped in a fog that deflected sound, so that sometimes Emma stared towards the brooding shadow of the bush, her skin tingling with unease.

Twice they sank into the rippling grass as the headlights of a truck swept a gap between the barrack-lines of houses. Their progress was slow, giving Emma plenty of time to contemplate what Dick would say when they arrived. Well, this time, whatever he had to say, she'd take it, all of it, without a murmur, Christ, she wouldn't blame him if he threw her out, when she thought of the way she'd run Mambo along the track in front of the fleeing crowd, the casual way she'd played with her life, the dark greed in her heart to expiate her guilt, to bear witness at this old woman's expense. As though Mambo were of no consequence. She bit down savagely on her lower lip, hardly aware when she drew blood.

'I'm sorry, I'm sorry, Mambo,' she whispered into the corrugated ear, her eyes stinging as the tears flowed again, the words repeated over and over in spasmodic bursts as they inched their way towards the patchy silhouette of the squatter camp tacked on to the southerly end of the township.

* * *

But Dick was not at home. It was the lithe shape of Modise which rose from the concrete step into the dark cabin as they finally stumbled down by the side of the church.

'You are safe.'

'Mambo isn't well. It's my fault.' The words blurted from her lips. She strained to see his face but in the darkness there was only the flash of his eyes.

'Where's Dick?'

'Detained.'

The word hit her in the solar plexus. She stood staring as he helped Mambo inside, the light from the small torch whipping desk, shelf, the clutter of unwashed dishes on the table as he finally tracked down the lamp. He lit it quickly, its blue glow quenching the torch's beam before he could snap it off.

'Come in. You have a blanket for the window? Quickly!' His urgent tone penetrated the numbness in her limbs. Only when she stepped inside, closing the door behind her, did she realise the cabin had been searched. The desk stood, its drawers gaping and empty. Apart from the old newspaper Dick sometimes used to shield the window from sunlight, not a page remained on the desk. Mambo, sitting with her arms spreadeagled across its surface, her head bowed with tiredness, didn't seem to notice. Just as well, Emma thought. She'd been through enough today without adding this. What would they do to him? She stood, the question hammering with her heart.

'A blanket? Quickly!' He nodded at the window, pouring some water for Mambo while Emma hurried into the lower room. It too, had been searched, their clothes and the sleeping bag on the floor, the bed overturned. There was no sign of Mambo's blanket. She grabbed the sleeping bag and hurried back out, draping it over the twine Dick had tied above the window. Modise went to close the door to the other room.

'It is best if no light shows tonight.'

Mambo's shuddering sigh as she drooped on the chair filled Emma with remorse.

'She should be lying down, will you bring her through? I'll get Dick's blanket.'

There was no protest from the old woman when they laid her on the bed, her hand patting Emma's as she tucked the bag about her.

'She's so quiet, I've never seen her so quiet. D'you think she'll be all right?' Emma stared up at Modise as they returned to the main room. The narrow shoulders shrugged. 'She is old, it is difficult to tell.'

The words were deadweight in her gut.

She watched the slim, graceful hands as he put some water on to boil. 'I ... almost killed her, I made her take me to the funeral.' She was afraid to ask him about Dick.

'Perhaps. But if you'd both been here when the police came ...' he shrugged, searching for the coffee, '... they've detained about thirty, mostly the injured who couldn't run away, and a few old women. Two young girls were killed. Some of the others they've taken were badly injured. But we can't be sure how many dead until the police decide to dump the bodies. It was just as well you weren't here when they came to search. Mambo wouldn't have stood a chance.'

'You think so?' She brightened a little. Perhaps, after all, what she'd done today had inadvertently proved the lesser of two evils. She grimaced at his back. Cold comfort. But she'd clutch it never-theless.

'I need the papers, they must be taken away from here.' He turned, bringing the steaming mugs to the desk. Somehow, they looked lost on the barren expanse of it.

She nodded. 'Dick told me if you ever came—. Will they ... hurt him?' There. It was out, the closest she could bring herself to the word that was gnawing at her bladder.

'Torture?' The dark eyes were enigmatic.

216

She rose, suddenly afraid she'd wet herself. 'I, I have to use the loo. Excuse me, will you?'

She was back a moment later, hands clutching her stomach, her mouth twisting as she fought to get the words out. He leapt from the edge of the desk, a startled rhebok alert to sudden threat. 'What is it?' Vaguely she registered the brightness in his eyes, the savagery of the gun in his hand. Where had it sprung from? His jacket? She hadn't even seen his hands move.

'What?' The word hissed in her face, his eyes scouring the room beyond as the gun jerked to attention.

'No!' Her hands flew upwards. 'It's the toilet?'

The dark eyes widened. 'Come?'

'It's, it's ...' She stared at the gun, the nausea rising again. If she didn't get out fast she'd throw up in front of him.

'Foul!' The word burst from the bile in her mouth. She hauled on the door and leaped outside, running to the back of the cabin as the heaving began, barely making it to the long grass that would hide the sludge of sour fruit spilling from her mouth. Even when it was over, she knelt, weak and shivering as the retching continued, the stench thick in her nostrils, her anger rising on the heels of her vomit, fuck them, fuck them, fuck them, their one small dignity stripped from their skins, besmirched in an act calculated to humiliate and degrade. Rising, she staggered away from the smell, and peed weeping into the long grass. She stared at the flesh of her thighs, faintly luminous in the starlit dark. I am black, she thought, black bandaged in a white skin, I am nothing, nothing more than the dark spasms of a bowel, and this is what it is to be black, to be Mambo's grey blanket stuffed into the toilet bowl, smeared with the filth of faeces until it soaks through the weave.

When she dragged around the front again, Modise was stepping back inside, the yellowed newspaper crackling in his hands as he wiped them.

'They must have taken a bucket from one of the latrines.' He dropped the crushed paper into the plastic bag they used for rubbish and picked up the soap, indicating the plastic container. 'Outside? You will pour a little?'

She picked up the water and followed him out.

'Close it.' The dark head bent gracefully towards the door.

'Tomorrow, I will bring it back clean.' The words were a whisper.

She whispered back, peering to find his hands as she poured a few drops. 'I don't think I could ever use it again.'

'That is what they want.' He worked the pale soap into a thick lather. 'That is why they do such things.'

'Yes, but I can't stand the filth!'

'Neither can I.'

The words were a rebuke. She grimaced, glad he couldn't see the heat rising in her cheeks. 'Yes, I know, I'm sorry, and you carried it outside, thank you. It's just that every time I look at that thing, I'll think of—.'

'Think this: they tried to make you shit like a dog in the streets or a baboon out on the veld, but you didn't submit.'

She shuddered, pouring the water slowly over his outstretched hands. 'What sort of fucking minds've they got? Why'd they do such a thing? I mean, it's not even as if—.'

'More water?' He rubbed his hands vigorously. 'It makes their job easier. If they treat us like animals, after a time they begin to see us as animals, they become conditioned. It makes it possible for them to do what they are doing without feeling guilt. Now rinse the cake.' He held the soap out, turning it as the few drops slithered over its smooth planes.

It was the longest speech he'd ever made to her, the logic of it irrefutable. In the dark, he might have been Solomon, seventeen going on ninety. She thought of the speech he'd made in the church, the single-minded intelligence in the dark eyes. The kind of bright young man the dean of any European university would enthuse about. So calm was he, it was difficult to believe he was of this place, a seed of its anger and despair. Where she had expected the impetuosity of youth, there was a cold patience, a clarity of vision that was unnerving. And still she was afraid to ask him about Dick. Afraid of the way he'd refuse to mince words.

'Your English's so precise. Where'd you learn it? — hold this will you? I need to rinse my mouth.' She gave him the container, cupping her hands as he poured.

'Somafco. I was there for several years.'

'Eh?' Turning from him, she sucked on the water, driving it in a furious whirl about her teeth, sending it spurting into the darkness beyond her feet.

'A freedom college in Tanzania. I was lucky.' Already he was opening the door, stepping swiftly inside. 'Hurry!' He held it until she was in, then locked it. She sat, rubbing her hands on her shorts. It was time to face what he had to say. She sipped the cold coffee, swilling it about her mouth before swallowing. 'Did they come here for him? You got a cigarette by any chance?'

He reached inside the light anorak he was wearing and pulled out a crushed packet. Instantly she thought of the gun. Yet there was no sign of any bulk.

'They took him at the funeral. With several others.'

'Where to?'

'He's here, at Andries.'

She thought of the concrete fort the far side of town, the rolls of bladed wire topping the high steel fence.

'Will they ... hurt him?'

'Yes.' He swilled the coffee in the mug.

'But he's white, they mightn't ....' She felt the flush rise from her neck.

But he didn't seem to notice. 'His skin won't save him. It didn't the last time.'

Her mouth was suddenly dry. 'You mean he's been detained before? For how long? What'd they do to him?'

'Both times he was released after a few hours.' The chiselled lips thinned. 'First they promised him a fine church in the official section if he would stop helping the squatters. When that didn't work, they roughed him up a little, promising they'd pay him a visit with a petrol bomb some night. They told him to go back to his church and pray to his God for a miracle.' He smiled suddenly, and she sucked in her breath at the childlike radiance of it. 'They might've asked Jesus to stop loving the poor.' The smile vanished, as though a light had been switched off behind his eyes. 'After a while, they get tired playing such games.'

The words chilled her. 'But you said, a few hours. So it's possible he might be back tonight. Surely?'

He jerked his head, his voice contemptuous. 'The warder who brings the food to the prisoners in the communal cell is easy to bribe. Father comrade is still in the interrogation room.'

She stared at the dark, impassive face. 'What does it mean?'

'It means he is standing naked, handcuffed to a grid since—.'

She flinched. 'Don't tell me, please, don't tell me!' She stared at the mug on the desk, vaguely registering the cracked handle.

In the silence, a low snore rumbled through the thin partition dividing the rooms. Outside, the chirp of crickets amplified, a frenzied weight pressing on the walls.

She jumped up. 'I've got to go there, see if I can help—.'

'No! You'll stay here!' He stood, body taut as whipcord. 'It is his wish.'

She blinked. 'How can you know something like that? He's in trouble, he needs—.'

'What else could be his wish? That you go there to be detained also?'

'Me? But they wouldn't—.'

'No?'

The word hung in the paraffined air, refusing to dissipate. She stared at his face, the black sheen of African granite in the lamplight. Impenetrable.

'How can you be so ... cold-blooded?'

His eyes shuttered. 'That is a question for the Boers.'

'Yes, it's a question for the Boers, that's why I should go there, somebody's got to help him—.'

'But not you.'

His words were a slap in the face.

'If he is needed, Thulatu will come. I have sent word.'

Thulatu. His name thudded in her chest. She'd managed to keep him at bay for the past twenty-four hours. Christ, it was too soon to have to face him again.

'Let's hope it doesn't come to that,' she said, her tone fervent. Instantly, she was ashamed, her wish for Dick's release intensifying in her desire to avoid Thulatu. What wonderful stuff she was made of.

'Yes. And now, the papers? If they keep him long enough, he will break.'

She shuddered, following him outside. Break. Such a small word. Long after he'd gone, the darkness enveloping him as he stole away with the bundle from the altar under his arm, the word drummed in her head. She wished he'd stayed, had even asked him back in for some hot coffee, afraid to be alone, afraid to lie in the dark thinking about Dick, afraid they might come for her and Mambo in the night.

But he wouldn't stay. 'You are safer on your own. If they found me here, you and Mambo would suffer. They'd accuse you of harbouring a terrorist.'

And are you a terrorist, she'd wanted to ask, remembering the gun in his hand, the way his body had coiled to spring when she'd rushed from the stench inside the toilet door, his quick eyes trained on the blackness behind her. As though he could see in the dark. As though he'd devour whatever might leap from it.

Lying now in Dick's room, her head resting on the frayed bag into which she'd stuffed the clothing she'd found spread about the floor, she blocked Dick and Thulatu from her mind, trying instead to concentrate on Modise, seeing him slip from shadow to shadow as he wound his way through the township, snippets of history welded to his chest, eviction orders, removal notices, minutes of committee meetings, testimonies of those tortured in detention, of those who'd witnessed the brutality of SAP in the streets, the clinic records, even the newspaper clippings she'd brought back from Durban, was it only yesterday? — pieces of the jig-saw that would one day bear witness to the grass-root truth of Apartheid.

Strange the way when she was in his presence, the dark perfection of that face, how she couldn't conceive him without a penis, warm and limp between his legs. A eunuch. Such a ... violent word. Like terrorist. How easily she'd pinned the label on him. It was she who was the terrorist, living under laws which ratified, even absolved her of her crime, laws she'd accepted without question. How could she dare measure Modise by such a twisted yardstick?

She sighed, drawing the sleeping bag more tightly about her, staring at the square of stars fading in the growing light. Could Dick see the sky? Could he see? Think? Talk? Feel? Feel pain? Breathe? Did he still have a penis? Christ, she couldn't lie here any longer, she'd go crazy. Better off up, doing something. She'd go through the medical supplies, see what she had available for the morning. How was she going to last here on her own? What if he didn't come back? What if he never came back? The thought spread like ice, numbing her. Suddenly, she was tempted to pray. The words would be easy. Simple. Let him return. Safe. A good man. Let him not be hurt. A small wish. Just one man, let him not be hurt. Dear God. Deaf God. Blind God. Dear God who is not there. No. It would be an act of treason.

Somehow, over the next couple of days, she managed, grateful for Modise's help, the youths he sent to assist her in the clinic. She fought a constant battle with Mambo, trying to make her take things easy. In the end she compromised, giving the old lady piles of mealie sacks to cut into bandage strips, a task she could sit at while she worked.

For the first time since she arrived, it rained: a torrential downpour that broke the oppressive heat, that brought the children out to dance barefoot in the lightning, to jump shrieking into the reddish pools forming in the cratered streets. That's when she found out in how many places the roof of the church leaked. She and Mambo rushed about, carrying in the containers they'd been using to catch the rain, finding they filled almost as quickly inside as out. Too much water all at once. Emma stared at it plopping into the plastic basins. Could nothing ever be moderate in this godawful place?

Still, it'd been wonderful to stand outside behind the cabin, washing away the stale sweat, lifting her face to the cool staccato rhythm beating on her skin, the laughter of children, the joyous upsurge of adult voices in her ears as water flowed endlessly, singing on corrugate, its applause slapping in the muddied street. The rain brought with it hundreds of frogs, as though by some magic stroke of nature, they had spawned overnight. She found she had to be careful where she stepped, but she couldn't understand Mambo's horror of them, despite the old lady's attempts to explain. In the end the most she managed to glean was that it stemmed from some deep-rooted superstition.

When Dick came, he came alone. The rain had eased, the late afternoon sparkling in its wake.

'Umfundisi!'

It was Mambo who alerted her, crying out the word from the door of the cabin as she climbed down to greet him. Emma dropped the clothes she was sorting on the desk and ran to see. She stood rooted in the doorway, staring at the staggering gait of the man making his way down by the side of the church, his right eye swallowed in a mound of swollen flesh, his clothes torn and soiled, the tattered collar trailing from his neck. But he was alive. She breathed, the iron hand that had gripped her skull for the past two days suddenly dissolving.

'Modise,' he was saying to Mambo, 'get Modise,' the words clenched in his teeth as he tried to wave her away. 'Quick, tell him to come quick. Modise!' The roar of pain galvanised Mambo. She nodded, reaching to touch his shoulder before she scuttled away.

'What is it, oh what is it?' Emma jumped down, reaching out to steady him as he swayed, catching the stale whiff of urine on his clothing. But as she touched him, he reared back, almost over-balancing. She might have tried to strike him.

'Don't, don't touch me!' His voice was an agonised snarl. Desperate, she stared at him, her hands flapping aimlessly as he struggled to get inside. If only he'd let her help him. Christ, what'd they done to him?

But it was Modise who told her hours later when Dick finally lay on his stomach in an intoxicated stupor on the narrow camp bed. They stood outside the cabin, the caked earth drying in the low sun. She scuffed a clump of pinkish grass at her foot. It blurred suddenly as the tears came.

'The bastards. The fucking bastards!'

Modise said nothing.

'Can't we lodge a complaint? Official? Get Thulatu to—?'

'If he signed an affidavit, he'd be more likely to disappear the next time they detained him. It is so for all of us. And he could not win. It is their word against his.'

She wiped her face with the back of her hand. 'Y'know, I thought he'd be safe, well, not safe, but I thought—. You said he'd been roughed up a little, I thought, the most they'd do, beat him maybe, what I mean is—.' She rubbed her eyes, trying to relieve the stinging.

'You thought his skin would save him?'

'No. His collar!'

Modise laughed, the sound harsh. It was the first time she'd registered any emotion in him.

'Because he is a man of God? You do not know these Boers. Do you know what they told him when they drove the nails into his buttocks? They told him every time he blesses himself he should thank them for putting the sign of the cross on his arse!'

She shuddered, visualising the studs nailed into the soft flesh. Afterwards, when Modise had removed them, Mambo had brought them outside to show her, shreds of skin clinging to the bloodied metal, his agonised roars still loud in her ears. He hadn't wanted her present. Spreadeagled across the desk, his white knuckles wrapped around each corner, he'd looked her way, his good eye registering embarrassment behind the pain as Modise snipped at his trousers. 'Please,' he'd said, his voice hoarse. 'Go away.'

And she'd gone, glad not to have to witness it.

'Shouldn't we get him to a doctor?' she said now, looking up at Modise.

He shook his head. 'The wounds are not too deep, they will heal, I have seen it often. There is more pain than injury.'

'What about tetanus? Shouldn't he have—?'

'The clinic from Lenasia gave everybody an injection last year, it is okay.'

'And his eye?'

'It will weep a little. But the swelling will go down. He will be all right, sisi.'

Sister. She looked at him, warmed by the word.

She scratched the thick stubble on her head. 'It's just that I feel so ... useless—.' The tears were threatening again. She turned away.

'The whiskey will make him sleep. Tomorrow he will be much better. You will see.'

And he was right. In the morning she rose early, wanting to bring him some coffee. But he was already up, clean-shaven and dressed, fixing the collar about his neck as he stood by the window. Coming from his room, where she and Mambo had spent the night, she stopped dead in the doorway.

'You're up.'

'Course.' He grinned, the bruising around his eye an iridescent swirl of colour, as though he'd been in a prize fight.

She felt awkward, unsure of what to say. She looked for pain in his face but found only tiredness. The whole thing seemed unreal. Seeing him standing there, bullish as ever, it was difficult to believe anything had happened. Except for his good eye, the dull impenetrability of granite. And the fact that he was standing.

'Coffee?' She moved across to put some water on to boil, careful not to brush against him as she slid past. She wanted to say how sorry she was, how terrible it must have been for him but he began whistling, a hard jaunty tune that excluded her. 'Shouldn't you be resting? I can manage the clinic today, and the crowd in the church.'

'What's this? Trying to do me out of a job? The church? You been preaching some more sermons while I've been away?'

She gritted her teeth at his teasing tone. 'We've been lucky, no raids since you were ... you were ....'

'On vacation? They the words you're looking for?'

The two of them glanced towards his room as they heard Mambo stirring.

'I'm not made of glass, Emma, I won't shatter if you say the word. I've been detained before.' His voice was light. He might've asked her to pour the coffee.

'Yes.' She stared at the steam rising from the water. 'You might've told me.'

'Why? What good would it've done you to know?'

'It never dawned on me they'd take you. Stupid, eh?' She banged the mugs down on the desk. 'I got a shock, can you imagine that?' She spooned the coffee indiscriminately, uncaring of whether they ran out of it or not. 'You could've saved me that at least.'

The good eye stared. 'What is it with you? You were warned before you came. You knew the risks. Nobody's sacred here.'

'Yes, but at least if I'd known you'd been taken twice before, at least if I'd—.'

'Modise's been filling you in.' He shrugged. 'I don't see how it matters.' He turned away to look out the window, something careless in his action spiking her anger.

'Don't you?' She poured the boiling water, slopping it on the surface of the desk. 'Damn you, Mambo nearly had a heart attack all thanks to ... to me.' Suddenly, she was crying. 'And you weren't here. You weren't here. And now you're here, acting like nothing happened, like it was all some light-hearted joke, what do we do now, sit down for breakfast and talk about the weather? No, not sit, not for you, forgive me, I forgot about your ... condition ... your little indisposition, I suppose you'll be telling me next you've a boil on your backside!'

He stood transfixed as she wept into the steam. What the devil had he said or done now? God in heaven, would he ever get it right? He shifted, trying to ease the pain in his buttocks. He'd played down what'd happened for her sake and Mambo's. For his own sake, afraid of the sympathy he'd seen in her eyes, of what it might unleash in him. He raised a hand to pass it over his face, wincing as he touched the bruised skin. The tears were running down the line of her neck, darkening the rim of her tee-shirt. If only he could walk across to her, press her small face against his chest, hold it there until the thin body quietened. Still, he stood, unable to move as Mambo came through the door, eyes flitting as she took in the scene.

'Why do you not comfort her?' she said to him in Xhosa as she passed him, the gap-toothed mouth set in a line of rebuke.

Quickly she went to her, wrapping her spindly arms about the heaving body, the gesture maternal. He felt his throat thicken. Suddenly, the walls began to close in. If he didn't get out, he'd make a complete ass of himself.

When the last shudders finally eased, Emma realised he was gone. How soon had he left? The moment she began to bawl, most likely. And who could blame him? She stood ashamed, her cheek pressed to Mambo's bony shoulder, unwilling to relinquish the comfort of it. What the hell was wrong with her? She couldn't seem to control herself anymore. Christ, what must he think of her, bawling her eyes out as if she'd been the one who'd been tortured? What sort of selfish bitch was she to inflict the pent-up fears of the last few days on him? Hadn't he been through enough without being forced to watch her wallow in self-pity?

Her remorse lasted right through running the clinic together, an awkward politeness between them as they avoided each other's eyes, her own red and swollen from the frenzy of her outburst. She'd have to apologise, later, when everyone was gone.

But he never gave her the chance. She began packing the medicine box as he walked to the door with the old man who'd been their final patient. She was so busy framing the words in her mind that it took a while before the silence registered. She looked up to find herself alone, sunlight streaming through the open door.

Dumping the rest of the rolled bandages into the box, she lifted it and hurried round to the cabin. Mambo had gone to help the family of the girl who'd been shot in the graveyard. Now was her chance to get it over with.

But when she entered the cabin, it was empty. Perhaps he was lying down? It was then she saw the note on the table, the scrawled words indisputably his — 'Back about six. Eat something.' She snorted in disgust. Blunt and bossy as ever. Nevertheless, she went to mix some mealie pap, surprised to find she was hungry. Where had he gone? As far away from her as he could get. She pounded the grey mess in the pot, suddenly lonely.

When he came through the door that evening, the first sight that greeted him was Emma sitting asleep at his desk, her head pillowed on her arms. For a moment, his heart thudded at her stillness, but she moved suddenly, snuffling through her nose, the sound reassuring him. He clattered about, putting water on to boil, unpacking the bread and chicken he'd been given because he couldn't attend the funeral meal after the ritual washing of the hands. Emma stirred, her dark eyes drunk with sleep as she peered up at him. She rubbed the numbness in one of her arms, flexing it as it bristled to life.

'You're back? Where were you?' She winced at the accusation in her voice. Christ, she was beginning to sound like a nagging wife. She rushed on, trying to justify it. 'Talk about me not eating, look at you, you're dead on your feet, you should be in bed, about time you took a dose of your own advice.'

His silence surprised her. She watched him measure the grains of coffee into the mugs, his face grey. Standing for the entire forty-eight hours, Modise had said. Under a bare bulb. Any time he closed his eyes, they'd thrown a bucket of icy water over him. At one point they'd given him electric shocks. She spoke again, her voice gentle. 'I thought you said you wouldn't be back till six?'

'It's after that now.'

'Is it?' She turned to the window, surprised to find the sun had already worked its way round to the back of the cabin. Outside the pink and violet clouds looked as if they'd been laid on with a palette knife. Sunset. Her eyes widened. 'I must've slept all afternoon, isn't that something?' She smiled. And there'd been no dreams again. Just a dark, restful oblivion. A miracle.

'Where'd you get it?' She stared at the plate of sliced chicken he handed her.

'We buried the girl this afternoon.'

'You what? Are you crazy? How many were there? What about the police? I thought you weren't supposed to—.'

'That's why we did it today.' He grinned, passing her the bread. 'Police'll have a long wait at the graveyard tomorrow.'

'Where's Mambo? Is she—?'

'At the sopolo.'

'Eh?' She bit deeply into the bread, its fresh, oven-baked smell thick in her nostrils.

'There's a meal after the funeral. She's stopping over, won't be back till morning. Haven't seen such a spread in a long time. Family's got quite a few relatives in the official section, all a them've got jobs. When I couldn't stay, the mother got Mambo to wrap us some food.' He pushed the chicken around his plate, staring at it as though it were a message he couldn't decipher.

There was something about him, she thought. Something ... extinguished. She shivered. 'What is it?'

He glanced up, his good eye surprised, the white of the other, jaundiced under the hooded lid. Perhaps she was wrong, perhaps it was no more than all he'd been through.

'I've just come from Modise.' He hesitated, his fork clattering on the plate as he dropped it.

'What is it?' She searched his face, the sheen of marbled flesh about his eye.

'He's just got his hands on a copy of a demolition order. Eight o'clock on Wednesday morning, the bulldozers move in.' His voice was deadweight thudding in her ears.

'Y'mean they're going to bulldoze—? They're going to break down—?'

'They're gonna flatten us, church and all.'

'But they can't, they can't just—!'

The good eye blazed. 'They can. And they will. Prevention of Illegal Squatting Act. When it's all razed to the ground, not a brick left standing, they'll round up the squatters and since homelessness is illegal in this fine country, they'll jail the ones they suspect run the street committees, the rest'll be shipped off to the homelands to rot. Only thing we're sure of is the Sothos're going to Gazankulu.' His lips twisted. 'Used to be Shangaan there, but they moved them on. That's the way the Afrikaner cookie crumbles.'

She stared around the clutter of the cabin, as familiar to her now as her own skin. 'And this, will they—?'

'Everything.' He picked up the fork, stabbing a piece of chicken. 'The collar's only sanctified when it's on their side.'

'Wednesday? But that's only three days away! What're we going to do, how're we going to—?'

'We're gonna fight it this time.'

She stared, wondering if she'd heard him aright, but the grey eye was fixed on her, cold as slate.

Her heart knocked against her ribs. 'You're crazy, they've got guns and trucks, they'll kill us, they'll—.'

'We're gonna make a stand. This is where these people belong. They get shunted into the homelands, they're dead anyway.'

In the silence a couple of dogs snarled in the street.

'She was sixteen years old. When we buried her, she still had the clay clenched in her hand.' His voice rasped in the gathering dark.

Chapter Seven

I

The sun beat down on the farm patio and as they knelt, the two blacks eyed the bottles on the table under the sun canopy. Murphy stared at the braai in the corner and for an instant allowed himself to conjure an image of meat roasting on the grill. He tightened the twine around the sack he was wearing, toying with the notion of taking a swig from one of the bottles. But would there be time before Verwoerd showed up wielding his whip? He dropped the rag into the bucket of cloudy water in front of him, wishing it were drinkable. The alcohol'd help him get through the day but it wasn't worth the price of being beaten. Besides, his skinny little companion Sipho, still wet behind the ears, didn't look like he could take much more, the cuts and bruises livid on his arms and face. He sat back on his haunches, deciding to sweat it out.

'But if your name's Murphy, why'd they keep calling you James? They never changed my name.' The new man turned to stare up at the large hulk beside him.

Murphy squinted at the bird soaring high above the ocean of sugar cane that rose towards the distant koppies to the north. An eagle, maybe, its powerful wings outlined against a slash of cloud. Free as a bird. Fly, brother, fly. One day I'll join you, we'll rise on the wind, glide together in the blue dome.

'It's a new kind of manacle to show you who's god here.'

'Ah, you won't be serious.' Sipho scratched at his chest and was immediately sorry, the rough fabric of the sack scraping against his swollen nipple.

'I've never been more serious, brother.' Murphy turned to look at him. 'You look like trouble, first thing they do is get rid of your name and give you one of theirs. That way you belong to them, see? A real baptism of fire.' He laughed, swiping the edge of his hand across his forehead, collecting the drops of sweat, shaking them onto the ground. Instantly they faded on the terracotta flagstones. The air rasped with crickets.

'How much longer?' At his side, Sipho shifted, his voice jittery.

'Keeping us waiting is all part of it. Patience!' Murphy glanced at the chess set on the table. Behind them, the French windows into the farmhouse were closed. He grinned, raising his voice, 'I say, d'you fancy a game of chess, old chum?'

But his companion was staring directly ahead, peering beyond the lawn to the small orchard of trees to see if the farm manager was coming. 'I thought "Scutta" was only played in the cells?'

Murphy looked at the tic racing in the older man's jaw. If he'd been capable of pity, he'd have felt it. But too many things had happened to bleed him. There was room only for anger now, and a black humour which helped him survive until his hatred could be channelled. 'The manager here was once a policeman. He's still fond of the game. But!' He wagged a finger at Sipho. 'He'll only beat us if we lose. A real bonus, eh?'

'I'll never get it done in time.' The older man screwed up his face, slapping his hands over his ears. 'Those fucking crickets!'

'The thought of that sjambok lashing your back is enough to move mountains. The secret is to push the rag back to the bucket, damming the water. I've seen men squeezing it out of sheer nerves before it's half-way back.'

Sipho lifted his shoulders, trying to ease the ache in his back. 'I'm still sore from that donkie piel.'

'The newcomers' welcome. So now you know who's baas, eh?'

'Those fucking crickets!'

Murphy raised a hand, flipping it over as he spoke. 'Switch them off.'

Sipho stared at him. Big prick. 'Ha. Ha.'

But already Murphy's eyes were closed, his hands over his ears, something about his stillness reminding Sipho of the old witchdoctor his mother had once brought him to when his skin had raged like hot coals. The old man had gone into a trance, his mud hut thick with the smell of what he'd ever afterwards thought of as boiled blood. 'Stop it, will you?'

Murphy's hands slid from his ears, the eyes opening slowly as he stared at the distant cane flickering through the trees. Swords, he thought. Spears. Millions and millions of them. Someday, someday. He turned, smiling. 'There, you see? What'd I tell you?'

Sipho stared at him, the crickets still ringing in his ears. He'd want to watch this one. 'Yeah,' he said, trying to make it sound like he was convinced.

'Ah, you didn't try hard enough, brother.'

'Yeah, and you tried too hard.' He was tempted to tap his head when he said it.

'You got to believe in the power.'

'There's only one power I believe in right now.' He jabbed a finger close to his swollen face.

'The power of the mind. Mind over matter. That's what it is.'

'Is that what it is?' He'd humour him.

'You ever been interrogated?'

The question took him by surprise. 'Is there a black who hasn't?'

'What'd you think about while they were——?'

'I thought about how long I could hold my piss before it'd come streaming down my pants.'

'What else?'

'How do I know? About being ten thousand miles away from every Boer in the world!'

'That's it!'

'Huh?'

'You switch them off same way you shut the Boers out. That's what it is, how you live through it. Come on, come on, try it. Concentrate.' Murphy grabbed Sipho's wrists, drawing his arms up until his hands were over his ears.

'You been here how long?'

Murphy's eyes flashed. 'Long enough to switch those fucking crickets off!'

Sipho stared at the quickness in the over-large eyes. Maybe this fellow wasn't off his head after all.

'Now, you interested?'

'Okay, okay.'

'Close your eyes. Concentrate. Squeeze those bastards out of your ears. That's it, that's it, that's how you do it.' Murphy's hands pressed hard over his own, the frenzy of the crickets suddenly swallowed in the low thunder of an ocean rolling towards a shoreline, the sound of the sea cupped in the shell of his ear. Drumming far-off on the shit-yellow sand. Beautiful, he could listen forever. Sail away to the dim horizon. Rising and riding on the back of a wave. Every time they got to him in future, he'd put his hands over his ears, take himself off to the sea. Maybe, just maybe, if he took his hands away slowly enough, if he concentrated on the waves, held on to them there, deep in his ears.... It worked. He opened his eyes, afraid the movement might shatter the peace. But it held. He stared about, knowing those crickets were still there, somewhere in the short sweet grass that ran to the trees, scratching in a well of silence. Had anything ever been so easy? 'Hey, brother!' He slapped his hunkered companion on the back, almost sending him sprawling across the flags. 'I'll get some sleep tonight.'

'Easy, easy! The bones are brittle.' Murphy straightened up and sat back, the stone hot under his buttocks.

'I'll never get it done in three minutes.'

Murphy looked at him. The same, all of them. No sooner'd they solved one problem, they were worrying about the next. He sighed. Why did they always stick him with this type?

'Y'hear me? Three minutes is too short, it's nothing.'

'That's what the last man said.' Murphy grinned. 'He was nearly shitting himself.'

'What happened?'

'He shit himself.'

Despite himself, Sipho laughed, the sound swallowed in Murphy's sudden howls of mirth. He scanned the path that led through the trees. No sign of the animal Verwoerd. He shifted a little to relieve the pressure on his knees. He could risk sitting back, as Murphy'd done, but sure as anything, the moment he did it, that son-of-a-bitch'd show. It was nice just sitting here chatting in the heat. 'What'd they get you for?' he asked Murphy, as much to bury his fear as out of a desire to know.

'Out without my Pass book.'

Sipho stared at him. 'But the Pass Laws've been abolished, don't you know that?'

'Then why'm I here?' Murphy's eyes were suspicious. 'Where'd you hear that?'

'It was in all the newspapers.'

'Ah, you don't want to believe everything you read in the papers.'

They laughed together. Sipho looked at the younger man, suddenly liking him. 'Yeah,' he said, 'now blacks can eat in five-star restaurants.'

'Ah, shit, just when I lost my credit cards! Ah, I'll eat in the cheaper places.'

'And end up back in jail? The cheaper places are still out of bounds.' Sipho stuck out his chest. 'Only the best for us, the very best. You need the works for those places, black tuxedo, bow tie.'

'That all? Here, get a load of this!' Murphy pulled at the twine around his waist. Before Sipho could think to stop him, he'd hauled off his sackcloth, a pair of frayed black shorts just about holding his credentials underneath.

'Stop, stop it! If he comes—.' Sipho craned to see through the line of trees. But Murphy, tying the twine in a bow about his neck, ignored him. He stood, his hand a sweeping arc as he indicated himself. 'Y'see?' He began strutting about the patio, his walk the exaggerated swagger of a peacock.

'Cut it out!'

'Y'like my black tuxedo?' He stopped, posing for his companion. 'Hand-sewn in Heaven by the great Tailor himself.' He swivelled, turning his buttocks to Sipho. 'Seat's a little shiny but shit, I've been wearing it since I first looked a wholesome piece of thigh in the eye.'

'He's coming!'

Murphy responded to the words as though his life depended on it. Within seconds, he'd donned the sack and was kneeling again, tying the twine around his waist. He closed his eyes, nostrils flaring as he dragged in air. When he opened them, there was no sign of the farm manager. 'My heart! He's not.'

'I thought he was.' Sipho tried to make the words sound emphatic. Murphy cast him a sharp look but said nothing. For a while there was silence.

'What about you?' Murphy eventually asked him.

'My wife works for a madam in Durban. Sometimes I sneak in. The bastards caught me without a "midnight special".' He winced as Murphy poked him in the ribs, his voice thick with innuendo. 'Before or after?'

'After.'

Murphy's belly shook as he roared with laughter. 'Jesus, brother, that was some expensive screw. How long've you got?'

'They selected me for parole yesterday. Eight months to do.'

Murphy nodded, wiping the tears from his eyes. 'Harvest time. Be glad it's sugar cane. I once got paroled to a wine farm outside Cape Town. They operated the "tot". Cheap wine twice a day instead of a fair share of food.'

'You took it?'

'It got me through the days, the smell of the compound, the sour mealie. We were locked in at night, same as here — forty men and a bucket. This isn't so bad. There's room to lie without touching off the next man.'

'Unless you stretch.' Something cracked in Sipho. 'It stinks!' Murphy glanced back at the French windows. 'Keep it down!' He lowered his voice. 'I heard about a man over in the Free State who complained. The farmer shot him in the face. The police made the other parolees bury him right outside the compound. None of those men ever stepped on the spot afterwards. Even though it was never marked. You'd imagine, in the end, they'd forget, wouldn't you? But they never did. Any of the newcomers ever stepped on it, those men beat them up. So even when they left, one by one, when their terms were served, everybody still knew where it was. And they still walk around it, even now. Funny, hey?'

'*That* wasn't in the papers.'

'All the more reason for believing it.'

Their laughter was low, bitter, both of them picturing the spot, the men stepping round it.

Murphy squinted up at the sun. 'Reading the newspaper gives you a very good idea of the situation. You want the truth, you just read between the lines. Then you—.' He jerked around, registering the swish of the glass door. But it was only Samuel, immaculate in his white jacket and dark necktie.

Sipho watched the old Capey walk to the table, setting down an ice-box. moving one of the chess pieces as though the set were his. Showing off, probably. He hoped they hadn't been overheard. You never knew where you stood with these servants. Sometimes they proved whiter than the Boers. He kept his head down as the man moved to stand before them. He'd be the one to get a kick if that was what was coming. No fear of Murphy getting it, even a servant wouldn't take a chance on a man as big as him. Maybe Murphy'd protect him, they were getting on quite well together. He looked up, his heart doing a flip as he saw what was going on. The servant was slipping a gun to Murphy, eyes peeled as he stared over their heads towards the windows. Murphy had the gun tucked away in his underpants before the servant had taken more than two steps back towards the farmhouse. All of it done without a word being spoken. Sipho began to pant, his voice strangled. 'What the—?'

'Now you know why I'm not complaining.' Murphy's voice was low.

'If you're caught—.'

'I'm dead.' Murphy grinned. 'Won't be missing much, right?'

'It's a life.'

'Yeah, but what kind? I've had all I can take, brother.' Murphy's face was bitumen. 'What are we? Blacks? Animals? Insects? Filth? What?'

'If you had a life, you wouldn't know what to do with it.'

'Give me a life, then I'll worry about what I'm living it for.' His elbow jabbed Sipho's ribs, making him hiss. 'That's luxury, hey?'

'I have a wife. Kids.'

'That's your excuse.'

'You calling me a coward?'

'I'm saying I've had enough.'

'You married?'

'I have a woman.'

Sipho shook his head. 'She wouldn't want you to get yourself killed.'

Murphy snorted, his wide nostrils quivering. 'For all I know she could be dead. I was working in the mines at Kimberley. When I came home for Christmas, the township was flattened.' His voice took on an officious note. '"This area has been re-zoned for whites only." Took me weeks to find out she'd been sent to the Transkei.

Then they caught me without my Pass.' He hissed through his teeth. 'Seven months in jail before they took me to court! If you're black and you don't fight, you'll rot.'

Sipho pointed a thin finger at him. 'You'll rot if you do.'

Murphy sniffed. 'At least the smell of myself'll be more pleasant.'

'I wish you luck, brother, but leave me out of it, I don't want any trouble.'

'If you're breathing, you're in trouble.'

Sipho stared into the shadows under the trees. 'I'm afraid of the police. I'm afraid of the army. I'm afraid of whites.'

'Blacks are afraid to piss in this country.'

'All I want is peace, time to watch my children grow up.'

Murphy spread his hands. 'To this?'

Sipho sighed. Always the same with the young. Quick and hot-eyed. How could he make him understand? 'I don't want to die.'

'We all have the skin disease. You either lie down and you die or you fight and you die.'

His words sickened Sipho. He searched his mind for a way to change the subject. 'You believe in God?'

But Murphy didn't answer, his eyes hooded as he stared into the bucket.

'Do you?'

'Believe?' Murphy turned his head, his gaze focussing. 'I've seen Him, brother! — a big black man, his fist raised, a spear in his hand, his eyes burning with the fire of the townships—.'

'Aw, you won't be serious.'

Murphy cocked his head, listening. 'You hear Him? Listen!'

Sipho shrank as he raised his hand in a clenched fist over his head, his other hand laid across his heart. 'God our Father,' he intoned, 'I kneel to say, thank you for this gun today, thank you for the bullets too, I'll use it wisely, promise you.'

'Stop it!'

But Murphy was beyond hearing, his gaze locked on something inside his head, the words spilling with the rhetoric of a psalm: 'God our Father, which art in South Africa, justice be thy name, thy liberation come, thy salvation be done not as it is in Mozambique, but as it is in Lusaka, give us this day our daily weapons, our military training, and forgive us our past timidity as we strive against our white oppressors and lead us not to Apartheid but deliver us from its evil, for thine is the non-racial kingdom, the power and the victory forever and—.'

'Those fucking crickets are back!' Sipho's heart hammered as he watched the small iron bulk of Verwoerd detach itself from the shadow of the trees.

Murphy nudged him, his voice a low hiss. 'Head down! Deep breaths, deep.'

Sipho drove the words through the corner of his mouth. 'You're not going to—?'

'Not now.' Murphy took the rag out, squeezing it until every last drop plopped back in the bucket. Before Verwoerd spoke, they heard the quirt, its plaited braid making a whirring sound as he whipped it through the air. 'You stinking munts had a good rest?' His feet thumped through the grass as he approached the patio. 'Well, you got *two* minutes.' Murphy gritted his teeth. The shit. Normally he gave them three. The two men backed towards the french windows and waited, bodies rigid at a starting line. Immediately the quirt cracked, they flung the soapy water, watching it gurgle across the tiles to spend itself in the grass beyond. The moment Verwoerd looked at his watch they began the frantic race to mop up, Murphy marking time by the crack of the quirt, one crack every four seconds, if he could reach the seventh tile by the end of the first minute, chances were they'd finish in time. Beside him, Sipho's breathing was hoarse, his erratic progress slowing them down. Maybe that's why Verwoerd always put him with the nervous ones, a way of ensuring he'd always be beaten.

'Who's baas, eh? Swartgatte!'

Murphy felt the air about him displaced as the quirt cracked close to his face. The prick, the fat prick, for two pins he'd—.

'Enough! I've told you before, I want none of that here!'

The voice was music in Murphy's ears. The son of the oubaas, a Boer who knew what it was to be a man also. Every night in the compound he heard the others praying they'd be one of the group put to work in his charge. Instantly, he slowed down, winking at Sipho to do the same.

'I take orders from your father,' Verwoerd was saying.

'My father isn't on this patio.'

'He leaves the men in my hands.'

'Does he know you beat them up?'

Murphy almost sniggered. Does a tick-bird feed on cattle?

'He's never had any complaints about my efficiency.'

Beside him, Sipho shrank as the Boer walked up to him, his face mottled. 'Look at this man!'

Sipho curved his back into a defensive shell as the Boer ripped the back of his sackcloth. For a moment there was silence as Piet stared at the raw flesh.

He turned to Verwoerd. 'You're an animal!'

Murphy grinned into the drying flagstones.

'Take him to the kitchen, those cuts need attent—.'

The new voice, hard as whiplash, cut in on Piet. 'Get these kaffirs out of my sight!'

Murphy tensed. The oubaas, stiff as a stone prick. Oh, for an iron mallet! He shifted a little, the barrel of the gun warm against his dormant penis. Soon. Some dark day or night.

'I've told you, Verwoerd ...' Claus was roaring, '... early morning when I'm not using it!' He stared at the puce face of the farm manager, wanting to smash it.

'Sorry, sir.' Verwoerd sprang forward, kicking at the two black men, the anger in his voice matching his boss's. 'Get a move on, you bloody commies!'

'Wait!' Piet turned to his father as the men jumped up. 'Those cuts need attention.'

Verwoerd hesitated, casting a quick glance at Claus.

'Are you mad, maan?' Claus dropped the file he was carrying on the table. 'Next thing they'll be looking for hot dinners.' He turned to Verwoerd. 'Get them out of here! And see it doesn't happen again!'

'Sir!' Verwoerd turned to the blacks but already the two men were hurrying towards the trees. The steel gaze flickered insolently at Piet before he turned to follow the men. Piet shoved his fists into the pockets of his trousers, watching the blunt shape trundling across the lawn. 'Why d'you let him?' The words spat through his teeth. But his father, standing over the chess set on the table, didn't seem to have heard.

'Hah! That Samuel's a clever little get. Thinks he's foxed me.' Claus snorted. 'He'll have a hairy wait.'

Piet began to pace, feeling the sweat ooze in his armpits. 'It's not the first time, Papa.'

But Claus was engrossed in the chessboard. 'Right, you smart little hotnot!' Picking up the white knight, he moved it forward, placing the black king in check. 'Let's see you squirm your way—.'

'It's happened too often since you hired that brute.' Piet pushed hard against the seams in his pockets, feeling them strain to hold his fists. Perhaps if he appealed to his father's business instincts .... 'Unproductive, even. How can they be expected to work after that?'

Claus nodded at the board. 'Black and all, I could almost admire how he plays. Best thing I ever did was teach him after your mother died.'

Piet clamped his lips. What was the use? He couldn't win, no matter which way his father played it, deaf man or preacher, it was all one.

'How many times've I told you? Forget them. They've skins thick as rhinoceros hide.'

236

Piet sighed. The preacher. What the hell was the use?

'I'm telling you, they're so used to it, they've become immune.'

'Or we have?'

'What?' Claus's eyes narrowed.

'Nothing, nothing, Papa.' Piet avoided his eyes.

'Get your priorities right, maan. Those are animals out there, lazy, good-for-nothing criminals who'd stab you in the back soon as look at you. The only law they understand is the whip. The day we stop sniffing their fear is the day we're finished. What's the matter with you anyway? You're like a man's got a bee buzzing in his pants.'

'It's Mia.' The words were out before he could stop himself. He shoved his hands back in his pockets again, anything to keep them still. There was a tinkle of glass as Claus reached for a bottle, the smoking ice fast extinguished as he splashed the whiskey over it. Piet took the proffered drink and sat, grateful for the hard kick of the alcohol in his gut. It made thinking about Mia easier. It made possible the idea of telling his father.

'Zo? She's still the same?' Claus poured him another drink, his eyes hawkish.

Suddenly the words spilled, the alcohol loosening his tongue. 'I found her wandering in the garden last night. Naked. Washing herself in the dew.' He swallowed hard. 'Good for the skin, she said. It was freezing, Papa!'

The table shivered as Claus slammed his hands down. 'You've got to deal with it before it gets any worse.'

'When she finally began getting up again, I thought she was better. Then, when I found her giving all the silver to Elijah—.' His hair stood on end as he ran his hands through it. 'What the hell'm I going to do?'

Claus leaned forward, the chair creaking under his bulk. 'I told you, that sanatorium up in Parklands is like a first-class hotel.'

'I, I .... She'll never forgive me.'

'Ja, I'll never forgive you if you don't. Even if you can cope, what about Jan? Y'think I want the only grandson I've got exposed to that kind of thing?' Claus's voice softened. 'Why not let him come here until you decide what to do?'

'I sent him to the Vorsters yesterday. He'll stay till—.'

'I see far too little of him.' Claus stretched his arms wide. 'This house should be full of children. If Yolande had lived—.'

'Helmut is his best friend. You know what boys are like.'

'You mean Mia wanted him to go there. That woman's always twisted you round her ... what in hell's wrong with her? How long's it been? Something must've brought it on.'

Piet stared at his own tired face in the window. 'Three, four weeks. Maybe more.'

'Anything unusual happen at the time?'

The head in the glass shook. 'I'm sick thinking back.'

'Something sparked it off. Think, maan. Did you quarrel?'

'She was like that.' He frowned, trying to remember. 'I came home one day. She was ... different.'

'When?'

'Feverish. That's it! The day we were last together for dinner!'

His father's eyes narrowed. 'Babo?'

'The row? You think ...?'

'I think nothing. Yet.'

'You and I ... I dropped you back to the farm.'

'She was with Babo when you returned?'

Piet shook his head. 'On her own. Talking gibberish.'

Claus's eyes were speculative. 'They used to be thick as thieves before Babo started her politicking. Could be she's been getting at Mia.'

'I don't know what she thinks I'm made of. The place is falling apart. Elijah keeps pestering me. He doesn't seem to have a clue. She won't even bother to get dressed most days now. Can you imagine! Mia, of all people, she was always so capable! I never thought—.'

'She was always weak. Like—.' Claus looked at his son. Nee, there was no point in going too close to the edge or he'd lose the ground he was gaining. 'You could never see it. She needs psychiatric help. Zo.' He spread his hands in a casual gesture. 'Having your wife in a sanatorium — it's no dishonour on a white family. The Americans have made it fashionable, acceptable. What would be terrible for an Afrikaner is to find black bones in the cellar, ja?'

Piet rubbed his eyes, refusing to meet the ones in the window. 'I'll be lost without her. I hate the house when it's empty.'

Sniffing victory, Claus held his breath. When he spoke again, he was careful to keep his voice expressionless.

'Zo. You and Jan can come here.'

Piet didn't seem to have heard. 'I always leave the radio on. It kills the silence.' There was a hard knot in the pit of his stomach. In his mind's eye, he roamed the empty rooms of the house. Christ, he'd go spare without her.

'Has Babo been?'

'Mia won't talk to her.'

Claus stared at the grey defeat in his son's face. Enough for one day. Something tingled pleasurably in his gut. More than enough, more than he'd ever expected in a month of Sundays. 'Come,' he said, picking up the file. 'Time to meet the broeders.' His lips tightened as he watched his son haul himself upright, the dark grooves cut below his eyes. That English bitch had a lot to answer for. And so did his hellcat of a daughter. Well, he'd get to the bottom of it, or know the reason why. 'Why not invite Babo over? Tell her you're worried. Get the two of them in the same room. See what happens.' He threw the last words over his shoulder as he crossed the patio towards the house.

'If there's a scene — I don't think I could face it on my own. Would you—?'

Sliding the glass panel, Claus nodded, pleased. 'Wednesday night?'

'Thanks, Papa. Maybe it'll sort itself out.'

'Don't bet on it.' His index finger jabbed the air as he faced his son. 'Say nothing to Babo about my coming. Otherwise she won't show. Ja, she's had a hand in this, I can smell it.' He placed a hand on his son's shoulder, ushering him into the room before him. Right into his hands. Perhaps his daughter had done him a favour, after all. It had been a long time since Piet'd confided in him, looked to him so freely for advice. A long time since he'd proved so malleable. He stretched, a luxurious tingling invading his limbs. How good it was to be alive, his body suddenly tuned to the least blade of grass that grew on his farm. Ja, this was one mess he'd sort himself, that way at least, he was guaranteed success.

II

But Piet didn't have to wait until Wednesday. That night, he stood in the middle of the softly lit room, the bed and all about them a dishevelled mess as he stared at his wife squatting among the sheets. Her head was buried in her hands, one thin strap of the silky nightgown trailing on her upper arm. He unbuttoned his shirt. The heat in the room was killing, she must've been at the thermostat again.

He gnawed at his bottom lip, wishing now he'd kept his mouth shut. 'Say something.' He stared at the dark tangle of hair. 'Will you say something?'

'Claus.' The word stabbed the air, but she wouldn't lift her head.

'I don't need Papa to tell me what to do.' He began to pace, hampered by the books and the clothing heaped on the floor. The only thing in place were the drapes, snug velvet blotting out the night, and even those, he'd had to draw himself.

'Claus,' she said again.

'You're crazy. He was right.' His face glared from the dressing-table mirror. He picked up a spray of perfume, catching a whiff of her skin in its fragrance. It had been a long time since she'd worn it. He dropped it back among the clutter, not caring whether he broke the small crystal bottle.

'You've always needed him.'

He turned, his arm swiping the air. 'Look at this place—.'

'Look at me!'

'I can't stand it.' Crossing the room, he began picking up her clothes at random. 'I've never lived in such a—.'

'Look at me.'

'You won't even let Elijah in to clean—.'

'Look at me!'

'I'm sick looking at you!'

'So you're going to have me locked away. Disposed of. Like I was—.'

'Stop saying that. For the last time — you need help.' He looked at her, finally, his eyes pleading. 'I want you to get better. I want everything to be like it was. We were happy, weren't we?'

Black, Mia was thinking. Like I was black. Picked up off the street — 'Idle and undesirable', which section was that? She delved among the newspapers at the foot of the bed, hardly hearing his voice above the rustle. There! Her eyes skidded over the blur of print.

'Undesirable?' she said aloud. 'That's easy — every black, every coloured, every Indian. Idle? Unemployed — most of them are that. A decorative domestic engineer might escape it.' She paused, tracking the words with her finger. 'Here. Section 29. But which Act? Internal Security? Blacks Act? I'm so confused. Oh, what does it matter? They've got him anyway, on one pretext or another. Fined 500 Rand, or 190 days in jail. Of course, he couldn't afford to pay. Which of us can?' She screwed the pages into a ball and flung them towards the door.

Piet stared at her, trying to decipher it. 'Has Babo been getting at you?'

'Which of us? Him? Or me?' She laughed, the sound teetering on the edge of something he couldn't see. Something dark. The hair bristled on the back of his neck. Babo. Yes, Babo, he'd cling to that, cling to the confines of what he knew he could handle.

'Has she been here? While I'm out?'

'Of course, I could afford to pay it. If it were me. But then, I'm accepted.'

She didn't seem to have heard. He'd ask Elijah.

'It won't last, though. Nothing ever does.' She looked at him, suddenly calm. 'I'm not mad.'

He tossed the bundle of clothing into a corner, his tone gentle. 'I'm not saying you're—. Look, it's no big deal. It's even considered fashionable nowadays to be seeing a psychiatrist.' He stretched out his hand, palm upwards, a mendicant begging for alms. 'What about Heidi Moulin? — she's been going to one for years.'

The name tolled in her head, conjuring the image of the woman in the church, the mink stole clutched to her throat, the lost eyes marooned in the sallow face. Drowning.

She shook her head, the hair whipping her cheeks. Not that, not that. Not yet. She stared about the room: plum cushion on the stool before the dressing table, walk-in wardrobes, nightstands, the row of book-spines above the bed, yes, if she concentrated hard enough she could coax back the familiar lines of it, and the man, the man who was standing, watching, her husband, there, all in order, all in its proper place again. Now she could talk from the calm. 'You can't lock me away.'

'Christ, this is a vicious circle.' He stared at her for a moment, then began picking up the books strewn about the carpet. Legal tomes, government publications, what the hell did she want with these?

Her laugh grated on his ears. 'They'll be angry.'

'Who?' He straightened.

But she was staring past him. 'She is incurable, they'll say. Take your wife away from here, Meneer Schuurman, or we'll remove her by force.' She wagged a finger. 'She is here illegally. Take her back to her homeland.'

'Of course they can cure you. Lots of people have breakdowns.'

'This is a breakapart.' Her voice was hard. 'Apartheid. There is no cure.'

'Nothing's that black and white.'

Her laughter shrieked in his head, mocking him. He strode to the bedside, his hand raised, anything to shut her up, he could bloody kill her! He fought the impulse, reaching instead to grasp her shoulders, to shake, shake her until her bones rattled beneath his fingers. Eventually, she sobered and he let her go.

'Clever boy.'

'Don't talk down to me!' He dragged the air into his lungs, his body shaking out of control. 'I'm my own man.' He had to fight his tongue to get the words out.

'You don't fart without his permission!' She crouched, cat-like on the bed. 'Oh, has my vulgarity shocked you? Forgive me!'

He stared at her, bewildered. 'What's got into you? I married you.'

'When he was in Lesotho.'

'For years afterwards — working with him on the farm, nothing but days of silence.' His eyes flared, remembering. 'Yes, he made me pay! But I never complained to you, never regretted it.'

'You never let me forget the sacrifice you made. I've never stopped paying for it.'

'What the hell's that supposed to mean?'

'Every time he came here, I could have been part of the furniture. And you ...' she raised herself up on her knees, '... falling over backwards, grovelling, "Goodbye Papa, thanks for coming, Papa".'

He winced at her mimicry, hating her.

'We've always stood in his shadow.' Her eyes glazed as she brought the word out. 'Darkening.'

'It was never like that.'

Staring into the soft pool of lamplight washing the nightstand, she didn't seem to hear him. She might have been talking to it. 'I've never been separate, ever. You've been my sustenance. Filtered through your father. Sometimes I've had a chilling dread that if Claus weren't around to look at you, you wouldn't exist. You feed on him.' She blinked at the light, as though it were blinding her. 'Then I wouldn't exist either. I'd fade away, blend into the wallpaper like your mother, smiling apologetically, too timid to open her mouth.'

He stuffed his hands into his pockets, closing his eyes against it. 'Mama was quiet. That was her nature.'

'I even dressed to please him.' She turned, her voice ugly. '"It's lovely on you, you know I like it, but you know how Papa is, he's so conservative. Perhaps something a little less revealing?" And like a fool, I'd change! Well, I can't change my skin. I can't!'

Opening his eyes, he stared at the carpet. The mud she was raking. If she were using a whip, she couldn't do a better job. 'That's all in the past. You're being neurotic. He accepts you now.'

'He won't accept me. Not when he knows.' She scoured the thin profile of his face, willing him to know, anything, anything to break out of the tomb that held her.

'I have to live with him, work with him.' He stared at the books he'd dumped on the end of the bed. Steps of stairs leaning drunkenly against the brass bedpost. Going nowhere. The farm was his life. One day it would be Jan's. She knew that! Couldn't she see that? Was it a crime to be fond of his father?

The bed shifted as she turned away, her voice little more than a whisper. 'I was afraid he'd win. That he'd take you away from me. Now he'll take me away.'

The words gnawed at the ache in his chest. 'No, he won't, I promise.' He moved to kneel at the side of the bed, taking her hands in his. 'It's all in your mind.'

'Is it? Is it?' She stared at him, her eyes suddenly darkening. 'Show me then.' Leaning over, she kissed him, her tongue flicking

242

over his lips in the familiar way that he loved, that never failed to arouse him. 'Make love to me. Make love to me now.'

Suddenly, he was suffocating. He pushed her away. 'I, I can't. I can't just switch on like that.' He tried to lift his head and look at her. But he couldn't. Rising, he moved away.

'Has your Papa been telling you sex with me is a fruitless activity, since I can't supply him with a grandson?'

'You bitch!' He swivelled, facing her.

Her eyes goaded. 'You can't switch on? You've never yet managed to switch yourself off.'

'Shut up!'

She pushed back the tangle of hair, staring beyond him, her eyes out of reach. 'You know, when I think of it, it's been the only ... constant. An electric current, you might say. But does it count as ... warmth?' The dark eyes focussed, accusing. 'Every night for ten years, not including lunchtimes? Oh wait, apart from these last weeks, and those shopping trips to Jo'burg with Babo. But that was years ago and even then you made up for it when I came back!'

'Stop it!' He was beside her, shaking her again.

'Did I ever tell you I had a headache? I was too tired?'

The bitch, the fucking bitch! Raising his hand, he slapped her face. 'You wanted it as much as I!'

She stared up at him, her eyes frenzied as she pressed her cheek. 'I didn't want it *half* as much as you!'

'You're lying!'

'I accepted it because I was afraid not to! I thought at least if I could keep you satisfied in bed, Claus couldn't get to you, I'd be able to hold you. Even when I didn't want it, I accepted it gratefully, a sign that you loved me!'

'You hypocrite, you bloody hypocrite! The whole thing was a lie, a fucking lie!' He drove his hands through his hair, wanting to tear it from his head.

'He was there, even in the bed between us. I might as well have slept with your father! It would've been a more honest prostitution!'

'Tart!' He flung the word, his spittle spraying her face. What, what had he married? This woman wasn't his wife, he didn't know this creature who sneered and jibed, who looked at him with wild eyes, full of hatred! How could he have lived with her, all this time, not knowing, not knowing.... He was losing her. The thought chilled him. 'Why, why didn't you tell me this before?'

'There's more. Oh, there's more.'

'I bought you clothes, jewels, this house — I thought you were happy. You were happy. You wanted those things.'

She sighed. 'I'd never had them before. I thought they'd ... warm me.'

'You can't blame me because your father poured all his money into a clinic for poor whites.'

'Not my father.'

He stretched out his hands. 'Did I ever complain when you ran up bills? You never stopped spending.'

'My compensation. I became a well-dressed mannequin, a ventriloquist's dummy, to tempt you, to woo your father.' The bed creaked as she scrambled to the far side, stepping onto the floor. He heard the satin gown rip as she hauled it off. She walked across to the wardrobes, the milky flesh of her buttocks jiggling below the tanned bikini line. He tried not to look.

'I lost my substance. It disappeared into my string of pearls ...' her words mocked him as she flicked through the dense rail of clothing, '... my mink stole, my shimmering gowns—.'

His lips curled. 'The way you've been dressing lately, I'd say you've lost your self-respect.'

'Wait till you see my new image!' She'd hauled out a black slip. 'It goes with my new substance.' She turned, her breasts rising as she lifted her arms to slip it over her head, the words muffled through the silk. 'The real me!' She hurried to the dressing-table, knocking over bottles as she searched. What the hell was she up to now? He stared in the mirror as she rubbed the black eye shadow on her cheeks, the patches a dark burlesque he couldn't handle. She turned, her arms flung wide. 'Well, d'you still find me attractive without the clothes, the jewels?'

'You're pathetic.' His voice shook.

'You can always sell them when I'm gone.' Strolling towards him, she might've been modelling designer clothes, her body angled in a grim parody of fashion. 'Or better still, use them for the next wife.' Her finger danced in his face as he stood beside the bed. 'But make sure it's another Yolande you marry, from a nice Afrikaner family. Otherwise your papa won't approve.'

Reaching out, his fingers bit deep into the buttery flesh. 'That's enough, enough, d'you hear?' He shook her, her face blurring as it see-sawed back and forth on the slender neck, but suddenly she was hitting him, the small fists like rocks pummelling his chest, the strength of her fury winding him, the words shrieking in his ears. 'Yes Papa, No Papa, three bags full, Papa!'

Heaving, he pushed her onto the bed, her fists trapped as he flung his full weight on her, Christ, he wanted to crush, grind her to silence.

'Notice it's Baa Baa Black Sheep!' Her breath tingled in his ear and he felt the familiar tightening in his pants, the old discomfort rearing. Grasping her wrists, he flung her arms above her head, his mouth covering hers as he knuckled into the swell of her breasts.

'You want me?' A whisper against his lips.

He had to fight to bring the word out. 'Yes.' He sought her mouth again, but she turned her head away. 'Like this? I smell. I'm ...' a small laugh sobbed in her throat '... undesirable.'

He buried his face in her hair, willing it to come right. 'I like the smell of you.'

'There's a dark side to my nature ... I'm tainted.'

He put his fingers to her lips. 'Don't talk.'

'Have you ever had a black woman?'

The question hit him like cold water. Straightening, he turned away. Suddenly he was exhausted, a terrible lethargy gripping his limbs, his head a monstrous weight in his hands as he stared at the grey line of his legs tapering to the neat jaws of the crocodile shoes.

'Tell me! Have you ever had a black woman?'

The words stabbed at his back.

'No.'

'You're lying!'

He turned, shouting. 'All right, I'm lying! Are you satisfied?'

She was looking at him through hooded lids. 'I hear if you close your eyes, it doesn't feel any different. You, you always make love with your eyes open. D'you think you can close them from now on?' Reaching, she took his hand, laid it against her stained cheek. He felt the sudden tremor in her body as she spoke, the words thick with innuendo. 'This is my new substance. And this.' She slid his hand down to her breasts cupped in the black slip. He stared at her, the sudden calmness in the wide eyes. What was she saying? He jumped up, wrenching his hand free. For a moment he prowled the room, fighting the fear that was rising.

'What're you saying?' Swivelling, he faced her. 'Spit it, for Christ-sake!'

Kneeling on the bed, her gaze searched the ornate brass bars of the bedpost. If she ducked down, she'd be peering through a cell window. She shivered. 'Paul is not my father.' She counted the bars. One two three four five. 'Paul is not my father.' Five four three two one. How quickly the numbers tolled. 'Paul is not my father.' The nail was home. How tedious to spend your days counting. Better a dark box and oblivion. No click-ticking tongues in a tomb. No breath, no beat, no sight. No bells.

Somewhere, outside herself, she heard him say her name, as though she still existed, his voice thick with incredulity, denial, threatening to drag her back into the sludge of deceit she'd been choking in these last weeks.

'... for Christsake ...' he was saying, '... you need help! Of course he's—.'

But the deed was done, the truth excreted, her mind limp and clean in the aftermath. 'Phone him. He'll tell you.' She looked at him. Still he couldn't take it in. 'Go on.'

He scratched wildly at the stubble on his jaw, the sound rasping with the hoarseness of a cricket. 'What're you saying? Just what the hell are you saying?'

She stared at the panic in his face. How dare he! How dare he feel panic after what she'd been through! 'I'm saying there's an accidental black spot in my lineage, a dark birthmark on my nether horizon. I'm saying my father is a Capey. Cape coloured. His skin's the colour of peanut-butter. I'm saying my grandfather was black. Black as the ace of spades.' The laughter rose like bile, threatening to overwhelm her. 'Just think,' she gasped, 'I had my very own life-sized golliwog and never knew it. Imagine what a difference that could've made to my wonderful childhood! I always loved music. D'you think I could've been a black and white minstrel in my youth?' She paused, dragging the air into her lungs. 'That's what I'm saying. Don't you hear what I'm saying?' She cocked her head, listening. 'I hear the words,' she whispered. 'They're outside my head, clear as a bell skewering the sky on a quiet morning.' She grasped the satin sheet, crushing it between her fingers. 'Oh, isn't innocence bliss! When I look back now I can see that compared to this, I was positively rapturous!' Her gaze followed the slope of his shoulders as he moved to the stool before the dressing-table. Lopped branches. Dead with the weight of her words. 'I have black blood in me,' she said to the branches. 'Black as coal. Black as pitch. Black as hell.'

Her voice dropped in the silence as he lowered himself onto the stool. He looked diminished, she thought, a marionette with its strings cut. How dared he look like that, as if it were his cross, his ... blight and the silence, thick with his distaste. Unbearable!

She swiped the hand-mirror from the nightstand, her face filling the gilt frame. Hard to believe, really, apart from the eyes and the hair. She turned to look at him, she must say it, first, before he thought it, there was something, a weak sense of salvaged pride in anticipating, voicing the thoughts that would vomit in his mind. 'That woolly hair! D'you suppose they're related to sheep?' Turning, she confronted the woman in the mirror again. 'Though she does tan easily — the merest whisper of the sun, you know?' The glass lips twisted in the semblance of a laugh. 'You've always said how lucky I am, in this climate!' She hurled the mirror, striking the panelled wood of the wardrobe, the tinny shiver of glass disintegrating as it sprayed the carpet. 'I had no words either. I have no pity for you. This should have been no tragedy. A mere hiccup. Take a deep breath and count—. Except I haven't learned to breathe deeply, I'll hiccup to death.' She looked at him, her head heavy. It was difficult not to let it droop with the weight of it. She might be dead already. No, really, he'd be more likely to dance on her grave, stamp the earth firmly into place, celebrate his escape, after what she'd told him. 'What? So quiet? No questions? You've been fucking a black bitch for ten years and you've nothing to say?' Her voice beat against the walls. 'All that fucking, was it worth the price?'

'Stop it!' The words were a low howl but she couldn't accommodate them.

'Why, this is my new language! It goes with my new substance. Why won't you look at me?' She laughed. As if she needed to ask.

'When—?' His head jerked sideways, eyes still trapped in the intricate lines of the carpet.

'You know when. Paul brought him that day. And Babo.'

'Who is he?' Again the question was asked of the floor. Maybe that's where she was, she thought, remembering how the negatives had spilled from the album.

'Who is he?' Cold. Interrogative. Hardly the voice of her husband any more. She'd killed his love, the love she'd given birth to in him. It lay, shrivelled and grey between them, like a dead foetus. She stared hard at it there on the snarl of sheets: the skeletal folds, the infant bird-breast were her own, her life gripped in rigor mortis. Who, who, who was she? — one of twenty-eight million, blacks, coloureds, Indians. Hard to find among such countless odds, the abandoned, the limbo legions shackled to eternity.

'We all look alike, don't you know that?'

'Who is he?'

'Who am I?' She shivered.

'My God, I can't believe it!'

'I can't not believe!'

'Who knows?'

'I do.'

'Who knows?'

'You do.'

'Nobody else?' Finally, he looked at her, his gaze searching. Searching for lies. She sighed. 'Not yet.'

His eyes sheered away, frightened. 'I, I don't know what to say, what to do.' He shook his head, flailing, as though he were caught in a net. 'I can't tell Papa.'

'You will.'

There was desperation in his voice. 'I can't. He'd—.'

'You'll tell him. You won't be able to stop yourself.' Her heart pulsed in her ears, almost drowning his reply.

'No, no, I have to think!' Jumping up, he began to pace. 'I can't—.'

'You'll tell him because you tell him everything. Because you're afraid.'

He stopped, his face livid. 'Hou jou bek!'

'Afraid he'll find out one day. Know you've lied to him, cheated—.'

'I can't take any more!' He strode towards the door.

Suddenly she was afraid. 'Where're you going?'

'Out!' He wrenched the door open. 'Anywhere! Away from you. You're driving me crazy!'

'Back to Papa!' she knelt screaming as the door slammed in his wake. 'Go! Go on!'

For a long time she stayed, staring at the whorls of wood in the dark panelling, the clock in the hall striking with venom in the silent house. It was done. Beneath her, the bed trembled. With shaking hands she dragged the coverlet about her shoulders, her skin goosed and clammy. Go quickly, Piet and tell him. I'm tired. So tired. So cold. The nail is home.

III

Piet paced the drawing room, unable to keep still under the watchful eyes of his father. How, how to tell him, bring the words forth calmly, matter-of-factly from his lips, the precise phrasing so important, the desperate need to find quiet words that might lessen the impact. Lessen the shock, the ... wrath.

Get it said before Mia came down. His lips tightened. If she came down. Difficult to predict anything with her now. For all he knew she could waltz in the door, naked as a new-born in front of Papa. The thought made him shiver. Get it said, just in case.

'What time'll Babo be here? Piet?'

'What?' He stopped dead. Papa was reclining on one of the couches, drink in hand. Calm. Primed. A hawk, sights fixed firmly on its prey. He pushed the thought aside. 'Papa, I've got to talk to you—.' The strident belch of the phone cut across his words. Babo? Perhaps she'd sniffed a rat? He strode across to the bureau and picked up the receiver. But the call wasn't for him. He held the phone out to his father, pacing again as he tried to concentrate, but the hard edge of Claus's voice cut through his thoughts.

'No, van Rensburg, you listen. You need your head read — I'm not interested in your ravings about freedom of the press, zo?' He paused, pulling a pen from his breast pocket, motioning to Piet to

248

find him something to write on. 'I don't care if 600 miners got it in the fucking back — 60, 600, it's all the one.' Piet handed him a couple of sheets of the perfumed stationery Mia always used for invitations. Instantly he'd given them, he felt remorse, as though he'd committed an act of treachery. He'd go crazy if he didn't get the words out soon. Time and again today on the farm he'd broached the subject, only to find his nerve had failed.

'If you still want your newspaper in circulation tomorrow morning ...' Claus was saying, '... you'd better pay attention to what I'm telling—.' He scribbled something on the page, the writing indecipherable. Piet stared at the groove it cut in the paper.

'Korrek.' The word snapped at the receiver. 'Ja, now you have it. And no page one effort. Keep it short, low-key, violent in-fighting between rival tribes, words to that effect.'

Words to that effect. Mia has mixed blood. Never could words be strung together to worse effect.

'No, halve it. You heard me, 30 miners!' Claus slammed the receiver back on its cradle. 'These editors, onnosel!'

Piet stared at the phone. 'I've got to talk to you—.'

'So where is she? You should get her down here now.'

'Who?' He passed a hand across his eyes. 'I, I don't think she'll come down.'

Claus tapped the desk with his pen. 'Then what'm I doing here?'

Piet moved away. It was difficult to stand so close to him. 'Those early days.... We were so happy. Were we happy?' The glass door of the bookcase threw back his blank face.

Behind him, Claus's voice was disgusted. 'You're beginning to sound as woolly as your wife.'

'I could never wait to get home to her.'

'Did you tell her I was coming?'

'I didn't get much sleep last night. Papa—.'

'I might as well be hitting my arse off the sky! Why isn't she here?'

'She's ... not the same, Papa—.' He turned.

'You mean she's worse? Did you phone the sanatorium?'

Worse. Piet nodded. Oh yes, it was worse, the worst his father could ever expect to hear. 'It's ... worse. But she's more lucid.'

Claus raised a hand dismissively. 'Go and get her.' He jerked the gold chain on his waistcoat, pulling the watch free. 'What time is it? Balls!' He glanced at his son. 'Did you hear who won that by-election up near Modderbee?' He strode to the coffee table, picking up the remote control, sitting as he switched on the television. Piet, unsure of what to do, went to join him as the set flickered to life. He stared at the brutish figure of Swanepoel outlined against the red flag, its white sun blotched with the three sevens, so close to the swastika it left no room for doubt, his arm-band branded with the same insignia as he spoke to the crowd. Suddenly, Piet was afraid. He wanted to jump up, switch it off, but his father was glued to the set.

'... in South Africa ...' Swanepoel was saying, the words burning in his eyes, '... where God is our king. Our loyalty is to our God, our Volk and our Fatherland.'

The mouth paused, a wet, pink pit consuming the tumultuous cheers as it gathered itself for the final onslaught: 'It is not just a struggle between Black and White. It is a struggle of our Christian civilisation against the powers of darkness, Marxism and the Communist threat. We must never allow ourselves to forget that we are God's chosen race, that our survival is sacred. This is the land of our forefathers, who fought bitterly, courageously, with God's benediction, for what we have today. We will die rather than surrender it.' The arm-band rose beside the mouth in a Hitler-salute. 'Within our arteries surges the blood of Aryans, Teutons, whites, Christians — Long live our purity of race! Long live the Volk! Long live Afrikanerdom!'

Piet rose, unable to stomach it. But before he could reach the control, his father had switched it off.

'That asshole Swanepoel!'

Piet stared at the dead screen, finally seeing what it'd been reminding him of for days: her eyes, the cold, hard blankness of them, the way she'd been switching on and off as though an invisible hand played her at random. 'She's— You'd think it was my fault. Is it my fault?' He swiped the glasses, taking them to the bar to refill, hardly aware he'd spoken.

'Ja, onnosel! Who the hell allowed that to be screened?' Claus was on his feet, striding to the bureau. 'You got SABC's number?' He searched, moving the pile of papers aside. 'I'll warm van Lelyveld's ear. We've too many enemies waiting to grab stuff like that, filter it out to the West.'

The ice cracked as Piet poured the whiskey over it. 'He speaks for most of us, Papa.'

Claus paused, eyebrows shooting upwards into the silver hair. 'That bloody neo-Nazi? It's his like have the world breathing down our necks, calling us racists. That goddamn election has a lot to answer for. A swing to the right is one thing — but to flaunt our solidarity — a red rag, ja? We've got to be seen to be making reforms.'

Piet turned to hand him a glass. 'She won't come down!' he blurted. 'She's been there all day.'

Claus stared at the jittery face of his son. That damned woman — verdomme, he'd see she answered for it! 'You should never've waited till it got to this.' He carried his drink to the coffee table.

'She's locked the door. Won't answer me.' Piet leaned on the counter, glad of its support.

'We may have to break it down. Babo!' The couch creaked under his father's weight as he sat forward. 'I'll get answers if I have to beat—.'

'I have the answers.' Piet looked into the rusty liquid swirling in his glass.

'What? What?'

He stiffened, feeling the weight of his father's eyes on his back.

'Out with it, maan!'

Now, he thought, now. He began pacing, the walls seeming to shrink, hemming him in. 'You, you won't find this pleasant, Papa.' He gulped his drink.

'Don't use those words! The last time you said them, your mother died.'

He stopped, facing the couch, his legs trembling. 'Sorry.'

His father's eyes were narrowed, watchful. 'Go on.'

'Mia,' he said. Now, he thought again. Now. Throw her to the white wolves, the hungry teeth yawning in the pink mouth. No hiding place in his father's jungle for injured things. 'Mia has mixed blood. Flowing in her veins.' The laughter rattled in his teeth. The words weren't language. Burning on his tongue, they were an act of desertion. Treachery.

Claus stared, refusing to entertain it.

'Impossible! I had her checked myself. Her mother's blood is English to the last drop.' He paused, his breath thickening. 'There's no black blood—.'

'Not her mother.' Piet stood, feeling the nausea rise. But his father wasn't listening.

'She has to be pretty sick to talk like that. Sooner she's in hospital—. We don't want rumours—.' The bloodhound eyes flicked over his son's pale face. 'Not her mother.'

'Her father.'

'There's no—.'

'Paul is not her father.' The words dropped like bricks in the silence.

'He's on the birth certificate. He's on it.'

For the first time in his life he heard a note of uncertainty in his father's voice. A strange sound, almost as strange as what he was saying. 'He's not her father.' The words repeating, a faulty gramophone, stuck forever in the same snatch of song, the slow revulsion eating into his father's face, the familiar features sharpening to snout, making something other of him than father, something brutish and alien. And all the time the pink mouth: gaping.

* * *

The roar catapulted Emma from her sleep, the camp bed whinging as she jerked upright, heart jigging. She blinked in the darkness to make sure her eyes were open. Christ, that roar, agonised. Had it come from her sleep? She shivered. She hadn't even been dreaming. Inside the cabin. Somewhere inside. The thought chilled her. Swiftly she reached down to shake Mambo, then remembered the old woman was staying overnight at the, what was it, sopolo? Only she and Dick were in the cabin. The police? Her skin bristled. Coming back for him? For both of them? Maybe they'd taken him already, while she slept, his one roar thrown to warn her before they silenced him? She peered towards where she knew the door to be. Any moment, any second it would come crashing in, hands covered by darkness, human hands, monstrous silent hands would haul her out, tearing at flesh and eyes. The bed squeaked, making her jump, her pulse battering her ears. But still no one came, the wait stretching to centuries. Christ, she couldn't bear it.

Easing her rigid legs from the sleeping bag, she swung them to the floor. Bastards, if they'd taken him again .... The patter of her bare feet was little more than a breath as she crept, hands outstretched in the darkness, to the door. The office was unlit but beyond it, the door to Dick's room stood ajar, the blue gloom of the paraffin lamp spilling out across a corner of the desk. She listened, the silence shrilling in her head. 'Dick?' she whispered. The word sat oddly on her lips. It was the first time she'd used his name. No answer. She stared at the slit of light. Was he there? Perhaps he was reading? Reading? The police had taken his books, his bible, even. She stood, hunched. A muffled sound caught her ears. Someone was there. It had to be him. Surely? 'Dick?' she said again, the word trembling in the quiet. She held her breath, moving forward between the dim outlines of the table and the desk to the door of his room. It was open sufficiently for her to see him standing splayed against the wall, his face pressed against it. A silent, weeping face, huge and awkward, the tears coursing down the blunt screwed-up features as he fought for control. She covered her mouth to hide the quick suck of her breath, turning to work her way back to her own room before he could register her presence. Her thigh struck the corner of the table in the dark and she winced as the wood coughed against the floor. Had he heard? Hurrying, she made it to her own room and closed the door. The sleeping bag was still warm. She snuggled down but could find no comfort in it, seeing only his face, there, in the blue light, the solitariness of it.

Gradually the darkness thinned, the window carving a density of stars. What had they done to him? He'd looked so crushed. Shrivelled. What kind of animals, what, what? Humans. Inhumans. She closed her eyes, ashamed, knowing it was in her, too, this cruelty, this savagery. Eichmann went home and stroked his cat. And kissed his wife and children, she had once written, always changing for dinner because he didn't like the smell of the ovens on his uniform. How was your day, dear? Oh, so-so.

She should have gone to him, tried to comfort, ease the shuddering from his limbs. She rolled her head, the stubble scratching on the plastic mattress. How could she? He wouldn't have wanted her to witness it. Look how he'd bantered with her this morning, glossing over his detention as though it were of no consequence, while she, true to form, had bawled in his face, no fear of Emma trying to hide her misery. Oh Christ, she should go to him, she shouldn't leave him to—. What was that? She sat up, ears pricked. A heavy step, his step, in the main room. Making coffee? Now was her chance, get up, pretend she couldn't sleep, talk to him, pass the black hours till dawn tinged the edges of the window. She was unzipping the sleeping bag when the door opened. He stood, the lamp a drunken arc of light in his raised hand as he strained to find her, his face a craggy mass of angles and crevices. And pain.

She was crying inside as she held out her arms. With a low howl he came to her, dropping to his knees by the side of the bed. She took the lamp from his hand, setting it on the floor, the balance of light altering, so that his face was in shadow. Reaching up, she tipped her fingers to the roughness of his cheek, feeling his jaw work as he tried to speak.

'It's okay,' she whispered. 'It's all right.'

'I, I don't want to talk.'

She drew his head down, cradling it against her breasts, knowing suddenly in the hesitant way he touched her that he'd never been touched before. They made love then, in the blue light, her skin raw with the memory of Thulatu's hands as she came finally, a little after him, release firing in spasms that left her more bereft than when they'd begun. For a long time they lay, still linked, his limp wetness inside her body. When she turned to look at him, he was asleep, chin resting on her shoulder. She wriggled free, a small gush of semen spurting between her legs. Christ, there was hardly room to breathe. She should get up, wipe herself, curl up in the bag on the floor. That's what she should do. Before her eyes closed, she reached and found the sleeping bag, dragging it across both of them. The last things she noticed were the rough dressings Modise had patched on his buttocks. Later, she woke to find him whispering, his tears scalding the hard stubble of her scalp, wracking them both as she lay beneath him, listening to the secrets of his life, her arms locked about the broad shoulders. As though she were priest, he penitent.

When she opened her eyes again, he was gone. The early sun invaded the window, a warm triangle cosseting her feet. She moved, the stickiness between her legs tightening across her skin. Where was he? She strained to listen. No sound in the next room. What time was it? She glanced at the window. From the angle of the sun, he had to be still in the church with the squatters. There was time to wash and dress, have some coffee. Find a face to greet him with.

He loved her. The thought saddened her. He hadn't said it, but it had been there, last night, enveloping her. Christ, why did he have to complicate things? She'd enough to cope with, without that. She was spent, every which way. Even sex had lost its lustre, a biological urge, an automatic response mocking from the vacuum, deepening, widening it to a chasm. She remembered once when she'd been young, her adolescent breasts budding out of kilter, her fingers kneading the tender flesh, coaxing the nipples erect as she thought of a boy's lips pressed to hers, his tongue pushing into her mouth, how she'd come then, a slippery explosion deep in her groin, the pubescent ache of longing for the first startling contact of skin on skin. Last night, with Dick, she'd been more alone than that. Tearing the child out by its roots had emptied her. Her body was a womb where no tree grew.

Wearily, she rose and washed. When he returned, she was relieved to find Modise with him, anything to prevent a post mortem being held on the night.

'Mambo not back yet?'

Sipping her coffee, she looked into the good eye, feeling oddly disgruntled at the strength of his embarrassment. Christ, she hadn't been that bad. Had she? She got up to boil more water, keeping her back to him. 'No sign of her.'

They spread the map on the desk, poring over it.

'We dig the trenches here. And here.' Modise's finger was a brisk black pointer, turning street corners, jabbing intersections marked in red.

'What's going on?' She placed the mugs at the edge of the map, Dick's handiwork, she could tell from the American seven in some of the street numbers. The map covered the official and unofficial sections, the squatter area a labyrinth of crooked lanes covered with slashes of red. She shivered. 'What is it?'

Dick looked up, a rainbow of bruised flesh about his half-closed eye.

'We had a meeting. While you were—.' She saw the dull flush spread upwards from his neck. 'Early, before people went to work. Tonight, soon as it's dark, we're gonna start digging up the streets to stop the bulldozers coming in.' He looked across at Modise. 'Should buckle a few wheels while we're at it. They want us out, they're gonna have a rough ride.'

Her eyes widened. 'But they'll see the trenches in the morning. What if they—?'

He shook his head. 'They'll see nothing. Plenty a zinc to cover the pits, a layer of clay on top.' His lips twisted. 'Never seen so many people willing to donate their roofs.'

Modise looked at her, nodding.

'It is true. Even in the official section. Everyone is backing us.'

'But why? Why?' She stared at each of them in turn, pulling hard at her fingers to make them crack. 'If they behave like that at a funeral, what'll they do when—?'

'We want to be free to live where we have always lived.' The dark eyes regarded her, the logic in their depths, simple. They'd been born, lived, buried their dead here. Their right, inalienable.

'How long'll it take?'

'Couple a nights, working in shifts, non-stop.' For the first time Dick grinned, his eye meeting hers. 'You any good with a spade?'

For digging? Or burying? She rubbed the bristling skin on her arms, trying to shake the thought.

'Aren't you afraid?'

Three eyes scanned her face. 'Yes,' Modise said and went back to examining the map. She looked at the steady grey eye, searching for a weak spot.

'Ditto.' His smile was crooked, his cheek bulging below the bruised skin.

'Then why—?'

'This is the end of the line for them, Emma.' His words were quiet, punctuated by the squeak of the felt-tipped marker as Modise cut another red slash on the map.

'The good shepherd laying down his life for his sheep?' Her voice was bitter. Suddenly she realised how close to the truth it might be. Her heart thudded.

He cocked his head, his voice a southern drawl. 'Well now mam, what've we got here? John 10:15, I do believe! You been dipping in my Bible again? Way you're headed, I'll make a convert outta you yet.'

But she scowled, refusing to join in his laughter. There was nothing fucking funny about it. What was it that drove him to make light of every—. Fear, she thought, knowing it was true.

'What sort a shepherd would I be if I cut and run?' The eye was serious again, a question with its answer in-built, denying her any inroad.

'But what if they come tomorrow, before we're finished?' A feeble protest. She sighed. Already, she'd given up.

He shrugged. 'Chance we have to take.' He sipped his coffee. 'Unlikely though. Only time they come in is when they're raiding. Right now, they got their sights on Wednesday morning, they're liable to be too busy stickshifting eviction orders to bother us meantime.'

But he was wrong. Twenty-four hours later, when the township was flattened to a blood and brick huddle of devastation, she thought again of his words, the lilt of hope in his voice, the eager dream in a grey eye fixed on justice.

But for the squatters, justice had never been thick on the ground. All night they'd worked, the women taking it in turns with the men, sleeping babies strapped to their backs. The dusty soil gave way easily. She had even shovelled earth herself, taking the spade from Dick after she'd watched him lean on it for two minutes, drunk with exhaustion. The youths were in the official section, keeping the tsotsis busy. The older children were posted as lookouts, the smaller ones alongside their parents, scraping clay with jagged pieces of zinc, chips of rock. The elderly were in charge of transporting the clay out behind the thorn bushes, a hobbling chain of plastic bags and buckets, weaving its way out onto the moon-bleached veld. Emma saw Mambo berating an old man carrying a small margarine tub. She swiped it from him, giving him her bucket instead, emptying the clay from the tub into it. Emma grinned. It was good to see the old Mambo again.

They worked in whispers, the night threaded with camaraderie, a sense of purpose that fused their strength into a single heaving body of energy. And despite her fear, she was part of it. She saw many faces and shapes that were strange, those from the official section who'd come to help them.

They stopped in the half-light before dawn, her bleared eyes taking several seconds to register the two-year-old spooning clay into his mouth before she rushed to stop him. They covered up the half-dug craters, the air alive with the scratch of clay on zinc and tin. There was to be no service in the church that morning, Dick told them. 'Tomorrow's the day we gotta worry about. So go on home, get as much stuff as you can hidden on the veld before nightfall. And remember, all the kids to the church by midnight.' He turned to look down at Emma as they headed back to the cabin. 'Tough night, huh?'

She nodded, too tired to speak as they wound their way through the moving crowd. She didn't realise she was leaning on his shoulder until he straightened her up to unlock the cabin door. She put her hand against the wall to stop herself from falling.

The coffee, hot and strong, revived her. She wanted to tell him he'd used too much, that if he wasted it like this, they wouldn't have enough for the rest of the week. She wanted to keep pretending, she wanted to go on forever, sitting at the desk.

'You sure you wanna stay?' He stood, his back to the window.

'I told you yesterday, I'm not leaving, lay off will you?' Her teeth clamped.

'One thing. You stick right by me, y'hear? Close as a shadow. I jump, you jump. I got enough on my plate without having to worry where you are. Same goes for Mambo, you keep an eye on her.'

'You told me yesterday.' She cracked her knuckles.

'Yeah, but mostly I wonder if I'm talking to a mule.'

She scowled at his grinning face.

'Time we hit the hay, clinic won't be for another couple a hours.'

'Where's Mambo?'

When he didn't answer, she looked up. His face was puce as he turned to look out the window. What the fuck'd she said now?

'She'll be here any second.' He paused, shifting a little on his feet and she remembered how his buttocks had looked, swathed in the rough patches. A mealie sack, she was sure that's what Modise had used. It couldn't have been pleasant on the tender skin.

'You don't have to worry, I won't bother you ... like that ... again.'

'Eh?' She stared at his profile. The swelling had died, the eye finally registering a pupil. The dark bruise was a classic.

Still he wouldn't look at her. 'You don't need Mambo to protect you from me.'

Her jaw dropped. 'I didn't mention Mambo because, because of that,' she gabbled. But she had, and they both knew it. Frig him, he was always guessing her thoughts before she thought them, almost as if he could plant an idea in her head, then suggest she think it. It made her feel stupid. Added to which, he was now giving her the injured pride routine, making her feel guilty. 'Yes, well, as you can see, sex isn't all it's made out to be. I've always found it a bit of a drag, actually.' She'd meant the words to sound blasé, but instead they sounded cruel. 'What I mean, is—.'

'You're sorry you made love to me?'

'Here, you had a hand in it too, y'know! You weren't exactly an unwilling victim. I seem to recall you were the one to come to me.'

He turned to look at her, his voice quiet. 'I wasn't trying to score a point. I was simply stating the obvious.' His lips worked to get the words out. 'Even at its best, you could hardly call my ... efforts, "making love," now could you? You made love. I ... floundered.'

Floundered. She looked at the pain in his eyes. It was a good word for the way he'd thrashed like a giant fish suddenly released from its tank into the open sea. And now he was drowning because she couldn't find a kind word.

Rising, she went around the desk and took one of his hands. It filled both of hers. She stared at the earth deep in the groove of the lifeline, the blunt, broken nails, the calloused palm.

'I'm glad it happened,' she said, realising it was true.

'But the earth didn't move?'

'It ... shook a little.'

They both smiled.

'He's still there, this ... other man?'

She looked down at the hand resting in her own. 'Yes. I, I wish—!'

Suddenly her voice was crushed against his chest as he held her.

'Emma.' His breath was warm on her scalp. 'When I say your name, it's different from the way I say every other word, you noticed that? It's a prayer. I wanna keep it safe, God in heaven, how I want to keep it safe!'

She kept her face there, buried in the staleness of his sweat as she heard his voice break. Incense, she thought, he should smell of incense, the sweet, sharp integrity of it. She hugged his body with the same fierceness she sensed in him, an urgent need to convey what words couldn't, in the face of her fear. Finally, she drew back a little. 'Someday,' she said, staring at the damp patches on his shirt, 'if there's ever, ever, ever enough water in this place, we'll take a bath together, I'm going to soap you all over till the lather's thick as fleece, I'm going to scrub you till your skin shines like a glossy red apple. And then I'm going to take a bite.'

He threw back his head and roared with laughter, the joyous lilt of the sound tugging her with it, refusing to leave her on the outside. Leaning weakly against him she began to laugh. When she heard the first faint rumbles she thought they were coming from his chest. Suddenly his hand was across her mouth to quieten her, his body rigid against hers.

'Sssh—!' The quick hiss seemed to spring from the narrowed grey eye searching her face.

Eyes wide, she shook her head, trying to decipher it.

'Listen!'

He'd stopped laughing, but the rumbling was still there, growing. She froze, her gaze tracking his face, begging for some kind of denial.

'Whatever happens, you stick right by me or I'll have your guts for garters, y'hear!' His voice was hoarse as he stared down at her.

Chapter Eight

I

Claus sat immobile, the drink gripped between his knees as he gazed into it. In the long silence since he'd said the words, Piet had drunk three neat whiskeys, hardly aware that he'd done so. He didn't feel drunk, although he knew he must be by now. He leaned on the bar, a numbness in his limbs, a sense that his pulse had gone underground so that when the question was fired at the back of his head, it took him a moment to react.

'Who?' The word hammered again, forcing him to turn and face his father.

'I, I don't know.' He stared into the air just above his father's head.

'My God in die Hemel, who, maan?'

'She wouldn't tell me. Only that he's coloured.' He wilted, his gaze skidding past the revulsion in Claus's face.

'A hotnot! Thank God your mother's dead!'

Piet frowned. Mia had said such hard things, he'd never seen her like that.

'You work, sweat all your life, for .... To see your son marry a ...'

If he concentrated, he might be able to keep his father's voice out, minimise it, somehow. 'Mama wasn't a—.' He broke off before he could say 'racist'. Fuel to the fire.

'Go on. Say it! If you have the guts. Tell me what I am. Tell me what you are, what that ... woman of yours is! How long has she known?'

Piet turned back to the bar, leaning heavily again, too enervated to pour another drink. 'That day. Before dinner.' His voice was sluggish.

'My God, how stupid we've been. The little slut tricked us. No wonder she got you to marry her the minute my back was turned.'

'No, no! She didn't know until that day.' He swivelled, gripping the bar to steady himself.

His father's eyes were granite. 'You believe that? She's tricked you!'

'That's why she's been behaving—.'

'You know why you married her.'

'Ask Babo, she was here.'

'You know.'

He moved about, banging into the furniture. If only he could shut out his father's voice. It was so hot in the room. The blasted air-conditioning wasn't working properly again, he'd swear it. Christ, it hadn't been that bad a marriage, had it? She was exaggerating, she had to be. Between them, they'd crush him, her eyes bleeding, his father's snarling, what the hell was he going to do? He knew what he'd like to do, open his own hall door and run from it, run and never come back. She was tearing strips of his flesh, that's what she was doing, even through the alcohol he could feel it, tearing, tearing, well, he should leave her to his father, let him gobble her up—.

'Verdomme, did you have to marry her? Why?'

Why? The question arrested him, bringing a surge of emotion that lodged in his throat. 'I fell in love.'

'You married her because you wanted to get her in bed! You couldn't wait. What was it? The smell of the munt?'

He blinked his way to the bar, his legs trembling. 'You, you shouldn't talk to me like that, Papa.' He held the whiskey bottle with both hands to stop it rattling against the side of the glass as he poured. She was white, white! Whiter than—. 'When we signed that trade agreement with the Japs, we didn't think twice about amending the definition of a white, all to save them the humiliation of being classified as Coloureds.' Christ, the whole thing was a farce, couldn't his father see it? He began to laugh, the sound hollow. Yes. Perhaps Mia'd smelled the racist in him. She'd certainly smelled the beast.

'Zo. She can't stay here.' Claus's words sliced through his laughter. 'You can't send her to the sanatorium.'

'She doesn't want to go.'

'It's out of the question now.' Claus slammed his glass on the coffee table.

'I can't manage her on my own.'

'Use your head, maan. If she sees anyone here, she'll spill it. It'd be all over the city in no time. Can you see the Vorsters inviting your coloured wife to dinner?'

His father's tone made him afraid. He struggled to avoid slurring the words. 'Every inch, every inch of her is white.'

'It'd be better if she went away.' Claus stared at him. 'For a time.'

He tried to look away, but his father held his gaze.

'The UK. She still has relatives there.'

His heart jigged. 'I can't, I can't do that to her, Papa.'

But Claus ignored him, his voice calm. 'I'll have no trouble getting her a visa.'

He gripped his glass, hoping it would shatter, cut his fingers, anything to take his father's mind off—. 'I couldn't.'

'Ja, face it, maan. If she stays, she'll ruin your life. Jan's.' Claus leaned forward, hands outstretched. ' Why d'you think she's been told now? Either Paul is up to something, or the bastard who fathered her. And Babo!' His finger jabbed the air, as though he would skewer the very name. 'You think she'll keep her mouth shut, hah? There's nothing Babo'd enjoy better than watching me squirm. As for her!' The finger jerked towards the ceiling. 'Y'think the state she's in, she'll sing dumb?'

Piet stared at his father's face. If he could only think straight, clear his head, but the voice ground on, dragging him with it.

'Her birth certificate's falsified. Right now, she's up in that bedroom illegally. She can't breathe without obtaining the right documents.'

'But the Mixed Marriages was repealed—.'

'I'm talking about the Population Registration Act, the Group Areas Act!'

'Married to me, her mother being white—. She might get away with being classified white.'

'Until the authorities take into consideration the lies on her papers. Our only hope is that you're not legally married to her, otherwise—. If you refuse to split from her, you could end up being reclassified into her population group. Jan would have to leave that school. Go to one for coloureds. And you know what they're like. You'd be forced to live in a coloured area, you'd lose your vote, you'd be a nothing.'

'You could try—.'

Claus's hand slammed the wood. 'Ja, I know all the right people. But the price? Y'think anyone'll want to know us after this? The Broederbond? We'll be out on our ear soon as they get a sniff of it. Left to blunder in the wilderness. It'd cost me everything I've built up for you, for Jan. If you can't think of yourself, think of Jan. It'd cost him his future. Can you really be selfish enough to—! He's the innocent in all this, the one with most to lose. His blood is pure, he's every right to his heritage.'

From somewhere in the garden, the dog barked. Piet wandered to the window, peering out at the floodlit lawn. His son. His throat thickened. A boy any father would be proud to name his own. Why, even Papa melted when Jan hurtled into a room, quick blue eyes dancing in his eager face. If only he were here now, if he could crush that gangling uncomplicated body to his chest, lay his cheek against the springy blond hair.

'Just for a while. A few months, I'll say.' The words tolled in his ears. Had he really spoken the thought aloud?

'... good,' his father was saying, the old note of confidence back in full strength. 'You'd better get her down here. The father must be silenced.'

Piet threw back his head, peering at the chandelier as it blazed out of focus. 'Give you time to get over the shock,' he said, as though the ceiling didn't divide them, as though she could possibly hear the words. Perhaps they were words she knew already, she'd anticipated so much lately, she seemed to know him better than he knew himself.

His father was saying something again, something about there being ways of dealing with Paul, but that Babo ... what? Babo was another matter. His wife's voice made him swivel so that he almost fell as the room swung out of orbit.

'And what are the ways of dealing with me?'

He squinted to see more clearly. Mia, a ramrod standing inside the door and Christ, she was, she was ... black! Shaking his head, he peered through the haze of alcohol. No, no, just the black slip again, and that dark gunge on her face. Like some awful aberration in a dream. How, how could she do this to him in front of Papa! 'You, you're ... not dressed.' His arm flapped, refusing to point directly at what he couldn't bear to acknowledge.

She smiled, the whiteness of her teeth monstrous in the blotted cheeks. 'This is my shadow. The Emperor's new clothes. Well, what you see you can believe is me!'

Despite himself, he was drawn to his father's face, wincing at the expression he found there. For a while, nobody spoke. A breath rasped suddenly and it took him a moment to realise it was his own.

Mia stared past him as she closed the door, parodying his father's voice. 'Good evening, Mia.' Hips swaying, she moved into the centre of the room, turning to face Claus. 'Why, good evening ... Papa!' Her voice dropped an octave as she continued to imitate. 'You're looking well, Mia. That black is most becoming.' She simpered, patting the dark tangle of hair as though it were elegantly coiffed. 'Why, thank you ... Papa! Black's always been one of my favourite colours. Didn't you know that? Not yours, is it ... Papa? Still, from what I hear ....' Piet turned away as she looked at him, '... it's most men's. Of course, I've had too few men on which to base such a definitive statement, but drawing from the wealth of my own private experience, when it comes right down to it, silky French knickers wouldn't be quite au fait in bed, if they weren't black.'

Piet felt the blood pulse in his face. 'Mia, please ...!'

She took a step towards him, her eyes feverish. 'Mia, please, go crawl under a stone, and don't come out. Stay there, Mia, stay there till you're—.'

'It's not like that—.'

'Then tell me what!'

He moved quickly to her, the floor heaving beneath his feet. But when he touched her, she shook her shoulders free and moved to sit before his father.

'Tell me!' She looked up at Piet as he crossed to sit beside her, the couch creaking under the sudden impact of his weight. He smelt the staleness of her skin and felt sick. How long had it been since she'd washed?

'You reek.' Her nostrils wrinkled. He stared, winded by the viciousness of her distaste. Yes, his breath was sour with whiskey but it was nothing to—. 'You don't exactly smell of roses yourself!'

'I was talking about a different kind of smell.' Her eyes mocked him. 'So? Tell me!'

He hesitated. Christ, why didn't Papa speak? Help him out? 'Look, it's not a very pleasant situation for any of us—.'

Her laugh cut through his words. 'Oh but it will be, won't it ....' she turned to look at Claus, '... Papa?'

Claus snorted, indicating her appearance. 'You've no shame.'

She laughed. 'But I thought you'd appreciate my honesty, my willingness to show my true colour. To be what I am.'

Claus leaned towards her. 'Who is he? His name?'

But Mia was staring at a small, unfinished carving on the coffee table, the tip of Claus's scouting knife buried in the rough end of the wood. 'Oh, what is it?' She picked it up, tugging the knife free, letting it drop back to the table. Piet watched the light in her eyes as she stroked the small animal head. He swallowed hard. 'It was to be a surprise. He forgot to take it to the Vorsters to finish it.'

'Jan, Jan!' Her hands caressed the carving, lifting it to her face. She moved it over her cheeks, something so gentle in her eyes that he looked away, unable to bear it.

'There's love in it. A child's love. Don't do it, Piet!'

'I'll find out!' His father's voice was a snarl. He tried to ignore it as he turned to her. 'Just for a little while.' He held out his hands in a plea. 'A little while. I promise. Not the sanatorium.' He paused, dragging in air. Now, he thought. Now, before he—. 'You've always said you'd like to visit those cousins-. This'd be a good time—. Just for a while. Until we, until you ... get over it. The shock. Then, when ... you come—.' He wiped the sweat from his palms on his trousers. Better if he didn't think, just said it. 'No one need ever know.' The words tripped like lamed steps.

Her eyes burned. 'You kept your word! After all these years. I'm to go, finally.' Her laugh screeched in the quiet. 'With one slight omission. My husband.' She placed the carving back on the table as though it were porcelain. 'For good.'

'Just until—.'

'For good.'

'Mia, please, try to understand—.'

'For good.'

'No, I swear it—.'

'I'm afraid for Jan. You and ...' she jerked her arm towards Claus, '... what will you tell him?'

'You, you're not well—.'

'What will you tell him?'

'I, I don't know.'

'Let me—.'

'Nee!' The word whipped the air as Claus straightened. 'You'll upset him.'

Mia leaned towards Piet, ignoring the interruption. 'Piet? I've washed him, fed him, read him stories. He's my son.'

'You have no son.' His father's voice was hard.

Mia gazed up at the chandelier. 'I have nothing.' She laughed. 'One of the lost tribe.' Rising, she went to pour herself a drink as the door opened.

'My God!'

Vaguely she registered the shock in Babo's voice. She laughed. 'I have no God either, come to think of it.'

'Jesus! What've they done to you!' Suddenly, Babo was beside her, arms warm, pliable, about her shoulders, the smell of fragrant skin like a breath of fresh air. Oh, it was good to be touched, freely, without reservation. 'Dear Babo.' She hugged her sister-in-law, then pulled away, trying to smile. 'It might be infectious.'

'Don't talk rot!'

'It's what they will do.'

'Oh why wouldn't you see me? I've been worried sick. Paul told me a little. But not this.' Turning, she flared at her brother.

'Damnit, why didn't you tell me? You just kept saying she wasn't well.'

Piet avoided her eyes. 'These last days — it just spiralled suddenly. She's been locking herself in, refusing to see anybody.'

Mia peered into the pale liquid in her glass. Yes, she was definitely still there, a little fuzzy, but present, nevertheless. 'Mia is here,' she told the face in the liquid. 'She is not a non-citizen. She has not been vetoed. Yet.' Her words hung in the silence.

'What's going on?' Ignoring Claus, Babo glanced from Mia to Piet.

'Reforms.' Mia laughed, unwilling to sip the face in the glass. How drowned it looked, resting there under all that whiskey.

'Stay out of it, Babo.' Claus shifted on the sofa.

'When you do!'

'Piet's made up his own mind.'

'And South Africa's a non-racial, multi-party state. Mark it.'

'Ja-ja!'

Babo turned back to Piet. 'What?' She searched the flushed face, the shifting eyes. Whatever was going on, Papa'd done the job thoroughly. As usual. Her lips curled.

Behind her, Claus spoke, her spine tingling as the words prodded. 'She's going to England.'

Piet jerked to life, his eyes pleading. 'Just until Papa ....' The flush on his face deepened. 'Until we ... sort things out.'

'Stuff! You bastards!' Babo looked from Piet to her father.

'I need his name.' Claus's words were a searchlight probing the room. Mia laughed. It would be a question neither she nor Babo would answer. Their one triumph. Quick now, if she swallowed the face in the glass, if she swallowed herself, he couldn't reach her, the wolf'd go away hungry. She gulped the whiskey, welcoming its scorch in her throat. 'I need a priest,' she said as she moved to pour another drink. 'I could call him Father, he could call me child.' She looked at Babo. 'D'you think he would, a white one?' She raised her glass. 'There's a bad taste in my mouth.'

'For God's sake, fight them!'

'With what!'

'Tell them to go to hell!' Babo pointed to Claus. 'You think he'll ever let you set foot in this country again?'

Piet stepped forward. 'That's not true—.'

'Ja, a thorn in my flesh.' Claus's eyes glittered.

Mia laughed. Didn't Babo realise? She was gone already. She could never come back.

Babo's voice was flat, deliberate. 'You'll never see Jan again.'

Mia pressed her fingers to her lips, afraid she'd laugh. Never see Jan? Didn't Babo know? Jan could no longer see her, she was a negative now. Sweet Jesus, couldn't she see how funny it all was?

'Don't give in. Come and stay with me.' Babo's hand touched her arm.

'Not "in".' Mia patted her hand. 'I'm giving "up". I'm no longer acceptable ... to myself.'

'None of my friends are racists. They'll all accept you.'

'Except me!' The anger rose like bile. 'You can't convert a racist, don't you know that? A question of acceptability? Yes. But whose?' Mia pointed to Piet and Claus. 'You think I care about their attitude?

Look at me! The stink in my eyes! I've been taught it — to hate, to fear, to despise. Now it's rebounded, caught me by the throat.' Her fist hammered against her chest. 'I've no courage to fight what's inside. The white part of me is filled with a revulsion, a loathing that's been learned with the alphabet!'

'You can unlearn!'

'All my life I've been flushing shit down the toilet. Do you think I can eat it now?'

'What you feel ...' Babo spread her hands, searching for the words. 'It's ... based on a ... a myth ... an immoral ideology—.'

'A, B, C, D, the blacks are not as good as we. W, X, Y and Z, whites are clever, they're thick in the head, let's shoot all the bastards dead. Don't you know? We've twisted it into a scientific fact!' Mia swilled the liquid in her glass, watching as it splayed across her hand. 'All I've come to face is a sense of what they suffer—.'

Claus snorted. 'Spare me the martyrdom!'

Babo fought her impulse to turn on him. It was exactly what he wished, anything to distract her from persuading Mia—.

'Listen ...' She leaned towards her sister-in-law. 'Even that's a start—.'

'It's counterfeit!' Mia pulled her arm away. 'Y'think I would've realised it if I didn't know I had mixed blood?' She laughed, half choking, the sound acid as the whiskey in her throat. 'You know the truth about truth? It's man-handled!'

Babo stared at the wildness in her eyes. A rabbit, she thought, thrashing in a snare. It was too late to get to Mia, the poison had soaked too deep. The battle would have to be fought now on the home front, if she were to save her. She opened her mouth to speak, but a small rock seemed to have wedged itself in her throat. Instead, she put her arms around her sister-in-law, hugging her fiercely.

'I'm happy to go.' Mia laid her cheek against Babo's shoulder. 'I, I can't stay. But promise me—. It's the children you must start with.'

'No way're you going to get your hooks into my grandson.'

At Claus's words, Babo broke away from Mia. 'Piet! Will you—!'

'Leave him alone!'

'And to hell with Mia!' She swung to face the venom in her father's eyes.

'Yes, to hell with her! More bloody trouble than she's worth!'

Piet stepped forward. 'Don't, don't say that, Papa.'

Babo's gaze flicked over her brother's swaying figure. 'The worm has spoken.'

'You shut up!'

But Babo was now staring at her father, her voice cold as she sat. 'She's your daughter-in-law. Part of your family.'

'Never!' Claus's face was apoplectic. 'She's a hybrid. A sin committed by black and white.' His finger jabbed in Mia's direction. 'Look at her! A slut! A mutation! She belongs to a bastard race—.'

'*Stop it!*' Piet's voice was a roar. Babo lifted the knife, grinding its point into the surface of the coffee table. It stood quivering in the wood as she rounded on her father. 'You animal, you filthy animal! How dare you! You, of all people. I know what you are, I've seen it, out there on the farm! Well, it's time Piet was told—.'

'Shut up!' Claus's fist rammed the wood and the knife twanged. So. She'd struck home, had she? — well, this was only the beginning, why she hadn't even warmed up yet! She hauled air into her lungs to steady herself, but before she could launch in, Mia's voice was floating in her ears, something so cold and dead about its tone that instantly she felt chilled.

'In the beginning was the thought, and the thought was with white, and the thought was godwhite—.'

Claus looked at Piet. 'Y'hear her? She's witless!'

'A sin.' Mia nodded. 'The elders preach it from the pulpits: God has proclaimed it. White is the mastery of race.'

Babo jumped up. 'You can't still believe that bullshit. Even the churches are finally admitting Apartheid's a heresy.'

'But not a sin. They won't say it's a sin.' Mia giggled, the sound making Piet flinch. He moved towards her. 'Mia, don't, for God's—.'

'God?' Babo's mouth was a sneer. 'God's a defrocked bone-man in every white man's cupboard!' She turned to Mia, her voice pleading. 'Can't you see? Can't you see what it's about?' But in the silence which met her words, she turned away, unable to bear the luminous strangeness in Mia's gaze.

'I'm in a prison, Babo. There's a wall in my cell. There's no light there, no light.' The words hung in the air, refusing to dissipate. Babo swallowed, half-choking on a sob. She would not, must not weep, not in front of Papa.

'We could all use a drink.' Piet backed to the bar, relieved to have found something simple to focus on.

Claus watched Mia pull the knife from the wood. She looked at it lying there in her hand. Freed. If only it were as easy to step out of the prison she was in. But perhaps it was, perhaps it was that easy after all. Yes, she had to go away, why couldn't Babo see it? Farther than countries. Farther than fathers. She nodded, moving towards the door.

'Mia, wait!' Piet reached out as she passed him.

'Don't touch me!'

He leaned towards her, eyes straining through the haze of alcohol. Christ, it was difficult to face her after the things Papa'd said.

He wanted to tell her how ashamed he felt, for Papa, for himself. 'Where're you going?'

'To break it down. My hands are bleeding from trying to climb it.' She moved past him, heading for the door.

'Wait! I'll get you a brandy.'

'One night in a dream, I straddled it, looked down into the humming silence, the talking dark.'

He slopped the liquid into a glass, her words making him jittery. 'We've got to talk—.' Turning, he held out the drink. But already, she was gone, the darkness of the hall spilling through the open door. 'Mia, wait.' He lurched forward, forgetting his drunkenness. He had to talk to her, he couldn't leave things like this, it was too—.

'Leave her!'

Claus's arm shot out, gripping his as he passed the couch.

'You stay out of this, Papa!' He shook his father's hand off and the room reeled as Babo spoke.

'Pigs've learned to fly!'

'Shut your mouth!' He tried to fix his gaze on his father, but the face before him separated into two distinct orbs, circling each other. Christ, as if one of him weren't enough. 'I won't send her away, Papa.' There, it was out, finally. He felt a sudden sense of exhilaration.

'You'll lose everything.'

But nothing could stop him, not even the threat in his father's voice. 'We'll manage.'

'Go, go!' Babo was on her feet, urging him. She watched as he stumbled into the hall, hardly daring to believe. Only when the door crashed shut behind him, did she breathe. And if Papa made a single move to follow, she'd fly at him with her bare hands. What they'd done to Mia—. What she'd done—. Unspeakable. She shivered. Never once had she stopped to think of her. Jesus, why'd she ever let Thulatu come! She could've stopped him, could have saved Mia from all of it. No. Unless she were the living, breathing image of her father, she couldn't have. And whatever she was, she wasn't quite that. At least, not yet. She stared at Claus, the hatred rising, her legs buckling under the weight of it, so that she dropped onto the couch, glad of its support. The only saving grace for all of them had been Piet's sudden stand. 'Dear Piet.' Her voice was warm. 'It was a long time coming.' She was hardly aware she'd spoken aloud until Claus answered her.

'It's not over yet.'

'Don't try to persuade him!'

'She can come back. When she's better. By then, there'll be improvements.' His mouth snaked in the glimmer of a smile, the old lazy charm. Oh, how well she knew it, how well to her cost! The charm of an adder.

The broad shoulders lifted in the lightweight jacket. 'Attitudes are changing—.'

'After an election rigged to create more panic among the whites so the Nationalists can rein in even tighter?' Her mouth twisted.

'These things've got to be taken slowly, or there'll be chaos.' He leaned forward, hands spread in a gesture of conciliation. Papa the diplomat, the mask slipping over the angular features. She shivered, the sweat trickling into the hair on the back of her neck. For all her bravado, she was still afraid of him. Difficult to swallow, that. As long as he never suspected it, therein lay her strength. Should she let him talk her through it before she kicked him in the teeth? The idea was tempting, the kind of trick he was expert at himself, except in his case, the kick in the teeth was never an honest one, rather an act of betrayal which turned air into sawdust in her lungs.

'... given the South African experience of the past ...' he was saying, already well into his stride.

She leaned forward. 'Shove it!' She watched with satisfaction as the even line of capped teeth clamped. 'Try it on your liberal friends, Papa. You can't reform Apartheid, it's like asking the moon to turn blue. D'you know how sick the blacks are listening to our white prescriptions? They want a fair share of the cake—.'

'Ja-ja, and I'm doing nothing? D'you have any idea how many people I'm supporting on the farm? Mostly the families of the men who work for me. These people would starve if—.'

'And I suppose you don't force the women and children to work at harvest time?'

Claus hissed through his teeth. 'You're as corrupt as the rest of us — playing your little paper games. Easy, isn't it, when you have a strong safety net?'

'If I'm ever detained, you'd be the last person I'd—.'

He snapped his fingers. 'I'll know about you before the kwela-kwela reaches the station.' Leaning forward, his voice was velvet. 'You ever asked yourself why you're doing this? Ever analysed those high-minded motives of yours?'

She felt a stab of fear. 'I don't know what you're talking about.'

'Ja?' His eyes blinked, snapping. 'You're not fighting for black liberation. You're fighting me.'

'It won't work, Papa.'

'You don't give a curse about the blacks.'

She shoved her hands between her denim thighs. 'That's not true.'

269

'You sell yourself to them — anything to escape it.' He rose, arms outstretched, an angry tree tossing its weight above her. 'You've become a tart, a black man's whore because you can't face yourself. You don't care if they live or die. All you're interested in's provoking me!'

'God, you're sick. If I were a man I'd—.'

'You might as well be! It's not my fault you were born without a penis!'

Babo leapt up. 'You bastard! You stinking, rotten bastard! How dare you talk like that to me!' The spittle sprayed from her lips as she sought to get the words out. 'You think you know what I am? You know nothing. I know what you are. I saw you! That day in the kitchen. With Ruth.'

'Shut up!'

Under the light tan, she watched the skin whiten as it stretched across the sharp cheekbones. So there was a chink somewhere, all she had to do was keep chiselling. She dredged it up in her mind's eye, nausea rising in a swift wave, the words spewing from a belly-clutch of memories buried deep in her gut. 'Your lily-white paws all over her. Ramming your filth into her. Mama on the verandah drinking herself to a stupor.'

'I'm warning you, shut up!'

'You forced her! Even then, a child, I could see it. Too clearly.'

'That's a lie.' His voice was a snarl. 'She was willing! She wanted it, strutting about, twitching her fat hips!'

'She was your servant. Would you've kept her on if she'd refused? Every black in this country is prostituted.'

'Ja-ja.' With a wave of his hand, he dismissed her. 'It fits.' The tendons in his neck stiffened to hawsers. 'A string of black men sneaking in and out of your flat! What were you doing? Evening the score?'

'Two men! There've been two! One's rotting in prison—. My God!' She stared into the glimmer of triumph in his eyes. 'You!'

Her legs gave way and suddenly she was sitting. No matter which way she turned—. Zach. Her throat tightened. Tortured? Zach. The tears welled behind her eyes and she fought to hold them back. No, she mustn't ask Papa, he'd be only too willing to tell her the truth about something like that, and she wouldn't be able to bear it if—. She swallowed, wincing, as though shards of glass were lodged in her throat. 'What, what are we?' She stared at her hands, wondering why they didn't bleed, why they should look so pink and healthy and normal. 'Goddamn you!' She rose, a crackling heat spreading under her skin, how she'd love to burn him, reach out and scorch his flesh until nothing remained of it but a shrivelled mass of cinders. 'Afrikaners? A Christian minority?' Her laugh was harsh. 'Dutch ingenuity, German efficiency, French civility? A race of mongrels, pimps, racists.' She stared at the smug face, her voice deliberate. 'I saw her eyes. When I opened the door. Staring ... wounded ... she didn't even see me.'

'Enough!'

'The pain, the sickening disgust—.'

The sharp crack across her face as he struck, brought instant pain, a dervish of leaping stars as it sent her reeling onto the couch. She shook her head to clear it. At least she'd had the satisfaction of seeing his face suffuse before he'd struck. She rubbed her glowing cheek, wincing as it stung. The room came back into focus, the large wall of his back facing her across the coffee table. Well, they both knew why he couldn't face her, didn't they? She felt a small surge of triumph. She'd done it. She'd managed to excavate it, fling it in his face. And the mud had stuck, not all of it, but enough to niggle in the mind's eye. Never again could he conjure up Ruth without seeing the child watching at the door. She'd given him that child, exhumed from her own memory to be interred in his. A small thing, oh but the relief of it. She reached for her handbag. Still, he didn't turn. Rising, she was surprised to find her legs still trembling. She felt so good, so ... lightweight. When she spoke, her voice was low, even. 'You're wrong about me. But it doesn't matter. You know why, Papa? Because you are the system incarnate. The whole oppressive, evil regime. Fighting you, fighting it, there's no difference. But you're right about one thing.' She stared at the rigid back, the proud, dismissive toss of the head.

'Playing paper games isn't enough. When it comes to a war between good and evil, human and animal, there's only one choice, one dignity. Remember that, Papa.'

The silver head jerked, but still he didn't turn. 'You've joined.'

She wanted to laugh. 'You're way behind. I left the Volk long ago.'

'Then you'll perish.'

'Preferable to rotting from the plague of Afrikanerdom.' Her legs were shaky as she moved past him towards the door. 'If Mia doesn't stay here, I'm telling Piet about Ruth. Mark it. You can try convincing him of how much she wanted it.' She turned back to face him, but he swivelled quickly, afraid of what she might read in his face. He was still reeling from the shock of knowing that she'd seen him—. He closed his eyes trying to push it out, but the image rose, more clearly than he'd remembered in years, taunting, savage. The door slammed behind Babo, and the sense of relief made him weak. His legs were unsteady as he moved to the couch. It hadn't been like

like that. Had it? Ruth had been willing, she'd never made the slightest murmur, the slightest protest. Verdomme, he wasn't a beast. 'Would you have kept her on if she'd refused?' He shook his head, trying to dislodge Babo's accusation. 'She was willing,' he said aloud, but his voice was the faint clatter of stones in a hollow well. He stared at the floor, forcing his gaze to make some sense of the pattern woven in the carpet. But the cold snarl of lines seemed to snap at his feet. He resisted the urge to move them, angered by the sudden weakness it suggested. Ja, she'd blame him for all of it if he let her, trying to imply that her mother had—. No, no, how dare she try to land that at his door!

Trust her to rake over dead bones, anything to keep him from concentrating on the real issue, the real skeleton in the cupboard, the thing that had to be buried deep if everything he'd fought all his life for, was to be salvaged. My God in die Hemel, didn't any of them realise what the implications—?

'... Papa, y'hear me?' Piet was standing over him, shaking his shoulder. Claus shrugged him off, squinting against the glare of the chandelier as he gazed upwards, but his son's face was in shadow.

'I, I didn't hear you come—.'

'She won't open the door.' Piet wandered across to the bookcase, speaking to his image in the glass. 'I told her. Again and again. "You're staying here. We'll sort it out. I promise. You're not going anywhere. I'll take care of you."' He turned to face Claus, his eyes sober. 'She wouldn't answer, not even when I promised to bring Jan home.' He looked about the room. 'Where's Babo? Papa? You listening? What I said.' He took a deep breath. 'Is that, I won't send her away. You hear me? Papa?' The word was almost a roar. Claus finally lifted his head, trying to focus on his son's heated face, the alcohol still playing out its bravura in his eyes. My God, but his daughter would've made a brave man in comparison to this. By tomorrow morning, when the alcohol was flushed out of his system, it'd be a different kettle of fish. But for now, better to humour him.

'I won't send her away.'

'It's late. Let's talk about it tomorrow.'

'I won't, Papa.'

'We have a regional meeting at ten. You haven't forgotten?'

Piet shuffled. 'What's the point? When they find out about Mia—.'

'Zo.' Claus stood. 'We might find a way of keeping it hidden.' He feigned a yawn. 'Let's sleep on it.'

Piet's jaw was a stubborn line, taking him by surprise. 'If she comes out in the morning, I'm not going. I have to talk to her, make her understand—.'

'This meeting's important—.'

'So is Mia! I want some time off, Papa.'

Claus's eyes narrowed. This was more than alcohol. There was an edge to Piet's voice, a hardness he'd never heard before. So he was finally going to make a stand, was he? Ja, he could almost welcome it, how often in the past had he hoped for it, how often had he deliberately provoked his son to bring him to this very point? But not over this. His lips twisted at the irony of it. This was an issue over which there could be no compromise. Otherwise, none of them would have any kind of future here that mattered, least of all, his grandson. The blood pulsed in his head. If it weren't for that slut—! Ja, no use crying over soured milk, not when an ocean of slime was threatening to overwhelm everything he held dear. But softly. His son had a lot to learn when it came to the wiles of an old dog. He smiled at Piet, his tone warm, persuasive, as he moved towards the open door. 'If she doesn't come out, come with me. We can talk then. Decide what to do. It'll be a short meeting, when it's over, you can come straight back here, ja?'

Piet looked at him, confused, a small tic racing in his jaw. Claus patted his shoulder as he passed him, 'We should all get some rest, we've all been inclined to ...' He paused, choosing the word with infinite care '... over-react ... perhaps.' He shrugged, smiling again, satisfied as he saw the hard edge leave his son's face, the hope flooding his eyes. Zo, let it flood, let him drown his sorrows in it, at least till tomorrow, at least until a plan could be hatched. 'We'll talk in the morning, zo?' Glancing back at Piet, he raised a hand in farewell as he moved out into the dark hall. Ja and he'd make sure he called early enough, before Mia was likely to wake. His lips twisted. Stupid of her to keep the bedroom door locked, pray to God she kept it that way until he'd whisked his son away.

He took a deep breath as he stepped out into the cool night, his mouth sagging, fear gnawing at his bladder. His heart wheeled suddenly, a planet out of orbit. He leaned back against the hall door, conscious only of the heavy fragrance of flowers in his nostrils until his pulse steadied again. Above him, the sky was a gauzed network of stars reflecting the glimmers of their dying hour, what was already past hurtling towards him at the speed of light. He too, was such a firmament, burning out, the presence of the past flickering in every living cell, a savage sepulchre of ghosts threatening to devour him. Ja, now, he was being morbid, if Babo had kept her mouth shut—. But there wasn't time to think of that. The question now was, how to get rid of the tarbaby before she began to squeal.

II

The door was closed, but Dick refused to allow them to lock it.

'Won't make a whit of difference if the security forces decide they wanna pay us a visit.' He didn't tell them the 'if' was a certainty. The only question now was that of time. He hoped there'd be enough for him to make one last sortie into the streets.

They were in the church: Emma, Mambo and the twenty-odd children he'd managed to haul to relative safety in dribs and drabs, most of them little more than babies. The older ones were out in the streets with their parents, or with the armed youths organised by Modise, hurling stones at the police and soldiers as the first bull-dozers moved in to demolish the huts.

But these children sat bunched together on the concrete floor in front of the altar, a group of little black Buddhas, pot-bellied from their inadequate diet of mealie pap, their stillness sending a chill down Emma's spine.

Mambo sat a little apart, watching the door, her gaunt frame twitching in response to the sudden explosions that penetrated tin and brick as though the church were no more than a shivering house of cards.

Dick stood pressed against the wall by one of the windows, waiting for the Hippos to pass before he went outside again. His shirt was smeared with the blood of those who'd fallen against him as the police had fired into the crowd sitting in the street which led into the official section. The shallow, unfinished trenches they'd dug had merely been hiccups in the path of the lumbering tank. But those few seconds delay had been a blessing, nonetheless, giving most of the crowd sufficient time to scatter before they could all be shot. Those who were injured or dead were crushed under the relentless onslaught of the caterpillar treads. One body had burst, the man's eyes still screaming for mercy as the thing rode over him, his blood spraying like rain, almost blinding Dick as he hauled two children by their hair out of its path, the attempt at a peaceful sit-in on the edge of the squatter section turning to mayhem.

As Modise had known it would. His mouth twisted. Modise had more faith in the presence of evil than he had in the existence of a second 'o' in his God. Something had snapped in him out there on the streets, snapped in a clean, unsplintered way while the air about him had writhed with pain. He hadn't told Emma or Mambo how bad it was, no point in panicking them. He'd been hoping their entrenchment would at least gain them a stay of execution on their eviction order. It had happened before in other places, the well-organised resistance committees taking the security forces by surprise, gaining some squatter locations as much as an extra few months. But his hope had bitten the dust. Lord, just let Modise get his hands on the little demon who'd informed on them!

He peered now through the window, wiping the sweat trickling into his eyes. His hand came away covered in brownish streaks. Must be blood on his face. No wonder the two of them'd gaped when he'd herded the children into the church.

From time to time as he waited, he made various soothing comments, feeling the children's eyes glued to his face, although he spoke in English.

Emma moved about, watching the children for any sign of panic. Panic? She grimaced. The children's eyes were round and wide with the coinage of a fear too huge to spend in tears or shrieks. Both she and Mambo were more likely to go into hysterics than these little polished statuaries, Christ, if any of the soldiers came into the church—.

'Emma!'

She jumped at the urgency in Dick's voice. He didn't turn from the window, but his hand flicked for her to come and see. She hurried across.

'Look, there!' He pushed her against the wall, a beefy finger pointing through the small begrimed pane of glass. To prevent them being shattered, he'd blocked the windows in the front of the church with wooden pallets. The only view now they had of the street was from the windows on the left side that overlooked the track leading to the Porto Cabin at the rear. From here she could see a small triangle of the church yard out front and a section of the street beyond, before it disappeared between the rows of tin shacks. A Casspir stood silent in the sunlit street. Through the glass she could make out the pale shadow of the driver as he sat, gazing ahead. What was he doing, were the police already on their way into the yard—? She shivered. It was then she noticed the black man in camouflage gear with the cardboard box at his feet. He was talking to a group of black youths wearing witdoekes tied bandana-fashion on their heads. He bent to hand each one of them something from the box, a small, dark object with the shiny carapace of a baby turtle .... Grenades! One of Modise's—? But how could it be, with the Casspir and the policeman—? She turned to Dick.

'Watch!' He jerked her back towards the window. The man was still talking, holding up one of the grenades, his hands gloved as he indicated how to remove what she could only guess must be the safety pin. One of the youths pointed to something on the grenade and the man removed his gloves to demonstrate more accurately. She stared at his hands, her mouth dropping open. White. White as the driven—. Her gaze travelled back up to his blackened face, the cap covering his head. Turning, she stared up at Dick. He gazed ahead, eyes cold as wet slate.

'Yeah,' he said without looking down at her. 'That's how they run the war, that's how they win it. Now you know what it means when they report black-on-black violence in Natal and other places. The Civil Co-operation Bureaus train some a the more right-wing elements in the police and security forces to deal secretly with blacks.' His lips twisted. 'The blacks who can be bought, that is, either for money, but mostly for political reasons.'

'Political?'

'Inkatha. It wouldn't be in their interests to see the government brought down, especially a government that grants them all sorts a special favours.' He nodded towards the street. 'That's a new batch of vigilantes the security forces've recruited — little tsotsi hooligans from the official section with an eye to the main chance. According to Modise, this lot call themselves the A-Team, can you believe it?' His voice rasped in her ears. 'Remember, Emma, for Chrissakes remember all of it and don't stop telling it till the day your fingers can't hold a pen anymore!' Together they watched the man climb back into the armoured wagon. Only when the youths moved ahead of them up the rutted street, did the driver start the engine, easing the Casspir in their wake at a snail's pace.

'Bastards!' As the word left her lips, the first blast came, their dusty faces quivering in the glass. In that moment it came to him, what it was Mambo had left unsaid, what she'd sensed as she stared at Emma's skull. But she'd got it wrong. The death he smelt was his own. He glanced across at the old woman as she sat watching the door waiting for it to enter. The thought should have spiked fear but all he felt was a sense of urgency for what must be communicated. He looked down at Emma. 'Remember!' His fingers bit into her shoulder. She looked up at him, struck by the oddness of his tone. Under the streaks of blood, his face was white.

'What's the matter, what is it?'

'You gotta promise me, y'hear?' The fingers tightened, making her squirm.

'Isn't that why I came here in the first place?' She tried to shrug off his grasp.

'Is it?' The grey eyes probed her face and she felt the heat in her cheeks.

'It is now.'

He nodded satisfied, his grip relaxing. 'I believe you.'

'That's kind of you.'

He brushed his hand across the short hairs on her head, loving the soft spikiness of it. 'Don't forget, will you, huh? You're my ...'

He swallowed, bringing the word out with difficulty, '... prayer.'

She frowned, searching his face, the still-swollen flesh about his eye. There was something peculiar about him, something—. 'Are you all right?'

He was half-way across the church, spreading like a massive shield in front of the children, before the door crashed inwards. She stared after him, petrified more by the speed of his reflexes than by the fact they were being invaded. Two young policemen in camouflage uniforms crouched by the benches, scanning the church for any sign of threat, assault rifles held to attention on their chests. She watched the shrine of sunlight framed in the doorway, but nobody else stepped into it. The men hurried forward up the aisle, rifles jerking right and left as they searched the rows of benches. The younger, a freckled boy who didn't look more than sixteen, kept whipping around to check behind him, something so childish and comic in the action, it made her want to giggle. As though he'd watched a surfeit of war movies. Even the guns looked too monstrous to be real. Christ, it was just too ridiculous for words, someone ought to tell them to go home and have their nappies changed. Again, she felt the insane urge to giggle. Glancing at Dick, she was amazed to find how drawn he looked. And Mambo, Mambo was trembling. Quickly, she made to move towards the old woman, wondering why their fear didn't touch her.

'Stay where you are!' The words were snarled in Afrikaans but even had she not understood them, she couldn't mistake the tone. She stood still as the angry blond boy with the face of a cherub circled the altar, dark boots snapping on concrete. It seemed to her his steps thumped harder each time he passed the edge of the tight-knit group of children. When he was satisfied no one else was hiding in the church, he returned to swagger in front of Dick. Above them, another blast rattled in the roof, the silence shrilling as the last echoes died.

The muzzle of the rifle flicked at the wooden cross about Dick's neck, lifting it, letting it fall again as the boy sniggered. Dick stared ahead, trying to keep his face expressionless. This little charade would continue until the boy felt him to be sufficiently intimidated. If that were all he'd to contend with—. But he sensed something in the youth, something restive, uneasy. The type who was easily spooked. His heart lurched. God in heaven, let the children keep still behind him, their fear pressing against his spine, palpable as the cold sweat soaking his shirt.

Across from them, Emma watched. The gun was cocked, the safety catch removed, something so careless in the way the policeman held it in one hand, his middle finger loose about the trigger as he swung the barrel to stroke the dried blood on Dick's face, that she knew she should want to shriek. But she didn't. She was so calm, it was unreal, as though her run-in with the tsotsis the day she'd stepped off the mini-bus on the edge of town had somehow made her immune to fear. But it was more than that. These youths were her own colour, her own kind, delicate pink skins as familiar to her as her own face. They had proper homes to go to, mothers and fathers who loved them, they were civilised, educated, nothing more than little toy soldiers playing at war. Surely? How could anyone take them seriously?

When Dick finally spoke, it was in Afrikaans. He struggled to keep his voice pleasant. 'I'm Father Carruthers.'

'We know who you are. We know all about you.' The last word was thick with innuendo as the boy turned to his companion. 'Don't we, Frikkie?'

Turning her head, Emma caught her breath. The freckled boy was sitting on the foremost bench in front of the altar, absorbed in mimicking Mambo's trembling. The blond boy laughed at his antics, as the one called Frikkie leaned forward, prodding the old woman's chest with his rifle barrel. Emma sucked in her breath. Little bastards! She took a step forward and instantly 'Frikkie' lifted the gun, pointing it at her, a grin on his face as he chewed a piece of gum. She stopped where she was, her hands clenching to impotent fists. The blond boy laughed again and turned back to Dick.

'Out of my way!'

Dick stretched his arms wide, the gesture placating. 'They're just babies — they've been here with us all the time, I've been keeping them outta harm's way.'

'You've been hiding them. Our orders are to take whoever's hiding in the church.'

'But they've been here all the time, they weren't involved in any of it, they've done no harm to—.'

'Then why're they hiding? You saying they're hiding from us? You saying they're hiding from their friendly neighbourhood police and soldiers? Now why would they do a thing like that? Unless they're some of the little shits who've been out throwing petrol bombs at us in the streets!'

The sweat dripped from Dick's chin, dropping onto his outstretched hands. 'No, I swear to you, I give you my word—.'

'Hey, Frikkie, go call Gus, tell him to radio for a kwela van to take this lot in.' The youth turned back to Dick, his voice harsh as he gestured to the sitting children. 'Tell them to stand up and put their hands behind their heads, tell them they're going on a little picnic.' He laughed as the other boy hurried down the aisle and out through the open door. Unnoticed, Emma sidled up to the back of Mambo's chair. Mambo's hands shot upwards to grasp hers as she placed them on the trembling shoulders. Christ, the old woman'd have a heart attack if she didn't calm down, if only she could shake off the peculiar lethargy which seemed to have invaded her own limbs, perhaps she could do something to help Dick persuade the policeman not to take the children, he was becoming angry, too angry, his face darkening as Dick, palms still outspread in a gesture of appeal, tried to argue with him. She opened her mouth to add her own plea but the words veered to a screech as the policeman swung the rifle upwards, smashing the butt against Dick's already bruised eye. His large body sheered sideways, reeling for a moment as his knees buckled. Some of the children shrieked.

'Bastard, you filthy ba—!' She tried to take a step towards the policeman but froze as he turned, his eyes narrowed slits above the rigid aim of the rifle.

'Shut up, you bitch!'

Behind him, Dick fell heavily and she winced as his head cracked against the concrete. His dazed eyes stared at her through the splayed legs of the policeman, his large hands pawing blindly at the air as he tried to raise himself up. The shrieking spread itself like a contagion, until all the children were howling. The policeman turned, screaming at them. 'Julle! Stilte! Fokkers, stilte, verstaan!'

When the shots rang out, the policeman realised before any of them the noise was coming from outside. He swivelled, facing the open door at the end of the aisle, his body gathered to a clenched fist as he crouched to face the attack. 'Frikkie!' he roared. The word drummed in the corrugate and some of the younger children began to cry. Another burst of gunfire answered him, louder than the last. 'Voetsak!' He fired into the empty aisle, his voice teetering. The noise reverberated, a pneumatic drill eating into the ears. Some of the children began to scream, drawing others with them into a deafening crescendo of panic. The policeman swung round, his face a white, pinched mask. Emma heard a long, shuddering howl as he began to fire on the children, only realising much later, the voice must have been her own. So instantly did it happen that she didn't have time to release her hands from the vice-grip of Mambo's, ten, twenty, thirty rounds, the barrel of the gun bucking and belching like a powerful fire hose, the small convulsive limbs jerking in a parody of dance, the screams extinguished in sudden sprays of blood that threatened to drown her. Finally, she broke free, fingers curved to talons, teeth bared as she ran to tear the flesh from his face. But Dick was already on his feet, staggering as he lurched forward. Sensing him, the policeman turned, eyes rearing. He fired, pumping the last ten rounds from the magazine, Dick's large frame juddering as each bullet struck home. He stood swaying as Emma reached him, her voice a sob in his ear. He felt a peculiar sense of something caving, splitting into its infinite parts. Yet there was no pain, only that his collar seemed to be strangling him. He put a hand up to tear it off, but his fingers sank into a warm, moist hole. Where was his collar? Perhaps Emma had removed it? Emma. His prayer. When he died, she'd cease to be for him. That was the thought he couldn't bear. Crazy, selfish. She was holding on to him, saying something, but he couldn't make it out. There was something he wanted to say to her, something important, but maybe he'd said it already? If he could breathe, then maybe he could think clearly. He clutched at his chest, and something scratched his hand. Looking down he saw the slivers of blood lodged in his flesh. One of the bullets must've splintered the cross. Apt, that. Crucified by his own religion. Something bubbled in his throat. He wondered if it were laughter. Or tears for the children he'd led to the slaughter. What a damn fool he'd been, helping these people to make eyes at the heavens, while all the time it was thickening around them, a dark fog of hatred destroying everything in its path. He lifted his arm, hoping he was pointing at the policeman, although all he could see was a blurred outline. 'You do not have the right ... you do not ....' Goddamn it, he couldn't breathe, what'd happened all the air in the church?

'Don't, oh don't! Don't talk, please, Dick, d'you hear me? — Christ, oh Christ!' Emma's arms ached under his weight as he leaned against her, but despite his injuries, his massive frame resisted her efforts to move him towards one of the benches.

'You do not have the right ...' He was speaking again, the words drowning in the blood collecting in the corner of his mouth as he pointed at the policeman struggling to re-load the rifle.

'Dick, Dick, don't—!'

'Lissen ... mus' be said, lissen! Tell him ... do not have the right to ... remain silent ... anything you say can ... and will be ... used against you ... mus' not ... remain ... silent ....' For a moment longer, he struggled with it as she held onto him. Suddenly, he slumped, dragging her with him as he fell. Even before they hit the ground, she knew he was dead, the warm, bloodied mass that was him, and yet not him, the grey eyes pinned to a vacancy that was beyond her. She grabbed the large awkward hand in both her own, chafing it. He must not get cold, he must wait for her, stay warm until she came, in another moment, she too would be dead, she could hear it in the policeman's hoarse sobs of fear, in the quick intake of his breath as the nervous hands finally managed to ram the new magazine into the breech.

When the shot came, she jerked, wondering which part of her the bullet had struck. Even when the policeman was thrown forward, eyes wide with surprise in the half-severed head, still it didn't dawn on her. He crashed to the concrete close to her feet, a crimson halo forming about the blond head as the blood spurted free of the torn jugular. She hoped he believed in hell, that he'd an endless moment to speculate on the horror of it before he died. Oh how she hoped it!

Someone was shaking her shoulder. She looked up into the calm, impenetrable eyes of Modise.

'He's still alive. Finish, finish him off.' The voice, small and cold, hardly seemed to be her own.

Modise shook his head, the AK-47 drooping in his hands as he gazed past her at the bloodied pile of corpses. Not daring to turn, she looked in his face to see what he saw, but his gaze registered nothing she could fathom. 'He is dead. The blood still runs, that is all. Come.' Reaching down, he hauled her up. Beneath her feet, the floor heaved and she clutched his arm, afraid she'd fall.

'We must go, now. There is little time.' His fingers gripped the soft flesh of her upper arm, pulling her towards the aisle.

'Wait, there's Mambo—.' She swung towards the chair, stopping as she registered the old woman's drooping stillness.

'There is nothing you can do. We must go.'

She groaned, breaking away from him as she staggered towards the chair. Mambo sat, blank gaze fixed on the children, her small chin resting on the bird-cage chest, the rigor-mortis of grief already cut in her face.

'Mambo, oh Mambo!' Kneeling before her, Emma buried her face in the bony lap.

'Come. We must go. There is nothing here we can do.' Again, Modise hauled her upright, urging her with him towards the aisle. She stood, pulling against him, agitated. 'Wait, wait!'

'Sisi, you must listen! They are all dead, we must go before the police and soldiers—.'

'How, how d'you know? Maybe one of them is still alive—.' She tried to bring herself to look at where the children lay.

'They are all dead, I've already checked it. Come!' He caught her arm and began to drag her towards the aisle.

'No, no! I'm not going with you, oh why'd you shoot that policeman, fuck you for shooting him!' She broke away, her eyes wild as she stared up at him. He'd cheated her out of her own oblivion. How she hated him, his dark perfection, his beating heart, his breathing lungs, while Dick and Mambo were—. 'Fuck you, fuck you for saving me!' She ran at him, clawing at his face. He struck her, a sharp crack across the cheek that jarred her whole body. Before she could see clearly again, his hand was flat against her back, propelling her down the aisle. 'They were my ... my family,' she sobbed. 'Don't you understand, I, I can't just leave them there—.'

His voice was low. 'They are not there, anymore, Sisi. But there are others who need your help.' Quickly he opened the door of the church, motioning her to be still. She caught the faint whiff of tearsmoke as she noticed the body of the freckled boy lying half-hidden between two of the benches inside the door.

'You—?'

His gaze followed hers. 'Yes. Come!' He drew her out into the blinding heat, the street wrapped in a conspiracy of silence as he hustled her down the side of the church. In the distance, she heard the continuous staccato of gunfire, faint cries that carried the echo of the children's screams. She shuddered, a blast from somewhere close by rocking the baked earth beneath her feet.

Only when they were belly-crawling through the long grass on the veld, did she ask him where they were going.

'You must get to Durban,' he whispered. 'The special branch are planning to arrest Thulatu at the demonstration on Saturday. He must be warned.'

III

Mia folded another of her dresses and placed it in the suitcase on top of the bed. Perhaps she'd be able to fit in some more? She went to the wardrobe, choosing a few elegantly tailored skirts. That should do it, the case was bulging with her best stuff already. Passing the mirror, she started, catching sight of a woman in a black slip, a small, thin golliwog with blackened cheeks staring hard at her through the glass. She raised her hand to wave and the creature waved back, a sad little jerk of bravado. 'Don't worry,' she said to it. 'You'll be gone soon, in a little while you won't see me anymore.' She laughed and the creature in the glass threw its head back, baring its teeth. She hurried away from it back to the bed to pack the last few items. There, her best stuff, it really was all her best stuff, a mixture of day and evening wear—. Mixture? Now there was a word. Close, it was close. But it wasn't precise enough. If she searched really hard, perhaps she'd come up with the right one. Medley, miscellany, mishmash, melange, merger ... mixture? No, no, none of them right, wait, go back and start with 'a,' after all everything she could ever remember started with alphabets, really, yes, 'a', well then, amalgam, alloy, admixture, blend, compound, combination, composite, conglomeration, fusion, skip 'h', no, wait, heterograft, that was good, infusion? Go on ... 'm', no the 'm's' already done ... but wait ... mongrel? Save that. Then ... patchwork, pastiche, pot-pourri, tangle. Transfusion? Hm. No, no, no. Really. Not even mongrel. Hybrid. Offspring of a tame sow and a wild boar, child of a free man and a slave, wait, free woman and a slave. Offspring of a tame boar and a wild sow, no, you just can't beat that. Hybrid. She giggled, tossing the last of the skirts on the pile in the suitcase. She'd never be able to look at another cross-bred plant. But then, she'd never have to, would she? She should send a memo: — 'Dear Piet, please, no plants, no flowers, or I'll turn in my grave, and most definitely no white Italian marble nor black South African granite.' Now, what was next? The jewellery, yes, yes, the jewellery, and the room was neat, neat, yes, bed made, clothes hung or packed, drapes pulled back, sunlight warm on the carpet under her bare feet, time to call him.

On the way past the dressing-table, she picked up the jewellery boxes, carrying them with her to the door, turning the key, stepping out onto the landing, the fog of silence rising from the empty stairwell to wreathe itself about her skin, let him not be out, not now, when she'd got it all straight in her mind, got it all organised.

'Thembalethu!' Ridiculous, the word ghosting the hall below, submerging itself in the rigid little cough of the grandfather clock, what an ugly piece it was, marshalling her hours, reminding her of the thing that waited on the edge of all she could see, but she wouldn't think about that, not yet, yes, things to do, to see to, first.

'Thembalethu!' Not loud enough. *'Thembalethu!'* There! Loud enough to wake clocks and drown the dead, if he were in the house he'd come now, his squat charred face worrying its way around the panelled door, so hurry, have it all ready when he comes, leave the door open for him, now, yes, the jewellery in the case, but wait, the knife on the bedside table, in the drawer, out of sight, out of—.

'Madam?'

She turned, startled. How long had he been standing there, how long'd he been watching, perhaps he'd seen the knife? Difficult to tell when he wouldn't look at her, his gaze bumping somewhere about her knees, she wished he wouldn't do it, it made her want to bend and scratch. Scratch his eyes off her skin, no, stop it, think, you called him here, why, think, think.

'Madam?'

Quick, say something, anything till you remember. 'It's you, is it? Yes, there you are. Come in. Come on.'

He hesitated, opening the door a little wider. 'I phone Baas now, Madam?'

Oh yes, he'd always avoided her eyes but the way he clutched the doorknob as though it were a lifeline, sweet Jesus, he wasn't afraid of her! Was he? Had he always been like this? Difficult to remember, no, no, perhaps it was the little creature in the mirror he was frightened of, she must reassure him, act normal, yes, yes, smile, switch the lamp on behind her eyes, yes speak, that was it, she was feeling very happy, wasn't she? Yes.

'Madam?'

'I'm going away, Thembalethu. A long way. Isn't it a nice morning? Don't you think?'

'I phone?'

'Did I say it right?' She turned her back to the mirror. No point in letting him see that thing.

'I phone?'

'No, I don't need a taxi.' A laugh. Careful. She didn't mean to do that, she didn't mean to let the laugh out. 'I'm going under my own steam.'

'Steam?' His eyes bulged. 'You catching train? First you talk to Baas.'

'Why?'

'Baas, he said to phone him. He said, Madam, if she unlocks door, Elijah must phone. He come home then. He left you note.' For a moment longer he hesitated. 'I have here.'

She stared at the piece of paper he held out. Whatever it was, she didn't want it, couldn't he see that? But he came into the room when she didn't move, shambling across to her.

'Home soon.' The folded paper proffered on the wide pink platter of his hand, too late, too late, whatever it was but she'd better take it to please him, home soon, he'd said, then there wasn't much time, so take it out of his hand or he'd stand there forever, drop it on the bed. 'No, forget about that.'

'He get angry if—.'

'It's okay, I'll phone him in a minute. First, I want you to—.' She stared around. What was it she—? The suitcase! 'I want you to take this. Everything.' Wave a hand at the stuff on the bed, then he would see, surely he would see?

'Where you want I should put it?'

'Your wife. What size is she?'

'Size?'

'Maybe these things will fit her.'

'No, no, Madam. She will not fit.'

The way he was looking at her — was she dead already? Speak slowly, don't forget that. 'The jewellery too. Maybe you could sell it, buy some things for your family.'

'No, Madam, I cannot. Baas, still he is angry over the forks. He explain you not well. I know this thing. Before I work, my wife in Soweto. When the small one died, she was strange for a long time. I know. But she better now. I have work. I send money every month.'

Couldn't he see? She'd no use for such tinsel anymore.

'You wear them. They for you. For here.'

When had he begun to look at her? She wished he'd stop staring like that, bland eyes like varnished pebbles, perhaps that's what they were, perhaps he'd stolen those eyes from Jan's rock collection, perhaps he kept his own eyes hidden behind them? What was it he saw? Well, whatever it was, she didn't want to know. Now get this over with, get him out of here quickly, quickly.

So smile. 'Wouldn't they fit your wife?'

'If she wear them, she in trouble. They not for the township. They for here. For you.'

He had to take them, he had to! But, calm. 'I'll tell Piet, you needn't worry—.'

'Baas, yes, but worse, our neighbours.'

'Neighbours?'

'They see my wife in these, they smell white, they ask questions.'

Smell white. His nostrils were flaring. Could he smell her blood? Could he? No, no, no, don't think about that. Concentrate. 'You can tell them—.'

'They find own answers. They make big trouble for us. We can die. If you black and you well-off, then you a sell-out. You doing something you shouldn't. Maybe informer.'

'Informer?'

'The police, the soldiers, they pay big money for names of people who protest, students who organise the boycotts, the committees for the evicted, you know? If you see a black with money, then you ask .... Where he find the money to pay high rents? To buy meat? To wear new clothes, drink in the shebeens? And you know. Only blacks you can trust is they stay poor. I stay poor.'

What, what had she been? Turn away, look out the window, how the garden dazzles. Hide, hide in the dazzle, don't let him see your eyes.

'You phone Baas now?'

'Did I get it right? Did I?'

'Yes, Madam.'

Yes Madam. Laughable, that ... if it weren't so heart-squeezing. Why, he hadn't a clue—! Then, turn and face him, at least afford him the courtesy of that. 'Do you know what I'm talking about, Thembalethu?'

'I know you not well—.'

'Do you?'

'No Madam.'

And his eyes. Shifting. Poor stick of charcoal. 'Your name.'

'Name is Elijah.'

'Babo said—.'

'The police, they put it on my papers. I cannot change. I am registrated. Registered. Thembalethu cannot work. Elijah can work. That is the way.'

'You have a right to be called by your name.'

'Madam.' Palms cupped in a pink wound. 'This good job. I happy with Elijah. Money is good. I need to work.'

'How can you say the money is good?'

'Money is good. Baas is good. Very fair. He pay more than most whites pay.'

'A lot less than any white would get. How can you be thankful for that?'

'I want no trouble.'

'I don't understand.'

'It is difference. For you. For me. I phone Baas now?'

No, no! He mustn't leave with nothing in his hands, else, how could she—? Her bag! Yes, there on the dressing-table! 'At least let me give you some money.'

'No, Madam.' Backing away. The horror in his eyes. What was he seeing? What? What?

'I cannot have it. This make trouble. I go.'

She couldn't connect. Anywhere. She was homeless. Didn't he realise, his denial would be the final desertion. Then try, one last time, swallow pride. 'Please, let me do something? I, I won't see you again.'

Lock his gaze in her own, hold it there as he hesitated at the door. 'The books, Madam. If you don't need.'

Books, relief soaking like rain in the parched earth, yes books, books? 'Books?'

'Of Master Jan's. Old ones.' A black finger prodding the ceiling. 'The box on the attic. School books you keep there.'

He wanted those?

'For the children.'

'Don't they have books?'

'Is not cheap, the books.'

'At school?'

'Is not free, the school, is not free the books.'

Legs abdicating, then sit, find a corner of the bed, oh it wasn't that she couldn't, she wouldn't, she wouldn't look.

'Is okay, Madam?'

Now she couldn't look at him. Her head was too heavy to hold up any longer. 'Take them. Take them all.'

'Thank you, Madam.' His voice honey in her ears. Dripping with gratitude.

'First I call Baas.'

'First take them. Bring them to your shed at the bottom of the garden. Then you can call him.' Go away, golliwog, don't stand there with your hand on the open door, sweet Jesus, make him go away now, what was he waiting for, why was he looking at her like that, he was right, it was too late to make reparation, go, go, go! 'Yes, what is it?'

'Is a good thing.' There, he was gone, the door closing like carefully handled porcelain behind him, as though the room might shatter if he slammed it. As though he knew. It's a good thing. Outside her ears, she heard a laugh. Coming from the mirror. Yes, yes, it was right to laugh at good things when you knew they were little blind stabs in the dark. But the nail was almost ... almost ... time, quick, suitcase out of sight under the bed, what a tidy room, yes, yes, pity she couldn't do it more neatly, but there wasn't much time, already he might be phoning Piet, so hurry, hurry, climb into the mirror, there, it was easy, so easy, not a scratch on the skin, at least not yet, yes and say goodbye to the stranger standing in the room, a little loose on the chin, isn't she? — a little flabby at the midriff, but otherwise ... not bad for a thirty-six-year-old hybrid, except ... except ... she's losing her colour, can't have that, can we so reach through the glass to the make-up box, come closer, c'mon, that's it, a little dark stain on your cheeks, can't have you going off looking pale and wan and miserable, now can we, now off you go and get the knife and the pills, yes, yes, that's it, in the bedside drawer and this, come back over here for this, you mustn't forget the eyebrow pencil ... that's it, now everything on the bed and go and get the water from the bathroom, careful, don't spill the glass on the way back to the bed, good, good, doing nicely, wait, wait, what about your blue dress, your lovely blue creation! It's been there weeks, how could you have been stupid enough to forget it, quick, find your handbag, search for it, find the ticket, there, there it is, Elijah can collect it, you can call Elijah, otherwise, otherwise, her fat black fingers drooling over it .... 'Dry clean, Madam? Certainly, Madam,' well, she can't have it, she can't! Keep your paws off it, you filthy munt! No, no, I can't go with you, I can't come out of the mirror, please, please, don't make me, no, no, I don't want to be here with you on the bed, please don't swallow me again I don't want to be in you. Can't you hear what I'm saying, she's a filthy black munt no she's not yes she is, not, is, not, is, I'm a filthy black munt a filthy black munt munt munt, each pill is a munt, swallow, swallow pill munt water pill munt water y'see Babo, y'see? I can't unlearn. To know it is not what I should be, that's the killing thing. To be what you should and not to know why is also a crime. Be careful, Babo! But then, the terrible, the terrible, is coming to know it only by default. How can I live with that put all the munts in your mouth, gag, swallow, swallow, swallow. There, bottle empty, thoughts slurring, won't be long, won't be long now. Perhaps mongrel is a better word after all since some hybrids prove superior in nature to what went before. Stop. Stop screaming. Let the verdict be given the sentence be passed. Mia Schuurman you have been found guilty: to have no conscience is to be sub-human, to come to know it by counterfeit is despair, to try to live with it is suicidal, to die with it is the solution and and and the desire to be that which I've never been in this house separate break out break away break apart Apartheid is der Zeitgeist yes yes yes the wherewithal to take my life's been supplied courtesy of my ex-fathers for which I humbly thank them a divine trinity united in my godhead blessed be their union no no no don't laugh no laughing matter the doctor's pills and the butcher's knife the one to anaesthetise the other to operate and something must be whispered of a third party a black spirit who's been shadowing me it was he who diagnosed me the carrier of an immoral disease fatal to humanity please note all three should be given an honourable mention in the credits. Now. The eyebrow pencil, there, yes, there on the sheets, good, good, there will be no post-operative phase no jaded re-runs so quick-quick do it do it do it make a ring around each wrist yes a bracelet of black blood about the bone the nail is home the pickaxe poised to ring the stone and the knife there winking in the sheets, a flash on the wrist someone someone gasping screaming something running Mia running Mia run run run, run from the wall, the song in the stone.

Chapter Nine

I

Doctor de Villiers, their family doctor, had promised to phone as soon as he had the results of the autopsy. As if they needed to be told. Babo wandered about the bedroom, her eyes avoiding the startling trickle of blood on the bunched sheets. No matter which way she'd gathered them, she couldn't hide it, every fold a gash that glared in her face.

Piet was seated on the large trunk at the foot of the bed, his head buried in his hands. The sun had long abandoned its invasion, and in the late afternoon the room was lustreless. Paul and Thulatu stood apart, each ramrod back closed to Babo as they stared out of separate windows. It seemed she was the only one in the room, as though the men had somehow managed to absent themselves.

Noticing a small heap on the floor, she went to pick it up. It was one of the lace antimacassars from the drawing-room. What was it doing up here? She frowned, staring at the fine filigree handiwork. It reminded her of something ....

'She was always so delicate.' Only as the men turned from the window, did she realise she'd spoken aloud. A doll, yes, that was it, the porcelain doll Papa'd once given her when she was little, how she used to throw it up in the air, quite casually, knowing—. When it shattered, its eyes ... just staring ... from a fine mesh of lace. She shivered, trying to register what the men were saying. Paul's face was puce as he pointed at Thulatu.

'No! This is your doing, you b-bastard!'

'Yes, that's it, isn't it? I'm the black bastard.'

'That's n-not it.'

'Then what? May I ask?'

'Any w-white man her mother would've slept with — I'd've felt the same—.'

Thulatu's eyes were pin-pricks of fury. 'Y'think by now I haven't learned to smell it!'

'She should've stuck to her own kind! But oh no. She always had a wild streak—.'

Babo stared, hardly believing it. 'Why, you're a—.'

'You s-stay out of it! You're no b-better than she was! You and—.' He pointed to Thulatu as he struggled with the words. 'Two years ago, he'd've been thrown in jail. There was a law against—.'

'Black-fuckie-white?' Babo's mouth was a sneer.

'My God, you've no s-sense of—.'

'Jesus, you're a racist!'

'If we're not on your s-side, we have to be against you!'

Babo stared at him, wondering if Mia had known how he felt. A cold fish, she'd called him, yes, she must've known. The bastard, the stinking—. Piet's voice sliced into her thoughts, a dazed, lost quality about the tone that made her bristle.

'Such a hat! Sprigs of wild flowers framing her face.'

'Oh, Piet!' She hurried across to him as he stood.

'Hey, beautiful lady!'

'Piet! Look at me!'

But he was beyond her, his eyes locked in some bleak place she couldn't reach.

'We'll go someday, I swear!' He stared past her, as though the empty space behind her was filled with ... someone ... a presence he could see. Weird. Her skin goosed.

'We will, I swear!'

'Piet, Piet! Look at me!' She shook his arm, suddenly afraid he'd never come back. First Mama. Then Mia. And, now .... She swallowed.

'Mia! Mia!' His gaze pleaded with something beyond her. 'Is that, it's Jan's future too. This is a fine country. Ours. There, we'd just be outsiders. Can't y'see?'

England! All those years ago. Relief flooded through her. At least now she knew where he was, trapped in the deadwood of old memories.

'That's a long time ago, Piet.'

Her words seemed to bring him back. He looked down at her, his eyes begging. 'Y'think she forgave me? I promised, I swore I'd take her away. I should've, shouldn't I?' His gaze drifted past her again. 'No! No! You're wrong! It's not just Papa—.'

'Piet!' She panicked, her hands pummelling his chest. 'Piet, listen! She was happy with you, you hear me?'

Again, her words brought him back. 'She *was* happy.' He nodded. 'I made her happy, didn't I, Babo? Despite—.'

'C'mon, sit down, you're exhausted.' She pressed him backwards until he dropped onto the cushioned seat of the trunk. He leaned his head on her shoulder as she sat, her arms about him. She looked across at the other two. Back in their brick-wall stances by the windows. Fat lot of good they were. Her lips curled as she spoke to Paul. 'You're a doctor, aren't you? Can't you do something? Give him a brandy or something?'

He turned, stung by her tone, but he said nothing as he moved to the bar. How could he when the blame was his? Still, he'd be damned if he'd let that black bastard come out smelling of roses! What her mother'd done with him, wrapping his filthy skin ... always there in Mia's dark eyes ... haunting. A diet of black nannies and white neglect, that's what he'd fed her. Every time she'd tried to get close he'd run the other way, run into funding the clinic, anything to hide the shame that was eating him. If that bastard had never been born—. He poured the brandy and took it across to Piet. But Piet wouldn't take it. Raising his head from Babo's shoulder, he pushed the drink away, burying his head in his hands as he leaned forward on his knees.

'Oh, Piet!' Babo rubbed the sloping shoulders. If only she and Thulatu hadn't—. She jumped up, looking across at the dark figure silhouetted against the glass. 'You and your anger! Goddamn you, you destroyed her!'

When she realised her father had entered the room, she could have bitten her tongue out. It was one thing to be angry with Thulatu, quite another to give Claus the pleasure of seeing it. He was making a beeline for Piet. She moved out of his way, afraid he'd brush against her.

'There'll be no publicity. I've seen to it.' Claus gripped his son's shoulders. When Piet didn't look up, he turned to Paul, his hand jerking in Thulatu's direction as he indicated him. 'The father, I presume?'

'What's this?' Babo's mouth twisted. 'An unwanted pregnancy?'

But Claus' gaze was locked on Thulatu. 'We've no need of you here. The funeral will be private. Family only.'

Babo almost choked. 'Where's the new-found loyalty springing from, eh, mijn Fuehrer? Excuse me while I throw up!'

Still watching Thulatu, Claus ignored her. 'Your name, kaffir?'

'Don't!' Babo whipped the word at Thulatu. 'He's liable to have you assassinated by the security police once your back is turned. Mark it: once your back is turned. Remember Khumalo — murdered one month after my father made casual inquiries—.'

'Shut your bloody mouth!' Claus clenched his fists, his icy gaze flicking over all three of them as he stood beside Piet. 'A nest of vipers. Ja, I might've known.'

His tone sickened Paul. He thought of Khumalo, a nice, mild-mannered man who'd worked himself to the bone to help those who'd been tortured, a doctor with good hands, healing hands. If they could do things like that, what hope was there for any of them? Unless, unless .... The thought filled him with fear, but he stepped forward anyway, surprised suddenly to find how easy it was to touch Thulatu's arm. 'Tell me what to do. The m-medical records. I'll publish them. It's all there: seven, maybe eight hundred cases.'

Claus hissed. 'You won't get away with this. None of you.'

Babo turned to Paul and Thulatu. 'Mark what he says. My father is clairvoyant. He can predict with great accuracy the dates of people's deaths. He, my friends, is the time's pestilence.'

Her words galvanised Claus. He swung towards her, his hand upraised to strike. 'You bitch! I'm sick to death of your—!'

'At your peril ...' Thulatu stepped forward in front of Babo. '... Baas.' The word was an insult.

Dropping his hand, Claus stared at him for a moment. 'I never forget a face.'

Thulatu laughed. 'There's no file on me.'

'Yet.' Claus resisted the urge to wipe the sweat from his forehead as the three of them stared at him, their hatred palpable as a strong wind on his skin. Suddenly, he felt old, his heart knocking again in that peculiar rhythm. He reached out to place his hand on his son's shoulder. But Piet wasn't there. When he turned, it was to see Piet kneeling beside the bed, his face buried in Mia's pillow. Verdomme, he wasn't a child, couldn't the only son he had behave like an adult ... like a Schuurman. He sighed. It had always been the way. Too much of his mother's blood in him, not enough of his father's. 'Piet!' His voice was sharp.

'Leave him alone!' Babo stepped forward, ready to do battle.

Piet heard someone calling his name, arguing over him. It seemed to come from a long way off. He raised his head from the pillow, her pillow, the scent of her skin, her hair, still branded in the satin cover. He must remember to remove it before Elijah came to take away the sheets. It must never be washed, he must keep it with him always. When the yearning came, he could take it out, bury his face in the smell of her, but not too often or he'd lose her, he'd lose her scent, it would dissipate in the air that invaded his lungs, forced him to live, that held itself aloof from her lungs, refused to enter. How he hated it! He gathered the pillow to his chest. Four hours ago, she was breathing. Four hours. Talking to Elijah. The seconds ticking, bringing her closer. Closer. Then, it's done ... the spilling between the seconds. Tick ... tick ... tick .... On and on and on, ticking further, further away from her breath, never pausing, never stopping all down the years away from her breath. Jan growing up in an empty house. Jan, Jan, where was he? How she had loved him! If he stayed close to Jan, then he'd feel it too, her love wrapping them like a warm blanket. He stood, looking around him, dropping the pillow on the bed. The room seemed crowded, the others, Babo and his father still arguing, Christ, they'd still be at it in the next millennium, enough to drive him crazy, all he wanted now was his son, where was his son, what had they done to—?

'Jan!' His voice was a roar in his head, but at least it shut them up. Babo came to him quickly, leading him to sit on the trunk, her voice soothing.

'No!' He jumped up again, hands outstretched. 'Where is he? Where's Jan?' He clutched Babo's arm. 'How? How can I tell him? What do I say?'

'Piet, oh, Piet!' Babo's voice was a whisper as she looked at the pain in his eyes. Claus watched, making no move to deal with it. Zo. Let his daughter comfort, his son whimper. He was patient. More importantly, he was winning. An old dog learns to bide its time. He noticed Thulatu and Paul as they looked away. Ja, he thought, too chicken-livered now to face what they'd done. Zo. Look away! It is while you look away the leopard stalks!

'The Vorsters!' For a moment Piet's face cleared. 'Yes, yes! Bring him home.' He stopped, the word burning his insides as he howled it. '*Home!*' It rammed the walls, driving Paul to the window. But he couldn't stay still. 'For G-god's sake—!' His voice broke as he went to stare at the bed.

'Pietie, don't, don't—! Sit down, please! Pietie, please! You'll fall if you don't—.' Babo pressed him until he dropped onto the trunk. He stared at his shoes. 'Life is a cheat. How will I tell him? How?'

Babo squeezed his shoulder. 'You don't have to, yet. I'll be here. I'll help you.'

'How did it get to this?' Piet gripped Babo's hands. 'He'll ask me. How did my mother get to this? Did she see my wood carving, Papa? What did she say?' He cocked his head as though he were listening. 'Is that exactly what she said? Exactly? It's not finished, Papa. I never finished it. Why wouldn't you let me see her? Why, Papa? Why? Why'd she do it?' His hands went limp, releasing Babo's as his body slumped. Before she could sit to comfort him, Claus sat, his long arm stretching about his son, patting his shoulders. Unable to bear the hypocrisy of it, Babo moved away.

'Ja, it's ... difficult, I know. He was ... fond of her.' The voice was low, dripping with sympathy. Babo felt sick, yet she couldn't block it from her ears. How far would he go in a pretence at emotion, just how far would he go? Jesus, he must be dancing inside, dancing with delight. Mia dead: all his problems solved. Well, not if she could help it. She moved to the window, her ears pricked. Outside, it was almost twilight, the bark of the trees a violent pink under the onslaught of a dying sun. She listened to Claus, curiosity spiking the dull lethargy in her limbs. How would he handle it?

'... but he's young, resilient. He'll get over it.' The velvet voice had an edge of steel.

Babo grimaced. Could Piet not hear it? Surely he wasn't so deaf that he—. The voice went on, cutting into her thoughts.

'You too, given time. I know you don't think it now, but look at me. When your mother went ....' The voice crumbled a little. 'But it passes. You pick up the pieces. You learn to live with it. You must, for Jan's sake. He needs his father. Even, one day ... you might find ... when you're over it ... you change ... you can't see that now ... but it's true ... you change ... you might even ... find someone else ... have children ... who can tell?'

She heard Piet jumping up even before she turned. The shock in his face was balm to her. Now, now, maybe he could finally see what their father was!

'What is this—!' Piet ran his hands through his hair as though he would tear it out. 'I killed my wife to please my father! It's not enough for him! Not enough, d'you hear that?' He stared at Babo, his eyes wild. 'He wants more. Two wives dead and he's looking to the next.' Turning, he looked down at his father. 'I've tried, tried. All my small, narrow life. None of it's enough for you.'

Babo pressed the back of her hand over her mouth, hardly daring to believe it. Look, Mama, she thought, look. A man. Was it really possible?

Claus stood, gripping his son's arm. 'You're upset—.'

Piet shook him off. 'And what do you call Mia's death? An unfortunate slip-up? What do you want? Natural causes on the death certificate?' He swallowed, the effort hurting his throat as he looked into his father's hooded eyes. 'We each took her wrist and slit it for her.'

'Ja, now, don't talk like that! You'll drive yourself insane thinking—.' He pointed to Paul and Thulatu. 'That pair! I've no doubt they've been in cahoots for years, though what purpose it served them by telling her—.'

Paul stumbled away from the bed, half-blinded as he made towards the door. If he didn't get out, he'd break down in front of all of them. He should have told her years ago, then none of this would have happened. It was the shock that killed her, her blood was on his hands.

'Y'see that!' Claus pointed, eyes glowing as Paul hurried out. 'If that isn't an admission of guilt—!'

Piet's jaw worked. 'You and I, Papa. She was close to the edge, yes, so help me, I couldn't see it. But we ... shoved, you and I.'

'It's shock has you talking—.'

'I've let you do it. What'll you say to Jan? What? How'll you tell him we killed his mother?'

'She wasn't his—.'

'She was more a mother than you've ever been a father!'

'Listen—.'

'No! You listen! I worshipped you! Strong, brave, the kind of man I wanted to be. You knew that! I wanted nothing more than to please you, win your respect. I even married Yolande! The Afrikaner daughter-in-law you needed to ensure the continuing purity of our blood. The only good thing that ever came out of it was Jan. The rest was hell!'

Claus threw up his hands, moving away from him. Ja, his son had always been weak. Even Babo had more—.

'Your scouting knife! Your knife!' Piet's words stabbed the air at his back. 'It's you!' Piet swallowed hard. 'Remember old Mothodi - he must've been seventy. You and those others, forcing him to sit in a slimy puddle, hacking at his head — he dared to have white hair! You took it then — after I spewed my guts up.' His gaze was trapped in the memory of it, voice deepening to imitate his father's. ' "You won't have this knife till you're man enough." ' He sucked in his breath, suddenly hating his father, fighting to control it as he spoke again. 'I'm not much, Papa. Mia was right. All my life I've been trying to hide it. I've been living a bigger lie than hers. I'm a sham, a weak, frightened sham! What is her lie in comparison to that! Nothing, it's nothing. There was no deceit — she wasn't even guilty of that! I'm the deceit! Don't you understand what I'm looking at? She died because I have no balls!'

'Pietie, listen—.' Babo stepped forward, but Claus waved her aside as he turned to his son. 'Don't put yourself through this.' He pointed to Babo. 'Y'think she couldn't've stopped it? All she had to do was come to me.'

Thulatu's laugh was ugly as he turned to Babo. He jerked his head at Claus. 'Pure poison, isn't he? God's my witness, I'd no idea!'

Piet passed a hand over his eyes, his voice low, trembling. 'A queen has died. A brave, troubled queen.'

Claus snorted. 'She—? She was—. Don't exaggerate, maan!'

'Get out, Papa!'

Inside, Babo felt it crumble, the hard little rock of fear that had been with her all her life, the fear that Papa would destroy them all.

But the strength, the fury in Piet's voice was a new shield, an unexpected weapon in the struggle against Claus. The tears flowed freely as she wandered to the bed. God, it had been such a lonely battle going against the grain of family, a kind of solitary confinement. How many times had she regretted it, how many times had she wished she'd been able to live her life without taking on board Papa's cruelty? Weird that it should be now, when she sensed Piet's presence by her side, that she should realise how alone she had been. How could she weep like this for herself, when Mama ... and Mia ...? Reaching out, she tried to touch the bed, no longer paying attention to the shouting match going on behind her. Piet was saying all the right things, that was all that mattered. Even if it was too late, still they had to be said, the words must gain admittance to Papa's ears while he had a breath left in his body. Only when Thulatu gripped her arm, bringing it to rest at her side, did she realise she'd had it raised in mid-air above the bed. Closing her eyes, she laid her head on his shoulder, grateful for the warmth of his embrace, wishing she could close her ears as easily against the roar in her father's voice. But Piet would be strong enough to bear it. He had to be, for all their sakes. Otherwise, Mia, Mia .... Oh Jesus if only she could find a way to stop thinking about it!

'You dare to speak to me, your own father—!' Claus was saying, his voice heaving.

'I have no father!' Piet pointed to Thulatu. 'I'd rather this man were my father!'

Claus stared, unable to believe it. 'I don't know you!'

'You've never wanted to! Something happened last night. Something you'd never understand.' Piet's eyes were overbright. 'I wanted to accept Mia exactly as she was. D'you hear me? I didn't care about her blood. When I found her there, on the bed, the revulsion, the shame I felt was for the colour of my own skin.' He paused for breath, struggling with it. 'Her death ... just the tip of the iceberg, the tip of it, that's what's most cruel. That is what I can't live with.' His lips tightened as he stared at his father. 'I never want to see you again!'

Claus flinched at the hatred in his son's voice. It took him a moment to find his own again. 'Y'think you can manage on your own? Zo. Try it! You can't breathe without me!' Turning on his heel, he strode towards the door, the words slung over his shoulder. 'You can't piss without me to hold your hand!'

'The death announcements will state who Mia really is.'

The words stopped him dead as he reached the door. Turning, his mouth moved in a lop-sided sneer. 'Ja? No newspaper will touch you after I make a few calls.'

Piet threw his arms wide. 'Word will still get round! I'm going to take a pickaxe to the ice. I'm going to hack and burrow and bore until chunks of it drift into every sea, become beached on every shore.'

'Zo, talk! You'll do nothing in the end.' He opened the door, fighting to hold back the next words, unwilling to show any kind of weakness, but they burst from him anyway, his voice faltering. 'After all I've done for you—.'

'*Because* of what you've done *to* me! *To* Mia!' Piet shuddered, the hatred pulsing in his veins, yes he could kill him, kill, kill, kill! He hauled the air into his lungs. 'Go,' he said when he could manage to speak. 'Go. Go on.' His legs suddenly refused to support him. He dropped onto the trunk seat, knowing had it not been there, he'd have fallen.

Claus made as if to speak, but the words lodged in his throat. He straightened his shoulders. He would not bend, he would not beg. His son had gone mad, that was the only word for it, my God, to talk to his father in such a manner—. Well, when he came crawling, snivelling back, ja, a price would be demanded. He sighed. No. He wouldn't make him pay, he'd be glad to have him back, show his son how magnanimous he could be. Perhaps Piet would never come back. His heart juddered at the thought. Raising a hand, he pressed it against his chest. Ja, now, he was foolish to think like that. A storm in a teacup, that was all. In a few weeks from now, Piet would be over the worst, a little time, that's all he needed, ja-ja. As for Babo .... He glanced across the room. She was leaning against the hotnot, his dark hand a blot on her pale silky head. Claus tensed, fighting the nausea rising to choke him. Hemelse Vader, this was his daughter, no matter what enmity lay between them. And if Piet didn't come back .... He held out his hand, looking across at her. 'Babo?'

She heard him call her name, heard the velvet in his tone. Lifting her head, she stared at him. There was something old about him now, the wolfish jaw slack. But the eyes were still scavenging. Poor Mia, what hope had she ever had against that? What hope had any of them? Turning, she looked up into Thulatu's dark face, her words defensive, as though he'd accused her of something.

'I, I wanted her to face what he was, what he'd made of Piet. Was that so wrong?' She pressed herself close to him as he stroked her hair. 'I was always at her. Niggle, niggle, chip, chip. Y'want to know? I couldn't bear to lose her to this ... this ...' she waved a hand towards Claus. '... carnivore! I, I couldn't bear to give him that satisfaction!' She began to cry into Thulatu's shirt.

Claus heaved the door open. 'My God, what I've spawned!' His gaze swept over her.

'What you've ... cultured!' Thulatu's voice was hard. For a moment the two men stared at each other. Thulatu felt his skin lift at the venom in the white face opposite his own. Zo! — the face told him silently: I will find you out. Wherever you go, whatever name you call yourself by, beware the hand on your shoulder.

Only when Claus turned and left the room, did Thulatu realise how tense he was. He jerked his head backwards to ease the cramp in his neck. His shirt clung to his chest in a damp, warm patch where Babo wept against it. He pressed his cheek against the top of her head, wincing suddenly as his gaze caught the abject stillness of Piet slumped on the trunk.

'Ssh!' he said to Babo, patting her back. 'He's gone now. God's my witness, I'd no idea just how bad he was!'

She lifted her head, her eyelids swollen. 'Put a spear in my hand! Put a spear in it! Oh, yes, I'll make the speech, the words will ... rip the air!' Her voice wavered. 'It doesn't matter, does it? Tell me, tell me! I knew it'd hurt her ... but that it should kill!' She shook her head. 'The war. I know right from wrong. That was my reason, wasn't it?' Her gaze searched Thulatu's face, the bleakness in his eyes. 'That was my reason for choosing?' The tears spilled again, blurring his features. 'Why must the "why" matter? It does, doesn't it? "Papa's casual enquiries" — d'you know who he made them from? Do you?' She swallowed hard. 'He had no respect. Not for any of us. People need respect. If they don't get it, it drives them to do ....' She shivered. 'The things he does ... somehow we're right there with him at the very core. All stained!' She clung to Thulatu. 'It wasn't just hating him. It wasn't just that ... was it? Oh, I want to tear my heart out!' She collapsed against him, sobbing. Half-dragging her, he led her to sit beside Piet, sinking down gratefully onto the edge of the trunk himself.

He stroked her back. 'It was by my hand, Babo. God strike me!' His words were low, hoarse with his own guilt. But she didn't seem to hear him.

'I, I do care. I do, don't I?' She stared across the room, searching the darkness gathering itself in the window frame, the tears drying on her mottled cheeks. 'I know what's right. Surely that counts?'

Thulatu patted her again, unable to speak. When he found his voice, he'd tell her, he'd tell her none of it had been her fault. The fault was his, his only. If he hadn't been so blinded by Thabo's death—. What, what had he done? His gaze searched the pampered walls, seeking for some kind of relief. This was his daughter's room: a warm, silken nest where she'd breathed, laughed, talked, made love. Screamed her way into oblivion, Elijah had heard her. Come running. But her blood was swifter, escaping behind the locked door. That's what she'd done, escaped him. Preferring death to having to own him, own herself. In trying to take possession, he'd destroyed her, a crime as rank as any Boer's. There was nothing now to live for, save the struggle. Even Sophie seemed very far away, a mother he could never own publicly, his whole life lived in subterfuge. Well, no more! From now on, he'd face the Boers, look them full in the teeth!

Beside him, Babo turned to Piet, laying her head on his drooping shoulder. 'We've got each other. We'll manage.' But her whisper lacked conviction. She looked up into her brother's closed face. 'Won't we, Pietie?' Lifting a hand, she pushed his hair back. 'You're strong now. You can see your way clearly once you face what you are.' She paused, seeking for the right words. How could she explain how lost she felt? As though she were blinded. In a maze. Oh yes, she'd arrive. But she wouldn't know why she'd travelled. She knew what was right. Surely that counted? God, she hadn't escaped! Despite what she'd said to Mia that awful night when Papa'd called her ... what was it he'd called her? She couldn't remember ... but the venom in his tone had spoken volumes: reams of hatred unravelling from the dark ages of their family. Someday, he'd open his eyes, realise that the presence of the past was no excuse. Would that she was around to see the misery in his face when that day dawned! If it dawned. Jesus, he couldn't get away with it, she wouldn't let him! There had to be some kind of justice, some way of bringing him to account. For Mama. For Khumalo. For Mia. For Piet. But most of all, for, for ... no, she wouldn't admit his name inside her head, she couldn't stand the pain of wondering what they were doing to him. Or if he were still alive. Beside her, Piet was saying something, his eyes trapped in the implacable night staring through the window.

'... five hours dead.' His voice quivered like a badly played chord. 'Small hours.' He shifted, his hand reaching to clutch hers. 'Is that why I feel I could step back? Be there before she—? I can't stand it! The drip of the seconds. Mia!' The word was a roar, beating against the walls, hovering about the bed behind them as darkness thickened in the room.

II

They were in the mountains, heading east, the air cold and thin in her nostrils, the terrain rougher than anything she'd ever set foot on before. How long they'd been travelling she'd no idea any more, the hours meshing into a body-grinding eternity from which she began to think she'd never escape. She'd had a nose bleed as they'd climbed, the blood splashing suddenly onto her hands and tee-shirt, taking her by surprise. She'd crouched, staring at it stupidly, the vivid drops telling her she was still alive. Modise had made her rest for a while.

When she had asked him what mountains these were, he'd shaken his head, reluctant to answer. He wore the rifle tied to his back, cradled between his shoulder-blades. At the front, tucked into his belt, rising like a shield across his chest, the strings about his neck, was Dick's bag of papers and clippings from the church. When had he removed them? In the church when the others were—? She shuddered. She watched his hands feeling for a secure hold in the dark, pitted basalt face as he moved above her. All about them, a medley of water rose from the deep ravines, making speech impossible. Once she had almost slipped from an overhang into a gorge. His hand had grasped her, hauling her back at the last moment. She'd stared down into the churning ribbon of water far below, the spray boiling to steam as the water hurtled over the rocks. She wished he had let her go.

Once, on the lower slopes, she was sure she heard the sound of traffic. Were they close to one of the mountain passes? That put them in the Drakensberg, surely? Yet there was no sign of any hiking trails, no sudden glimpses of any hotels nestling in the nature reserves. All she could see were more bleak cliffs rising around and above her, spartan with clumps of erica and rough grass. Below, in the gullies, sago palms and ferns clustered like frightened children about the shuddering trees, the wind keening in the branches as though time in this place had only ever been grief expanding through the slow, painful haul of centuries.

They climbed higher. Even the animals seemed to have deserted the graveyard of these upper slopes. She supposed she should be grateful for that. The noises lower down at night had been terrifying, piercing the numbness that coated her skin.

Just how much further would he accompany her? He'd already indicated he'd be leaving her soon, that somebody else would direct her to Durban.

'It is not safe for you to be with me, my face is known. And I must go back. I am needed,' he'd said when she'd begged him to come the whole way with her.

'But they'll be looking for me too, after what happened in the church.' Her hands were raw, the bloodied knuckles missing bits of skin. She stared hard at them, trying not to see the children jerking in a parody of dance. As the child in her womb must have done.

'We will change that.'

She was too tired to spend a breath asking him what he meant.

At night they rested in caves, the smell of trout as he cooked it over a small open fire making her retch. She made him burn her share till it was crisp as a cinder and no longer tasted like food. She couldn't bear to watch him as he filleted and cleaned, the ooze of bloodied entrails bringing her back to it. In the scorching heat of the day as they climbed, there was no room for thought, Dick and Mambo lying tense with silence somewhere in the far reaches of her mind. But under the icy eye of the moon, she couldn't escape it. Often in the same night, he woke her from her dreams. She lay close to him, his body a hard, warm shell she couldn't penetrate, the papers from the bag tucked under her tee-shirt for warmth in the absence of blankets, the weight of township history leaden on her chest. Suffocating. In her sleep she dreamed that was all the papers were for, Dick's meticulous keeping of the records, the risks he had taken to keep them hidden, reduced to nothing more than a patchwork of words to keep her warm, to help her stay alive. And she must keep going, at least until she'd managed to contact Thulatu. She owed him that.

Provided neither she nor Modise stepped on the next bed of snakes. She shivered, seeing again how he'd frozen in mid-stride along the wide grassy ledge that morning.

'What, what is it?' She'd stared at his transfixed face as he stood, nostrils quivering.

'Go back.' His mouth hardly moved.

'But—!'

'Puff adders.' The words were barely audible on a whisper of wind. She stiffened, afraid to look down at his raised foot, the variegated blur of light and dark scales writhing just beyond it.

'Christ, I—!' Her voice was a breath, low as his own.

'Go! Back to the end of the ledge. Wait at the small outcrop we climbed to the left of the ridge.'

Then she heard the hissing. She shivered, wiping the sweat from her palms against her shorts.

'Go!'

'But what if—?'

'Go back.' The voice denied her any inroad. She backed away, sensing her delay was sapping his strength as he stood, his body locked in an awkward stance that robbed it of its natural grace. He wouldn't fire, she knew, the sound would carry too far. Only when she was at the beginning of the ledge, did she realise what it was she found so odd. He wasn't even sweating, his bare arms smooth as marble. She waited, feeling nothing. The thought that he might die, his body bloated with poison, only left her wondering how she'd find her way on her own. She closed her eyes. Perhaps they were dead already, perhaps that was it?

When she opened them again, he was beating the snakes with the butt of his rifle, sweeping them from the ledge into the deep gorge below, the muscles rippling across his back, a tension about him that was palpable. She stared at the thin, boyish shoulders: an adolescent body fed a diet of cruelty and hate, when his imagination should have been fired only from the safe ground of myth and legend. Poor child. Poor, poor child. Orphan of Africa, blood-cold in the foetus of his eyes. In her tears, his back quivered out of focus. Please. Oh, please. Let him not die. Raising her arm, she rubbed her eyes, catching the stale whiff of her own sweat. It smelt of blood. And death — the same clogging of the air about her in the church when—. For the first time she was afraid, the fear spiking a quiver of heat deep in her groin. It rose, radials of guilt and grief for all she was, for all she had ever been and seen, clutching, gnawing, scorching her insides as though it would tear her limb from limb.

When Modise turned and saw her still standing there, sagging against the rock face, she thought he would complain. But he didn't. Instead he said, 'From now on, we climb, much climbing.'

She nodded, unable to speak as he moved towards the crumbling buttress that flanked the wall of basalt. He stopped a moment, staring up at the creviced cliff. Alone, he'd make it to the camp by nightfall. But in her exhausted state, it would take them till noon tomorrow.

The cave they rested in that night was alive with Bushmen paintings. They'd used up the last of the fish the previous night. She chewed the leaves and berries he'd hoarded in his pockets for the higher slopes, finding them more palatable than the trout he'd caught in the streams lower down. The smoke from the small fire eddied around the cave, making her cough. Gradually the flames took hold, making it easier to breathe. Around her, fierce hunters with poison-tipped arrows crept through the bush, stalking their prey while women wove baskets or collected wild fruit, here and there the colours still vivid in the dripping walls. But mostly they were fading ... dying. She stared, her eyes drowsy, the flickering figures moving about her in a painted dream: the centuries-old rituals of birth and death, joy and grief and defiance captured in mime and colourful dance, a brushstroke evocation of a race which once had roamed, exulted, in freedom. She stole a glance at Modise squatting the far side of the fire. His dark eyes moved over the images as though he were reading a book. Or learning. The flick of his gaze pausing, lighting on some detail: the pattern of repetition in the beads about a woman's neck, or the painted symbols on a boy's chest in some kind of initiation ceremony.

'They're very beautiful.'

The dark head inclined, but he didn't turn to look at her. 'There are many more. In many other rock shelters. The tourists come to see. But they do not know about this one.'

'Did Dick ever see—?' She swallowed, his name stabbing at her insides.

Modise shook his head. 'Not this one. He saw some of the others. There are more than 150,000 such paintings in these mountains.'

'Why are they dying, why, why?' She was sobbing, the figures blurring and flashing through her tears. Modise was silent. Since they'd left the church, neither of them had referred to what happened. Here, death, sudden and violent, was a way of life: keeping one step ahead of the police and soldiers, the focus of all his strength. There was no room for love or grief.

'They are discolouring because the caves are open to the elements — the wind, the damp ....' He lifted a hand. 'You see the dripping rocks. And even the smoke from fires such as this takes its toll.'

His calmness, his refusal to discuss any of it, arrested her tears. For a moment, she was angry. How could he be so unfeeling? She stared at the dark, impassive face. Sexless, that was how. They'd butchered his humanity along with his penis, leaving him a dark, cool automaton. Suddenly, it seemed a miracle he wasn't a fiend.

'Well, I'm glad I saw it ... your, your ....' She lifted an aching arm, wincing as she swung it to indicate the gallery about them. 'Museum.' She was pleased with the word, as though it more correctly defined this place than the Bushman caves appropriated by the Tourism Board to entertain holiday-makers, or the staid Sunday buildings closing their fists on an airless, State-approved past.

'I, I won't forget about it, even when it fades. I'll tell others about it, and they'll tell others so that even when they're dead, when there's no trace ... no trace ....' Her voice faltered. '... people will remember ... they'll remember ... that once there were ... people ... Bushmen ....' She was crying again, thinking of Mambo and Dick. Modise rose and went outside, stepping far out to the edge of the overhang as he scanned the starhung sky for his bearings. When he returned, she was asleep, a bone-tired moan ebbing and flowing through her half-open lips. He began to memorise the pictures again.

III

When Babo finally surfaced, the doorbell was ringing. Thulatu! At last! She struggled to rise from the bed where she'd fallen the night before, the picture of Mia clutched in her hand as she'd tried to peer through the haze of alcohol. Last night? She glanced out the window. Dark. She must've slept through the whole day. She wished he wouldn't keep his finger on the bell like that, it seemed to be scraping the inside of her head. Lurching across the room and out into the hall, she cursed him again, the pain radiating in her head. When she hauled on the front door, she was already screaming at him to stop it. The words died on her lips. A strange woman stood in the dusky communal hall, blond hair drenching her shoulders in an unruly mass. Babo frowned. What the—? There was something about her, something familiar .... The dress, though, weird, old-fashioned, like something Mama would've worn in her youth.

'Babo?'

Her jaw dropped. Leaning forward, she peered at the woman. Emma's voice speaking from Emma's face. Jesus, what was happening?

'Quick, let me in!' The urgency in Emma's tone woke her up fully.

'Why're you wearing—? What happened?' Reaching out, she pulled Emma into the hall, closing the door behind her. 'You being followed?' Her eyes searched the pinched face before her, the blond luxury of the wig only serving to enhance the pale violet of exhaustion. Emma shook her head.

'Come into the kitchen and tell me. Oh, yes, your hair, I'd forgotten.' Babo hurried into the small room ahead of Emma. If she didn't take something, her head would split. She opened cupboard doors at random, searching for the pills. Emma pulled out a chair and sat down, her legs trembling. 'Where's Thulatu?'

'I don't know. I've been trying to contact him since—.' She popped the pills in her mouth and went to get some water. She hadn't seen him since Mia—. Swallowing quickly, she turned to Emma, her tone flat, lifeless.

'Mia is dead.'

Emma stared, trying to take it in. The second hand on the wall clock kept moving, something sinister in the silent little jerks of time. Why hadn't it stopped? Why hadn't it stopped when Dick and Mambo—? It wasn't possible, surely it wasn't possible? In this city? This neighbourhood? Surrounded by every kind of protection—?

'But, but—.' She avoided the younger woman's face, unable to bear the rawness in her eyes. 'How?' Even as she asked, she knew the answer.

'Suicide.' The word hung obstinately in the air. Babo went to make some coffee, her movements wooden.

Emma cracked her fingers, the sound snapping at the silence. Christ, she should've known. Warned Babo. She'd sensed it that day, seen it lurking in Mia's floundering eyes, in the odd tilt of her laughter. And the scissors. Snapping like jaws. All she'd done was run from it. Tried to use it to ingratiate herself with Thulatu, an excuse to see him again. While all the time Mia was moving ... moving .... Fuck. Oh, fuck!

She stared into the steam as Babo poured the coffee. 'Does he know?'

'Yes. But I haven't seen him since the day she died. The funeral was yesterday. He didn't even show up for that.' Babo's voice was bitter as she brought the mugs to the table and sat facing her. Emma picked up one of the mugs. It seemed pointless to say she was sorry. Pointless and ineffectual. But she said it anyway. Babo looked at her, trying to smile. 'Thanks. I know you mean it.'

Emma stared at the wavering mouth. Did she? Did she really mean it? No, if she were honest she'd say it, shriek it aloud. She was glad Mia was dead, glad, glad! Who'd want to live in this goddamn world, who? Christ, she was glad she'd killed the child, glad! She peered into her coffee. How black and rich it looked. And the smell. Heavenly. Not like—. No. She mustn't think of that. There were too many other things to deal with. 'What time's the demonstration in the morning?'

'Ten o'clock.' Babo glanced at the wall clock. Almost midnight. 'Jesus, I've been out for the count for almost twenty-four hours!'

'Y'mean you haven't tried him—?' Emma leaned forward, her eyes anxious. 'Try him now, please, will you?'

Babo rose, moving to the phone on the breakfast bar. 'What's wrong?' She glanced at Emma as she dialled.

'They're looking for him. Modise has a friend who managed to smuggle a message out through one of the warders at the police station in Rhaumsfontein. It seems he was detained with the group that included Thabo. Thabo talked. Not in the beginning ... but later on ... near the end ....'

Babo stared, the receiver jammed to her ear. 'But he lived for a few hours after the police'd dumped him, he even managed to tell what they'd done to him, if he'd talked, he'd've told Thulatu, I know he would, he was always—.'

'Modise says they can mix you up so bad you don't know what you've told and what you haven't, they can even make you think you've told nothing. He says he warned Thulatu but Thulatu wouldn't listen.'

'Hah!' Babo grimaced. 'Doesn't surprise me, he's done nothing but take risks since Thabo—. Go on, what did Modise find out?'

'It seems Thulatu had a string of false names ... addresses ... you probably know. Anyway, Thabo told about the ones in Cape Town ... and Pretoria.' Emma rubbed her eyes, remembering how surprised she'd been to discover the breadth and scope of Thulatu's deception. In Cape Town he'd been Sipho. She bit her lower lip. As in London. Aeons ago. Worlds apart.

Babo held out the receiver, its tinny cheep mocking the bleakness in her eyes. 'He has an answering service, but he must've forgotten to switch it over.' Hanging up, she shook her head.

'Maybe they've got him already.' Emma ground her nails into her palms.

'I don't think so. That day, the day Mia—.' Babo scratched her head, trying to remember. Jesus, she could do with a shower. 'He said he was going off for a while, yes, I'm sure that's what he said, he was pretty cut up, he wanted to be on his own, but he said he'd be back in time for the demonstration. At least, that's what I think he said. I was so screwed up myself I—.' She paused, gritting her teeth. She hadn't even acknowledged him leaving the bedroom that day, so engrossed had she been in herself and Piet. And she'd blamed him. Dropping onto the chair, she closed her eyes. She hoped he hadn't realised it, but she had. Anything to escape what lay behind her own willingness to tell Mia the truth.

'Then we'd better get there early in the morning, in case he shows up.' Suddenly the wig was more than Emma could bear. She dragged it from her head, the small spikes flattened under the weight of it.

'It, it's, growing, coming along ...' Babo's gaze sheered away, remembering Mia with the scissors in her hand. At least then she'd been alive. Oh if she didn't get out of the room, she'd—. 'Listen, are you hungry? D'you think you could make a couple of sandwiches while I take a shower? I haven't eaten since—. You look like you could use some food yourself. You cut it a bit fine for the demonstration, didn't you? I thought you were supposed to show up this morning.' Gabbling at top speed to cover it, she moved towards the door, trying to grin. 'Not that you'd've been likely to get an answer. I was dead to the world.'

Emma looked away from the misery in her face. 'What's in the fridge?' She stood.

'I don't know. Have a look, will you? Thanks.' She almost ran from the room, her bare feet muffled in the carpet as she hurried to the bathroom. Emma sighed, tossing the wig onto the chair behind her. It landed, a halo of curls clustering about the sunny crown. A real frigging goldilocks effort, Christ, where the hell were they going with their wigs on the freezing Alpine slopes? Frigging crazy, all of them. That fellow Tambo, the bald one, had told her he wore one of the wigs every night, to keep his head warm. She supposed she was lucky they hadn't produced a nun's outfit for her. The thought made her giggle, the sound quivering in the quiet room.

She closed her lips, stifling it. It was Modise who told her that when they'd taken the box of wigs from the theatre in Jo'burg, none of them had thought to check the colours. They'd put them on to cheer her after she and Modise had eaten: four big black men ridiculous in Titian and blond wigs, their bodies writhing in a sinuous parody of womanhood.

How they'd stood staring at her when Modise had hauled her over the rocky outcrop. She'd thought it was her whiteness which'd taken them by surprise. One of them muttered something to Modise. She asked him what the man had said.

'Blood and bone.' Modise looked past her, raising a hand to shade his eyes as he gazed out over the vast sweep of cliff hurtling to the deep gorge below. She'd shivered, chilled more by his words than the cold wind whipping her skin. Dick's blood. The children's. Perhaps even some spatters from the policeman. It had even soaked through to her underpants, her bra. The first time she'd squatted behind a rock to pee, when she'd seen the dark stains, she'd thought she was menstruating. But the bloodstains were dry. The pools on the church floor, seeking a lower level as they snaked across the uneven concrete. No wonder the men were gaping.

She stood, bleary-eyed at the mouth of the cave, too weak to be afraid of the dark eyes that seemed to penetrate her bones as Modise explained, a gunfire rapidity in his strange accent. She'd leaned back against the dripping wall and instantly it had soaked her tee-shirt.

'Has anybody got a cigarette?' The words croaked from the dryness of her throat. They laughed, as though she'd made some huge joke. They gave her water to drink and told her to strip behind the boxes of ammunition stacked at the back of the cave.

They waited inside while she washed, far out at the end of the ledge where water sprang in continuous icy jets from a crevice in the rock. The clothes they'd given her were clean: men's clothes, patched and darned, but the jumper was warm. She rubbed her sneakers till the blood faded to a uniform mud, as though she'd stepped in something foul.

When Modise left, he came to say goodbye. It was almost night-fall. He squatted down beside her on the sisal mat by the fire. She licked the last of the mealie pap from her fingers, knowing he was leaving her even before he spoke the words.

'I must go back.' He nodded at the dusky mouth of the cave. Rhaumsfontein might be just beyond it the way his gaze was focussed.

She folded the leaf on which the pap had been spread, wiping her hands in its warm underbelly. 'You should eat more. You're too thin. A boy your age should—.' Her voice broke on a shuddering sob. She stared at the leaf clenched in her fist, fighting it. Gradually, the spasm eased and she was able to look up at him, dry-eyed. The heat burned in her cheeks. A foolish thing to say. As though she were his mother or something. As though she had the right. He was holding out his hand. Smooth and hard against her welted palm. If only he'd smile. Do something which was human. If only she could put her hand to his face, press her cheek to his. But he didn't like being touched. She had discovered that when they'd had to lie close together at night for warmth, his skin seamless as black basalt.

'How will you—?'

'I have many who will hide me.'

'If you can—?' She shuddered. 'What about ... their bodies?'

'I will see to it.'

They both knew he was lying. It wouldn't be the first time the security forces helped bodies disappear into unmarked graves.

'If you get as far as Babo, you will make it, she will know a way. But keep the wig on till you get out. They know you were in the church with Dick. They will want to question you about the policemen's deaths. If you are taken, tell them everything, tell them I kidnapped you, that I threatened to kill you. That you escaped. If you can manage it, say nothing about Thulatu when they ask. Tell them the only time you ever met him was when he came with the mobile clinic. You've memorised his phone number?'

She nodded.

'His address?'

Again she nodded.

'Try his number from Pietermaritzburg before you board the bus. The men will give you money. Go straight to Babo when you get to Durban, it is the safest place. Good luck.'

She stared up at him as he rose. 'Goodbye, Modise.' Her voice was a whisper against the hardboiled lump in her throat. Goodbye. Goodbye. 'And, and, thank-you.' Her gaze searched the exquisite features, hungering to find what Dick had loved, so that she could love it too, feel Dick's presence in the dark face. The eyes, perhaps it was the eyes? Wary. Waiting for the next piece of wire to be tightened on his flesh. Goodbye. Goodbye. He turned, moving away from her out through the mouth of the cave. Don't! Oh, don't! Don't go. Don't leave me here alone. Dick! Dick! Please, oh please, come back. Through her tears, the men moved in a blur out onto the overhang to see him off. Later, the bald one, Tambo, brought her something hot to drink. He thrust a rag into her hand, embarrassed at her grief. 'Modise, he say to say you remember about the ... mus-ee-um, yes?' So he had remembered what she'd said. He'd been listening. She stared into the steamy drink. Something she'd said had meant something to him. She nodded, unable to speak, grateful for the small ball of warmth inside that had nothing to do with the drink.

'Drink, you drink!' Tambo grinned. He indicated the tin mug. 'Put hairs on your head.' He threw back his head and laughed, a deep belly-rumble that reminded her of Thulatu. 'Wh-what's in it?' She gasped as the alcohol hit the back of her throat.

'Something make you sleep. You need rest. We take you down before light comes. Me and Tambo-Two.' He pointed at the other men already stretched out on the sheets of plastic. She peered to see which one he meant, but already her eyelids were drooping.

When they woke her, the sky was lightening towards dawn, the moon an opaque sickle in the sky. She shivered, glad of the old jumper as they headed down, Tambo weaving over the rocks in front of her, keeping up a low barrage of instructions as to where she should put her hands and feet. She was glad she'd slept, else she could never have kept pace with them. Behind her, Tambo-Two, a tall, taciturn man with a slight stoop, corrected her any time she lost her concentration. Often she stumbled, pitching forward against Tambo's broad back, feeling it solidify to a brick wall as he strained against her weight. Each time she muttered an apology, he hissed the same words over his shoulder. 'Don't talk — waste breath.' Every so often, he called a halt, the intervals so regular that she began to be able to anticipate them. They stood silently, the breaks lasting for the time it took her to manage twenty deep breaths. Then they were moving again. Time became a battle with rock and stone, noisy streams that soaked her to the skin, animals startled as they stood to drink, antelope, eland, a red hartebeest, and once, even a zebra. The sun was well overhead before they reached the easier ground of the lower slopes, a cacophony of wings greeting them as they entered a dense cluster of trees. In front of her, Tambo stopped. 'Rest. You can sit.' He pointed to a clump of rocks where the trees thinned a little. She nodded, her breath burning in her lungs and throat. She wasn't sure when she'd lost the wig. But when she and Tambo turned, Tambo-Two was trotting up behind them, his eyes peering from the rich blond curls bobbing about his dark face, lending him an air of frozen astonishment. They stared, unable to believe it. Despite herself, Emma began to laugh. Pressing a hand to her mouth, she held onto her breath, the tears rolling down her cheeks.

'Why, it's, it's Blondie!' She collapsed against Tambo, giving herself over to it as they both doubled up. Tambo-Two put his finger to his lips, his eyes popping as he indicated the need for silence. Christ, it was funny, the funniest thing in the world, oh make him take it off or she'd wet herself! She rushed off in among the trees, still howling as she struggled with the belt on the oversized trousers.

When she returned, Tambo was gone. Tambo-Two was standing with the wig in his hand, his gaze sheepish. He held out the wig.

'I'm sorry we laughed, it's just that you ... and you had it on backwards.' She giggled again, unable to help herself. 'Look! Like this! See?' She pulled the wig on her head, patting the curls into place. He almost grinned, touching his own woolly helmet. 'You keep yours, I keep mine. Come.' He gestured ahead towards where the trees grew denser.

'Where's Tambo?'

'We will meet him on the other side of the yellow woods. He is gone to find a truck.'

They moved forward more leisurely now, the trees alive with the chatter of long-tailed birds in the dappled light. She wondered where the laughter had come from, how it could still be possible to laugh after all that had happened. Strange. Weird, Babo would say.

'No talk, no sound, from here.' He squeezed her arm to emphasise his words. A loud bark startled them. His hand delved inside the breast of his khaki jacket, towards the bulk in the shoulder-holster. She watched his listening face, his gaze roaming the trees ahead as the bark came again.

'A dog, is it—?' She gripped his arm. Suddenly he relaxed, withdrawing his hand.

'Baboon. Quiet, now!'

They moved deeper into the forest, taking what appeared to be the most tortuous path, the prickly undergrowth clawing at the old trousers she was wearing. Here at least it was cool, the sun seldom penetrating the vaulted roof of leaves that swayed far above their heads. Her arms and legs ached. If only she could lie down and rest. When they reached the dirt track, she stared, her eyes popping. Tambo sat grinning at the wheel of an old jalopy, a crate of chickens squawking on the back seat. He handed her a plastic bag, nodding at the trees. 'Change.'

She stared at the ancient dress, the platform shoes. 'Where'd you get them?'

He put a fat finger to his lips, his eyes dancing. 'No questions.'

They got her to Pietermaritzburg by dusk, dropping her in a deserted side-street near the bus rank. She crawled out from where she'd wedged herself between the back and front seats, her buttocks half-frozen from the windy holes in the floor of the car. They were gone before she could thank them properly, Tambo stuffing some notes in her hand, the warm pressure of his generous spirit still clutched in her fist as she hurried to the bus station.

She had tried Thulatu's number three times before the bus for Durban arrived.

And now it was after midnight, and still she hadn't managed to contact him. Going quickly to the phone, she dialled his number again, only giving up when she heard Babo moving about in the bedroom. She wouldn't, couldn't tell her about Dick. At least not tonight. Not on top of what'd happened to Mia. Tomorrow, there would be time enough tomorrow, after the demonstration. Time enough in all the long tomorrows to brood on it. Babo was yelling something. She strained to hear. Food. Asking her to do something about food. She gazed about the small kitchen, trying to concentrate.

IV

When they were ready to leave in the morning, it was Babo who spotted the car outside, hauling Emma back from the balcony doors as though the glass would scald her skin.

'Don't let them see you!'

'How do you know? Maybe they're not—.' Emma cracked her fingers, not wanting to believe it.

Babo's lips curled. 'A present from Papa, I can smell it a mile off!' She turned to look at Emma, the colour draining from her face. 'Was it there last night, when you—?'

Emma frowned, trying to remember. 'I got the taxi to drop me at the corner.' She frowned, trying to visualise herself clumping up the dark street in the oversized shoes. 'I don't think so, it was dark, I was hurrying, what I mean is ....' She shook her head, uncertain. 'I was trying to keep the shoes on my feet.'

'Then you'd better start praying.' Babo went to find the yellow pages. 'A demonstration this big is not something you can hide from the police. I'm sure Papa knows about it. Either those men are here to follow me, or he's asked them to see I never get to the demonstration.' Her voice was bitter as she rifled through the phone directory, the pages snapping. 'He did that once before, when—. Listen, if they know someone's with me, one of them'll hang around to find out who you are, neither of us'll make it to the university. And the police aren't the only ones looking for Thulatu. Papa wants him too. I saw the way he looked at him when Mia—. You'd better start praying.' She dived among the clutter of books on the floor of the living room and found the phone.

When the taxi turned into the street, they gripped each other in a fierce embrace.

'Soon's I get in the taxi, I'll make him call on his radio for another cab to come and get you, that way, if the phone's tapped—.' Babo broke away, grabbing her bag. 'I'd better go. See you.' She nodded at Emma, her eyes full. Emma nodded back, unable to speak. She touched her shaking fingers to her lips, trying to smile. But already Babo was gone, the door slamming in her wake. Emma turned to the window to watch as Babo skipped lightly down the empty drive and out the gate to the waiting taxi. See you. Someday. Maybe. She wiped her eyes, straining to catch a last glimpse of Babo's blond head as the taxi accelerated away from the kerb. Five shallow breaths later, the dark car pulled away, U-turned in the quiet street and headed off in the direction the taxi had taken. Emma hauled the air into her lungs.

She stuffed the money Babo had given her into her pocket, going to examine herself in the mirror: a blond woman with a well-made up face, dressed in cotton blouse and slacks, stared back at her, the face a thin, peaked cliff between the cascades of hair. Luckily Babo's clothes fitted her. The sneakers were a little large but clung firmly to her feet once she laced them up tightly enough. She went to the kitchen and watched the second hand crawl around the face of the clock. If the men were just instructed to follow Babo, she'd go straight to the campus, get somebody to warn Thulatu. If he were there. If Babo were stopped, questioned—. If the men came back—. If the taxi didn't come—. If the taxi-driver's radio wasn't working—. If nobody managed to warn Thulatu in time—. If, if, if .... She went back to the window in the living room to wait, the sunlight already probing the edges of the glass, the blue sky gazing at her blankly, feeding its reflection into the still-life of the sea beyond the sloping roof tops. Her stomach felt queasy and she was shivering, despite the fact that the room was overwarm. Nerves, that was all. She wasn't going to be sick, fuck it, not now—. The bile rising into her mouth galvanised her. She ran from the room, barely making it to the toilet before the vomit was spilling from her lips, her hands pushing the hair back to prevent it being soiled. When she was finished, she leaned against the tiled wall, afraid her legs would give. Gradually the spasms eased and she felt better. What had brought that on? All she'd had for breakfast was coffee and even last night, Babo'd had to coax her to eat half a ham sandwich. Nerves, yes, that's what it was, she was all screwed up inside, worried about finding Thulatu, thinking of Dick and Mambo. Turning the tap in the sink, she filled a glass and quickly rinsed her mouth. She was lucky she hadn't cracked up, never mind being all churned up inside. Inside. Sick. Sickness. Morning-time. She moaned, pressing the cool glass to her hot cheek. No, it couldn't be, it couldn't, too near the end of her cycle, she'd thought of that when he'd come to her in the cabin, knowing she was safe. Yet, yet, the last time, in London, she'd been ill from the very beginning, almost it seemed, from the very instant—. No, no, it couldn't, couldn't be true! She moaned again, the tears spilling in a fever of grief. Dick. Oh Christ, Dick. Oh please please come back come back. When the doorbell rang, it made her jump. She rushed from the bathroom to look from the window, her heart thudding. Outside on the steps, a coloured man with a peaked cap had his hand on the bell. Grabbing a tissue, she dried her eyes, and rushed outside, afraid he'd leave without her.

'You want taxi?' His gaze glanced somewhere off her left shoulder as she stepped out and for once she was glad his submissive attitude prevented him looking her in the face. In the taxi, as he drove uphill towards the university, she patted the last of the tears from her cheeks, hoping the make-up was still in place. When they crossed the toll bridge, Emma began to peer out, the tall cypresses in the suburban gardens still screening the university buildings from view. Look for the greenish dome, don't you remember, when I brought you there, Babo had said, you'll be able to spot it from the main road that cuts through the campus. But in the end it wasn't the dome that arrested her gaze. On the extensive lawns before the main buildings the crowds were massed, the banners and flags a rippling ocean of protest. Ahead, a road-block of bodies greeted them, the taxi-driver swearing under his breath as he slowed down. He threw her a filthy sideways glance as she paid him. Leaping from the car, she was gone before he could offer her the change.

The first thing that struck her was the silence. People were swaying, waving their banners, but nobody spoke, something so unnatural, eerie in the stillness that it goosed her flesh. She began to run, unsure of where she was going, swerving right as she circled the group sitting in the road, each with a letter printed on their chests. Her eye spelled out the word 'injustice' as she swung onto the grass, the 'j' and the 'c' belonging to two whites blending in a rainbow of skin shades. Sitting ducks, all of them. She shivered. Didn't they realise what'd happen when the police arrived? If he's there, he'll be at the front near the science block, with the representatives of the students' council. But which was the science block? She couldn't remember. Or maybe it was the library, was it the library Babo'd said? Christ, why hadn't she listened more closely, why hadn't she paid more attention the last time she was here, instead of brooding over Thulatu? This place with its roads and buildings was more like a city than a frigging university campus, what the hell was she going to do, the police'd be here soon, she could smell it in the silence, the same kind of chilling expectancy she had felt among the women and children, among the shivering dogs in the church. Dick. Dick. Oh Christ, where was Babo, where was Thulatu!

She jumped up and down, trying to see over the heads of the crowd. All she could see from here was the dome and the roofs of the buildings, too many heads and banners cutting off her view. Suddenly, a sweet, clear voice began to sing, the purity of the notes washing out through the loudhailers over the crowd in familiar, haunting strains. Instantly, she was back in the township, Dick's strong voice enveloping her as he joined with the squatters, giving himself up to it. About her, the crowd stilled to attention. She stood, her eyes closed, her face lifted to the notes threading the air, as if through the song she could somehow regain him. Repossess. When the song finished, the crowd hove in one exultant wave of continuous cheering. Somebody prodded her arm. The Indian beside her was holding out the corner of his flag.

'Use it to wipe your eyes!' He had to shout to be heard above the tumult of the crowd. Smiling, he patted her shoulder, as though he knew what she'd been crying for.

Forgetting the make-up, she wiped the tears, the sudden sting of mascara almost blinding her. She dropped the flag and knuckled her eyes, waiting till the stinging eased. Christ, she'd look a sight after this. When she could see again, she turned to thank him. The crowd was hushing as the first words came over the loudhailers, a female voice bidding them welcome, thanking them for their courage ....

'Please, please—!' She tugged at his arm. 'Where are the speakers, the speakers? Can you tell me—?'

Several heads turned, hushing her. The Indian stepped back a little, embarrassed by her intensity as the voice droned overhead, condemning the government's systematic banning of every organisation that was active in political protest.

She clung to his arm, the gesture reminding her of Mambo's vice-grip as she whispered. 'Please!' Looking up into his face, her eyes begged him. 'I can't see! Can you see where the speakers are? It's important! Please, please!'

She saw him register the urgency in her face. Or perhaps it was her mottled skin, the flatulence of the wig that did it. He stood on tiptoe, dark eyes scanning the heads of the crowds. She sagged, willing him to see, the seconds as he gazed seeming interminable.

Finally, he pointed, his voice an undertone. 'Over there, by the administration building.'

She jumped up, trying to take a quick look. 'That roof on the right, the one with the—?'

'Yes, yes!' He threw a nervous glance at the students in front of him, afraid her voice would make them turn again.

She gripped his arm, her voice a hiss. 'You sure?'

He pulled his arm, trying to free it. 'Yes, that's it!'

'How can I get around to it?'

His face lit up. At last he sensed the possibility of getting rid of her. He pointed. 'That way, to the edge of the lawn, turn left, past the small car park, you will be in front of the crowd. The speakers are there.' He paused, forcing a smile as she thanked him. He didn't tell her that the organisers had stewards flanking the sides, that there was no way she'd be able to get close to the speakers. Already she was running from him, something peculiar in the way she held her hand on her flying hair, as though she were wearing a hat. He shrugged. Crazy woman. Relieved, he turned to immerse himself in the brave rhetoric rolling above his head.

She ran along the fringe of the crowd, glad of Babo's sneakers. At regular intervals, she gave a flying leap to keep the roof he'd pointed to in sight. Christ, if only she weren't so small! Following his directions meant leaving the crowd, cutting away from them across the car park. Please, please, let him have told her the truth! Beyond the car park, the ground dropped away to a vast shrubbery of bush and trees. She veered left again, weaving among the parked cars, swearing as her knee struck a protruding tow-bar. She stood winded by the sudden pain, her fists slamming the boot in anger. She dragged onwards, leaving the cars behind, her breath coming in hoarse sobs as she swung back towards the crowd. Through the windows of the building on her right, she caught sight of walls of bobbing bookshelves, a dancing coat of arms. Ahead, the crowd had blurred to a forest of swaying colours as they applauded the first speaker. She paused, bending over, her hands resting on her thighs as she dragged air into her lungs. No good to anyone if she ran herself so ragged that she couldn't see where she was heading. A few beads of sweat dropped from her chin onto the concrete, fading almost immediately. Christ, the wig was stultifying, her scalp hot, itchy and soaked. How she longed to tear it off, throw a bucket of icy water over her head! She began moving again, afraid she was wasting time.

She was now on a stretch of concrete before the lawns, ahead, a barrier of chairs strung like a fence from the front of the crowd to the edge of the administration block. The next speech had begun, this time a man's voice, the words soaring in angry flight over the heads of the crowd. Running up to the barrier, she dragged one of the chairs from the top of the pile and climbed up on it. Inside, several youths stood wearing arm-bands with the word 'steward' printed on them. Beyond, almost in line with the centre of the building, were a row of people standing on a bench, facing the crowd. A white sheet was pinned over the entrance to the building with a slogan printed in bold type. On the steps below it, some youths stood in UDF tee-shirts, arranging their musical instruments. Before the speakers, a couple of photographers were pressing back into the crowd as they sought the best angles. Beyond them, towards the far corner of the block, several men were checking the technical apparatus that fuelled the loudhailer-system. Her gaze skidded over the faces but couldn't track him down.

She breathed deeply, forcing herself to begin again, this time moving more slowly. No sign of him. Her heart lifted. Perhaps he wasn't here? Perhaps he was safe somewhere? Perhaps he'd already been detained. She began to shake, holding on to the legs of the upturned chair in front of her, afraid she'd fall. She scanned the faces again, unwilling to believe she'd come this far without some hope of success. She turned to the crowd. Though he'd been the one to organise the demonstration, perhaps he'd decided to stand with them instead. Her gaze ranged over those standing in the front-line, willing him to be there. So engrossed was she in searching that she almost missed him. Gradually, the small flicker of movement on the edge of her vision registered. When she turned to look, the white sheet had been lifted up, allowing a white man in a black cap and gown to step out among the speakers. Behind him was Thulatu, ready to drop the sheet as he withdrew inside the building. The white man turned, whispering to him, delaying him a moment longer as the dark head bent to listen. She shrieked, unable to believe how close she'd come to missing him. The stewards turned, startled as they looked up at her. If he should go inside, now, before she could make him see her, the police'd be here any minute, Christ, don't let her be too late to warn him. She shrieked again, the sound a howl of fear rather than speech as she pitched forward against the mountain of chairs, pushing them inwards onto the yelping stewards. Thulatu turned. She screamed his name, crying with relief as she fell inwards, knowing he'd heard. Overhead, the speaker's voice faltered, then continued, trying to drown out the disturbance.

The stewards were pulling at her angrily when Thulatu came to her aid. 'It's all right, I'll deal with it.' He waved them aside, peering down at her. 'It's you.' He frowned. 'What's going on? I thought you were Babo.' His voice was dull, lifeless, the question asked mechanically, as though it didn't matter whether she answered him or not.

She stared up at him, wincing. Mia's death engraved in his eyes. 'Dick is dead.' She whispered it, knowing she'd wanted to jolt him, but the words seemed to have little effect. He nodded, his face expressionless.

'Didn't you hear me?'

'I heard.'

The sudden wail of sirens in the distance made the speaker's voice falter again.

She grasped his arm. 'Modise said the police are looking for you, that you should—. Thulatu, please, listen to me! The police are looking for you, you've got to get away before they—.'

'No.' He pulled her hand from his arm, his mouth resolute. 'I am finished. Let the police do what they like.' The sirens grew louder, drowning out the speaker's voice. Behind them, the crowd was shifting, straining to peer over the heads of those behind them, their voices rising to an uneasy pitch. The group of musicians in front of the sheet began to play, competing with the sirens as they struggled through the first strains of 'Mayibuye i'Afrika.'

She gripped him again, mouthing the words. 'You've got to come!'

'No!' He pushed her and she staggered back, almost falling into the heap of chairs.

She jumped at him, filled with a sudden intense hatred that blinded her. Beating at his chest, her voice was a scream. 'You bastard! You fucking bastard, we've been climbing frigging mountains, hiding from the police, getting ourselves blown to pieces while you, you go off on your own where nobody can find you, feeling fucking sorry for yourself! Mambo's dead, dead! You know what she died of? There wasn't a mark on her, not a mark, the mark was inside! It made her heart stop, she looked at the children and her heart stopped! And even when it stopped, she kept her eyes open, she kept looking at them, so she'd never forget, not even when she's deep down somewhere in an unmarked grave!' She began to howl, clawing at his shirt. 'You bastard, bastard, don't you dare say "no," don't you dare say it!'

He thrust her outwards, gripping her upper arms so that her hands flailed impotently. 'Shut up!'

Behind them, shots rang out and the crowd surged forward, screaming. Still gripping one of her arms, he dragged her towards the snarl of chairs, kicking them out of his way. 'C'mon!' They turned into the alley by the side of the administration block, several students already making a dash for it in front of them. She ran as fast as she could but still it wasn't fast enough for him, her bones straining in their sockets. The alley seemed endless, the wall of buildings on both sides hemming them in. Above her, the sky jerked and shuddered as she gasped for breath. If he didn't slow down soon, she'd collapse. As they reached the end of the alley, he swerved away from the group of fugitives in front and into a car park. They hunkered down, exhausted, her breath rasping the metal as she leaned against a car door. Her nostrils twitched against the first hint of tearsmoke. She tried to breathe more shallowly, but it was impossible. Shots sounded close to them. She clutched his arm. He eased his body upwards, peering through the car window. She watched his eyes narrow as he whispered. 'Fools!'

'What?'

'Ran across an open space.' His lips thinned. 'They're picking them off one by one. Come. Keep down. And stay close to me.' He crept ahead of her between the parked cars and she crouched low, following him, her limbs still juddering from the long run. When they crawled into the shrubbery beyond the car park, he made her take the wig off. 'It'll get caught in the thorns, slow you down.'

She opened the top buttons of her blouse, stuffing it in, glad to be rid of it.

'They're in the car park already, quick, keep your head down, try not to disturb any of the bushes!' He moved ahead of her on all fours, bending branches as he eased between them, handing them to her before he moved on to the next, whispering to her not to let them snap back when she released them. The ground was sloping downhill, the shrubbery widening to a valley of dense bush amid clumps of trees. Behind them, something thrashed in the undergrowth. A dog barked, a wolfish growl of triumph that made them both freeze.

'Hey, maan! Over here! He's got a scent!'

Emma watched Thulatu's face, the way his gaze searched for possibilities in the network of bush.

'No sign of any disturbance, not even a broken leaf. You sure it's not a dassie or a squirrel he smells? Place like this must be crowded with them.'

'I'm telling you, maan, he smells blood. Give him his head!'

There was a sudden thrashing in the distance that told them the dog had been let loose.

'Quick. That cluster of trees on the right.' Thulatu began to move forward at the same snail's pace.

Emma knelt, petrified. It took Thulatu a moment to realise she wasn't moving. Swiftly he backtracked and shook her. 'Emma! Wake up!' Her eyes were beyond him, terror blinding them to the still gaze of stippled glass. Her mother and the dog, it was written all over her. Reaching out, he pinched her cheek until he saw the pain registering in her face.

'Quick! Quick! Follow me!' He jerked her arm and she began to crawl forward in a jumpy, mechanical way, as though he'd wound her up. Behind them, the men moved into the shrubbery after the dog, swearing at him when he lost the scent, praising him when he seemed to pick it up again, the different pitch between the dog's barks and the voices, telling Thulatu that the dog had moved ahead of the men. Good. He kept on at the same cautious pace as before. The men would be scanning the shrubbery ahead of the dog for any sudden movement of bush, their guns on the alert. The constant barrage of gunfire and screams in the distance told him this was a day for more deaths than arrests. Well, they weren't getting Emma.

He lifted his head a fraction, gaze tracking the bush for an acacia thorn. If he were going to die, he'd at least like to give them a run for their money. There was one a little way ahead to the right. When he came what he thought to be level with it, he turned to Emma. She was gazing trance-like at the bushes in front, the taut skin stretched to breaking-point across her cheeks. He felt a sudden rush of sympathy, the warmth of it taking him by surprise. He put his mouth to her ear, the words little more than an echo of the sea in a shell. 'You go on. The trees are dead ahead. I'm going to leave a scent for him around some thorn bushes, shove my jacket right in the centre. He'll try getting it out. Should bloody his snout, slow him down a little.'

He thought she'd panic at the idea of parting from him, but her eyes were blank. Good. At least she wouldn't suspect his real plan. 'If anything happens ....' He hesitated, choosing the words. 'When you get to the trees, keep going until you're right in the heart of the valley, where the ground's even. Wait there for me.' He paused, trying to gauge from the barking how much time he had. 'If I don't come ... wait there, stay put until dark. The police'll be gone by then — once they've rounded up everyone they want, they usually clear out quickly. This place's surrounded by white suburban homes, they like to keep a low profile, it stops the locals getting shifty. Emma, are you listening?'

She nodded, her eyes glazed. Shock, he thought, his heart thudding. She probably hadn't heard a word he'd said. Reaching out, he pinched her cheek again, waiting until she was ready to shriek. Swiftly, he slapped a hand over her mouth, repeating the instructions as fast as he could. 'You should be able to slip out into the suburbs once it's dark, you hear me?'

She nodded again as he took his hand away, the same glazed look creeping back into her eyes. He would have to hope that later, when he didn't show up, something of what he'd said had registered with her. If she didn't go now, they'd both be caught. Reaching out, he touched the angry welt on her cheek. Half-starved sparrow flapping in the dark. Fly away. Fly free. Twitter above the graves till your small beak snaps. He swallowed, fighting the emotion as he shook her. Behind, the sounds were closing fast. If she were to have any chance—. 'Go! Go!'

She responded as though hypnotised, scratching forward through the soil, the wig inside her blouse a bird-breast curving above the stick arms. When she was out of sight in the bushes ahead, he whipped off his jacket, rubbing the lining against the earth, dragging it along the ground as he crashed into the bushes on the right. Those Rottweilers were trained to sniff out blacks before whites. With any luck the dog would follow his scent in preference. And the noise he was making should clinch it. A burst of gunfire suddenly minced the glossy leaves to the right of his ear. The shreds rained down in a dense green mist, blinding him for a moment. He flung himself forward, hoping to reach the thorns before the dog found him. When the dog stopped barking, he dropped the jacket, knowing it was too late for his original plan. Behind him, the undergrowth crackled. He saw the acacia ahead at the same time he heard the deep purr of the dog's breath. He thrashed on, sensing the dog gathering itself behind him, his ears filled with the distant jubilant voices of the handlers between the staccato bursts of fire.

He flung himself forward and sideways as the dog leapt, impaling its soft underbelly against the thorns. Kneeling, he crouched facing the brute as it pulled itself free, howling with rage and pain. Come, then! Tooth and claw and brain against tooth and claw! Try me. Try me and I'll tear your heart out. For Thabo. For Mia. My heart is a graveyard. I will fill it with strips of your flesh, with your smashed bones.

He stiffened as the dog sprang, sinking its teeth into his shoulder before he could grip the huge head. The pain was instantaneous, radiating into his chest, his fingers twitching in nervous spasms. He brought his left hand down over the dog's head, searching for the eyes, digging deep at the bulbous flesh. The great head swung, releasing his shoulder, snarling at his hand. Thulatu whipped his hand under its lower jaw, pushing the head back. The snapping face lunged against his hand, aiming for his throat. He dug his fingers deep into the flesh below the jawbone, the twitching fingers of his other hand tearing at the bloodied underbelly. The dog flinched, its flesh already tender from the spiky thorns. Thulatu thrust all his weight against the beast, driving it up and back into the snarl of thorns, the powerful legs drumming at him as it writhed on its back in the bush. He didn't release the underjaw until he'd buried the head deep, the thorns sinking viciously into the eyes. The dog howled, thrashing, embedding itself more deeply. He pulled his hands out, hardly aware of the thorns ripping him from elbow to fingertip. He stood, panting, his shirt-sleeves in bloodied tatters about his wrists as the two policemen burst upon him, one of them butting him in the side with his rifle. Thulatu's legs buckled and he dropped to his knees.

'Ah Jesus, Hennie, look what he's done, look what he's done to Jupiter!' Above the dog's howls, the scream was thick with horror and grief. A sudden shot was fired over Thulatu's head and the howls stilled.

'You bastard! You fokking bastard! That was the best dog I ever had!'

Thulatu put up his hands, shielding his head as the blows rained down. When the boot caught him in the solar plexus, he doubled up, the air driven from his lungs. Above him, two heads were pinned against the bright sky, the faces featureless.

'What sort of fokking animal would do that to a dog?'

'A fokking hotnot, that's what!'

He started to laugh and they kicked him again, the pain fusing to a solid core that seemed to connect his head and groin.

'Who else is out here with you? Who? Who? How many of you?'

Emma. Spread your wings.

'Fok you! How many!'

Thulatu opened his eyes, staring up at the police badge glinting on the hard blue ocean. He opened his mouth, dragging the word from beneath the pain. Thabo was close. And Mia. Not hating him any more. Death had cured her. Waiting for him. Hovering on the fringe of all he could see. And the others, millions of them staring across centuries, the dark eyes begging him to come before they found out who he was, before they tortured him to find out what and whom he knew.

He thought perhaps they were kicking him again, but the boots jerking about his head didn't connect to the pain.

'How many? How many!'

He opened his mouth, dredging the word from the depths of the river in his throat. 'Millions,' he said and smiled.

Something crunched in his ear, the sound of a boot on gravel. The pain left him, drifting into the air like a wreath of mist. He closed his eyes, staring into the line of shackled faces.

* * *

For a long time she waited. He did not come. He did not come because he was dead, his blood soaking the earth, making the trees weep. She had heard him die behind her in their shrill rage, their guns belching round after round of spite. She did not stop or try to look back. She crawled forward, her gaze fixed on each new bush, her hands lifting to press aside each grieving branch with mechanical precision as she held herself inside the dream. When she reached the level floor of the valley, she stitched the part of the dream that had unravelled in his death. Then she lay down, staring at the blank sky. Something crawled across her arm but she did not turn to look or shake it from her skin.

When night came, the sky punctured with a myriad stars, she dragged herself up to check her bearings. In the distance, headlamps crawled along the main road through the campus. Beyond the road, the residential blocks showed only the odd rectangle of light. Kneeling, she began the long haul to the edge of the shrubbery, the bedlam of crickets shutting out the quick scuttle of unseen creatures in the bush.

Near the edge, she wriggled out of the light cotton slacks, turning them inside out, pulling them on again, the caked stains of earth scratching her skin. The wig, when she put it on, was warm about her ears. She waited for a sufficient gap in the thin stream of traffic before stepping out on the pavement, her limbs stiff and aching as she made for the King George exit and the walled gardens of suburbia nestling beyond the campus.

Chapter Ten

I

When the taxi-driver had radioed for a cab for Emma, Babo asked him to give her a tour of the city. He glanced at her in the rear mirror, his eyebrows disappearing from view. Her smile was warm as she leaned back against the upholstery.

'Make it slow and leisurely, I've got to do an essay on all the historical buildings and monuments, you can drop me up to the campus afterwards.' She took a pen and her address book from her bag, flicking the pages noisily.

'Oh, you're a student?' The Indian's tone was distant, polite, but she could see he was pleased she was speaking English.

'Yes.' She took out her compact, powdering her cheeks as she held the mirror up to catch a glimpse of the back window. Right on her tail, the dark car several yards behind. Making no bones about it. She hoped the Indian wouldn't notice.

'I, myself, am hoping to go to the University of Natal next year.' He swung the car downhill towards the beach.

'Oh yes? What'll you study?'

'It is my wish to study English.'

'Let's start with Dick King's statue on the Embankment, okay?' She closed the compact, but kept it on her knee. 'English, yes, really?' She chattered on as he drove through the busy streets, maintaining the same slow pace while she pretended to make some quick notes. She glanced through the blank address book, a smile playing about her lips as she scratched at the leather-bound covers. Papa had given it to her one Christmas, no doubt hoping she'd fill it with interesting addresses. She'd carried it with her everywhere, knowing he'd searched her bag whenever she left it lying about. She stared at the message she'd written inside the front cover: 'Those who snoop will find fuck-all in this book.' And, in smaller print, underneath, 'But if you can't resist, try turning to page fifteen.' On page fifteen were the words 'Fuck-All.' Underneath, she'd drawn a hand with a carrot teasing a buck-toothed donkey. What would the two automatons following her make of it? She surfaced to hear the Indian telling her of the previous job he'd held.

'... waitering in one of the big hotels on the sea-front, lots of tourists, you know?'

She murmured a response and powdered her nose again. In the small circle of glass, a yellow Mercedes was between her and the dark car. She stared, hardly able to believe it. Ahead, the approaching traffic lights were flashing orange. The car in front accelerated to take them. Reaching swiftly, she gripped the Indian's shoulder. 'Can you take those lights, quick! Quick, it's urgent!'

He sucked in his breath, hesitating.

'Please, quick!' She squeezed his shoulder.

He pressed his foot down and the taxi leapt forward, crossing the line as the lights changed to red. Opposite, a bus easing to turn right, honked as it was forced to brake. Several horns sounded simultaneously as the bus, now stuck in the middle of the intersection, blocked the traffic from the adjoining streets.

'Sorry, but I've just remembered, I have a lecture ...' She glanced at her watch. '... at eleven. I forgot all about it. Could you hurry? I'll give you double the fare. Turn left here, I know a quick way.' She was still gripping his shoulder as they swung into the street on the left.

Sensing his unease, she released him. 'I'm really sorry, I must've given you quite a fright. But I've missed several lectures lately ... right at the next junction, yes, that's it.' She turned, looking out of the back window. No sign of the dark car. With any luck, she'd still be in time to make her speech.

They climbed uphill, the Indian asking her questions about the university, her answers automatic as she wondered if Emma had found Thulatu. A dark-haired woman window-browsing on the pavement suddenly reminded her of Mia. Her heart lurched and she stared hard, aching as she caught something of Mia's graceful walk in the slender figure. Oh, she could weep. She'd have to call round to Piet later, see how he was doing.

When the Indian dropped her on Francois Road, the speeches were already in progress. She'd just begun to skirt the massive crowd, when the first sirens wailed. Turning, she stared in disbelief. From both ends, the Casspirs were driving at full speed towards the group of sitting students. Till the last moment, the students stayed, arms linked, faces set as they tried to sit it out.

Babo screeched at them to get out of the way. But already they were scattering, one girl managing to roll free seconds before the wheels of the carrier coming from the right struck two of her friends. Babo closed her eyes, the screams of a man whose legs had been ridden over, cutting right through her. When she opened her eyes again, the people on the fringe of the crowd had already begun to run, slamming into her in their efforts to get away. A string of kwela vans and military personnel carriers faced each other behind the frontline Casspirs like opposing armies. Already the police were pouring from the vehicles, dressed in full riot gear, assault rifles pointing at random into the crowd. She stood, open-mouthed as the first rounds were fired, the coloured woman who'd pushed past her, pitching forward onto the grass, a black man leaping across her body in his anxiety to escape. Babo began to shake. It wasn't possible, no warning to disperse, nothing. This was Durban, for God's sake. Not some squatter township in the back of beyond. Not Rhaumsfontein.

When the handlers leapt down from the trucks with the dogs straining on the leashes, she began to run, taking refuge in the crowd. Emma. She had to find Emma. If Thulatu were here, he'd be able to take care of himself. If Emma had found him, he'd take care of her too. But if she hadn't managed to find him ... she hadn't a clue as to the layout of the campus, where it was best to hide. And this was no ordinary show of police strength. Today, they meant business, anyone doubting it was likely to have his head kicked in, black or white.

The bulk of the crowd still swayed stupefied, unable to believe the police were firing indiscriminately. Those on the fringes who realised they were in the front line of fire, radiated outwards, panic spurring them in all directions. Behind them, others peeled away in succession so that the central mass began to disintegrate, shedding its layers like a great onion. Babo, as she tried to beat her way forward, was almost lifted off her feet in one such surge, borne backwards towards the wall of riot shields hemming them in. Behind the shields, from elevated positions aboard the carriers, came the rattle of gun-fire.

Here and there, the momentum of the crowd carried them through, forcing cracks in the ranks of police which gradually widened to reasonable avenues of escape, with only the possibility of a blow from a knobkerrie as they hove through the gauntlet of baton-wielding arms. Or so she thought. She was propelled forward in one such wave of bodies to discover that the line of shields had merely been a spearhead, breaking formation to allow the crowd through in manageable doses to the men waiting behind. Both police and army, Jesus, a couple of soldiers holding sub-machine guns. BXP 9mm's? — it wasn't possible, was it? Shorter, more squat than the R4's and 5's, that much was certain. What was it Thulatu had said? — you'll recognise them by their long magazine, only used by the special forces, the elite. But this was Durban, damnit, not some sealed-off township—!

Something struck her, something with sharp points that punctured the soft flesh of her upper arm. A wave of screams engulfed her as others were struck. She swerved, hoping to avoid a second blow, trying to curve around the buttress of men ahead, something alien and brutish in the gas masks that hid their faces.

If she could just cut between the two Kombis, make it across the road towards the student quarters, she might stand a chance. When the dog sank its teeth into her calf, she dragged her leg, still trying to run. The flesh ripped like a strip of cotton, the lack of pain surprising her as she tried to drag her leg free of the vice-like jaws. Her head was suddenly yanked backwards as a hand reined in tight on her long hair. The pain brought her up short and she screamed as the policeman held her head far back, his gloved fist punching her breasts. The dog was still gnawing at her leg and she tried to kick out, wondering why it felt like a wooden stump rather than one of her limbs. The policeman kneed her in the stomach, his voice a muffled scream through the warthog mask. 'Don't you dare kick my dog, you bitch!' He began dragging her towards one of the waiting vans, but the dog's grip on her leg was slowing him down. He snapped an order at the wolfish ears and the dog released her. 'You're the worst, you women, out begging for a piece of black prick, should ram a gun right up your anus, you fokking whore! What's the matter with a white man, eh, eh?' Each word was accompanied by a vicious tug at her hair and she moaned as he flung her towards the open van, her pelvis slamming against the metal edge of the floor. It was already half-full and she tried to climb in as he kicked her buttocks, but her injured leg refused to function. She clawed at the floor, anything to be out of range of the rock-like boots. A black hand reached down to haul her aboard, the dark eyes sympathetic in the bloodied face. She clutched the fingers, sobbing as she struggled in, the urine streaming from her errant bladder, dyeing her jeans to ink.

* * *

The house was in darkness and the gates were locked. Emma made the driver wait while she pressed the bell. She looked back at him sitting in the taxi, drumming his fingers on the steering wheel. If Babo's brother weren't at home, she'd ask him to take her back down towards the beach, make a run for it when he pulled up at a traffic lights. Then, then ....

'Yes? Is who?' The voice over the intercom was suspicious. Probably the man who'd admitted them the day Babo had brought her to see Mia.

'I, I'd like to see Mr Schuurman.'

'Is who?'

She hesitated, hardly aware she was cracking her fingers. If she said her name, it would prove meaningless to Babo's brother.

'He, he doesn't know me, but—.'

'Not home.'

The speed of the man's response made her suspect he was lying.

'Please. Tell him—.'

'Not home.' The buzzer clicked and she knew he'd cut her off. She began to sweat, feeling the eyes of the driver boring the back of her head. She rang the bell again. Nothing happened. Putting her finger on the brass button, she held it there until the intercom clicked.

'He not home. You go now.'

'Please, it's important. I'm a friend of ...' she leaned close to the microphone, almost shouting the word. '... Babo's?' Drawing a deep breath, she went on. 'Tell him I have a message from his sister. Babo?'

In the long pause which followed, she forced herself not to glance back at the taxi, its engine still whining. From somewhere within the grounds, a dog barked. She stepped back a little from the gates. Instantly, she was in the shrubbery, the brute tracking them through the undergrowth. And Thulatu ... Thulatu .... She forced her mind back to the voice as it came over the intercom again.

'You got car?'

'Yes.'

'You come in gates, you stay in car. Dog is loose.'

She shivered, running back to the taxi as the tall gates creaked inwards and the drive was suddenly floodlit.

They were about halfway up it when the huge dog appeared from nowhere, bounding across the wide expanse of lawn on their right. She stiffened, watching the animal as it paced them to the sweep of gravel in front of the house.

A tall, thin man stood framed in the light cascading through the open hall door, his grey-blond hair a frizzy helmet about his narrow head. Even at this distance, the resemblance to his sister was striking. She stared through the car window, a sudden rush of warmth seeping through the numbness. Oh, if only it were Babo!

He strode out to the taxi, peering through the window as she rolled it down.

'Ja? You know my sister? How do I know if this is true?' He squinted, looking her over, the large dog stiff with menace by his side.

Her fingers plucked at her blouse. 'She loaned me this.'

She glanced at the driver. He had his ears pricked. It made her afraid the way he'd stopped complaining, begun instead to listen. 'Could, could you keep hold of your dog if I get out? I, I need to talk to you in private.' She gazed up at him, her eyes begging as she indicated the driver's alertness.

Piet stared for a moment at the floral pattern on the blouse. Like so many others he'd seen on Babo. Difficult to tell if the woman was lying. But at the very least, she seemed to know the kind of thing Babo wore. Besides, she might know where Babo was — he'd been trying to contact her all day, people kept calling the house, offering their condolences, he couldn't stand much more. Calling to Elijah hovering about the front door, he reached down, opening the car door for the woman. 'Take Brutus and tie him up.'

Emma waited until the servant came and took the dog, disappearing with it around the side of the house. She climbed out, the words awkward on her lips. 'I know it must seem an awful imposition, but would you ... could you pay the driver? I'm afraid I have no money.' She shuffled the gravel, her cheeks burning as he stepped back a little. Her nails bit into her palms in the small silence which followed. The driver looked straight ahead through the windscreen, muttering a figure with his hand outstretched through the window.

'Please,' she said, staring at her sneakers. From the corner of her eye, she saw him capitulate, dipping his hand in his pockets as he searched for some loose bills. The amount surprised him. What'd she been doing? Driving through the streets all night? What the hell was going on? Well, she'd better know Babo at the price he was paying.

'Come into the house.' He strode before her back to the open door and she hurried after him as the taxi made a U-turn, crunching its way back down the curve of the drive.

She followed him into the drawing-room, her gaze travelling over the furniture as though she almost expected to see Mia as she'd seen her that day, the beautiful gaze teetering as she strove to maintain some kind of inner balance. Dead. The word tolled in her heart. De-dead-de-dead. De-dead. Dead-fetus-dead-children-dead-lover-dead-mother. Dead daughter. Dead father. Dead wife. Standing in the middle of the room, she began to shake, her teeth rattling. 'C-c-could I ... a b-brandy?' The bookcases on the opposite wall grew monstrous, leering as they swung towards her, hurling their blurred titles in her face. She flinched, stepping back, knocking against the coffee table behind her. And could you give me some money? A bed for the night? Can you hide me? Find Babo? Can you get me a passport? An air ticket? Get me out? Out of this fucking place? Out-out-out-out-out! No one can live here, no one. It's a wild place, speechless, churning, a place where the air bleeds, where the trees weep, a place where the heart is dead, where hate is the only certainty — oh bury me deep in the cold language of rock, beyond the burial of roots, the slow soak of pain trickling in the mind's eye.

'Are you all right?'

When she could see again, he was holding the brandy to her lips, the glass tapping against her teeth. She took it and drank, gagging as it fired the back of her throat. When she was breathing normally, she spoke.

'I, I'm sorry about ... your wife.'

The words stabbed him, again confirming her death. 'You knew ...?' He stared at the feverish eyes in the skeletal face, his heart jigging. Mia, he thought, the throb of her death pulsing in the narrow throat. He turned, feeling his way to the couch opposite her.

'Who are you?'

She hesitated, wondering where to begin. In the end, he decided it for her. 'Where's Babo? D'you know where she is? I've been trying to contact her all day.'

'I was hoping she'd be here.' She took a deep breath, the brandy spreading its numbness throughout her body. 'She told me last night that I could trust you. If anything went wrong.'

'Wrong? What—?'

'There was a demonstration on the campus today. Babo was to give a speech, but the police turned up. I'm worried she might've been detained.'

Piet stood. 'She was there? I heard something about it on the news—.'

'I don't know for sure. Did it say who they'd detained?'

Piet's mouth twisted. 'The police never give names till they're ready. Or numbers.' He moved towards the phone. 'I'll see what I can find out.'

'Wait! Babo was followed when she left the flat this morning. Two men in a dark car. She said they were Special Branch, that your father was probably having her tailed. The car's there again tonight. That's why I asked the taxi-driver to bring me here.'

Piet nodded, his eyes bitter. 'It figures.' He sighed. A wonder Papa hadn't decided to have him tailed as well, after what had happened the day of Mia's death.

'I'll call my father, see what he can find out.'

Emma leapt up, the brandy slopping in the glass. 'Please—?'

'Don't worry, I won't mention you.' He picked up the receiver, his finger moving reluctantly to dial the farm. He'd sworn he would never speak to him again. How Papa would relish this.

Emma wandered about, trying to understand the stilted conversation he held in Afrikaans. When he hung up, he turned to her. 'Don't look so worried. My father's had her tailed on and off in the past as much to protect her as to find out what she'd been up to.' His voice was glacial. 'Or, I should say, "as much to protect his own reputation." An errant daughter who believes in democracy isn't exactly a big advantage in his neck of the government. However ...' He went to the drinks cabinet. 'Bad as he is, he wouldn't want her picked up.' When he'd poured the whiskey for himself, he reached automatically for the sherry Mia normally drank. He winced, staring at the familiar label, his hand arrested in mid-air. How, how could his mind play such a cruel trick — how could he have forgotten even for the least second, the weight of his grief multiplied ten-fold in the reawakening to her death. It was all this woman's fault. If she hadn't come to distract him—. He lifted his glass and drained it in a couple of gulps.

He turned, trying not to take too much notice of her gaunt face. 'Now.' His voice was hard. 'While we're waiting for my father to call back, perhaps you'd tell me where you fit into all this? You're English, aren't you?' He stared at the mound of tangled hair. Ridiculous. Its luxury obscene against the malnourished face. Suddenly, he spotted it. 'Is that a wig?'

She looked at him, startled. 'Is it so obvious?' She put her hand up to touch it.

He considered it, frowning. 'Not really. It's just the way your face looks ... against it.' His gaze shied away from the dark orbs of her eyes, the smudged skin underneath reminding him of Mia. When he looked back, he froze, his skin crawling. Mia's bloodless face stared at him from death, her dark hair shorn to the shape of her skull.

'What? What is it?' Emma rose, taking a step towards him as he dropped the glass, backing away from her.

'Stay back!' His voice was hoarse with a fear she couldn't decipher.

She stood, uncertain, staring at his white face. 'What, what is it?'

'Who are you? Who the hell are you?' He put his hand out, feeling for the couch and sat down abruptly. Finally, he registered the wig in her hand.

'You took it off.' His voice was an accusation.

She looked at the wig. 'I'm sorry. I thought when you mentioned it, you wouldn't mind if I—. It's very heavy ... and, and itchy.' She sat, silent, bunching the hair on her lap. Christ, just how bad did she look? She'd almost frightened the wits out of him. Even still, his colour was unnatural, his face drawn—.

'Tell me.'

She hesitated, wondering what she should say, what she should omit. You can trust Piet, Babo had said. 'It's ... a long story.'

'I've got time.' The sadness in his voice moved her.

Once she began talking, she couldn't stop, the whole story spilling in one huge avalanche that drained her, as though she'd buried herself beneath the words so that by the time she'd got to where she'd picked up the taxi, the words were limping from her lips. Lying back against the plush cushions, she closed her eyes, yearning for the oblivion of sleep.

He stared at her, hardly able to believe what she'd told him. He had asked her the odd question, but mostly he'd listened, aware of how tired she was. Here and there, she'd been careful, despite her exhaustion, a certain reluctance to mention names and exact locations that convinced him her story was genuine. He couldn't get his mind away from the scene she'd described in the church, the stark horror in her eyes as she relived it. Over and over, he kept seeing Mia's slashed wrists, the river of blood on the sheets.

'You've got to get out.' He looked across at her, wondering how she'd managed to stay sane. She didn't answer. He rose, switching the phone off before he left the room. Let her sleep. He'd wait for Papa's call in the study.

When Emma opened her eyes, the window was flooded with morning. She blinked, staring down at the blanket which covered her as she lay outstretched on the couch. Someone had entered the room. She squinted up at the servant as he placed the tray down on the coffee table before her. Coffee, triangles of lightly buttered toast. Her mouth watered.

'Is for you.' He kept his eyes averted as she thanked him. 'Baas, he said you must to eat all of it.' Elijah's lips clamped as he turned to leave the room. How many times had he said the same words to his mistress before she'd—?

'Mr Schuurman, where—?' Emma struggled to rise, her limbs still leaden with sleep.

'He come now.' He was gone, the door closing on her words of thanks.

She poured the coffee, saliva flooding her mouth at its sudden pungency. She added milk, sipping it quickly, its clean heat cutting through the gunge in her throat. Tackling the toast, she was ashamed of the way she wolfed it, licking her fingers lest she miss a single crumb, small moans escaping her lips as she ate and drank. When she was finished, she found she was crying.

'You ate it all.' Piet's voice was relieved as he stood looking down at her.

She looked up, startled, rubbing the tears from her cheeks. How long had he been in the room? Had he seen the way she'd torn at the food? She looked down at the blanket on her lap, the heat rising in her cheeks. 'Yes. Thank you for ...' She plucked at the blanket. '... the food ... everything.' Suddenly, she remembered. 'What about Babo, did you find—?'

'Papa says she's not among the lists of names.'

'Lists? How many were—?'

'Don't ask.' His mouth closed in a thin line.

'Then where is she?'

'That's what I've been asking myself.' He moved across to stand in the floodlit window, his hair forged in the sun. The pattern on his light sweater was peculiar. Then it dawned on her. He was wearing the thing inside out. Like her slacks. She wanted to weep. Had he dried earth on the inside too? Maybe he'd been clawing at his wife's grave in his sleep, trying to exhume her. She wanted to tell him she still had the earth under her own fingernails, that she was still burying the child she'd killed, his wife's half-sister or brother, Christ, if she didn't get out of this country, she'd go crazy.

'... have a few contacts within the force myself,' he was saying when she dragged herself back to the room. 'They're not as high-ranking as the people Papa knows, mind. Still, it's worth a try.' He roamed the room, ill at ease. Something about Babo was nagging at the back of his mind but he couldn't put his finger on it. Perhaps if he left it alone, stopped trying to force it, it would slip through the snarl of memories of its own volition. He stopped, looking at Emma. She was looking a little more alive at any rate. Except for the eyes, a familiar desperation in them that gnawed at his heart. He went to the coffee table, pushing the tray out of his way as he sat on it, facing her.

'We've got to get you out of here, I've been thinking of the best way—.'

'D'you think she's okay, Babo?'

'I'll find her, don't worry. Is that, according to Papa, she gave those tails the slip. When they realised they'd lost her, they drove up to the campus, hoping to pick up her trail again. But by then the police were all over the place.' Reaching, he picked the wig up off the floor. 'She's probably lying low for a couple of days in case someone in detention blurts out her name.' He tossed the wig onto the couch, wishing he felt as reassured as he sounded. Why hadn't she come to him? Was she afraid Papa'd put a tail on him too? Didn't she realise that bad as Papa was, he'd see she wasn't harmed? She knew that, surely she knew that? Whatever his father was, he wasn't one of those brutes in the truth room.

He tried to shut it from his mind as he looked at Emma. 'That Mission Society your friend Carruthers worked for ...' He looked away, the sudden misery in her face reminding him of his own grief. So she had loved the man. God help her. God help them both.

'I sent Elijah to them with a note. Apparently, they've heard nothing from the township, they didn't know about ... the deaths. They're sending someone, a Scottish priest by the name of ...' He pulled the scrap of paper from his pocket. ' "MacLeod". With any luck, they'll be able to figure out a way to get you out. I'm sorry I can't be of more help.' He hesitated. 'Is that, the people I know would run to my father.'

She rose, feeling sick, afraid she'd soil the beautiful carpet. 'The ... bathroom?' She pressed a hand to her mouth. He went with her to the door, pointing quickly as he stepped into the hall.

She made it just in time, the same heaving, retching pattern as the previous morning, telling her it was true. When the spasms eased, she sank to the floor, pressing her face against the cool enamel of the bath, waiting until her heart slowed to its normal pace. She dragged herself upright, refusing to take it on board, rinsing her mouth, returning to the drawing-room so that she would not be alone with it. When she walked back in, a grey-haired priest was sitting with Piet, their heads close as they pored over the map spread on the coffee table. She was brought up short by the stiff dog collar, the grey cotton shirt. The man rose, his face creasing in wrinkles as he tried to smile. She could see from the shock in his eyes that already Piet had been filling him in. Had he known Dick personally?

'This is John MacLeod.' Piet stood, gesturing, a verve in him that he hadn't felt since—. Christ, it was good to have something to do. He sat, jotting distances in the margin of the map as Emma told the priest what had happened in Rhaumsfontein.

'I didn't know him, I'm afraid,' The priest was saying. 'I'm only here a couple of months.' He stared at the dead eyes, barely recognising the woman whose face he had studied in the photograph back in his office. Her file said little, other than that she was an English lay missionary, gaining work experience under Carruthers, her permit valid for six months.

'Your first assignment? That's tough.' His voice was gentle. He didn't tell her that he'd had more or less the same experience on his first posting to Chile when he was little more than a raw recruit.

Right now, there was no time for anything other than to get her out. It was a wonder he hadn't been paid a visit yet. Unless they were still searching for her among the rubble of the township. But they'd come, the moment they realised they couldn't find her body. His lips clamped. Sure as Judgement Day.

While the priest told her how he went about getting people like her out, Piet stared at the map. Luckily Elijah could drive. He'd take her himself if it weren't for his worry that Babo might show up needing his help. And then there was Jan. His throat tightened. That his own son should've chosen not to return with him to the house after the funeral, that he should prefer to stay with the Vorsters—. He knew Jan blamed him, blamed him for all of it. He'd have to deal with it soon, go to him and try to explain. He tapped Pretoria, staring above it at the frontline states. Botswana. He gauged the distance between the small mark the priest had made, and the border. A couple of hours, drive? 'If you can get her to the mission here ...' he'd said, his waxen finger prodding the spot. '... there's somebody who can take her through.'

Piet raised his head and looked across at the chalky, elf-like face. Would she make it? He swallowed, trying to ease the sudden dryness in his throat. She had to. For Mia. For all their sakes. He'd sworn himself to take a pickaxe to the ice. To hack and burrow and bore. And he would, as soon as he knew Babo was safe. As soon as he'd talked to Jan, made him understand. This woman had a weapon too. She'd been here to collect the words and pictures in her head, smuggle them out uncensored. A small thing. But a beginning. Even in Botswana, she would have to travel under an assumed name, but the priest had said his friend would see to that. An assumed name. The words rang a bell in the corners of his mind. Warning. Something to do with Babo? Something she'd said to him once. Threatened. What? What? Suddenly he was trembling, unsure of what it was that made him afraid.

II

Police Commissioner Reunert stood on the farm patio, hugging the file to his glittering buttons. He wished he were anywhere else right now, even in one of the lousy townships, rather than where he was, facing Schuurman across the table, the bull-neck taut with fury. Reunert resisted the urge to wipe away the sweat trickling from under his peaked cap as the silence lengthened. A cool breeze eddied about his ears and he lifted his face, trying to take advantage of it. Despite his resolve to appear calm, he jumped when Claus spoke, the words snapping at his face.

'The report, maan!' Claus held out his hand, the grizzly arm rigid as a hawser.

Reunert shuffled, his boots tapping the flags. 'Look, I'm sorry, sir, deeply—.' He flushed as Claus walked past him to the French windows. 'Samuel?' The word was a roar. 'See if she needs anything ... a drink ... zo?' For a moment longer, Claus stared into the cool darkness of the living room, listening. He swivelled suddenly, his hand again outstretched as he faced Reunert. 'Verdomme, give it!'

Reunert's heart thudded as he forced himself to hold out the file. 'Look, I realise you're upset. I mean, if she were my daughter—.'

'Ja-ja.' Claus swiped the report, moving with it to the table as he spoke. 'Remarkable powers of observation. Is that why we gave you the job of police commissioner?' He opened the file, leaning on the table as he began to read. Reunert stepped forward, a cold fist gripping his heart, the words tripping from his tongue as he tried to explain. 'Unfortunately, she was taken to one of the smaller stations across town.' He dashed the sweat from his eyes. 'We were swamped. Literally swamped. We annexed the sports complex at the university. A lot of them were held there, initially.' Unable to watch Claus, he began pacing. 'If she'd been taken there, I could have .... It was mayhem, mayhem, sir, believe me. It took us days to find out who we'd detained, who'd slipped through.' He paused for breath. 'Of course, the smaller stations don't have photographs. Lists of names, certainly, but ... a question of the administrative cost, you understand?' His voice was an appeal as he watched Claus sink onto the chair, his eyes fixed on the pages before him. Reunert pulled at his tie to loosen it. It wasn't his fault, though he could bet Schuurman would make him a scapegoat if he let him. He took a deep breath, stressing it as he spoke. 'If she'd given her name, it wouldn't have happened. It was unfortunate ... in the general melee — if she'd been taken to me—.' He paused, searching for the words least likely to offend. 'It was an unfortunate oversight.'

'Oversight!' Claus lifted the file, slamming it back down on the table. 'You dare to call this ...' His fist smashed the table. '... an oversight!'

Reunert flushed. 'I mean, you, I, we didn't foresee her being taken out of my jurisdiction—.'

'Burn marks? Animals!' Claus put a hand over his heart, his face congesting as he fought to draw the warm air into his lungs. When he could speak again, he pointed at Reunert. 'I want that bastard's hide!'

Reunert released the bit of flesh he was nagging between his teeth, suddenly tasting salt. 'I don't suppose you'd know ... has she had a, a ... tetanus shot recently?'

'Tetanus?'

'The dogs were let loose on them in the courtyard.'

'My God in die Hemel!'

Reunert waded on, desperate to find something that might calm him. 'That servant of yours seems a capable sort of ... of .... He seems to be able to ... manage her .... Though perhaps you might like to consider some private nursing .... I can give you some names—.'

'His hide, d'you hear?'

'Actually, she was quite ... fortunate. If it hadn't been for your son and his enquiries, she might still be—.'

'My son?'

'He became quite a nuisance I gather. Just as well, for her sake. He insisted she might be using an assumed name. When his name was brought to my attention, that's when I put two and two—.' He broke off, turning away as Samuel stepped out onto the patio, moving to the folded wheelchair half-hidden behind the potted orange tree in the corner. He pulled it by its handles, snapping it open as Murphy carried Babo out, her body limp and silent in his huge arms. Nobody spoke.

Murphy stood waiting, his anger gathering like a storm in his chest as he remembered how Claus had had him 'christened' by his henchman Verwoerd. And now the bastard stood far out on the edge of the patio, unable to look at his own daughter, preferring the sight of his ocean of cane rippling in the dying sun. Soon, he thought. Soon. He wriggled a little to ease the pressure of the gun against his sleeping penis, hardly aware of the deadweight in his arms.

When Samuel finally had the wheelchair positioned, Murphy lowered his burden gently onto the seat. They'd broken her, snapped her like a sapling, he could see it in the rambling eyes, the lolling tongue. She smelled of the same disinfectant soap given to detainees to clean themselves up the day they were being released. The police didn't like to broadcast the fact they let most people pee in their pants to humiliate them. He nodded, moved as he'd never thought he could be by the sight of a white reduced to a state he'd come to expect only among his own race. What chance had she, a gilded bird among the beasts?

He stood while Samuel straightened her in the chair, positioning her head in the centre. His eyes never left the older man's face. When Samuel finally glanced up at him, his eyes flicking in mute consent, Murphy held his breath, afraid he'd misread the sign. When the eyes flicked again, Murphy nodded, turning to leave the patio. Before Samuel had risen from his knees, he was gone, the powerful legs making short work of the sweeping lawn as he headed towards the trees.

Even after Samuel had returned to the house, it was several minutes before Claus could bring himself to turn and look at her. Behind him, Reunert had begun to move about, his faltering steps conveying his unease.

'A, a few weeks rest ....' The commissioner glanced at the granite face. '... all this will be just a, a, memory.' He gulped, eyeing the whiskey bottle on the table. 'You think they won't recover, but I've seen it, yes sir. I mean, some of them, no matter how many times they're detained, and you think, that's the end of them, they're broken, once and for all, a couple of months later, there they are, large as life, boycotting shops, spouting about freedom.'

In the silence which followed, Reunert avoided looking at Claus. He turned as the french window slid open, relieved at the possibility of some diversion.

'Where is sh—?' Piet stood transfixed, his gaze locked on the figure slumped in the wheelchair. It wasn't true, none of it was true, Babo's hair, but not Babo, never her, someone else with an exclamation mark just visible under the bruises on her cheek as though she too had been startled by savagery. She was marked, from the very beginning, why couldn't he have seen it, why couldn't he have protected her? He opened his mouth, his jaw working, but no words came. He moved across to stand before her, his body leaden under the weight of her suffering. Forgive, forgive me. She seemed to see him, her hand flapping on the arm of the chair, a mumble drooling through her lips, her tongue lolling in a moist pink swamp. His legs buckled, bringing him to his knees before her. Raising a hand, he tried to touch her, to ask her if she knew him, but her eyes had slipped away again, peering into dark spaces he couldn't reach. He bowed his head, unable to bear it.

Behind him, Claus stood, uncertain whether to go to him. He was afraid now as he'd never been since he was a child, his daughter's blank eyes staring at him, unfathomable as the black folds of his mother's skirt. He turned, his heart leaping from some vicious pattern of treachery repeating itself. Treachery. He glanced at Reunert standing well apart near the orange tree. Treacherous.

'I want his hide!' Eyes narrowed, he stared at Reunert.

Reunert glanced down at his boots, wishing he were at home facing the certainty of a stiff drink before supper. 'You're upset.'

'You bastard, I'll nail you for this!'

'I, I make allowances. A man has a right to ....'

'Where is he?'

'... be angry.'

'You owe me.'

'He's ... being transferred.'

'I want him out!' Claus crossed to the table, staring down at the open pages.

Reunert raised a hand, placating. 'It's the best I can do in the—.'

Claus rammed the file with his fist, the table shivering under the impact. 'Out!'

Reunert took a deep breath. There was just so much he could take. If the stupid bitch had given her name—.

'Out! D'you hear, maan?'

'I suggest you ... control yourself, sir.'

'That bastard's been walking around scot free—.'

'He wasn't to know she was your daughter.'

'Is that any reason to treat a woman—?'

'He was doing his duty, like any other policeman. He had his orders.'

'Ja? You think I'll leave it at that? Zo, watch. I'll make waves enough to drown both of you.'

Something snapped in Reunert. He stared at Claus, his voice equally harsh. 'Who will you complain to? Yourself? Sir?' In the silence which followed, he stared, unable to believe it as Claus wilted, the chair shrieking its protest under the impact of his weight. So he had got to him, finally. He felt a sudden stab of fear. Schuurman had a long memory. When he got over this little business, he'd make him eat his words. Or his badge. He took a step towards the table. Perhaps he should apologise now, before—. The long, low sound rumbled in the flags beneath his boots. It seemed to come from everywhere at once. He swivelled, terrified, scanning the empty lawn, the gaping entrance to the darkening house. Finally, he registered it: Piet, still on his knees, his face contorted in an anguished howl that rent the air. Reunert backed towards the table, trying to distance himself from it. Time to get out. Definitely. He glanced at Claus, the granite eyes full of his weeping son. Good. Sliding a hand across the table, he picked up the file, slipping it under his arm. Not the kind of evidence he could afford to leave in Schuurman's hands. He retreated, inch by inch, until he'd stepped back into the house.

Claus stood, vaguely aware that Reunert had skipped it. Unable to look at Piet's shuddering frame, he moved to the edge of the patio, staring out into the gathering darkness, the sky veiling the last streaks of the setting sun.

Wiping his eyes, Piet laid his head in Babo's lap, staring at her hand as it flapped again on the arm of the chair. 'Mia was right,' he told her. 'There are no words.' He buried his face in her jeans, the disinfectant choking his nostrils. 'Babo, oh, Babo!' He fought the tears that threatened him again, raising his head to stare at the wall of his father's back. 'Do you know what she was saying when she slit her wrists? Do you!'

Claus didn't turn.

'Beyond words.' Piet fought the pain welling in his throat. 'These things are beyond words. D'you know what that makes us? Do you!' He struck his chest. 'Well, Mia's here now ... here! Every time you look me in the face, she'll be staring at you!' Babo's sudden mumble brought him round to face her. Reaching out, he stroked her hair, its straggling, singed edges rasping like steel wool in his palms. What the hell had they done to her? 'Oh, what is it? What is it? Babo?' He touched her face, trying to decipher the fleeting glimmer in her eyes. Was she crying, was that it? Oh, Christ, Christ, somebody help her! 'Are you in pain? Is that it? You should be lying down.' He rubbed her hand, its limpness defeating him. Hauling himself upright, he turned to Claus, his voice cold. 'Has Samuel made up her bed yet?'

Claus jerked his shoulders, unable to look at him.

'I'm staying.' Piet's voice was thick with disgust. 'Much as I don't want to be under the same roof as you. I'll put the camp bed up in her room.' He strode towards the house.

Claus turned, panicking at the thought of being left alone with her.

'Where is Jan?'

But Piet, already stepping into the living room, wouldn't answer him. Claus glanced at Babo, then looked away as he moved to the table. He sat heavily, staring at the bottles on the tray. Perhaps a drink might help. He poured a large measure, the whiskey slopping over the rim of the glass as Babo stiffened suddenly, her mouth contorting in a silent scream that jerked his heart. He turned towards the house, his voice a roar. 'Piet! Piet!' Ja, what was the matter with her, why was she doing that, she mustn't do that! He wiped the sweat from his face. Hemelse Vader, why didn't Piet—? 'Samuel! Vinnig! Vinnig!' He rose, taking a step towards the wheel-chair, freezing as Babo slumped again.

'Wanted something, baas?' Samuel stood just outside the french windows, the sloppy, threadbare tee-shirt and pants emphasising his tall, spare frame. Claus stared. What was he doing out of his uniform looking like every other hotnot?

'Something, baas?'

He gestured at Babo. 'She's saying something again.'

Samuel looked at the wheelchair. 'Not now. Only silence.'

'She was.'

'She needs help.' Samuel's gaze was level as he looked at Claus. Claus blinked, surprised to find himself looked in the eye. But then, Samuel had always been his wife and daughter's servant more than—. 'The doctor said—.'

'Not his. Proper kind.'

'Zo?'

'You know.'

'He's the best there is.'

'No.'

'What d'you want? A bloody medicine man?'

'Miss Babo needs proper kind.'

They both turned to Babo as she mumbled again, the sound low, unintelligible. Claus glanced at Samuel. 'What? What is she saying?'

'Not sure.' He shuffled across the flagstones. 'Miss Babo?' Leaning down, he smiled in her face. She mumbled again.

Claus took a half-step forward and hesitated. 'Ja, what is it?'

'Think she's cold.' Samuel straightened, moving towards the french window.

'Where're you going?'

'Get rug.'

Claus stood, holding himself stiffly, staring at the glass in his hand until Samuel returned with one of the travel rugs. His old slippers whispered on the flags as he went to tuck the rug about Babo's lap. 'There, warm.' He looked across at Claus, his voice hard. 'Proper kind.'

'He's the best there is.'

'Can't help. Doesn't know this sickness.' Samuel looked down at Babo. 'Doesn't know torture.'

'She wasn't ... wasn't ....'

'I know. Samuel knows. Seen many. Only one man ....'

'Who?'

'... can help. Takes time. Works.'

'Who?'

'Black man.'

In the silence, Babo's arm slipped from the arm of the wheelchair, her body tilting a little to one side. Samuel bent down again, propping her upright.

'Takes time. Long time. But works.'

'Get him.'

'Can't. Too busy to come. I take Miss Babo. Go there.'

'He can come here.'

'Won't come. Too busy. Clinic. Treats many. There.'

'Get him!'

'Can't.' Samuel straightened, looking him in the eye.

Suddenly Claus was afraid to push it. 'When?'

'Tomorrow. Morning. Early.' Samuel moved towards the house.

'He'll make her better? Won't he?' Claus panicked. 'Wait! It's your move!'

Samuel paused as Claus pointed to the chess game laid out on the table. 'You haven't taken it.'

'No.'

'Make it now.'

'Have work.'

Babo mumbled again, her tongue lolling in her mouth. Samuel hurried to her, bending over to listen.

'What is it?'

'Wants water.' He came towards the table but Claus was already pouring it, handing him the glass. Samuel took it, returning to Babo, holding it gingerly to her lips, her slobbers amplified in the silence. When she jerked her head back, Samuel moved to the table, placing the glass down. He turned again towards the house.

'Wait! I, I need you here ....' Claus tried to shrug, but his shoulders wouldn't lift. 'If she talks ... I can't understand.' He didn't want to be alone with her, he couldn't be alone with her. He didn't know how to handle—. He looked at Samuel, trying to keep the appeal out of his voice. 'We might as well play the whole game. Pass the time.' He held his breath as Samuel hesitated. The old man had been with him donkey's years, since the children were knee-high, obeying orders, going about his business like a good hotnot, quite a bright one, even. Yet, something had changed, here now, on the patio. He wasn't sure what it was, but there was something in Samuel that hadn't been there before, something rock-hard and resolute. Except when he looked at Babo. He'd better go softly. Right now he needed the old man too much to risk losing him. No one knew Babo like he did. Zo. He looked at him, keeping his voice even. 'It'll pass the time.'

For a moment longer, Samuel hesitated before going to the table. He made his move quickly, without studying the positions of the pieces. Claus stared at what he'd done, hardly believing it. Reaching down, he castled his king. Samuel's response was instant, his dark queen glowering the full length of the board as she threatened his king.

'Check.' The word shot from Samuel's lips like a small, hard bullet.

'What?' Claus stared, unwilling to believe he hadn't anticipated every possibility. 'I taught you everything you know, everything! Y'must be mad if you think you can beat—.'

Samuel sat down. 'We see. No more, the old way.'

Claus sat, his legs trembling with anger. So he thought he could get the better of him, did he? Ja, he'd soon show him. Lifting his knight, he sideswiped, cutting off the black queen's access to his king. The play continued, but he found it hard to concentrate, the sudden gurgles from Babo as she drooled distracting him. He poured himself another drink, glancing across at her. 'You think she's okay, ja?'

'For moment.' Lifting the bottle of whiskey, Samuel poured himself a drink, his movements slow, deliberate, his eyes like brown polished stones mocking the sudden fury in Claus's face. The glass almost at his lips, he waited for Claus to tell him to put it down, to get out of his sight. Claus stared, suddenly seeing it. Ja, now, that was exactly what he wanted, if he told him to get out, he'd be playing into his hands. Right now he couldn't afford to lose him. Later on, when the time came, when he no longer needed him, verdomme, how he'd make him pay! He lowered his gaze to the chessboard, making another move, his lips twisting as he heard Samuel gulp the drink. Zo! Gulp! One day I will make you chew the glass! When my daughter is better! When she is ... better. She will get better. When he spoke, he was careful to keep his voice even. 'I'll come with you. Where is this clinic?'

'You stay here.'

Claus leapt to his feet as the shot rang out, a staccato of echoes beating the air, drowning the first stirrings of cricket-song. 'What was that?' He peered at the black line of trees beyond the lawn. It seemed to come from further afield, from the direction of the compound.

Opposite him, Samuel was still sitting, calmly sliding one of his chess pieces, his mouth hardly moving as he spoke. 'Probably wild animal. Not good on farm.' He raised his head, cocking it as he listened. 'They shoot to kill.' Suddenly, he swung his head to stare at Babo. Claus followed his gaze to Babo's silent face. He turned back to Samuel. 'What? What?'

Samuel put a finger to his lips. 'Sssshhh ....' Rising, he hurried across to her, bending down, his ear close to her mouth as he appeared to listen. Finally, he straightened. 'Tired.' He turned to look at Claus. 'She says, very tired. She wants to lie down.'

Claus stepped back a pace. 'I didn't hear her.'

'I did.' Samuel held his gaze.

Claus swallowed hard, setting his drink down. He forced himself to move across to the wheelchair, but as he stretched out his hands to lift her out, Babo's arms flailed at him, her hand glancing off his shoulder. He stopped, cut to the heart by the terror that suddenly streaked her eyes. That she should fear him, her own father, ja, didn't she know he wouldn't harm a silky strand of her hair, oh how he loved her hair, how he'd loved to stroke it when she was little, when she'd rush to climb aboard his knees, settling there, her head content against his chest as she'd sucked her thumb, small bubbles leaking in the corners of her rounded mouth, his lap a ship he'd built for her safety. My God in die Hemel he'd kill the bastard who'd done this to her, kill him with his bare hands! He turned away, unable to look at what was in her face. Gesturing to Samuel, he dragged the words out. 'Will, will you ...?'

While Samuel lifted her and carried her indoors, he moved to the table, his legs suddenly weak. Sitting, he buried his head in his hands. So good, all of it, until she'd opened the kitchen door that night. He raised his head, looking across at the wheelchair, speaking to the darkness which blurred its hard edges, as though she were still sitting there. 'Your mother never knew. That's not why she drank.' He passed a hand over his eyes, as though he could blot out the memory of it. 'She was willing. Willing! Verdomme, d'you hear me!' He slammed his fists on the table, the small huddle of bottles tinkling as the table shook. It was then he noticed the file was missing. Reunert! The bastard'd made sure to take the evidence with him when he'd sneaked away. Well, he'd have his revenge, he'd—. He stopped, the policeman's accusation ringing in his ears. Yourself? Sir? Mocking all he had ever done, all he had ever tried to be. How dared they judge him? How dared she point at him with her flailing arms! Damn her! Damn her courage! Zo! Damn her eyes! He swiped his hand across the table, knocking everything to the floor, his ears filled with the screak of glass on stone.

* * *

It took Murphy a long time to stop laughing.

It was the first time he had killed. Sober now, he stared at Verwoerd's body propped against the stout trunk of the cypress. Two things had surprised him. The fact that one bullet had done the job. And the fact that he hadn't missed. Verwoerd now had a wine-dark pit where his heart used to be. He'd noted several things about the killing: the force of the recoil when he pulled the trigger on the Magnum .38; the way Verwoerd's body had jerked upwards as the bullet struck, and lastly, the way the stain appeared on Verwoerd's chest simultaneously with the sounding of the shot.

What interested him most of all was what he had been thinking at the moment he was ready to pull the trigger. He'd lived this killing so often in his mind, planned it down to the finest detail, especially the part where he would tell Verwoerd that the bullet was for all the beatings he'd inflicted on every single man in the compound. Yet, when the moment came, the only picture he'd had in his mind was of how Verwoerd laced the buckets with his own urine to stop the men from drinking the water they used to swab out the concrete floor of the compound.

'It's because you pissed in the buckets, see?' he'd said, right before he'd pulled the trigger. Verwoerd had stared, his eyes bulging as he tried to grasp it, taking Murphy's laugh with him as he jerked into eternity. For a while, Murphy had gone on laughing, his pleasure at puzzling his enemy at the last minute outweighing the pleasure of wiping him out.

He raised his face to the darkening sky. Already it was pricked with the promise of a thousand stars. Samuel would've heard the shot, got the woman out of harm's way. Schuurman would be drinking his whiskey, star-gazing at what he considered his patch of sky. Murphy smiled. How many stars did you see when the gun was aimed at your eyes? Millions, he'd imagine, just for a split second before all went dark. Lowering his gaze to the line of trees skirting the edge of the lawn, he began moving towards the farmhouse, the tune he whistled hardly audible above the noise of the crickets.

III

For days after she'd arrived back in England, Emma drifted in a half-world between dreams and madness. When her skin raged, she stayed in the dreams, too weak to open her eyes and escape. But when the sweats chilled and dampened the sheets wrapping her, she opened her eyes, staring at the walls of the vault in which they'd placed her.

Once she thought she heard her name whispered. It made her remember that someone had said it was a prayer. But she couldn't remember who. The not remembering made her cry. When the tears escaped through her closed lids, they sizzled on her cheeks, drying back into her, leaving her hotter than before.

She travelled long distances in her dreams, in rundown trucks over dirt roads under a blinding sun. Sometimes there were pigs in the trucks, sometimes chickens. Once there was even a priest with a white body and a black, infant head. Always, the head was crying. Once it dropped from the body, rolling like a turnip on the floor of the truck. The pigs rushed at it, squealing with hunger. She reached out, trying to take it from them, but they snarled, gnawing at her hands. She screamed, knocking her head against the little rear window of the cabin, begging the driver to help. When he turned to look, he had no face.

Sometimes, when the fever cooled, when she opened her eyes in the vault, God was standing at the end of the marble slab, a chalky little gnome, white from head to toe. She told him what a shite he was, what a lowdown, spiteful little shite. He asked her if she had a permit for language like that. He ran around the marble slab, shrieking at her to show him her permit, freaky! — he kept saying, freaky, freaky! She screamed, closing her eyes, running back inside the dreams to escape him.

One day, when she opened her eyes, the vault was gone. She was in a room with pale walls, a small, sickly sun staring through the window. She blinked at the figure in white standing by the end of the bed. This one was taller than God. When it came around the side, peering in her face, she saw it was a nurse, a little white boat sailing on the blond curls.

'So we're awake at last!' The face smiled at her. Emma closed her eyes, trying to get away from it. But it went on talking, bland phrases uttered in a gentle tone so that she realised it meant her no harm. Before she drifted away, she felt a hand wipe a tear from her cheek and knew that the touch was real.

The next time she opened her eyes, the sun was a little higher in the pane of glass. The same white figure was there again, jotting something on the chart she held in her hand. Emma opened her mouth, trying to dredge her voice through the mire in her throat, but the sound she made startled the nurse into dropping her pen. She shrank a little at the speed with which the woman came to fuss over her, the cheerful voice booming in her ears. Emma nodded at the glass pitcher on the nightstand beside the bed, her eyes pleading.

'So we're thirsty at last!' The nurse smiled as she poured the water. 'Here we are, then.'

Emma sucked long and hard on the straw, the water hitting her stomach in little icy slaps that shocked her fully awake. The nurse was tutting at her, telling her to slow down as she lowered the glass out of the straw's reach so that at times Emma found herself sucking air. Christ, but it tasted good, so good, hacking a path through the thicket in her throat. When she finally released the straw, the glass was almost empty.

'There now, we've done very well.' The boat bobbed on the blond curls as the nurse held up the glass.

The 'we' was beginning to grate. She gritted her teeth, trying to raise herself up in the bed.

'Oh don't do that! There's a drip in our arm.'

Emma wanted to tell her to fuck off. She turned her head as the door opened, glad of the distraction. A white-haired woman entered, her stick thumping the carpet as she moved across to the bed.

Emma stared. Somebody's grandmother. The thought made her want to weep.

The nurse smiled again. 'We're awake!'

'Yes, I came as soon as I heard the bell. Leave us, will you?'

The nurse wagged a finger. 'A few minutes, that's all. We're still very weak.'

The old lady nodded. 'Yes, yes!'

Emma lay against the mound of pillows, hardly believing it was true. Sophie Chamberlain. She watched the old lady drag a chair close to the bed as the nurse sailed out.

'Well, child?'

The quiet words opened a floodgate. Emma burst into tears, her body gripped in a sudden paroxysm of grief as she remembered. Thulatu's mother. The car sent to meet her at Heathrow. Arriving at Holbrook Hall. Telling Sophie the news. Watching the life drain from her eyes. She'd thought the old lady would die there and then. But instead she'd risen, walked stiffly to open the french windows, stepped down into the garden beyond the terrace, her flimsy sweater and tweed skirt no match for the winter afternoon. She'd stayed out a long time, her thin hand resting against the bark of a tree, her back to the house as she stared out across the vast expanse of her property. When she'd returned, she found Emma sprawled in a heap on the floor, unconscious.

'Dysentery,' she told her now. 'That and dehydration. Not to mention lack of food, shock and exhaustion. The doctor pronounced a list as long as my arm, he's been here every day. Plus, of course, the fact that you're pregnant. That at least was good news. More than I could've hoped for, at my age.' Sophie gazed at her, eyes bright.

Emma plucked the sheets, wondering if she could avoid it, at least for today, at least until she got her strength back. She cleared her throat, her voice husky, strange in her ears, as though it might belong to someone else. 'How long've I been—?'

'Over a month.'

'A month!'

'Sometimes I wondered if you'd ever come back.' Sophie's hands twittered about the handle of the walking stick. 'After a while, when you didn't respond, the doctor thought maybe you didn't want to come back, that you'd lost your will .... I sat up with you all that night, calling your name, hoping you'd hear me. You didn't. But after that, you seemed ... quieter, more at ease somehow.' Sophie swallowed, trying to smile. 'God is good.'

Emma closed her eyes. God my ass. God was a bomb that'd self-destructed in the thickness of township bodies.

'... feeding you intravenously, and the catheter, of course. Thank God for modern medicine.'

And piss-bags. Emma shifted in the bed, feeling the thin tube that trailed between her legs. If she had the energy to lean over the side, somewhere, under the pretty quilt, she'd find a yellow sunburst of piss waiting to be whisked away in its cloudy little bag to the nearest toilet. Neat. Discreet. Civilised. The blush-saving grace of medical jargon wrapping up body odours and effluence.

'... was surprised you didn't lose the baby.'

There it was again, the hope in Sophie's eyes. She sighed, hating to kill it. But it had to be said. 'It's ... not Thulatu's.' In the silence which followed, she couldn't bear to look at the old lady.

'It's ... Dick's,' she said eventually.

'Maybe.'

'What?'

'Maybe ... physiologically speaking.' Sophie patted her hand. 'But you went there because you loved my son, that's true, isn't it?'

Emma nodded, unable to speak.

'And he saved your life, didn't he?'

Again, Emma nodded.

'It's thanks to both of them this child will be born. You won't deny an old woman her right to spoil her grandchild, now will you? Well, child?' Sophie patted her hand again.

'After I had the abortion, he stopped—. He didn't love me. I don't want you to believe—.'

'Of course he did! How can you say he didn't love you after what he did? It may not be the kind of love you wanted from him, but it was a better kind ... purer, don't you see that? Yes, he hated what you did. Even when he was a little boy, he was always like that, he never saw the shades of grey, there was no middle ground to be travelled between bad and good. But the only things he was ever selfish about were his principles.' Sophie's hand fluttered to push back a snowy wisp of hair, the gold band sliding on her marriage finger. 'This child had two fathers.' Her voice was firm. 'I want you to stay here with me. Both of you.'

'I, I can't do that.'

'You owe me a grandchild.'

Emma winced.

'I'm sorry, but at my age, there's little time left for niceties.' Pressing on the stick, the old lady stood up. 'Think about it, child. You need looking after. Where better than here? According to the doctor, you're lucky you didn't miscarry, he says you'll be even luckier to carry it full term.' She hesitated, trying not to frown at the wan face, the tufts of hair defining it against the pillows. Perhaps it was enough for one day. Let her become used to it by degrees.

Emma stared at her. She'd expected the shock of Thulatu's death to unhinge the old lady. Instead, she was planning the future, a stubborn general refusing to surrender in the face of all his defeats.

'You're ... not bitter?'

'Of course I'm bitter!' For a moment the bird eyes glowed. 'But history has a habit of repeating itself, the good parts as well as the bad. Haven't you noticed? I make what I can of the good. That's all any of us can do.' The stick thumped time in the carpet as she went to the window.

Emma chewed her bottom lip, wondering if she should tell her. She'd made up her mind in the endless blur of being passed from hand to dark hand on the long journey back. The child wasn't hers. It was Dick's: conceived out of his anguish, her own despair. And Thulatu's: redeemed by his sacrifice. The old lady was right about that, they had both given it life. But the child belonged to Africa.

She sighed. How could she make her see it? The words had to become flesh. Oh yes, her articles might help. In the same way that the plastic bag in a cave in the Drakensberg might one day be found, food for an avid historian long after the blood had faded to sepia. But the real words were the burial grounds between the paintings in the caves and the modern crap of the constitution.

'As soon as I've finished the articles, I want to go to Tanzania. That is, if they'll have me.'

'Tanzania?' Sophie turned from the window, her hands perched on the handle of the stick.

'Maybe I could get a job teaching English, I don't know, will you help me?'

'But why—?'

'There's a school there, the ... Solomon ... something ... freedom college, Thulatu told me about it ... he wanted ... the first time I was ... pregnant—. And, and ... Modise went there.' She looked up at the liquid dripping its seconds along the tube towards her arm. Two to a breath. Twenty breaths to a rest on the side of a mountain. Or was it thirty? Or ten? And how many shit trucks? How often? How many people to a single tap? Grains of coffee to a cup? Bowls of mealie pap to bloat your stomach? Days in incommunicado detention? Hours to fix a single borehole? Minutes for the police to fuck it up again? Children missing? Mothers crying? Trees weeping? Studs to make a cross in Dick's buttocks? Hours of tight wire about a penis? Lost childhoods? Cracked hearts? Seeking shelter in a church? Missing, presumed butchered? That was the trouble when you stepped outside, when you stopped living it. You forgot. The words stopped being flesh. That's why she had to take the child back. History must be hewn from the inside. As Dick had done. And Thulatu. Otherwise, all she was doing was paying lip service to justice. What was it Dick had said? — I can't see no other way of living with myself. She hoped the old lady would understand.

Whatever Sophie was about to say was interrupted as the nurse returned, fussing over Emma, telling them both it was enough for now.

In the days and weeks that followed, they argued about it. But it was the doctor who settled it, refusing to consider her fit to travel until after the birth, although she was rapidly recovering. And getting fat. Her laziness confounded her, the writing sapping all her strength, making her more anxious than ever to go as soon as the child was born.

In the end, there were eight articles, two more than she had planned, published over eight consecutive special Sunday supplements, the newspaper dredging up what they could in the way of photographs, and even commissioning some etchings to accompany the baldness of her words. But though they were reaching a wide audience, even picked up by the press abroad, she had no interest in the hundreds of letters that began arriving at Holbrook Hall, the controversies that raged in the media about how accurate or reliable her uncensored accounts might be. It certainly stirred mud, those with vested interests in South Africa refuting her statements in vicious personal attacks aimed to discredit her. She was glad when Sophie took the whole thing over, hiring a second secretary to help her deal with it. The old lady was in her element, appearing on talk shows on radio and TV, making statements to the press, her stick abandoned as the days lengthened into summer. Better still, she seemed too busy to argue any more about wanting Emma to stay in England after the child was born.

In the final months, at Sophie's insistence, she visited a specialist in London, Rafiq taking her there and back by car, the 'Mr Harrington-Smythe' she was attending, the same kind of smooth, pin-striped effigy she'd attended for the abortion. She hated going, hated facing the reminders, but it pleased Sophie. Besides, the pregnancy was doing something to her, dulling her, she thought, even dulling her guilt. And underneath, a feeling was growing, almost an excitement now that the time was drawing close, a curiosity, wondering if it would look like Dick. As soon as it was born, no matter how difficult it'd be to compose the letter, she would write to his mother, Sophie had got her the address. Dick had told her about his parents that night after they'd made love. How did you tell a mother that her son who'd been a priest, a son, moreover, whom she'd thought had become a priest to hide his homosexuality, had made her a grand-mother posthumously?

On her final visit to the specialist, neither she nor Rafiq noticed the dark car with tinted windows parked at the end of the tree-lined street. Rafiq gave her the second set of keys after he'd helped her scale the steps into the spacious reception room.

Usually, she was no more than an hour all told, just giving him time for a pleasant stroll in the park opposite, a read and a smoke on one of the benches facing the duck pond. Usually, he was there, his large frame leaning against the sunny chrome of the radiator when she came out. She never wanted his help coming back down the steps. But today, he ran out of cigarettes, realising it just as the hour was up. He hurried from the park, glancing across at the Georgian facade that housed the doctor's rooms. No sign of her yet. If he were quick about it, he'd be down to the corner shop and back before she made it to the car. And if she got there before him, well, she had her keys. Perhaps he'd buy her a cone if the shop sold them, the day was a scorcher. He glanced at the blurred outline of the two men in the dark car as he strode into the shop. Nice car, but he didn't envy them in this heat with the windows rolled up.

While he was waiting to be served, a taxi turned into the street. Sophie sat in the back, peering over the driver's shoulder, pleased when she saw the car still parked outside the doctor's. Good. It would save them driving all the way to Rudi's office to pick her up. Besides, it would give her an opportunity to have a word with the doctor about how Emma was doing. She paid the driver, waving aside his offer of help as she mounted the steps to the hall door.

Inside, Emma was mutinous as she sat across from the specialist's desk. The examination was over, but she was still panting a little from the effort it had taken to dress behind the silk screen. A two-year-old would've got dressed twice over in the time it had taken her. It made her feel helpless, this inability to move with even a reasonable degree of speed. Nor was it just the change in her body. Her span of concentration on any one subject seemed to equal that of a brain-dead flea. Perfectly natural, the specialist had said, his smile blasé, happens to the best of women, glancing at his watch, the clock in his face already alarming for the next patient, think no more of it, don't worry your pretty little head about it. He'd stood, looking through her, arm outstretched to shake her hand, goodbyes already phrased in his gaze, his eyes saying it all: you dummy. Christ, how she'd wanted to spit on his manicured hand. Instead she'd told him she'd no desire to win 'Miss Senility of the Year.' That had ruffled him a little. He'd even sat down again, unsure of what to do when she wouldn't rise, her bloated belly resting like a giant egg in her lap, the tension she'd created between them palpable as the pall of township heat.

She stared at the shaft of sunlight spearing the window, not knowing why she was doing it, why she was delaying when normally she couldn't wait to get out of this stuffy, overdressed room. Weird .... Babo would say. Dear Babo. Sophie was still trying to contact her. And Piet. But Thulatu and Dick had been the only direct links, the silence from every avenue, killing. And what of Modise? What news was likely of him? Was he still slipping from shadow to shadow in the unlit streets, his dark gaze unwavering? Finally she pressed down hard on the desk as she hauled the cumbersome weight of her body upright. The doctor sprang up in relief, rushing to open the door for her, the speed of his movements an insult. Waddling into the long hall, she was surprised to find Sophie chatting to the young, pink-faced receptionist. She opened her mouth to greet the old lady as the bomb exploded outside, rocking the house. For a moment they stood transfixed.

'Rafiq!' It was Emma who whispered his name, but Sophie was already at the far end of the hall, pulling on the heavy, panelled door, flinching from the heat, the rippling wall of fire framed in the open doorway as the flames engulfed the car parked below them in the street, the small tree beside it already a mesh of smoking charcoal. A furnace, Emma thought as she moved forward, Africa come to haunt an English summer, the groaning metal below her blackened and twisted as the tin roof of any township shack. She stood dazed at the top of the steps, oblivious to the sudden bedlam around her, the shrieks of the young receptionist.

Please, she thought, please. Let him not have been in the car, let Africa not come home to roost. Please. Her legs buckled as the flames shifted, exposing him in the distance, his spine a grotesque arc impaled on the park railings opposite, the specimen tree a halo of quivering blossom above his rigidity. She closed her eyes as someone rushed past her down the steps. Rafiq. Sweet Rafiq. Meant for her. All of it. She should've been the one catapulted by the blast to lie draped across those railings, their spiked tips severing her spinal cord, piercing her heart ... heart ... heart ... let it stop now ... let it beat no more ... let it ... let ....

She was falling, the pain streaking in radials from the base of her spine. She lay at the bottom of the steps in the scorching heat, a river oozing between her legs, giving herself up to the pain, welcoming its punishing grip. But someone was calling her name. If she sank deeper into the river, she might be able to drown it out, deep, deep into the river of pain, into the very core of it, aeons of pain stretching, grinding, ripping, burning, burning, but the voice was there too, inside the pain, calling, calling and calling, fuck it, how dared it call her, this was her pain, hers only, she must keep it, contain it, consume it, never never let it go from her, never let it escape, poor pain, poor poor pain, and grief, grief enough to drown the world, so stay, stay safe on the inside, but the voice was there again, prising it from her, squeezing her face in a vice-grip, refusing to let her go, fuck, fuck it!

'Emma ...!'

She opened her eyes, gasping as the cold compress stung her cheek.

'... for God's sake, child ...!'

Eyes floating above her, pleading for something, the voice filling and fading in her ear.

'... in an ambulance, we'll soon have you at the hospital, but you must do what the doctor says ....'

Ambulance? Emma frowned at the swaying interior. No-no, the voice was wrong, this was the mobile clinic, the one from Lenasia, but she had to get out of it, get out before Modise came and handed her the child, she had to tell the voice. 'When you get to the trees ...' she whispered, the tears sliding into her ears, '... keep going until you're right in the heart of the valley, where the ground is even. Wait ... wait for me there ... wait, wait ...!' She closed her eyes against the two heads orbiting above her as someone stroked her brow. 'But he never came!'

'Then you'll have to make do with me, my dear.' The tone brooked no argument. Emma opened her eyes. Sophie's swaying head was suspended in mid-air, streaks of blood and smoke pigmenting the lines of her face.

'Now push, child!'

Beyond Sophie, a stethoscope swung from the second head, a pendulum over the naked globe of her belly.

'Now!' the head said, an urgency about the mouth that cut through her stupor.

'You heard him, child. If we're ever to get to Tanzania ... the freedom college ....' Sophie's eyes were overbright. Fixed, Emma thought. Unquenchable.

Then let the key be turned in her womb. Heaving a deep breath into her lungs, she began to push.